CW00429984

Out of the Northern Mists

# THE CIMBRI APPEAR

## Book 1
### The Cimbrian War

JEFF HEIN

RED WOLF BOOKS

The Cimbri Appear

Copyright © 2021 by Jeff Hein

Published by Red Wolf Books

All rights reserved.

Book 1 of The Cimbrian War

Paperback ISBN: 978-1-737553922

eBook ISBN: 978-1-7375539-1-5

No part of this book may be reproduced in any form or by any electronic or mechanical means, including information storage and retrieval systems, without written permission from the author, except for the use of brief quotations in a book review.

This book is a work of fiction. The names, characters, and incidents portrayed in it, while based on historical events and people, are the work of the author's imagination.

Cover design by Dusan Arsenic

Torque image by The Crafty Celts

Edited by Homestead Publishing Company

Formatting by 341 Enterprise

# Dedication

*This book is dedicated to my wife Dawn. I will be forever grateful for you putting up with my endless hours of reading, writing, and talking about "my people". Without your patience, this would never have happened. Thank you, I love you.*

*and*

*To my mother Alice Reuss. Your strength and perseverance have been an example to me throughout my life. Thank you, I love you.*

*Special thanks to:*

*Kevin Wellman, John Willman, and Bob Marschke*

# Table of Contents

Part III - Rome

# Table of Images

# Character Trees

# Germans and Celts
## (* Fictional Characters)

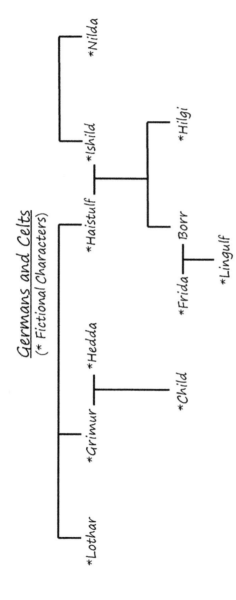

Claudicus – Hunno of the Boar Clan
Caesorix – Hunno of the Raven Clan
Lugius – Hunno of the Bear Clan
*Skalla – Borr's friend/Freki's brother
*Freki – Borr's friend/Skalla's brother
*Hrolf – Borr's friend
*Gorm – Blacksmith
*Glum – Brewmaster/Frida's father
*Gudrun/*Eldric – High priest
*Skyld – High priestess

Teutobod – Chieftain of the Teutones
*Amalric – Chieftain of the Ambrones
*Magalus – Chieftain of the Boii
*Theobald – Sub-Chieftain of the Boii
*Aodhan – Chieftain of the Scordisci
*Epatus – Chieftain of the Taurisci
*Viranus – Taurisci ambassador to Rome
*Talla – Nubian warrior/Vallus' friend
*Anik – Indian warrior/Vallus' friend

# Romans
(* Fictional Characters)

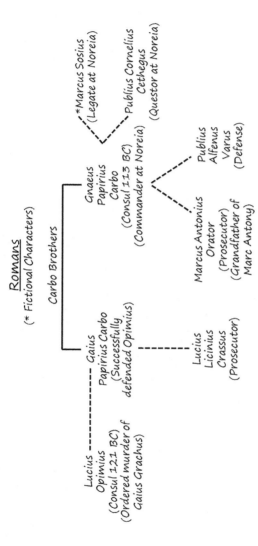

Carbo Brothers

Lucius — Gaius Papirius Carbo
Opimius (Successfully
(Consul 121 BC) defended Opimius)
(Ordered murder of
Gaius Gracchus)

Gnaeus Papirius Carbo
(Consul 113 BC)
(Commander at Noreia)

*Marcus Sosius
(Legate at Noreia)

Publius Cornelius Cethegus
(Questor at Noreia)

Lucius Licinius Crassus
(Prosecutor)

Marcus Antonius Orator
(Prosecutor)
(Grandfather of Marc Antony)

Publius Alfenus Varus
(Defense)

Lucius Aurelius Cotta – Consul 119 BC. His daughter Aurelia would become the mother of Julius Caesar.
Sextus Pompeius – Grandfather of Pompey the Great. Killed in Macedonia in 118 BC.
Marcus Aemilius Scaurus – Consul 115 BC. Princips Senatus for twenty-five years.
Gaius Porcius Cato – Consul in 114 BC. Led two legions to their death in Thrace against the Celts.
Marcus Junius Silanus – Praetor in 113 BC. Will be consul in 109 BC and charged with fighting the Cimbri.
*Lucius – Young legionary recruited to fight the Cimbri.
*Titus Romanus, Vulca, Decius, Foligio, Porcius, Aulus, Marcellus: Lucius' friends and tentmates.

IX

## Family of Gaius Marius

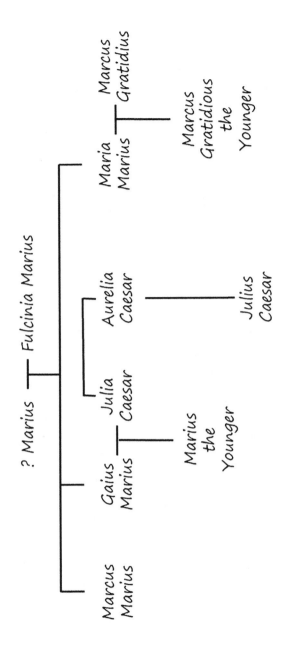

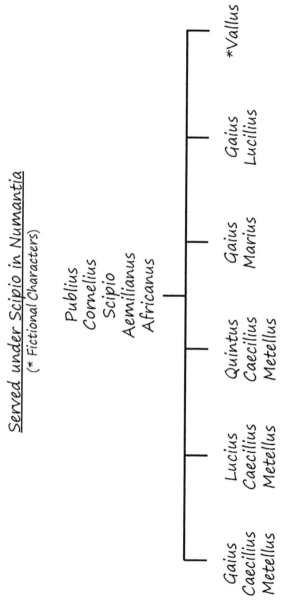

## Served under Scipio in Numantia
### (* Fictional Characters)

Publius
Cornelius
Scipio
Aemilianus
Africanus

Gaius
Caecilius
Metellus

Lucius
Caecilius
Metellus

Quintus
Caecilius
Metellus

Gaius
Marius

Gaius
Lucilius

*Vallus

# EPIGRAPH

In the same corner of Germany, nearest the open sea, dwell the Cimbri, a name mighty in history, though now they are only a little state.

Widespread traces of their ancient fame may still be seen: huge encampments on both sides of the Rhine, by their enormous circuit, still give a measure of the mass and man-power of the nation and demonstrate the historical truth of that great exodus.

Rome was in her six hundred and fortieth year when the alarm of the Cimbrian arms was first heard, in the consulship of Caecilius Metellus and Papirius Carbo.

Tacitus: The Germania, 98 CE

# PREFACE

This story begins twenty years before the birth of Julius Caesar, while Rome was still a republic at the cusp of its expansion into Iberia, Gaul, Illyricum, Pannonia, Macedonia, Germania, and Britannia. It is told by Borr, a boy of the Germanic Cimbri tribe of Jutland, today's Denmark, who will grow into the warrior and tribal king Boiorix, the Cimbri leader that bested Rome's legions time and again. In the second century BC, the Cimbri emerged onto Rome's borders from the dark and mysterious north. They were among the first of the Germanic tribes to begin the great barbarian migrations that contributed to the eventual fall of the Roman empire centuries later.

In this novel I stayed as true to the original sources as possible, while filling in the gaps that exist in our knowledge of this time. Inevitably there will be details that will be questioned as accurate because so few original sources exist. Some were written centuries after the events in question, and many differ about life in the world of ancient Germania and Rome.

Borr's story parallels the life of Gaius Marius, the Roman general who will one day bring the story of the Cimbri to a disastrous end. Historians have often credited Marius as the man who laid the groundwork that led to the fall of the Roman Republic and the rise of the Empire.

Using bits of archeological evidence, ancient and modern historical sources, and a generous imagination, I hope that I have provided the reader with an enjoyable story.

# PART I
# THE FLOOD

# Chapter One
## Jutland
## September 120 BC

The morning that changed my life forever began no differently than any other.

My mother, Ishild, pushed an errant strand of blonde hair back from her face, leaving a dark smudge on her forehead as she added a piece of wood to the fire. She exclaimed and looked up in alarm at the thatch roof when a shower of sparks rose, watching for any that may have settled into the dry straw.

She was tall and fair, sturdily built with a strength of character that made her a perfect match for my father. The two complimented each other in every way. Golden blonde hair, bright blue eyes, and a quick smile or a laugh for a joke, but just as quick to anger when provoked.

Smoke from the morning cooking fires hung low over the village, creating a haze just above the rooftops. A sudden breeze cleared the air, and with it came a feeling of unexplained foreboding, as the people outside looked about, sensing something was amiss.

My family was seated at the solidly built roughhewn table my father had built before I was born, laughing at something my three-year-old sister Hilgi had just done, when the sound of the sentry's warning horn jarred us from our breakfast.

Borremose, the fortress of the Wolf Clan of the Cimbri, sat on high ground, an island within a man-made lake, near the northern end of the Cimbrian Chersonese. The only approach was a stone causeway that crossed the shallow lake and entered the village through a large gateway framed by oak timbers. Thick doors of oak planks hung from iron hinges, and a great oak beam barred the gate.

An earthen embankment rose from the lake, on top of which stood a double walled timber palisade with a platform around the inside that allowed defenders to keep watch and fight over the top of the wall.

My father, Haistulf, hunno of the Wolf Clan, dropped what he was eating, seized his weapons and raced outside to see men running to the walls, expecting an attack. I was a few steps behind him and stopped abruptly when a shadow passed overhead. Thousands of birds of every kind were in panicked flight, passing over the village, racing eastward as if Hel herself were chasing them. The animals in the village added to the racket assaulting my ears, bawling and bleating as if they had seen a predator.

When I reached the walkway, I was shocked to discover the surrounding lake had disappeared, rushing back down the streambed that led to the Limsfjord, exposing the mud and deep pits, sharpened stakes, and other defenses under the surface.

The base of my skull tingled, and the hair on my arms stood up as my body reacted to the signs of impending danger. In stunned silence, we all looked westward as a growing rumble filled the air. A thin dark line formed where the sea met the horizon and as the noise grew, so did that line until it disappeared behind the trees between us and the shore. There was a distant crash of sound, accompanied by spectacular fountains of water splashing skyward as we all realized we were watching a monstrous wave impact the outer islands and banks. I stood transfixed; my feet rooted to the planks of the walkway as I watched helplessly.

Men ran and jumped off the wall, some injuring themselves when they landed. They ran for their homes and families, slamming doors behind them in a futile attempt to shut out the approaching doom. Trees fell before the tremendous force as wheat to the scythe, cracking so loudly it rivaled Donar's thunder. Enormous oaks that stood for hundreds of years were splintered and stripped of branches as lesser trees were toppled and swept along in the deluge.

The colossal wave slowed, its force somewhat diminished when it struck land and forest, but it continued to surge up the unobstructed streambed to the edge of the protective lake. I was finally jolted to action by my father's shouts and turned for the stairs leading to the courtyard. Half running and half falling I stumbled down until he grabbed my shoulder and shoved me against the earthen bank that formed the lower part of the wall.

The deafening roar of the wave and its terrible destruction drowned out screams of panic from man and beast as the ground trembled beneath my feet. When the wave impacted the fortress walls it broke or pushed over the palisade timbers above our heads, creating a cave-like space that protected us from the debris that topped the wall. Water slopped over the earthen rampart into the courtyard, filling the basin within the fortress like a barrel. We were spared most of the force of the wave as its momentum slowed, having traveled miles inland.

Its last strength died on the ridge of high ground at the center of the peninsula, and it gradually slowed, then paused for a few moments, and began draining away into the river valleys and fjords back to the sea. The retreating waters swept away untold numbers of houses, wagons, animals, and people into the sea, leaving still more lying across the land covered with thick layers of sand and gravel.

All low-lying areas were covered in standing water. Bogs retained the sea water in their basins and fields were flooded, any unharvested crops were ruined. The seaside communities on the western side were destroyed. Most of the farmsteads were built in protected areas to avoid the winds and now were either swept away or covered in the remaining water. The defensive lake around the fortress was refilled, but now it contained the broken remains of men and animals, along with all the detritus that came from the flood. It had taken only moments to transform our land from the bright colors of fall to a dirty brown. The trees that remained standing were broken and twisted like the teeth of an old crone.

The fortress was flooded chest deep, and we waited until most of it receded before crossing the draining current to return to our home.

My mother had followed us to the doorway and watched wide-eyed as the wave crested the palisade. She ducked back into our home, slamming the door in a hopeless effort to keep the water out. She screamed at her sister Nilda to get into the rafters and threw Hilgi to her, scrambling up behind them. When the water entered, they were safe and when my father forced the door open the water came rushing back out, carrying many of our belongings with it.

Relieved that the family had survived intact, my father and I joined the people outside who had already moved several palisade logs that blocked the gate when the water rushed out. Nilda and my mother helped the injured.

Everywhere there was shock and despair as the people tried to comprehend what had happened. Among the injuries and death, we discovered that the wave had swept away the buildings where meat and grain had been stored for the winter. The dirty seawater had destroyed everything in the storage pits inside the various homes.

A sudden shout warned us of a second wave approaching and the people ran for something to hold onto, but this one weakened quickly and only rolled through the area and did not crest the top of the earth rampart.

Storm clouds gathered on the horizon, a sign that our ordeal was not yet complete. Within the hour the people had to seek whatever shelter they could find as the sea god Njoror followed the great flood with a frightful storm. Wind and rain, lightning and thunder threatened to destroy those that survived the flood.

By nightfall, the terrible fury subsided, and a soaking downpour set in. Our people spent a sleepless night huddled in fear under whatever shelter they could find, praying to the gods for mercy, fearing it was the end of the world. The buildings inside the fortress were mostly intact and provided some shelter from the cold and rain, but there were no fires, and many died before morning, cold and wet, shivering uncontrollably, and slipping into a deep sleep they would never awaken from.

When dawn finally broke, the clouds were low and gray, and a light mist blanketed the earth. The rain had stopped, but the air was damp and thick. Moisture clung to everything, and it was cold enough to see my breath. We all shivered in our wet clothes, and my family huddled together with Hilgi in the middle for warmth. There was no sun that day to disperse the haze, and in the weak light my father gathered his men and issued instructions to scatter and search for survivors.

People climbed from the sodden wreckage of their homes, calling for loved ones, gathering the remains of their belongings, trying to round up their surviving animals, weeping over those who were lost. Most of the cattle and other livestock that had not been slaughtered for winter were still pastured out on the heath. Because it was higher ground, it had escaped the worst of the flooding.

When I emerged from what was left of our home, I stood frozen in place, hardly able to comprehend the carnage that had occurred in such a short time.

The wrath of Njoror was spent.

---

My father sent riders to the surrounding communities to learn the extent of the damage to our people. I listened in disbelief when they returned with their reports. The village of Lyngsmose, closer to the open sea than Borremose, was completely gone. Audo, the hunno of Lyngsmose, had been swept away and his son Lugius was gathering their people and moving them toward Borremose. The survivors walked aimlessly, still reeling from the disaster, and set up a makeshift camp on the heath among the cattle. The once proud and defiant people looked defeated, ambling along silently, their shoulders bent as if carrying a heavy load, their vacant eyes on the ground.

I found my friends Freki and Skalla weeping over their parent's bodies near what was left of their homestead. They were twin brothers, two years younger than I was, and I had known them my whole life. Their father had been one of my father's retainers. Most of the tribe's military strength consisted of men who on any other day were fishermen, farmers, or tradesmen, but who, when need-ed, were called upon to pick up their spears and shields and answer when their hunno called. All were trained for war, but the retain-ers, also called companions, were professional warriors whose life consisted of military training and provided the core strength to the clan's formation in war and were always ready to defend against raids. These men typically lived in or near the fortress and I had grown up knowing many of them and their families closely.

The twins and I had shared many adventures, often earning us a reprimand from our parents. Today, we would share the sad task of providing the last rites for theirs.

We used the abundant wood that was scattered about to build a pyre and reverently placed their bodies beside each other along with as many of their belongings as could be found. We were no priests but did our best to give them a decent service, according to our traditions. Freki prayed aloud, asking Wodan to accept the souls of his parents as Skalla lit the oil-soaked wood. The wood was so wet it took several efforts to get it to burn, but eventu-ally it took. Once the fire was hot enough to dry out the wood, the flames leapt skyward. I stood with them silently as they wept, sharing their grief. After a time, I turned for home, leaving them to their misery for the night. I returned at dawn with some food and an undamaged clay urn I had found among the wreckage. The ashes were still warm as we scooped the remains into the urn; the twins found comfort that their parents would be entwined together for all eternity. While Freki muttered another prayer, we buried the urn at the base of a large boulder behind their destroyed home. Then we turned away and continued to help others, making our way about the district.

For days following the great wave an oily, black smoke hung low over the land as funeral pyres burned. We were facing the onset of winter without proper food, clothing, and shelter; and I watched, helpless, as the people fell into despair.

---

Several days after the flood the surviving leaders of the Cimbri nation were called to attend an assembly at Borremose. The assembly of the leaders and senior men of the tribe is where decisions regarding law and custom are made. Elections of tribal leaders, decisions to go to war, and trials of great importance were heard at the assembly. The Cimbri were facing a situation never before seen, and the decisions our people faced now were momentous. The hunnos and senior warriors of each clan were present, and the mood was somber as the leaders recited the losses in their various districts. I had never seen a gathering such as this and felt insignificant among the presence of so many wizened and battle-hardened men.

The hunnos were clan leaders who led districts that belonged to each clan. These districts normally could field around one hundred fighting men when called, and they fought in their clan groups, led by their hunno. My father was hunno of the Wolf Clan of Borremose, and last to address the leaders and senior warriors of the tribe.

I admired my father greatly and hoped that one day I would take his place as hunno, though I knew that was unlikely. He was tall and well-built. His long hair and drooping mustache were blonde, as was common among our people. A heavy brow gave him a near constant impression of deep thought. A wide scar crossed his face from behind his left ear to the corner of his mouth, where a sword stroke had nearly ended him. He stood before the senior members of our tribe, not aloof, but with ultimate confidence in himself. He had the ability to make others want to hear what he had to say, and all eyes were upon him.

"Long ago, our ancestors came from the mountains and plains of the lands far to our south and east," he began in his strong, deep voice.

"Our people, great warriors, feared for their courage in battle and renowned for their many victories, came north. Our legends tell us how Wodan, god of the sky, appeared to them and directed them to follow the great rivers west and north until they came to the northern sea, and once they found it to make this land their own.

Sitting in the rear of the council, I leaned forward, fascinated by his recitation of our history, as were the rest of the people present.

"Our fathers encountered a race of people who did not possess the secrets of iron or steel. Those people hunted and fought with bronze weapons, many still used wooden spears and stone axes. They lived in simple huts. They wore animal skins, for they did not know the loom. They were mound builders and stone work-ers and our people conquered them, took their land, and settled it as Wodan instructed them. Those first people that remained were absorbed into our own and the cultures mixed and became a new people, unique from all others, yet tied to their ancestors and their neighbors. They became the Cimbri, the people of the coasts.

"This new land was good to them, and they spent many years here content with its rich bounty. After so many years of good harvests and good hunting the people thrived and had many children. The Cimbri spread across this land.

"In time, we reached across the waters and became friends with the people to our north and east in Scandia. We reconnected with our cousins the Teutones and others who had come north behind us."

His voice dropped in tone. "But, in more recent years, the harvests have been poor and the game less plentiful. Our hunters must travel for days to return with meat. The fish and seals and shellfish have dwindled in number. The grain no longer lasts the winter, and our people grow hungry before the last snows are gone. Each winter is colder than the last and the summers wetter. The sea has slowly crept closer toward our homes and now, in one bold stroke, our communities are destroyed, our crops are ruined, and our fields have been flooded with sand and saltwater. It will be years before they are able to grow crops again. Hundreds are dead and thousands are without homes."

He paused for a few moments, an orator's trick to build anticipation for what was to come. The council silently waited for him to continue.

"This is my son, Borr," he said, beckoning me forward. "Before the flood, he told me of a dream that I did not understand. I asked him to share it with you so that we may determine its meaning and if it should have any bearing on our decisions here today."

I was fifteen years old, an unbearded youth, and I was about to address the most experienced warriors and leaders of our tribe. I could tell from the faces that looked back at me that they were not impressed with the young man before them, skinny and weak with pale skin that looked even paler against my copper-colored hair. I had suffered from a breathing sickness since the age of three, when I was playing with my friends at the seashore and was caught in an undercurrent and pulled out to sea. My father plucked me from the ocean floor, and when he placed me in my mother's arms I was no longer breathing. She pressed me to her, thinking she had lost another child when I suddenly coughed up seawater and raggedly breathed again. From that day on I did not grow well and was unhealthy, at times struggling to breathe. The sickness often reduced me to lying on my bed gasping for air, coughing and spitting out gobs of infection, and praying not to die, while my mother suffered, listening to the rattle in my lungs.

I looked at my father, who had moved to the back of the ranks surrounding the fire. He met my gaze and nodded his reassurance, straightening his shoulders and throwing out his chest to remind me to stand up tall and face my fear.

I stood up straighter, took a deep breath, gathered my courage, and began nervously. "Before the great flood, Wodan came to me in a dream."

My voice threatened to embarrass me by its quavering, and my mouth felt as if I had swallowed a handful of dust. Men were leaning forward, and I understood they could not hear me well.

Swallowing dryly, I continued, this time in a stronger voice. "He woke me with a shake and extended an arm, beckoning me to ride with him. He pulled me up behind him on his eight-legged steed, Sleipnir, and we flew above our lands. It shocked me to see our homeland devastated, just as it looks today. At the time I did not understand that I was seeing what was to come.

"We flew southward over the great estuary of the river Albis, and the devastation was present anywhere that was close to the sea. We followed that river eastward and passed over the lands of many tribes. I saw a great caravan of people and herds of animals as we soared over majestic mountains and grasslands. Thick forests teemed with game and rivers were so full of fish you could walk on their backs from bank to bank.

"We passed over mountain top villages, many times the size of Borremose."

Most were listening with interest now, but many still were skeptical. I continued with more confidence.

"At last, we came to a land of wondrous cities filled with a strange people, protected by warriors made of gleaming metal that shone in the evening sun. The metal warriors moved about in large squares responding to the calls of their horns. We watched through the rising dust as they fought a host of warriors from many tribes. Swooping low over the warriors Wodan hurled his spear, Gungnir, toward the shining enemy. The tribesmen looked up and saw the sky god, and a great cheer rose to our ears as they surged against their foe. The metal warriors fought valiantly but were defeated, overwhelmed by the great numbers of tribesmen. After the battle, the victors returned to their camp as a flock of ravens descended upon the battlefield.

"My eyes were drawn to the large raven that led the flock. When its feet touched the ground, it shape-shifted into an old crone who walked among the dead, encouraging her minions as they plucked an eyeball or tore into the spilled guts of a fallen warrior. As the sun set and the bright day turned to twilight, the ravens seemed to grow in size from their feasting, and at the crone's command each grasped a fallen tribesman. With great flapping wings they lifted the warriors from the ground and flew skyward, ever upward, until they vanished from sight into the darkening sky, leaving only the enemy dead. The crone was the last to leave the battlefield in a swirl of her black cloak as she resumed the form of the large raven and followed her grisly flock into the blackness."

After a moment of shocked silence, a murmur of disbelief traveled around the council as men considered the story and challenged why Wodan would appear to a weakling boy, until my father called for quiet.

I licked my dry lips and nervously continued. "Wodan said nothing to me during our flight and later returned me safely home to my bed.

"When I awoke, I remembered the dream vividly, but did not understand what any of it meant. I told my father of the dream, and he took me to a priest to interpret the meaning. That priest sits

11

among you now," I said, pointing to Gudrun.

Two young priests helped Gudrun to his feet, for he was an old man with thin white hair and a long, wispy beard. His back was bent, and he shuffled his feet, but his eyes were bright, and his voice was strong. He took my place and spoke to the gathering as I gratefully returned to the shadows at the edge of the council, next to my father.

"As Borr has told you, I interpreted his dream and I believe he tells the truth," Gudrun said. Another murmur rippled through the crowd.

"Just as in our past, Wodan has shown us the way. Though it was meant as a warning to avoid the disaster that has occurred, it now reveals what will come to be. I believe Wodan chose the boy to avoid the fractures that would have naturally arisen if he had chosen anyone in power to bring us this message.

"Wodan has shown us that the path forward is to retrace our steps along the great rivers back toward the south, to the lands of our ancestors. He assured Borr that fish and game will be plentiful once again, and he has shown that we will have great enemies to conquer. These men of metal that he describes can only be the soldiers of Rome who we have heard of for many years. His vision of our victory over them is a sign that we will regain our former strength and glory. The raven goddess assures us that our honored dead will be taken to feast with the gods in Valholl until the end of days!" he shouted, followed by the first sounds of consensus.

"Leaders of the Cimbri, the time has come for us to leave this land. We must seek out a new homeland that will allow us to begin a new life, as our ancestors once did," Gudrun said, as he finished speaking and was helped back to his seat.

There was a low rumble of feet stamping the packed earth in agreement. I was proud that Wodan had chosen me to deliver this message and that the men gathered round had apparently accepted it.

The Cimbri do not recognize one tribal leader. Each clan is led by a hunno, who receives that leadership by right of birth, and keeps it through personal strength. In a time of war, we elect a chieftain to lead the combined effort, but that leader's power is limited to the time it takes for the conflict to end. Claudicus, hunno of the boar clan, rose to be recognized and pointed out that though this was not a time of war, under the circumstances faced by all, the tribe needed a single leader and put forth my father's name.

Lugius stood. "I and the people of Lyngsmose support Haistulf as chieftain until we are past this crisis, and we find a new homeland. If he will lead us, we are prepared to follow."

One by one, the other leaders swore their support and allegiance to my father until each clan leader had agreed to join the exodus.

At last, he rose to address the assembly. "I am humbled and grateful for the trust you place in me. I accept the responsibility to lead our people, and we shall linger no longer than it takes to construct the necessary wagons and carts and gather our supplies and livestock. Let each clan in the north assemble on the heath outside Borremose when they are ready. We will travel southward along the ancient trade route, and the other clans will join us as we travel. When the new moon begins, we shall begin our search for a new homeland."

This time the clash of spears and seax on shields indicated their approval. Now, as I looked about, the smiling faces looking back at me held a measure of respect that I did not expect, and my father looked at me with pride in his eyes.

———

The next morning the twins and I, along with hundreds of others, searched for carts and wagons that were undamaged or could be repaired and hauled back to Borremose. The ones too damaged to move were torn apart, placed in a working cart, and taken to Gorm, the blacksmith. He had been assigned dozens of men to repair and rebuild carts and wagons and harness out of the parts of others. The wagon assembly worked day and night and produced a great number of usable carts for the journey. Any iron that could be found was scavenged and fashioned into the axles, hubs, and other parts to build the many carts needed for the journey. Weapons, tools, and cookware all went back to the village to be distributed to those who needed it. There was so much debris lying around we simply picked up anything that looked useful and threw it into an empty cart.

The twins and I were searching for iron when we heard a child's scream from the other side of a rise. We raced to the top and saw a man standing over the body of a woman who lay motionless on the ground. A girl of about ten ran towards us. Breathlessly, she told us the man had killed her mother and pleaded for our help.

We spread out and approached the man. He stood there, watching us silently, his eyes filled with madness, his chest still heaving from the effort he had made to kill the woman. He suddenly shook his head and blinked, as if waking up from a dream. Looking about, he realized we intended to capture or kill him.

He ran toward Skalla who slowed him enough that Freki and I could get to them. I swung a chunk of solid wood I picked up from the ground against the man's temple and knocked him unconscious. We bound his wrists and dumped him unceremoniously into the cart. After burying her mother in a shallow grave, we accompanied the girl back to Borremose.

"We found him standing over her mother's body," I explained to my father, gesturing toward the girl.

"Tell me what happened. No one will harm you now," he said.

The girl told us her mother had been sifting through the carnage of their ruined homestead. "She lost her senses and was wandering about searching for my father," the girl managed between sobs. "He was swept away in the storm, and she could not accept that.

I was looking for food as we had not eaten in days when he appeared," she said, looking fearfully toward the cart.

"He demanded food and held my mother by the neck, shaking her. When I told him we had no food either, he became enraged and shoved my mother to the ground, shaking her and hitting her head against a rock until he killed her."

The girl shook with grief as she retold the story; the tears leaving jagged streaks through the dirt on her cheeks. As she spoke a crowd gathered, and my mother took the child away to comfort and feed her as my father considered what he had been told.

"Put the prisoner into the cell and guard him," he instructed me. "I will send a warrior to relieve you."

Freki removed the wooden grate that covered the prisoner's pit and we shoved the man into it. He fell awkwardly and injured his ankle, but no one cared. He was already pleading for mercy, and had been since we captured him, knowing what was likely in store for him. His calls fell on deaf ears; there was no mercy to be had for murderers.

---

Several days later I walked beside my father as the high priest led a procession out of the village by torchlight, along the causeway, and out past the ruined fields. The flames flickered in the sea wind, casting ominous shadows upon the grim faces that marched in the darkness. Amidst the group of white clad priests, a cart drawn by two white oxen carried a silver cauldron, displayed for all to see.

The cauldron was a magnificent work of art and the most sacred possession of the tribe. The Scordisci, a Celtic tribe that fought side by side with us in the war with the Hellenes, had taken the cauldron from a Thracian tribe encountered during the invasion. The Scordisci, in turn, gave it to the Cimbri as a sign of brotherhood between our people and it was brought to our new homeland in the north when the campaign was over, along with weapons, livestock, slaves, and some silver and gold.

It was the Scordisci that we hoped to rejoin and request new lands to settle, and my father dispatched several ambassadors to find them. He had some idea of where they now lived from reports of travelers over the years, as the Scordisci were at war with Rome, and news of conflict with Rome traveled far and wide.

The cauldron was made entirely of silver, with a bowl-shaped base. Rectangular plates were attached upright around the rim with detailed artwork inside and out. Some images were familiar and others unknown to us. One panel depicted a procession of warriors with spears and large shields, mounted warriors, and a figure holding a man over a cauldron. Another panel showed the horned god of the forest, Cerunnos, sitting cross-legged and holding a torc in one hand and a snake in the other. The plates on the outside depicted several men and women, probably gods, as the main figure of each panel, surrounded by smaller figures of humans or animals. Parts of the designs were gilded to show the details of hair and ornaments, and the eyes of the larger figures were decorated with gemstones. The cauldron had come to be an object of great religious significance, and it was used by our priests during important ceremonies. This day it was to be sacrificed as an offering to the gods.

Behind the sacred cauldron came a second cart in which the prisoner sat within an iron cage, rocking back and forth with the motion of the cart over the uneven ground.

The prisoner's hands were bound behind his back, and a rope hung from his neck. The priests had crushed dried mushrooms into his last meal of gruel to keep him calm, and now he could only watch silently as his fate approached.

The procession moved to the north for an hour and stopped just before midnight on a spot of dry ground surrounded on three sides by a bog. A platform stood in the clearing and a large bonfire was lit by which to witness the night's events. The spectators formed a half circle facing the platform, and the wind caused the torches to cast a flickering light on all present. Recognizing his time was near, the prisoner anxiously searched the crowd for a sympathetic face. He caught my eye and pleaded silently for help, his lips quivering with fear, nostrils flaring. I stared at him until he turned away. There was nothing that could change what was to come.

Now resigned to his fate, the prisoner was silent and watched wide-eyed as two warriors took the cauldron from the cart and placed it carefully on the platform. The guard, followed by a young priest, then led the trembling prisoner up the stairs to the edge of the cauldron and forced him to kneel behind it, maintaining a tight two-handed grip on the rope around the prisoner's neck.

Gudrun, the high priest, stood before the raging flames that reached high behind him, silhouetting his spare frame. He chanted slowly at first, building to a great crescendo as he prayed to Wodan. At the end of the prayer, Gudrun folded his arms across his chest and dropped his chin. There was a loud crash of weapons against shields and a great shout from the onlookers.

"Hoosh!"

With the prayer completed, an ancient priestess stiffly climbed the stairs to the platform where the prisoner knelt. This was Skyld, the high priestess. She was given ultimate respect, though most also feared her. She was very thin in her dirty white shift and wore nothing on her feet. Her leathery brown skin was the only cover to the bones and sinew in her arms and legs. Her eyes were milky white, so common in the very old, and her thin, white hair looked like a bird had been caught in it and struggled to escape. She pursed her lips in and out over empty gums. She was a seer, a sorcerous, a matron. She was good and evil all in one and a woman who held mystical powers that the common mortal could not understand.

At a nod from her, the young priest approached the prisoner from behind and with a mighty swing, smashed the back of his skull in with a single blow from a heavy club. The warrior holding the prisoner pushed his head forward, while Skyld drew a large knife and deftly slashed his throat, directing the resulting fountain of blood into the cauldron.

When she determined there was enough blood for her purpose, she gestured impatiently to the guard and executioner with a flick of her hand and the body was dragged away.

I watched without expression. I was no stranger to violent death, and I accepted it as an important part of our religion. It is through the dead and dying that our gods speak to us.

Skyld bent over the cauldron, examining its contents carefully. She moved slowly about it, stirring the foaming dark liquid with a twig, and mumbling to herself, interpreting the signs that she saw in the flickering reflections of the blood. Slowly she stood, the hump in her back keeping her from rising all the way up as she raised her spindly arms above her head. The air was palpable, and I held my breath as we all stood awaiting her words.

"Wodan understands why his children must leave this place," Skyld announced in her shrill, cracked voice.

"He is pleased with the gift of life we have sent him and promises to watch over us and protect us as we search for a new homeland. Wodan warns us that it will be a long and difficult journey and that we must be strong. We will suffer many hardships, but we will survive, and we will conquer if we trust in him."

A murmur of hesitant agreement rippled through the crowd as they heard her words. Then the priests began to chant, signaling the end of the ceremony.

While the procession returned to the village, I delayed long enough to watch two young priests as they scrubbed the platform clean and emptied the cauldron. They cleaned it and reverently disassembledg the silver plates from the bowl, placing them gently inside it, while another stepped off to the side and began cutting a hole into the peat. When the hole was deep enough, they placed the cauldron in it and covered it back up with the peat they had removed, the excess scattered about until there was no sign of where the cauldron had been left. On the way back to the village, the body was unceremoniously thrown into a watery bog. The pale, bloodless face reflected the light from the torches as it slowly sank below the dark water. By the time we returned to the village there was no sign of the sacrifice to be seen and the sun was pinking the eastern sky.

# Chapter Two
## Mid October 120 BC

I stood beside my father on a small rise, looking down on Borremose and the surrounding devastation, knowing there would be no returning to my boyhood home. The sky was heavy with the threat of rain, and our cloaks snapped in the sea-wind. Closing my eyes, I breathed deeply, committing the sights, sounds and smells to memory. I looked toward the coast and saw none of the ever-present gulls or puffins or pelicans wheeling about, and I wondered if this was an omen of things to come. A large caravan of two and four-wheeled carts drawn by oxen wound its way along the ancient trade road, plodding southward.

In each district and in many villages, some people remained for their own reasons. There were those too old or unable to travel, and those who remained to care for them, intending to catch up to the main tribe later. And there were those who simply did not wish to face the unknown future and preferred to stay and rebuild as best they could. After the tribe departed, these groups gathered into new communities that allowed them to protect and provide for each other.

Grim-faced mounted warriors led the caravan. Foot soldiers carrying spears and shields with a single-edged seax in their belts walked with the column. The brightly colored shields were a stark contrast to the dour mood of the procession.

In the rear, thralls herded the cattle and other livestock. Geese and ducks waddled amongst cattle and swine and carts and people,

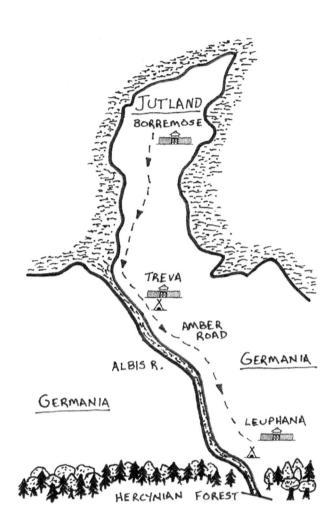

Figure 2.

all moving at their own pace, bewildered at leaving their familiar places, and creating a great cacophony.

When the last of the carts finally passed, my father turned to me and ordered, "Find your mother and help her with the oxen."

I desperately wanted to stay with him and ride with his retainers. I opened my mouth to protest, but as I did, I remembered I was not yet a warrior, and hung my head in disappointment.

"Yes, father," I replied obediently.

At fifteen, I was the age that most young men became warriors, but because of my illness, others looked at me as weak. Taller than most my age, I was gangly and awkward, never able to put on the muscle they did. I did not have their stamina when running or learning to fight, gasping for air before the others even began to sweat heavily.

Rather than point out my weaknesses, he grasped my shoulder and looked directly into my eyes.

"Borr, there are enough scouts and warriors. I need you to stay close to your mother and sister and protect them. These are dangerous times and I need to know that they are safe in your care."

My chest swelled with the trust he had placed in me. With a boy's prideful boast, I assured him I would protect our family until my death, then turned and ran to catch up to them.

Smiling, he mounted his horse and cantered down the hill to the head of the column where he took his place in the vanguard, riding beside his brothers Grimur and Lothar.

My uncle Grimur was usually beside my father. He was a formidable warrior and was liked by everyone who knew him. He ate most meals with our family and was particularly fond of my little sister, Hilgi. Grimur was always kind to me, despite my physical ailments, and did his best to train me in the warrior's skills. Lothar, like Grimur, was seldom far from father's side.

These two, along with ten others, made up the core of my father's retainers. They were battle hardened professional warriors who had faced death a hundred times. They served as his personal guard and would never allow themselves to be surpassed in bravery on the battlefield and would never willingly leave the field alive if he fell. They served as his lieutenants, ambassadors, and liaisons, as he required.

A few days prior, Lugius and his followers had encamped on the heath south of Borremose near the refugee camp. Clans from the nearby islands had also staged close by, waiting to join the caravan when it moved out. They fell in behind our people as the caravan swelled to many thousands of people.

Following the Amber Road meant we could take advantage of a well-traveled path the wheels of trader's carts had packed for centuries. The path avoided the worst terrain and crossed numerous streams and rivers at shallow fords with gravel bottoms.

The great caravan of carts, animals, and people grew larger daily as more and more joined. Such was the number of hooves, feet, and wheels that trod the earth that the rearmost were having a hard time crossing the churned-up streams and negotiating obstacles along the trail.

The ground changed from mud that stuck to my foot coverings and covered my legs up past my knees, to a dry powder when it had not rained for a few days. We choked on the dust on still days and were thankful on the days the sea breezes whipped it away. Then the rain turned the dust back into the clinging mud in a constant cycle.

We entered the lands of the Teutones a fortnight after leaving Borremose, now with tens of thousands of our people in tow. My father sent Lothar ahead as a messenger to Teutobod, chieftain of the Teutones, to let him know of our intent to move peacefully through his lands, and that we wished to meet with him.

Lothar returned one cool evening while my family was eating supper.

"Teutobod will welcome us," he began in his blunt manner.

My father waited patiently, knowing that Lothar would continue in a moment.

"He has been talking with the Ambrones who live west of the Albis. Their chieftain, Amalric, is aware of our plight and has offered to host a council for the three tribes."

The Teutones lived in the south of Jutland and among the eastern islands and rocky shorelines. Like many of the surrounding tribes, they were related to the Cimbri through ancient ties. Their influence spread from the shores of the Suebian Sea south across the plains and lowlands to the land of the Langobards and stretched between the Albis River in the west and the Suevus River to the east. Though the Cimbri had borne the worst of the great storm, the Teutones along the coasts had felt its direct impact as well. The surrounding islands had all experienced flooding as a result of the following deluge of rain.

Neighboring settlements of the Cimbri and Teutones communicated and traded often, and after the disaster they were soon aware of each other's situation.

The bulk of the Ambrones lived farther inland and had escaped most of the flood that had caused so much carnage for the tribes who lived on the peninsula. But it had wiped out their barrier islands and coastal areas.

A few days after the caravan was settled into camp, the Cimbri and Teutones leaders joined the Ambrones in a council at Treva, their main village at the confluence of the Albis and Alster rivers. It thrilled me when I was allowed to accompany them.

It was an overcast day of gusty winds and passing showers that were enough to keep most people inside. I sat quietly behind my father, trying to remain inconspicuous as the leaders and several others met in Amalric's home. The rest of our party was welcomed in the mead hall.

At the meeting, we discovered that both the Teutones and Ambrones had already held council. The tribes as a whole had each voted against leaving their lands, but as a free people, individuals, family groups, and even a few clans requested to join us on our quest. My father readily agreed, and a rendezvous was set to meet the newcomers the following spring, farther along the Albis River where he intended to camp for the winter. After renewing agreements of friendship, the council adjourned to cement those friendships with a feast.

Amalric's mead hall was large enough to comfortably hold two hundred warriors, but it was packed wall to wall with many more. There were rows of long tables with benches and a raised dais at one end for the head table. A whole boar roasted over a large hearth on the opposite end while several women tended it. Girls weaved their way among the tables and kept the horn cups full of ale. Several chickens and geese roasted on a second hearth, while a few large fish baked in the coals. A stew of beef and pork bubbled in a large cauldron. The air was hazy from the smoke that was hesitant to escape through the smoke hole and out into the drizzly rain and the smell of roasted onions and garlic mingled with that of the wood smoke, roasted meat, and sweat. There was a cry of welcome as the three leaders entered the hall where the warriors of all three tribes intermingled as they boasted of feats of bravery and strength, laughed at crude jokes, and sang songs of heroes' past. The Ambrones suffered no shortage of ale, and the golden liquid flowed freely as the men ate their fill.

I sat with my uncle Grimur watching my father with Teutobod and Amalric who were seated at the high table. The three head men talked and laughed with easy friendship, and I saw my father for the first time in a different light. He had been the hunno of our clan as far back as I could remember, and it was no surprise that those who knew him so well voted him chieftain of all the Cimbri. The calm strength that he had exhibited during the aftermath of the flood and thus far on our journey was something I took for granted, as it was his way. But the way he conducted himself now and his ease around these other leaders, strong men in their own right, was something new to me.

Teutobod was perhaps thirty, younger than my father and with a thicker build. Where my father was lean and loose-jointed, Teuto-bod always appeared tightly coiled and ready to spring into action at any moment. His long blonde hair was tied up into a knot tight to his scalp above his right ear. He was without a doubt the hairiest man I have ever seen, covered in fur over his chest, shoulders, and even his back. His beard was a magnificent, thick, blonde mop that hid his mouth and covered his neck. Bright blue eyes shone with an intelligence that belied his rough exterior, and one could say his expression appeared as if he was always thinking, planning something. He seemed to have the more vibrant personality of the three chieftains and was always the loudest in a group, roaring with laughter when one of his men belted another in the mouth for bragging about winning an arm-wrestling match.

Amalric, older and more reserved, was a large man with the scars of a warrior and the carriage of a man long accustomed to leader-ship. He stood and banged an ancient bronze war hammer on the table, causing the clay pots and platters to jump and clatter loudly. The gathering of warriors quieted and looked in his direction.

Raising his cup in a toast he intoned, "I dedicate this feast in the name of Wodan, the spear carrier. Welcome to our guests the Cimbri and the Teutones, who are our brothers by blood, descended from the same forefathers. Alike in custom and beliefs, we will grow to know one another again through our nearness in the coming winter. The Cimbri have suffered greatly, and I ask my people to help them gather food and supplies. I encourage our warriors to hunt and train together, so that you may know each other by name and manner. I encourage you to foster the bonds of brotherhood. In the spring, the Cimbri will depart to the south. Some of our people will accompany them, and the Cimbri have agreed to accept them as their own. Some day in the future we will meet again, of this I have no doubt, but for now, eat! Drink! Skal!"

"Skal!" the room shouted as one as they raised their own cups in salute.

The room burst back into noisy conversation as everyone drank heartily from their own cups, foam dripping from their thick mustaches and running down their beards.

When Amalric sat, my father leaned toward him, "I am grateful, we…are grateful for your generosity, Amalric, and to you, Teutobod. It has been hard on my people to lose everything, and they fear the unknown future."

Amalric looked at him with a guarded expression and said, "We are brothers, Haistulf. It may come from far in our past, before anyone here was born, but our people are family. All of us." He looked to his left and tipped his cup to Teutobod as well.

"We have always traded, and at times inter-married," Teutobod offered. "It is only right that we help if we can. It is good to have allies, and there may come a day when we will need your help."

It relieved my father to know that there was no tension between the tribes and was grateful for the words of support.

I noticed a passing shadow behind Grimur's dark eyes as he watched the head table. He was the opposite of my father with his dark hair and thick beard streaked with strands of gray. He always had a more somber expression but was usually open and friendly. But the look I saw gave me pause. If I had not known my uncle so well, I would have thought he was angry, or perhaps jealous.

It passed in a moment and when my father looked our way, Grimur gave him a wide grin, raised his cup in salute, and was soon caught up in the mood as the mingled tribesmen around him toasted the future.

In the morning, the delegations were invited to witness a sacrifice to Wodan. We were led to a small lake not far from the village where a ship had been dragged inland and deposited. A priest prayed to the sky god for strength and courage and to grant us good fortune during our journey. Each warrior then passed by the ship and threw in a spear, or sword, or a shield that had been captured in battle. The sacrifice of these weapons would ensure that Wodan would look favorably upon them in the times ahead. Holes were chopped into the bottom of the ship and it was covered with its leather sail, then pushed out into the lake to sink slowly into the murky water.

---

A few days later, a grinning Amalric and Teutobod approached our camp at the head of a caravan of carts with hundreds of men and women walking behind. We were shocked to find that they had brought grain, salt, and ale, as well as some tools and desperately needed clothing. The people wept with gratitude. Never did we expect such generosity, especially as winter approached.

"Now," Amalric grinned, "you have arrived in time for the eels' return to the sea. We've already taken our fill over the past few days and these people will help you catch as many as you can carry. If you will prepare as many as care to come, we'll spend the night fishing for eels!"

Pointing at the rear of the caravan Teutobod said, "Make sure you bring that last cart, there are several barrels of ale in it."

All those within hearing rejoiced, and they ran to tell others about a night of catching the snake-like fish that provided so much food for those who lived on the northern shores and rivers. Soon, hundreds of people appeared with carts loaded with sacks, empty barrels and baskets, bags of salt, spears, and nets. Each year in late fall the rivers teemed with the eels as they returned to the warmer waters of the sea. They could grow to be longer than a man's arm and their delicious meat could be smoked and preserved for months.

Amalric led the way to where a large tributary spilled into the Albis, and the people spread out on the banks. The tribes mixed, chattering excitedly, making new friends. Bonfires were lit and ale was passed out as we prepared for an evening of catching eels. Freki and Skalla sat and fashioned spears out of willows while I helped build a smoking rack. I had never been fishing eels because after I nearly drowned, I always had a fear of water, but now, I was looking forward to it. It had been a while since we did something enjoyable and the mood was light, our troubles forgotten for a time. As day turned to night, the river churned with eels. The twins waded into the shallows, spearing the wriggling fish, and throwing them onto the bank for me to catch. A young Teuton boy had been watching me struggle to pick them up and fell to the ground, his chest heaving with laughter. He was watching me try to hold onto the slippery eel that was desperately fighting to keep from being captured, slapping my arms and chest and drenching me with water, sand, and slime.

He walked up to me, still chuckling, and said, "I'm Hrolf. Here." He was holding out a bit of rough woven cloth and showed me how he used the cloth to grasp the eels.

Laughing at the obvious solution, I said, "Thanks for that. I'm Borr, those are my friends Freki and Skalla."

I toasted him with the cloth.

He acknowledged my thanks with a casual wave of his hand, and we immediately were scooping them up by the dozens and putting them in the baskets, sprinkling salt on them in layers to remove the slime and kill them.

The ones not fishing held torches or carried baskets to people at the carts who were swiftly gutting and washing them. The eels were then tossed into barrels of salt brine to soak for a short time and then placed on the smoking racks over the fires.

Throughout the night, young girls carried around platters of the eels roasted over the open fires and we gorged on the flaky white flesh. The eels were so plentiful, and there were so many people helping, that by the middle of the night all the carts and containers were full, and the people were drying out around the bonfires, laughing, and drinking.

One girl seemed to keep appearing by our fire, a small slip of a thing with a long chestnut braid falling down her back. I took notice of her, and Hrolf took notice of me noticing her.

He nudged me after one of her visits and said good-naturedly, "That one has been coming back here again and again, offering you more food. She doesn't seem to care if any of the rest of us are hungry." He laughed and took another swig of ale.

I could feel my face burning and said nothing. But I could not remove the stupid grin from my face, so I took a drink to hide it.

"When she approaches, she seems to only see you. I think you've an admirer," Hrolf teased.

"Frida!"

A group of giggling girls near the smoking fire called to her. She rushed over and shushed them, looking over her shoulder at us.

Hrolf laughed and took another drink, punching my arm and spilling my cup onto my lap.

Someone had brought a flute and people were dancing to the lively music, while other groups broke into bawdy drinking songs or told stories over the fire. Hrolf, the twins, and I talked and laughed the night away, our cups never empty. It was the first time any of us boys had gotten drunk and when we were shaken awake the next morning, all four of us had pounding headaches.

We returned to the caravan with months' worth of food and between the grain and other supplies as well as our own livestock, we would not starve this winter and we owed it to the Teutones and Ambrones. This was a debt that could never be repaid.

———————

The day before we were to leave the encampment at Treva, my mother was up before dawn to prepare breakfast. She moved silently, careful not to wake my father as she rolled out of their coverings and dressed in the crisp morning air. I was sleeping under the cart and heard it creaking as she moved, and I joined her when she stepped down.

I have always loved that part of the day when things slowly take shape as the veil of darkness is lifted, and the stars fade in the sky against their backdrop of inky black that fades to gray, then to a bright blue. The birds woke in their trees and sang to us as the sun came up. Even the air here was so different from the windblown heath of Borremose. I gave thanks to the sky god for blessing us with this fine day and breathed in deeply, coughing twice when the cool air hit my damaged lungs.

I missed the sound of the surf and the smell of salty air and the sea, but I was already growing accustomed to this new experience. I could hear the stirring of others as the day dawned, and they moved to the edge of the caravan to relieve themselves. Here and there a metallic clang rang out as fires were rekindled and iron pots were stirred. My mother was rewarming a stew from the previous evening's meal when I returned from the nearby bushes.

Yawning, I looked skyward and watched a large flock of geese fly south. I caught my mother watching me and grinned, causing her to respond in kind. The smell of the warming food caught my attention, and I walked to the fire, my mouth watering as she filled a wooden trencher for me. Shoveling the food into my mouth, I smiled as the familiar flavors of my mother's cooking pleased me. I greeted Freki and Skalla as they walked up to the fire, and she handed them each a meal. My family had more or less adopted the twins. They took their meals with us and helped with the work that needed to be done, and we were growing ever closer with the time spent together.

The twins were so much alike, most people could not tell them apart. Their looks were nearly identical, and they wore their hair the same way, their movements and speech were the same and they often finished each other's sentences. They thanked my mother simultaneously and sat by the fire with their food.

Hearing movement behind her, mother turned in time to see my little sister Hilgi, a rag doll clutched firmly in one hand, climbing down from the family's second wagon she shared with aunt Nilda. Mother put a finger to her lips, motioning silence to Hilgi, so she did not wake my father. He had attended a meeting the previous night with the other leaders and then, after spending some time speaking with the sentries, he had not returned to the wagon until very late.

Hilgi smiled and nodded her head as she allowed mother to lift her to the ground. She was off immediately to chase a chicken that was scratching in the grass a few feet away, her laugh a piercing squeal as the chicken fluttered and scrambled away, squawking loudly.

Rolling her eyes and shaking her head, my mother sighed, then looked toward the wagon as father threw back the leather flap.

"Good morning," she said with a wry smile.

Rubbing his face with both hands and yawning, he asked her groggily, "Why didn't you wake me when you got up?"

"You needed to sleep," she replied. "You've not slept well since we left home. You're no good to anyone if you cannot function. I intended to let you sleep until you woke on your own, but your daughter saw to that," she said, turning back to her makeshift table.

My father came up behind her and slipped his arms around her waist and nibbled on her ear. She yelped and rewarded him with a slap from a wet rag she was using to scrub a pot. He laughed and ducked away, putting his hands up in mock surrender.

His attention shifted to my sister, as she quickly tired of chasing the hapless chicken and ran over to sit on his lap by the fire. He shared some of his breakfast with her before she was down and off again.

The sun was fully up above the treetops now and mother turned toward it to enjoy the warming rays on her face. Her hair reflected the light, single strands sparkling like strings of gold, defiantly refusing her attempts to smooth them down. My father was watching her, smiling. My parents had both felt from a young age that they were destined to be together, and secure in that knowledge they had grown unusually close.

Grimur was next to join us. He had spent the night away from the family again, and when he sat down, my father raised a questioning eyebrow. Grimur's face broke into a grin and he shrugged self-consciously, not bothering to offer an explanation. Along the journey, my uncle would disappear for hours at a time without explanation. We all knew that he was helping a young widow whose husband had been killed in the flood, but he offered nothing further, so no one asked. My mother and father shared a knowing look across the fire, then she busied herself with packing up our belongings and preparing to move.

Nilda quietly stepped around the rear of her wagon. Mother looked up and immediately knew something was bothering her sister when she saw Nilda's pale and drawn face.

Gripping Nilda's elbow, mother drew her aside and questioned her, "What is troubling you, sister? Are you ill?"

"I didn't sleep well," Nilda replied tiredly. Her thin frame seemed so fragile.

"Another dream? Tell me," mother said as she guided her sister to a seat by the fire.

"It was the three matrons again, a warning of death. It wasn't clear to me, but I fear we will soon know what they've been trying to tell me. It's never a direct message, just a feeling of foreboding. I can see them through a watery veil. They are reaching out to me as I move farther away from them, then it fades to darkness. When I awaken, I'm left so cold and tired, I can hardly move."

"I want you to rest in the wagon today," my mother told her. "We will leave in the morning, and you need to regain your strength. Can you eat?"

Nodding her head in agreement and smiling weakly, Nilda accepted a few spoonfuls of stew and allowed my mother to help her back into the wagon and cover her with a thick stack of warm furs.

My mother's sister and I shared a bond from the time I was born and now she shared that with Hilgi as well. She never married and having no children of her own, she found the family she desired with us, and she was a great help to my mother.

Nilda was an Idessa, a midwife and healer, someone who knew the herbs and potions that helped the sick and injured. She was present at my birth and my sister's, as well as most of the clan for nearly twenty years and had often relieved my pain from the breathing sickness with a poultice on my chest and a tea of herbs and roots she dug from the forest. She was also a dreamer, and I believed that my vision came from my connection with her. Or perhaps the gods chose those who suffered illness, I do not know. But she was often ill, and the events of the past month had drained her.

We spent the rest of the day preparing to continue our journey as the weather was changing quickly. We had only weeks left to reach the border between the Teutones and Langobards, where the coastal plains, marshes, and scrublands met the dark Hercynian Forest. My father had decided that we would camp there, on the edge of the great forest, where the winter would be milder and there would be forage available for the herds through the cold months.

The next morning we woke before dawn and renewed our journey.

# Chapter Three

## Late October 120 BC

I was walking beside my mother while the twins followed with the other cart when we approached yet another tributary to the Albis River. The caravan disappeared ahead of us as it dipped into the small river valley. When our carts reached the ford, my mother climbed into the back as they plodded ahead methodically.

We had crossed many small rivers on our journey already, but this one was bigger and swollen with the fall rains. I still held a fear of the water, but I had learned to trust the oxen, and as long as I was not in the water, I was confident. Hilgi was sitting in the rear of the cart near Nilda, excitedly chattering and watching the water rush past.

She half stood to reach for her doll when, without warning, the cart's wheel dropped into an unseen hole tipping it dangerously to one side and sending everyone flying into the air, jarring them roughly when they came down opposite from where they had been sitting.

A heavy iron pot struck my mother on the head, knocking her unconscious. The violent movement slammed Nilda against the edge of a wooden crate and knocked the wind from her lungs. Hilgi fell backwards out of the cart and into the icy water, her eyes wide with terror as her hands grasped desperately at empty air.

Nilda was unable to grab my sister and shouted at me as she leapt into the water after Hilgi, heedless of her own safety, trying to keep sight of the little blonde head bobbing to the surface.

Without thinking, I leapt into the water after them. The cold quickly sapped my strength as I was swept downstream.

Freki, mounted on the second team of oxen, heard the screams, and alerted several nearby horsemen. But we were moving much faster than the riders could manage through the heavy brush alongside the river.

Nilda struggled to stay close to Hilgi and managed to get a grip on a flailing arm. She found purchase with her feet and gave a mighty heave, pushing Hilgi into an eddy that formed behind a large boulder. In the effort, Nilda lost her footing and was pulled under the surface, spun around by the current and slammed into a rock. The impact dazed her and cut a large gash in her forehead before she slipped under the churning surface.

"Borr!" Hilgi screamed as I swept past her. She was crawling through the shallow water onto the bank, and I was struggling to keep my head up. My chest constricted as visions of when I nearly drowned as a child entered my mind.

I was carried downstream toward the same rock that Nilda had crashed against but managed to get my feet against it and push off. Something caught my leg and the current forced me under the surface. While I struggled to free myself, my fingers went numb, and my chest felt as if it were about to burst.

The torrent battered me about, and I was struck by something being carried along in the water. The impact dislodged my foot, but by then the pale light from above was fading and the last thing I was conscious of was the cold. I was so cold.

The riders found Hilgi sitting on the gravel at the edge of the river, shivering and crying out for Nilda and me. Others searched farther downstream to where it flowed into the Albis, but Nilda was never seen again.

She had unknowingly seen a vision of her own death and, in saving Hilgi, had fulfilled the destiny she had dreamed.

Word was passed to the front of the caravan and my father returned at a gallop to find Skalla holding a compress to my mother's forehead, and the rest of the family missing.

"They're searching downriver!" Skalla shouted over the noise of the water, pointing his arm in our direction.

Urging his horse back across the river ford, my father met a mounted warrior making his way back toward the caravan holding Hilgi on his lap, wrapped tightly in a wool blanket.

"Papa!" she cried.

Father swept her into his arms, relieved to find her safe and unhurt. When questioned, the warrior knew nothing about me or Nilda and my father joined the search.

"Over here!" someone called.

My father forced his way through the alders at the river's edge and joined the men who found me washed ashore on a sandy bank. Thinking I was dead, he choked back a sob of relief when I retched up a lungful of water that contained a thick, greenish pus; the infection that had plagued me since I was a child.

I sat up, weak and bruised, but unhurt, and regained my feet in a few minutes.

Freki and Skalla had stayed with both ox teams and were tending to my mother when we arrived back at the caravan. She had awakened, stunned and confused, and was just realizing the extent of what had happened.

A pall hung over our family for many days as we mourned Nilda's death. She had been a vibrant part of our daily existence and so much was different now. Hilgi was deeply affected and withdrew into herself. She refused to speak to anyone, and her eyes had lost their mischievous shine.

That night, in the light of a waxing moon, my father called me to accompany him. We walked away from the caravan to a nearby grove of oaks where he knelt on the ground and placed a small bronze brazier on a flat rock. He lit a nugget of amber incense and as the smoke and piney aroma slowly rose and swirled about, he placed a loaf of bread on the improvised altar.

He gave thanks to Nehalennia, water goddess of the north, for the lives of his family. Then he offered a prayer thanking Nilda for her bravery and sacrifice and asked the goddess to watch over her. A single tear of gratitude and pain fell down his cheek.

I watched as he stood, raising his arms in supplication to the goddess. He thanked her again and promised to love and protect his family for all his days and bade me to swear the same.

---

North European Plain

Early November 120 BC

Dry leaves swirled in the chill wind as the caravan spilled out onto the lightly wooded rolling hills and grasslands east of the Albis River, not far from the village of Leuphana.

Our forward scouts led the clans into a sheltered area they had found near a stream that fed into a small river that then emptied into the Albis. The wagons dispersed in a haphazard gathering that provided no organization and little defense. The herds were pastured between the two rivers, and we settled in as a swift drop in temperature announced the coming of winter.

The next morning, I awoke to a cold and clear sky. The sun sparkled brightly on the thick hoarfrost that covered all the foliage. My father and his brothers, Grimur and Lothar, were talking quietly at the fire. The frozen leaves announced my approach, crunching loudly with each step.

"Borr, after you eat, you and the boys take the axes to that stand of aspen," he said, pointing toward the river. "I want enough logs cut today to start work on a house that we will build there. Grimur and I will be around later to help, but you three can get started."

"Yes, father," I replied.

My brow furrowed as I tried to calculate how many trees it would take to build a house.

Grimur chuckled. "Don't look so sad, boy! You will be happy to have a stout house when the snow comes to stay, instead of sleeping on the ground under a cart."

I smiled back, embarrassed, and sat down next to him, accepting the chunk of smoked eel he handed me. I ripped off a handful of bread from the loaf sitting by the fire and chewed silently.

In the weeks since I had nearly drowned a second time, I noticed I was breathing easier; I was not coughing or spitting up the phlegm that had plagued me most of my life, and when I felled the first tree, it felt good.

At the end of that first day, I came back to the fire with red and broken blisters on my hands, wincing in pain as I opened and closed them.

My mother rummaged through Nilda's medicine crate until she found some dried plantain leaves. She ground a few in a quern stone adding a bit of water to make a paste, then spread it on my tender palms and wrapped them with a strip of cloth. A tear ran down her cheek and when I asked her what was wrong, she replied sadly, "This is something that Nilda would have taken care of if she were here."

In a short time, the pain in my hands eased.

Freki and Skalla took turns the next day and they, in turn, developed their own blisters. Within a few days our hands had formed calluses and we could chop the trees from morning to night. Grimur showed us how to properly sharpen the axes and each night we sat by the fire talking and laughing over the sound of the sharpening stones rasping on the iron axe blades. I felt stronger every day, and in my newfound strength I worked harder. I swung the axe longer and took deeper chunks out of the trees. I was developing the muscles in my shoulders and arms.

We worked for six days just to cut down and limb enough trees, then notched and placed the logs. The cabin took shape quickly and by the end of the second week the walls were chinked with moss, the rafter poles were up covered with birch bark shingles and overlaid with chunks of sod. We built a stone hearth in the center with a smoke hole above it and sleeping pallets around the walls to keep us off the ground. We covered the doorway with an old bearskin cloak, which we would later replace with a plank door when there was time.

It was not nearly as cozy as our home in Borremose, but it would keep us warm through the winter and I was proud to have done a great deal of the work.

Grimur and Lothar helped with our cabin and then we all pitched in to build theirs nearby. As always, they shared our meals and were present whenever my father was home. Freki and Skalla would join them in the bachelor's cabin.

With the cabins done, we unloaded what little provisions we had from the wagons and shortly a routine set in. The work never stopped. There was always firewood to be cut, water to be carried, and many other tasks and chores.

We hunted, and we culled our herds. We tanned every hide to make clothes and bedcoverings. Food was never as plentiful or as varied as it was before the flood, but with the smoked eels and the grain our friends had given us, we did not starve, though we all tightened our belts.

At first, clothing was in short supply. Our woven clothing was mostly tatters and could not be replaced. My mother's loom had been lost and there had been no time to replace it or the wool and other tools and materials required. The clothing given to us by the Teutones and Ambrones was not enough for everyone, so we wore buckskin leggings, leather foot coverings, and fur covered tunics, hats, and gloves.

One day Grimur announced that he and Hedda, the widow he had been helping, were to be married and asked permission from my father for them to join our family in our small cabin. He readily agreed and congratulated his younger brother, and we had a small celebration to welcome her into the family.

To make room, I took Grimur's place in the bachelor's cabin. My mother was happy to have another woman around and they soon became fast friends. She missed the company of her sister, and Hedda provided the salve to that wound as they grew closer throughout the winter months.

As the days became shorter, there were times during the dark hours to sit by the fire and replace the many household items that were lost in the flood.

My father and uncles made a butter churn and wooden buckets, and a new loom for mother. Some nights they would care for their weapons or discuss some situation in the camp. Hilgi helped my mother churn the butter and bake the bread, and the twins and I scraped hides or carved wooden spoons and trenchers. My mother and Hedda made tallow candles, or ground flour, or fashioned clothes from the hides.

Before the heavy freeze came, the twins and I collected acorns and dug up the tubers of bulrushes to be crushed, rinsed, and dried to supplement the grain given us by our allies. Every week, the cabin was filled with the smell of fresh bread on baking day and there was always a stew bubbling or meat roasting over the fire at the end of the day.

In all, we made a comfortable camp, and we had already come a long way in recovering our strength and our pride. The herds were able to scrounge for grass through the light snows, and though it was not as good as cut hay and they lost weight, they lived well enough. The winter was milder here, and they found shelter in the nearby woods. Though we had to keep a careful watch for wolves.

---

The day Vallus arrived, heavy dark clouds threatened the first real snow of the season.

Vallus was an old friend of my father's. He was born in the ancient Etruscan city of Clusium and, as a young Roman soldier, had witnessed the fall of Carthage to Scipio Aemilianus. Some years later, he was in Hispania, a commander of scouts during the war with Numantia.

His patrol was ambushed, and he took an Iberian arrow to the chest and lost half his left hand to a falcata sword. It took more than a year for him to recover, but he survived his wounds and was retired honorably, discharged with a missio causaria.

The usual retirement to a farm did not appeal to him so he sold the farm he was granted and became a traveler, a trader. Not in goods, but in information.

He was not a spy; he worked for no one, and he gave away no great secrets. Rather, he was a listener, an observer, and he freely gave his news to any who asked, sat him by a warm fire, and fed him a good meal.

I did not know it then, but Vallus was a wealthy man. His tattered clothes and unwashed body, the old, worn-out cart and tired looking ox were all part of the identity he used to put those around him at ease, to assure them he was no threat. It loosened their tongues and made his business much easier.

Vallus said people wanted to talk, all you had to do was give them the opportunity. A little ale or wine never hurt either.

"Vallus!" my father called, genuinely pleased to see the old man. "It's so good to see you again. Come inside by the fire and warm your old bones," he said fondly.

"Haistulf," Vallus said, embracing him. The top of the old Roman's head barely reached my father's chin. "Thank you, my friend. First, I must tend to my wagon and ox, but I would welcome your help. I'm eager to hear how your family is doing. I was staying with friends in the Marcomanni lands when I heard of the flood and your flight from Borremose. I had planned to come north in the spring, but I struck out immediately in hopes of finding you well."

"There is much to tell," my father replied sardonically. "But it can wait until we get you a warm meal. Suffice it for now that Ishild and the children are safe."

"Thank the gods. I have prayed for your family, Haistulf, and I am thankful they have heard my prayers. Now, let us go and see them."

---

Having been introduced to and apparently bored with Vallus, who she did not remember, Hilgi was sleeping on my parent's pallet. Throughout the evening my father told Vallus about the flood, the losses to our people, and our alliances with the Ambrones and Teutones. It saddened him to hear of Nilda's death and he was glad to hear of Grimur and Hedda marrying. He introduced himself with mock sincerity to Freki and Skalla, who were full of confidence and self-importance. Sitting with the family for the evening meal, Vallus sucked in his breath to cool the hot stew burning the roof of his mouth and reached for his cup of ale.

"You might slow down to keep from blistering yourself," my mother said with a wry smile. "There is plenty, and no one will take it away from you."

Grinning broadly, Vallus replied, "It is worth the pain, my dear. This is by far the best food I have eaten in a very long time. If you were my wife, I would weigh as much as my ox."

She cocked an eyebrow and said, "If I were your wife, you would be required to bathe more."

I grinned at Vallus when he winked at me. I liked the old man and loved the stories that were always a part of his visits, and the banter between him and my mother always brought a laugh to whoever heard it. It embarrassed Hedda when he flirted unashamedly with her as well, but she warmed quickly when she saw how the rest of the family accepted him without question.

Growing serious, my father asked, "So, Vallus, what news do you bring? People say that Rome has been more aggressive and is invading Gaul. I also wish to know more about the people whose lands we will enter next year as we move south."

It seemed odd that, though we seldom traveled far from the place of our birth, we should know of a people so far away. But Rome was a mighty city and word of their conquests traveled far along the trade routes, along with their wine and fine pottery and other goods that they traded for the amber found on the shores of the northern seas.

Vallus reached into his pack and unrolled a vellum map on the table. "Much has happened in the world since last I saw you, my friends," he said as he pointed to a spot on the map.

"Here, in Gallia Transalpina, west of the Rhodanus River, live the Arverni, a powerful Gallic tribe who has opposed Rome for many years. Last year their neighbors and allies, the Allobroges, angered the Romans by harboring Teutomalius, king of the Salluvii. The Romans had previously defeated all three tribes in separate battles, but now they were united in a common cause against Rome.

"After several indecisive battles with the Roman consul Quintus Fabius Maximus, the Arverni king Bituitus raised a large army that he was sure would finally defeat the Romans.

"The combined force that awaited the Romans near the confluence of the Isara and Rhodanus rivers was well over fifty thousand warriors. The Romans were badly outnumbered and Bituitus, confident in his overwhelming numbers, led his men to the battlefield.

"I was returning from a journey into Hispania when I met up with the legions and found myself with the camp followers.

"The commander of the Roman cavalry, Gaius Marius, whom I knew as a young officer in Numantia, sat with the cavalry, hidden in the trees on the army's flank.

"He commanded twenty war elephants and two ala of cavalry. The young officer was given the responsibility for attacking the flank of the Gauls as they clashed with the Roman infantry."

Freki interrupted him, asking, "What's an elephant?"

Vallus smiled, bending over a bit to get closer to us boys, who sat on the floor. "An elephant is an enormous beast that stands as tall as a house. Taller! Its feet are as big around as this," he said, holding his arms in a wide circle.

"It has ears as big as your cloak and a long snout, like a snake, that it uses to snatch grass and shove in its mouth," he said, pretending to use his arm like an elephant's trunk.

Holding two fingers to the sides of his mouth, he went on. "Long white tusks protrude from its mouth that it can use to impale an enemy. Some come from Africa, but they live in India too. It is a fearsome animal used by Hannibal to fight the Romans, and now the Romans use it in battle whenever they can."

We listened intently, mouths agape, transfixed at the description of such a strange animal. Surely it was a beast only the gods could have imagined.

Vallus sat back and continued, "Many of those cavalrymen served under Marius in Numantia and were now his subordinate commanders and senior cavalrymen. The Roman infantry, in all its shining splendor, marched out onto the field as the Gauls across from them took up their fearsome battle cry, beating on their shields and blowing their carnyx, screaming and shouting obscenities at the Romans.

"One huge warrior, naked but for a bronze torc around his neck and a wide leather belt that suspended a sword, raced out to the front of their formation. He held a large oval shield on his left arm and several short spears in his right hand and stopped just outside javelin range of the Romans.

"Standing with his feet apart, he spread his arms wide, exposing his impressive muscular torso. He shook the javelins and pointed them at the Romans, offering a challenge of personal combat, daring them to send out their champion.

"The Romans held their formation and watched from over their shields as the berserker continued his display, shouting obscenities, leaping about, thrusting his hips, and pointing at the erection jutting from his groin, and then pointing at the Romans.

"With a great roar, the Gauls began their charge surging up behind their champion who led them straight into the shields of the Roman formation.

"Both sides exchanged missiles as they came within range, the Gauls suffering heavy casualties. The Romans released their pila and closed ranks, taking the return volley on their heavy shields with few casualties. The front lines of the infantry, supported by those behind, absorbed the impact of the human wave as it smashed into them.

"Many of the lead warriors leapt upon the Roman shields and ran across them to the rear ranks, launching themselves into the center of the legion's formation where they thought they would cause chaos, but were fell upon instead and killed without causing much damage.

"From the rear of the legion came the command to begin the forward movement, and the slaughter began. Heave, step, thrust, heave, step, thrust; the battle rhythm of the Romans as they pushed the Gauls back, gutting the ones in front of them. Slowly they inched forward, stepping on guts and over the slippery bodies. They thrust their gladii between their shields into the soft bellies and groins of their enemy. On command, the second rank moved forward and the first fell back through the ranks behind them to the rear to rest, always keeping the front line fresh. These were veterans of the Numantine wars and were well versed in the business at hand.

"Enraged Gauls were pressed behind one another, the rear ranks unable to reach the Romans, the front ranks falling like wheat. Packed closely together, they were unable to bring their longer swords to bear, not having enough room to swing their arms while the Romans continued to thrust the shorter gladius between their shields, their second rank shielding the heads of the first.

"Marius watched the Gauls commit their reserves to add weight to the battlefront, and when he saw the signal flags from his commander, he gave the order for the cavalry and elephant corps to charge into the enemy's flank.

"The elephants let loose with a horrendous trumpeting as they rushed forward, the horse cavalry surging around them, lances lowered. A great dust cloud arose from the battlefield and neither side could see the cavalry charge, as a rumbling thunder seeped into the consciousness of all the combatants. The ground shook under hundreds of hooves and the great weight of the fearsome elephants. They smashed into the flank, wreaking havoc among the Gauls, whose own cavalry horses panicked and bolted at the sudden appearance and frightful sound of the elephants.

"Bloody tusks cut through their ranks and men were crushed beneath their feet as the archers and spearmen who rode atop their broad backs added to the gruesome harvest. The elephants picked up warriors with their serpentine trunks and smashed them into the ground or threw them bodily into the air.

"The Gauls turned in panic, unable to fight the huge beasts, and began fleeing by the hundreds, and then the thousands back toward the Rhodanus River. Thousands of terrified Gauls rushed the pontoon bridge they had constructed to cross the river, their numbers capsizing it and throwing all on it into the water. Many were dragged to the bottom under the weight of their armor, only a few reaching the far side.

"Turning his legions, Fabius' infantry trapped the remaining Gauls against the river and the Roman cavalry completed the slaughter. Fabius achieved a one-sided victory, wiping out most of the Gauls and capturing Bituitus and thousands of his followers. Bituitus, the defeated king, was taken to Rome and paraded through the streets in chains. He was eventually sent into exile."

Vallus paused and drained his cup. With everyone listening in anticipation, he continued long into the night, telling the news of Rome and the rest of the world as he knew. There was never a shortage of that news and always an interest in learning what occurred beyond our small world.

---

The next day Vallus was tending to his ox when I found him.

"Good morning," I greeted him. The ox stretched its neck out as I scratched it. "Would you like some help?"

Vallus turned and greeted me with a smile that exposed his few remaining teeth. "Well, I certainly would welcome your help, my boy. You've grown tall in the past few years. How old are you now?"

"I'm fifteen," I said. I could feel the color rising in my face. "I should be a warrior by now, but I have been unwell and still have not fully recovered."

We stood in uncomfortable silence for a moment until I went on.

"But, last month when I nearly died in the river something happened when I coughed up the poison with the river water. Since that day, my breathing has gotten stronger and I've been gaining weight," I said proudly.

"I can see that. Your color is much better, and you are becoming a man of your father's size," he said.

"I was hoping to hear more of Rome," I blurted out, eager to change the subject.

I was fascinated with the Romans. Not just the military but their leaders, their laws, the city itself. I had heard of them since I was a child and I wanted to learn everything I could about them.

Vallus, encouraged by my curiosity and always willing to talk about any subject, was more than happy to oblige.

"I'll tell you what, my boy. If you can find some cheese and bread, and a pitcher of ale, I will be happy to tell you all you want to know about Rome. I'll be waiting under that large oak behind the village."

It had snowed in the night, but by mid-day the snow was gone. We spent most of that pleasant, early winter day beneath the oak tree, sitting beside a small fire, talking of wonderful things.

A piece of bread lodged itself in his beard as Vallus chewed and pointed to his map.

"Here is Rome. The eternal city. Ah, what a beautiful place. It's like nothing you have ever seen, Borr."

Vallus made expansive motions with his hands, and his eyes lit up as he recalled the great city.

"Buildings as tall as the tallest trees, made of white stone called marble and glittering with gilded statues. Hundreds of thousands of people, all mingling in the streets, the markets, and the temples.

"Beautiful men and women dressed in the plain white toga virilis of the citizens and the purple striped toga praetexta of the curule magistrates. Slaves going about the business of their masters. Foreigners in rough woven clothing and furs, or beautifully colored robes and headdress. Dark men from the eastern deserts, even darker men from Africa. Strange looking men with almond eyes from Asia and even barbarians from the north such as you," he said, nudging my shoulder.

"And the forum – ahh... the forum. The beating heart of Rome. The site of grand speeches, momentous elections, religious ceremonies, and criminal trials. Goods are exchanged here from every possible place, brought by ships and caravans. It is truly a wonder. Yet, the city can be very cruel."

I listened intently to every word as Vallus spent the rest of the day telling me of the great men of Rome. The generals, the senators; their battles, their politics, and their intrigues.

Over the next few months Vallus spent countless hours passing on his knowledge of Rome and the many inhabitants of the lands that he traveled. He taught me to speak several dialects of the Celtic language, which was remarkably similar to our own. He taught me to speak Latin, and even some Greek. I learned I had a gift for understanding languages and a passable talent for speaking them.

One day, he produced a scroll with markings on it I had not seen before.

"What do the marks mean?" I asked as I ran my fingers over them, mesmerized by the hundreds of small marks in straight lines across the scroll.

I had seen such markings on his map and wondered about them, but this was no map. There were no pictures on the scroll. He explained to me that this was how the Romans preserved their words. It was used to record their laws and their history, and to send messages to one another. The idea fascinated me.

I had seen rock carvings in Jutland that told a story in a series of pictures, but the concept of writing down the words we spoke was incredible. I was a slow learner but eager and Vallus was a patient teacher. By spring, I could read and write the language of the Romans and the Greeks.

At the time I only knew that my curiosity was being satisfied, but one day I would realize that what I learned from Vallus would become even more powerful than the battle skills I was learning from my uncle and father.

# Chapter Four

## Rome

## 120 BC

Gaius Marius and Gaius Lucilius were sitting in Marius' modest apartment in Rome, enjoying a cup of expensive wine from Lucilius' personal stock. They were reminiscing of days past and catching up on the news of their personal lives. They had both been young cavalry officers in Numantia under the command of Scipio Africanus. The friends had not seen each other in years.

The two came from equestrian families of the same social status. Marius was now a military tribune and had just been returned as plebian tribune for next year, beginning his climb on the cursus honorum. After Numantia fell, his friend Gaius Lucilius had decided an army career or a life in politics was not for him and followed his heart to become a well-known satirist and poet.

"Have you heard?" Marius asked. "That fool Carbo is going to defend Lucius Opimius in the murder of Gaius Gracchus." His face was twisted into a grimace as though he had bitten into a lemon brought to Rome by the Arab traders.

Already well into his cups, Gaius Lucilius snorted, "Good. They deserve each other. Gracchus was a fool to trust Carbo. Of course, that's politics, to seek support wherever you find it, and Carbo supported the laws that Gracchus wanted. Still, Carbo has ever proven to be a snake, and this, Carbo defending the man who caused the murder of Gracchus, is just the latest proof."

Gaius Papirius Carbo had been elected consul for this year and immediately moved to defend Lucius Opimius, consul of the previous year who was charged with the murder of a citizen without a trial in the death of Gaius Gracchus and his followers.

Carbo had also long been suspected of having a hand in the death of their former commander, who both Marius and Lucilius adored. Despite there being no evidence discovered to support that rumor, they both hated him for it.

Scipio had been an example to both Gaius Marius and Gaius Lucilius, in personal and professional life.

Unfortunately, Scipio proved to be naïve in the intrigues of Rome and when he returned from Numantia, he had a falling out with Gracchus over the new laws and was dead just a few years later. The official statement was that he died from natural causes, but those closest to Scipio suspected he was murdered.

Marius recalled that fourteen years after Scipio brought about the defeat of the hated Carthage, he was elected consul a second time. The people were confident he could bring an end to the war against the Numantians, who had rebelled more than a decade earlier and fought Rome to a standstill in a prolonged, bloody, and expensive war.

Scipio went to work immediately retraining and refitting the legions that had been content to lay siege to Numantia for years and had become lazy and unfit. Marius had chafed under the incompetence of his prior commander, and he observed the difference that a new commander made in a short time as Scipio transformed the legions largely by the strength of his own character and example.

The new commander immediately set about restoring the iron discipline the legions were famous for. Removing and even executing commanders that were responsible for the current state of the legions and replacing them with men from the ranks who showed promise. The replacements became very motivated when they saw what happened to their former officers.

Scipio instituted an intensive program of training to restore the combat effectiveness and physical fitness that had lapsed. He ordered his men to construct a series of fortifications that surrounded the city, cutting it off from their allies and starving them into submission. After months of siege the Celt-Iberians finally decided that it was better to die than surrender to the Romans. They committed suicide by the thousands. Only a few were left to surrender to Scipio, and those were taken prisoner and enslaved.

Having no children of his own, Scipio took a liking to the young Marius and sat for many hours during the siege discussing wars of the past, military tactics and leadership, and the insights of Roman politics.

Gaius Marius absorbed it all, using his prodigious memory and intellect to store each tidbit of information for future reference. He remembered how the old man had mentored him. Encouraging him and preparing him for a bright future.

Scipio was of the old school. An honorable man who respected the arts, had compassion for the poor and above all showed loyalty to Rome, declining many opportunities to enrich himself.

Scipio came from an ancient Roman patrician family. His family line included senators, consuls, and generals. Marius was an unknown equestrian knight from Arpinum, a back-country town in Latium, and leaned toward the ideology of the populares. But despite their difference of status and origin, and their opposing viewpoints, the two enjoyed many lively debates on how best to deal with the political issues of the day.

"I miss the old man," Marius said morosely.

Lucilius raised his cup in salute, saying nothing. Marius blinked slowly, then inhaled suddenly and went on.

"If I ever find that Carbo had anything to do with his death, I will kill him, you know. Scipio was like a second father to me," he vowed.

Gaius Lucilius, recognizing the danger of discussing the killing of a consul even in private company, immediately changed the subject.

"Speaking of old friends, I spoke with Quintus Metellus a few weeks ago," he said smiling, knowing the use of the term "old friend" would get under Marius' skin.

"That bastard," Marius swore bitterly. "He reluctantly sponsored my own election for tribune after I had to kiss his arse for more money."

Gaius Lucilius chuckled as he remembered the day young Metellus had arrived from Rome to join Scipio's staff, green as a spring shoot. Metellus had grown up in one of the most privileged houses of all Rome, while Marius' father was an equestrian farmer with little money or land.

Metellus' head was swollen with the fame of the family name created by his ancestors, and he wasted no time in alienating his fellow staff officers and Scipio's subordinate commanders. Educated in Graecia as a young man, he was determined to ensure everyone knew of his superior status and intellect, as he perceived it. Metellus never tired of putting down anyone not born a patrician, and Marius, himself a client of the Metelli, was often a target for Metellus' comments.

To be fair, Quintus Caecilius Metellus developed into a respectable staff officer under Scipio's tutelage, and was now well on his way to the highest ranks of power. Marius was shrewd enough to hold his tongue, realizing that his future may one day rely on the favor of the Metelli, though his personal pride made it extremely difficult.

Marius' friend, Gaius Lucilius was also from a wealthy family, unusual for a poet, but he never put on airs about it. He was as comfortable around his high society friends and acquaintances as he was around those of lesser birth.

Gaius Marius, though, was ever sensitive of the limitations of his family name and finances and, at the age of thirty-seven, had begun to doubt that he would ever reach the rank of consul. That doubt was making him bitter.

Lucilius was aware of his friend's ambition as well as his potential and disagreed with the idea that his career might be stalled.

Their visit went deep into the night while they reminisced of friends and comrades long past, until the wine was gone, and the first rays of the sun peeked above the horizon.

# Chapter Five

## December 120 BC

The time for Samhain came and went while we were on the march. Once we settled in for the winter, everyone looked forward to the Yule festival to end a year of great loss and celebrate the beginning of a new future.

Gudrun, the ancient priest, tasked a group of acolytes to find and bless the oak tree that would be used as the ceremonial Yule log. Several warriors accompanied them with a team of oxen to cut it down and bring it to where the ceremony would take place. On the eve of the winter solstice the bonfire was lit with the end of the great Yule log lying in the fire. For the next eleven nights, the log was moved further into the fire to burn anew.

As a boy, I had always loved the feast days that were filled with eating, drinking, singing, and storytelling. While this year would be different in many ways, it was a reminder of home and better days.

For a fortnight before the celebration, we hunted and fished, foraged, and gathered to supply the feast. There were dozens of species of fish from the surrounding rivers and lakes. There were geese, ducks, and waterfowl of all kinds. There was wild boar and venison and rabbit and grouse; hazelnuts, chestnuts, beechnuts, and walnuts. The freezing rain had covered and preserved the late season rose hips and other berries in a coating of ice, and the women had made jams from juniper berries, hagedorn berries, whortleberries, and blackthorn berries mixed with honey. There were mashed bullrush roots dripping with butter. There was fresh cream, milk, and cheese from the cattle and goats, and boiled chicken and duck eggs.

There was hot tea made from pine needles, ale, and mulled mead.

Glum, the clan's brew master, spent most of his time after we arrived searching out trees that contained beehives. With the help of his daughter Frida, the girl I met while fishing eels, he used the honey to make mead. He warmed the brew in a barrel by submerging hot stones and now distributed large portions with a big smile.

He enjoyed watching the people try to guess the different flavors of wild herbs and berries that he used to flavor the drink. He even used mashed bulrush roots to make a passable ale that he flavored with boiled spruce boughs.

He found enough honeycomb to share with the women who used it to bake honey cakes and sweetened breads, and made sticky sweet glazes for the ducks, hams, and other meats. Though everything was in less quantity than usual, there was enough for everyone to enjoy the feast.

After the Yule fire was lit and Wodan properly honored, the first night of the festival passed with food and drink. Priests orated for hours on the virtues of the matron, and the symbolic birth of the new year. At midnight, the Modranicht sacrifice began when a bull, a boar, a stallion, a buck goat, a rooster, and a gander were killed in the name of Freya, the holy mother, goddess of love and marriage, and wife of Wodan. A portion of the blood of each animal was gathered into a bronze cauldron and blessed by the priests, who then walked amongst the crowd, using oak twigs dipped in the cauldron to sprinkle the onlookers with the sacrificial blood and blessing them with good fortune. Several couples were married in a mass ceremony and blessed by Freya, goddess of love and fertility. The meat of the animals was later boiled and added to the next night's feast.

The drinking and celebration lasted until the first gray light of dawn and gradually the people found their way back to their homes to sleep the day away. No work was done during Yule, and the festival would begin again at dusk.

Each night of Yule honored a different god, and the priests retold their stories so that our young people were reminded of them; my favorite was Wodan's night. Wodan had the ability to appear to humans as he chose, and he often appeared as the sky god riding upon his eight-legged steed Sleipnir. He also appeared as a hunter, warrior, and at times a wanderer. At midnight of the second night, a man dressed as Wodan the wanderer with a patch over one eye and an oaken staff appeared at the yule fire.

"On certain nights," he began, sweeping his arm across the sky, "when the sky is very dark and filled with storm clouds, Wodan the huntsman gallops across the sky, following a pack of baying hounds on the trail of some mystical beast. He is accompanied by his wife Freya in a chariot pulled by her two male cats, and his son Donar, the thunder god, pulled in his chariot by the magical goats, Tanngrisnir and Tanngnjostr. They are followed by a horde of lesser gods and the ghosts of great warriors, as well as fairies, elves, dwarves, and trolls.

"Woe to the mortals who look upon the wild hunt, for they will be captured and taken to the underworld, or, if they are lucky, carried far away and dropped to the ground for offending the sky god. And if one is so foolish to speak to him, the huntsman shall strike him down where he stands.

"A horrible din of hooves, howling, and shouts of the joy of the hunt announces their coming. It is best you stay in your homes on such a night.

"But if you are caught unawares, you must drop to the ground and close your eyes tight. Cover your head, and pray they pass you by."

As his story ended, there came the rumble of a great number of running horses and baying of hounds in the distance. The children in the crowd looked into the darkness with apprehension as the adults smiled knowingly at each other. When the crowd turned back toward the fire, the wanderer had vanished.

On the twelfth night of Yule, the warriors renewed their oaths to the hunnos and the hunnos to my father. Gifts were exchanged between family and friends, and a last evening of feasting and drinking took place that would usher in the new year. From that point on, the days would continue to get longer, even though some of the coldest days of winter were yet to come. We knew we would see hunger by spring, but for now we looked forward to the challenges ahead.

---

## January 119 BC

Shortly after arriving at our winter camp, Gorm the blacksmith found the clay he needed to rebuild his forges.

There were repairs to be made to the wagons and carts, and there were always cooking pots, tools, and weapons to be mended or melted down and recast.

The smithy was always warm and was a gathering place for the men throughout the winter. Ale was drunk, jokes were told, and knucklebones were thrown. Advice about all things, especially relations between men and women, was freely given. For a young man, there was much to be learned about life in the smithy.

I loved to sit and watch Gorm as he transformed the shapeless lumps of bog iron by first smelting it in the tall clay chimneys of the furnace to remove the impurities. This created a porous bloom of raw iron that could be heated and shaped. The real skill began as the blacksmith re-heated and cooled, twisted, hammered, and chiseled the various pieces of red-hot iron into sickles, axes, needles, spades, wagon hardware, and other useful items. Occasionally he took the time to make decorative pieces of jewelry or hardware, but mostly his work was practical, with little beauty involved.

To me, the beauty was in the transformation of the raw ore. I often worked the bellows that supplied the heavy airflow to the charcoal fire, creating the awesome heat required. I was mesmerized by the red, orange, then white-hot glow of the iron as I moved the leather bags. The rhythmic ringing of the hammer striking the glowing metal against the anvil stone reminded me of home and was a comforting sound in the camp.

One of my jobs with Gorm was to watch the charcoal heaps that made the charcoal needed for his forge. Sitting alone throughout a quiet winter night, amongst the warmth of several smoldering heaps allowed me time to think, my only responsibility to ensure they did not begin to burn with an open flame.

The charcoal heaps were shallow pits in which oak logs were piled, covered with dried grass, and then capped with a layer of dirt to contain the heat. Air holes at the bottom of the mound and a chimney at the top allowed some airflow, but not enough to create flame. Once lit, the heap would smolder for weeks, slowly transforming the wood to charcoal, which burned much hotter in the forge than peat or wood. The heaps had to be watched night and day until the charcoal was ready. If a flame did burst out, I would smother it with buckets of dirt that sat nearby. Because of the thick, acrid smoke they generated, the heaps were a good distance from the village.

On these nights, my mind wandered. I dreamed of leading my people, making decisions that affected so many, and of great battles against formidable enemies. Enemies like the Roman armies that Vallus told us of, or strange and terrifying wild tribes yet to be encountered. Alone in the dark, I recalled Vallus' teachings about the Romans and did my best to remember all that he told me about their ways.

I observed the night sky and watched the movement of the stars, fascinated as each night they changed slightly, except for the bright northern star that remained constant high above the village.

And suddenly, I thought of Frida. It was a night much like this that I first saw her at the riverside, and I hadn't thought about her since.

I leaned back with a smile on my face as I thought of the impish girl with the dark brown eyes.

Stuffing another cheese curd in my mouth I jumped as my father silently materialized out of the darkness.

He seated himself next to me as I watched him warily, waiting for him to speak. It was obvious he was troubled, and we sat quietly for a few moments while he sorted his thoughts.

"I could not sleep," he started haltingly. "I have many advisors and they all have their opinions and suggestions. Your mother is always there to listen and offer support. But tonight, I just need to speak to someone, without judgment, argument, or interjection. Do you understand?"

"Yes, father."

And so, for hours, I sat and listened to my father as he vented his worries, his frustrations, and his anger at the gods for forcing us to leave. At the loss of so many during the flood and along the journey thus far. He spoke of his self-doubt, then countered with the recognition of his own strength and the feeling of responsibility for his people. Finally, he exhausted his need to release the pent-up emotions that had built since the flood, but that he could not express for fear of showing weakness. After he finished, we sat quietly for a time.

I looked sidelong at him. Seeing that he was in no hurry to leave, I took advantage of this time that I had his undivided attention.

"Father, how did you and mother meet?" I asked him.

He looked at me curiously, surprised by the sudden change of subject. His thick mustache rose just a little as a smile curled the edges of his mouth.

"Well, when we were children, her father Arnulf was one of my father's retainers. You already know my father was hunno of the

Wolf Clan before me. They lived near the fortress on a small farmstead and as children we played together whenever her father came to Borremose.

"As I recall, I was about fifteen when I first saw her as more than a childhood friend," he said, looking off in the distance as his mind drifted back to his youth.

"She would have been fourteen, I think. It was during an assembly that summer, and Arnulf brought her along to the assembly. Her mother died when she was young, and she was the only surviving child of the family. Arnulf's brother and wife helped raise your mother when she was a child, and Arnulf never remarried. He was killed in battle before you were born.

"But, you asked how we met. I was too young to attend the assembly, and my friends and I had challenged each other to a wrestling contest to pass the time. Several other young men from neighboring villages also took part in the competition and we were having quite the time. I won several matches before I drew an opponent that was much bigger and faster than I was.

"In the beginning I was holding my own against this other young man. I observed during his earlier bouts that he had a habit of wrinkling his face up just as he was about to make a move toward his opponent's legs, and I used this knowledge to set a trap. We circled each other warily for a while, coming to grips and parting, testing each other's strengths, searching for a weakness. Then I saw his face contort and I prepared to counter the move I knew was coming.

"As his head dipped to come in low, a flaxen-haired vision appeared behind him. She was wearing a pretty, blue linen dress, an uncommon enough thing amongst our people, who mostly wore rough woolen clothing of dark colors. Her long fair hair was unbound, falling past her waist. Her piercing blue eyes locked with mine, diverting my attention. I froze, only for an instant, but that was enough. Before I knew what was happening, my opponent drove his shoulder into my stomach and locked his arms around my knees. In an instant I was looking skyward as he threw me to the ground, landing solidly on top of me, driving the air from my lungs.

"I don't remember the move," he chuckled. "But I remember thinking that the sky was the same color as your mother's dress, as I lay flat on my back, gasping for air."

He shook his head, smiled at the memory, and continued.

"I lay on my side for a time with my knees curled up to my chest, my mouth opening and closing, gasping like a fish out of water. When I finally forced a bit of air back into my lungs, I rolled onto my back and my tear-filled eyes again looked skyward. Only this time, the vision that had caused this calamity was looking back at me.

"She was kneeling beside me, her delicate brows knit with concern for my condition. My breathing had still not returned to normal, and when her hair fell forward, I sucked the ends of it into my mouth, causing me to gag and succumb to a coughing fit.

"She jerked away, falling over backwards into the dirt, and watched me through narrowed eyes until my breathing finally returned to normal. I thanked every god I knew that I had managed not to die. I had to dig several long strands of hair out of my throat before I could recover completely. When I did, we just sat there looking at each other, tears streaming down my blood-red face. We both suddenly burst into uncontrolled laughter, as I groaned and held my belly in pain, trying not to laugh, but unable to stop.

"When we finally regained self-control, she helped me to my feet. My stomach ached so badly I could barely walk. My voice was hoarse, but I slowly regained my faculties, and we found a place to sit. We talked for hours, and if the day had not faded into night, we would not have noticed the passage of time.

"We had been friends and playmates from our youngest days, but that day, something changed. I saw her differently. I was captivated, and from then on, I saw her as often as I could. By the next summer we were betrothed, and we married in the summer of my seventeenth year. We have seldom been apart for more than a night ever since and remain the best of friends and lovers."

---

On a cold and clear morning when the charcoal heaps had completed their task, I went to the smithy to watch Gorm, following the familiar ring of hammer and anvil to its source. The blacksmith wore only a pair of short pants under his thick leather apron and gloves as he hammered at a white-hot piece of iron, shaping it into a spearhead. His forearms were taut with the effort, as he gripped the tongs with one hand and swung the heavy hammer with the other. Large veins pulsed up his forearms and crossed his biceps, bulging from his neck and forehead as he concentrated on his task. Sweat ran from his brow, across his chest, and down to his waist, leaving trails of lighter skin through the black soot that covered him. Gorm wore his nearly white beard short, and his hair pulled back tight to prevent it from falling about his face or catching a red-hot piece of metal to smolder and burn. Muscle fibers twitched beneath the skin that was scarred and pockmarked from the hot spall that flew off his work.

Seeing me enter, he set down his tools and straightened. He rolled his shoulders, and stretched his back, his chest muscles jumping with release from the tension. The two large round globes that sat atop each arm, and the thick neck muscles made him appear wider in the shoulders than possible, even compared to his ample midsection.

Gorm was shorter than most. Standing there in the red glow of the forge, holding his blacksmith's hammer with his chest still heaving from the recent effort, I imagined that this was how the dwarves Brokkr and Sindri must have appeared when they forged Donar's magical hammer Mjolnir in their underground home of Nidavellir.

"I've a surprise for you, Borr," he greeted me with a broad smile. "Today you will begin to learn about smithing. Get your forge going and prepare your tools," he said, gesturing toward a second chimney forge I helped him build a few days ago. He had begun a fire already and laid out another set of tools and a second anvil that was used when he needed help.

Surprised and excited, I rekindled the forge and within the hour had it going hot enough to place the iron ore. After a while, the tremendous heat had burned off the impurities and left only the bloom, glowing a bright red. Using the smith's tongs, I removed the bloom and carried it to the anvil stone where I laid out the tools I would use.

"First you must hammer off the slag," Gorm instructed me from across the smithy, where he had begun his own new project so that I could observe how he worked.

I hammered it, turned it, and hammered it again as he offered advice, returning it to the heat whenever it cooled.

"First you are going to make a flat plate to be used on an ox yoke. Look behind you, there is one hanging on the wall."

I took it down and placed it next to the anvil.

"Now, look closely at the bloom," the smith said. "Picture in your mind what the plate will look like and make it so."

Working the hammer, I flattened and lengthened the bloom. Slowly it began to resemble the plate, but its thickness was uneven, and the edges were too thin.

I returned it to the forge many times to be reheated, folding it over again into a mass, and starting over. The smith hovered, watching, and occasionally offering a piece of advice as I slowly transformed it into a flat piece about a foot long. After starting over several times, I became consistent with the thickness, getting a nearly true flat piece in the correct shape. Gorm showed me how to shape the edges and punch several bolt holes, and by the end of the day, I had created a reasonably good replica of the one I had taken from the wall.

I was bathed in sweat. Dirty streaks and large smudges covered my torso and face where I had rubbed it away. I had small burns from the spall that flew up when the hammer fell, and my forearms and shoulders ached with the work. I was getting stronger every day since I coughed up the infection, and I was proud of how far I had come in such a short time.

Gorm commented on how I switched hands from time to time, using both hands for all tasks as the urge struck me. I shrugged at him and told him it had always been easy for me to switch between hands.

The next day I returned to the smithy and began work on a spade. It took several days to learn the finer skills that it took to create a more complex tool, but Gorm was pleased with my progress.

After several weeks of making simple, useful objects and tools, and learning more of the process and science of smithing, the black-smith greeted me heartily when I entered the heat of the smithy.

"I think you are ready to try something more challenging. How would you like to make a seax?" he asked with a large grin.

I could feel my cheeks stretch with the smile I returned to him, and excitedly bobbed my head in speechless affirmation.

The work began much the same as the others, and by the end of the first day I had created a straight flat bar about the thickness of my thumb and the length of my forearm.

While I worked, Gorm explained to me that the bog iron we collected back in Jutland was a low-quality ore. It was adequate for making tools and hinges and such, but made inferior weapons compared to the ore that came from the mountains in the south and the bog iron was never found in the quantity that we needed.

The owners of those mountain mines jealously guarded their secrets as it provided them with a military and economic advantage. Traders sometimes bargained for that better iron, but it was expensive, and seldom made it as far north as Jutland. As a result, we had few weapons made from it.

The second day, Gorm told me to pulverize some of the charcoal to a fine dust, then instructed me to sprinkle it onto the anvil and the reheated bar. This was done repeatedly for several days while I folded it, reheated it, and hammered it out again into a similar shape. He explained that this changed the raw iron into what was called steel. It made the metal harder, but more brittle. I was hammering it out a final time when the blade suddenly cracked, breaking in half. I was crestfallen and looked sadly at Gorm.

He simply shrugged his shoulders and said, "Too much carbon. That makes it too brittle. Start over."

For six days I repeated the process until late one evening when the smith proclaimed the bar was ready to be shaped. The next morning, I began the final shaping of the seax and by the end of the next day, the blade was complete. Gorm filled a container with water and instructed me to reheat the blade.

"When it is red hot, dip it in the water and leave it there until it cools," he instructed. "This will harden the blade so that it will keep an edge." The heat caused steam to rise and quickly cooled the metal.

"The last step is to temper the blade," he went on. "Heat the blade one last time. This will toughen the metal and remove the brittleness so that it won't shatter when it strikes a shield boss or another blade."

Finally, it was finished. It had a thick spine that tapered to a thin cutting edge. It had a drop point at the tip and a full tang that would pass through the handle I would make for it. Gorm told me to let the furnace cool and go home. I was exhausted but exhilarated to see and hold the result of my efforts.

I honed it for several days until the edge could shave hair from my arm. I polished it using a sandstone slab, moistened with water to make a slurry, and I fashioned a handle from a piece of antler. I had already made a wood and leather scabbard for it, lined it with sheep's wool to keep the blade from rusting, and hung it from a new leather belt. With great pride I showed the finished blade to the smith who grinned widely, clapped me on the back and told me to show my father.

"You have done well. This is a fine weapon," he said proudly. Hefting it and fingering its edge, he swung it through the air and thrust it at an unseen enemy. "It will serve you well, Borr," he told me as he reversed it and returned it to me, handle first.

In fact, it was heavy and was not perfectly straight or balanced. An unskilled first try by a boy who knew little of making a weapon, but I felt my chest might burst with pride. My father was not free with praise, and it meant a great deal when a compliment was given. He handed it back to me and I hung the weapon on a peg near the entrance where his weapons hung.

I had not only learned to make a weapon, but I had received an important lesson. How even something as solid as iron could be molded, shaped, and changed. Removing the unwanted and unproductive slag, bringing forth the pure iron beneath. Strengthening the iron core within while creating a tool, a weapon, that is useful, beautiful, and deadly.

---

## March 119 BC

On a day when it was our turn to help mind the herds, the herdsman instructed me to get the twins and round up several stray cattle that had wandered off. We rode toward the west where the cattle were last seen and followed a clear trail in the fresh snow. We continued toward a rounded hill on the horizon, and as we got closer, we realized it was not a hill, but a burial mound left by the ancient ones. Small trees and shrubs had taken root on the mound and disguised the actual size of it until we neared. I knew of several such places back in Cimberland but had never viewed one up close.

I felt a cold shiver run up my spine. Licking my lips, I glanced aside nervously at the twins and saw the apprehension on their faces as well. After crossing the open plain, the air was suddenly very still. When a sudden gust of wind rattled some dry branches, the sound reminded me of the old bones that the priests hung from the oak trees in their sanctuary back home. My horse balked restlessly, dancing sideways.

"Skalla," I said. "Come with me around the north side of the hill. Freki, you stay here and gather the cattle together when we push them out."

As we rounded the base of the hill, one of the missing cattle suddenly bolted out of a thicket, bawling loudly, the whites of its eyes showing. My horse reared, and I lost my seat, falling heavily to the ground as the panicked animal raced off toward home. I picked myself up and shook my head to clear it. Skalla trotted up, having trouble controlling his own horse. Dismounting, he walked with me around the back side of the hill, his horse reluctantly allowing itself to be led.

"Ugh," we exclaimed simultaneously, recoiling as we came around the hill. Our hands covered our faces in an effort to block the smell. An overpowering stench of death and decay assaulted us physically.

"Look," Skalla pointed ahead, peering through watery eyes.

Several dead cattle lay on the ground, dozens of ravens flapping and hopping around the carcasses. Our sudden appearance startled them, and we watched in horror when the entire flock took flight, passed over the burial mound, and suddenly dropped from the sky. Dozens of black bodies hit the ground in a rapid succession of dull thumps, already dead when they landed.

I nearly leaped out of my skin when another gust of wind blew through the treetops, conjuring up thoughts of long dead spirits whispering evil things.

We quickly rounded up the remaining cattle and headed back to the camp. I rode double behind Skalla, as my horse was already beyond sight. I could not help glancing nervously over my shoulder as we eagerly left the mound behind us, the sun setting behind its summit.

When we arrived back at the camp, we sat around the fire to eat supper and told my parents of the mysterious deaths of the cattle and the birds.

"I wish my sister were alive to interpret these signs," my mother lamented. Then, she drew a deep breath and began a tale that she vaguely remembered from when she was a child.

"The old ones say that when the ancient kings died and were placed in their tombs, they were buried with much treasure. Gold, silver, and gemstones, as well as fine weapons and armor, were all buried with the king. Many took the tools of everyday life as well as religious items; elaborate wagons, horses, and even slaves and family members went with them to the grave to serve them in the afterlife.

"It is said that a draugar, the spirit of the dead king, sleeps in the tomb and guards these treasures. People and animals that are near when a draugar is awakened can be driven mad and even die an unexplained death."

I shivered, remembering the odd sounds of the wind in the trees, the actions of the animals, and the smell of death at the hill.

My mother continued in a hushed voice. "The draugar can pass through the solid rock and packed earth of its tomb to material-ize into a giant being that resembles the dead king. This creature shambles about, spreading death and disease unless stopped. It can only be stopped by a hero worthy of the task. If someone has trespassed at the mound you saw, they may have awakened the creature."

I lay awake deep into the night, afraid to close my eyes, my heart jumping at every sound. When I eventually slipped into a troubled sleep, I felt a lightness come over my body as if I were floating in water. I fought to open my eyelids, but as hard as I tried, it felt as if they were sewn shut.

I was enveloped in an inky blackness so thick I felt a claustropho-bic panic begin to build. A shimmering point of light appeared and slowly filled my vision with a ghostly green glow. In the distance I could make out the black silhouettes of trees and a round hill on the horizon. I realized I was floating toward the ancient burial mound that we had seen that morning.

The green glow became brighter until it faded into the pale, gray light of morning, as the dawn broke on an overcast, sodden day. I was soaring high above the hill in wide circles among a flock of large black ravens. Looking down to my side, I was shocked to see an iridescent black wing coming from my shoulder, and I realized I was flying in the body of a raven.

I looked down and watched a group of strangely dressed men ride up to the hill. They circled it before dismounting and then began to climb it. They were looking around as if searching for something. Eventually, the men gathered together and began digging into the ground. They had found the entrance to the mound and were at-tempting to enter the ancient burial site. That is when I realized they were grave robbers, come to seek the ancient treasures.

A wisp of smoke rose from the top of the mound and glided swiftly around the hilltop, hovering over the men for several moments. The cloud increased in size, taking on a human shape several times more than the size of the largest warrior.

The spirit solidified into flesh and bone, still hovering silently above the intruders. The men reacted to the terrible smell and as they looked about for its source, they finally took notice of the creature above them. They stood frozen in horror, unable to believe what their eyes were seeing.

The spirit was dressed in a combination of furs and armor, including a strange bronze helmet with large cone shaped horns jutting outward from each side. Two pieces of ruby red glass shined from the front of the helmet like a pair of fiery eyes. The creature's flesh was blueish-gray and moldered. Two points of white light shone brightly from the shadow just below the rim of the helmet where its eyes would be. Its petrified lips receded and revealed sharp yellow teeth in an evil grimace. A thick mane of red hair spilled below the back edge of the helmet and onto its broad shoulders.

With a piercing shriek, the spirit swooped toward the men who in their terror finally discovered the ability to move their feet and turned to race down the hill. The last of them to react was lifted bodily into the air, soaring so high and so quickly he could not breathe, until the creature released him to fall screaming to the earth far below.

The remaining three men raced down the hill, stumbling toward their tethered horses. The terrified animals were pulling desperately on their ropes, trying to break free. Their eyes were wide with fear and foam frothed at the corner of their mouths.

Two of the horses escaped and raced away when the body of the first man slammed into the ground between them and their approaching riders. As the men reached the remaining horses, another was snatched up as the first had been, screaming as he rose out of sight, knowing what his fate was to be.

I watched the last two disappear over the horizon, whipping their horses savagely, pursued by the draugar whose screeches echoed over the land. The gray light faded, and I turned homeward. When I arrived back at the camp and returned to my human form, I fell into my bed, completely exhausted.

Sometime later, I awoke in fear, unable to breathe, feeling a great weight on my chest. When I opened my eyes, the draugar was sitting on me, its glowing eyes fixed on my own. My heart nearly bursting from the pressure, I felt a strange familiarity with the creature as it stared into my eyes. Its head was tipped to one side as if in curiosity, or perhaps recognition. It was so close its fetid breath gagged me. As I struggled to breathe, still in the depths of my nightmare, my vision slowly faded and returned to blackness.

---

The next morning, I awoke with a start. Detecting a lingering foul smell, I looked around in sudden fear, seeking its source. After a moment, I saw Lothar looking at me curiously. I did not discover a reason for the smell, but I noticed a small red object on the ground next to my sleeping pallet. I did not know where it came from, but it was something unusual and after examining it for a moment, I slipped it into my pouch without another thought.

Dressing quickly, I left the cabin to find the twins. I found them nearby, looking pale and upset. The boys had both had a version of the same dream, but they had not been transformed into a raven or seen the draugar after we left the hill. When it was my turn to relay the story, I kept that information to myself.

# Chapter Six

## Rome, 119 BC

Pro-consul Gaius Papirius Carbo, still dressed in his senatorial white toga praetexta, the wide purple stripe indicating his rank, paced back and forth anxiously in the atrium of his luxurious home. His younger brother Gnaeus looked on uncomfortably. Though separated by several years, the likeness of the brothers was striking. Their close-cropped hair and clean-shaven faces were common to the Roman upper class. They were alone in the house, save for the servants. Gaius had sent his family to their villa near the coast.

Gaius Papirius Carbo had been brought before the senate for impeachment on almost the same charges for which he had successfully defended pro-consul Lucius Opimius the year before.

"Ohh, what shall I do, little brother?" moaned Gaius. "The verdict will be read tomorrow, and I know I shall be found guilty. This Lucius Licinius Crassus is a lion. Who would think that such a young man would have such a quick mind and sharp tongue?"

"He has studied law with none other than Antipater and he was obviously an astute pupil," Gnaeus replied dejectedly. "It is an obvious attempt at revenge for your brilliant defense of Opimius. These false charges result from the influence of those men who still support the laws of Gaius Gracchus. They want revenge on Opimius for instigating his murder. When you exonerated him, they substituted you as the focus of their anger."

Gaius went on. "There are also those that still whisper that I was involved in the death of Scipio Africanus, though I was not. I respected and admired the general greatly, though we disagreed politically. No evidence has ever been produced that implicates me because there is none.

"Ohhhh," Gaius moaned again. "I cannot bear the shame of being exiled or imprisoned. To have the state confiscate all my property and leave me and my family destitute, without a home or money. To be turned out into the streets like a beggar. I fear that I have no recourse, Gnaeus—I must avoid the verdict. If I stay, they will convict me and seize my property. If I flee, they will convict me in absentia, and force it upon me in any case. But...if I die before the verdict is read the trial is over. The state could not seize my property and my honor would be preserved. The choice is clear. I shall commit suicide to save the family honor. Tonight...before the verdict is reached."

Shocked, Gnaeus exclaimed, "Brother, no! We do not know for sure they will find you guilty. You succeeded in acquitting Lucius Opimius, please, your defense is very competent. Please, wait for the verdict."

"I cannot take the chance Gnaeus, I am sure we have already lost. This is the only way. Please respect my decision."

Turning back to his younger brother, Gaius rested a hand on his shoulder and continued.

"Do not worry, brother. This is my decision. I know you will carry on in the senate, you are destined to be consul one day. I have updated my will, and my estate will be preserved. My wife and son will be provided for and will not be a burden upon you. All I ask is that you look out for them and provide a father's example for my son, he will need your guiding hand."

Gaius grasped his brother behind the neck, and they touched foreheads in a last embrace.

"Go home, Gnaeus. Tomorrow you will start anew, and you will return the family name to respect and prominence. Remember always, brother, that I love you. By this time tomorrow I will have paid the ferryman and when it is your time, I will be waiting for you in the fields of Elysium."

The brothers bid a tearful final farewell, and when Gnaeus departed, Gaius returned to the atrium.

"Marcus," the elder Carbo quietly called for his body servant.

"Here, master," the slave answered, materializing immediately.

"Fetch my gladius and a wax tablet and stylus."

When the slave returned, the man's face was darkened with sadness, having overheard the brothers' conversation. Not so much with concern for his master, but rather for himself. With the death of his patron, his own life would suddenly be very uncertain.

Taking the wax tablet and stylus from Marcus, who stood waiting silently, Gaius wrote a letter to his family expressing his love for them and an explanation for what he saw to be his final duty. Leaving the letter on a ledge of the small pool in the center of the atrium, he stood near the brazier that warmed the room, hands clasped behind his back. He stared into the glowing embers, his mind at ease with his decision, the tension and worry now gone from his body, while Marcus stood impassively nearby.

Gaius Papirius Carbo, former consul of Rome, took his sword from the slave.

"You have been a faithful servant, Marcus. In return, I have given you and your family their freedom. It is decreed in my will; you will be provided with the proper papers when it is read."

The slave's heart leapt, and he fell to his knees in gratitude. He wept openly as he thanked his master, who then dismissed his servant for the last time.

Gaius calmly walked to the edge of the pool, where he placed the pommel against the ledge and aimed its point at his chest. With a last breath to fortify his courage, he let his weight fall onto the sword, driving the razor-sharp tip deeply into his chest, through his heart. He fell sideways, the sword pivoting against the ledge, dead before his body hit the marble tile.

# PART II
# THE JOURNEY

# Chapter Seven

## June 119 BC

I woke before dawn to the sound of a bronze lur announcing the new day to any who had managed to sleep. Throwing back the covers, I immediately dressed and rolled up my bedding. Then I tossed it into the back of the cart on top of the crates that contained the cooking pots and other camp gear we packed the day before. Skalla and Freki hitched the oxen to the carts while I helped my mother and Hedda load the last of the camp goods.

Aside from the barrels of smoked spring salmon that had been caught just weeks before, the carts were filled with barrels of ale, woven bags full of bread loaves, and small casks of butter and salt. Axes, spades, buckets, and other tools hung from the sides to access them quickly when they were needed on the trail.

Mother's new loom and butter churn were in one corner and a few bags of wool from the spring shearing formed a comfortable bed where Hilgi would ride when she was not walking and where my mother and father would sleep. The women would process the wool during the trip to make new clothing as we traveled.

The leather covering was cinched down tight over the staves to keep everything dry and provide us with shelter, if necessary.

My friends and I each grabbed a handful of goat cheese and dried beef, and a goatskin canteen of water and trotted off to help get the herds moving. The camp was a place of purposeful and enthusiastic activity and was obviously quite different from the forlorn

Figure 3.

people who left their homeland behind just a few months ago. Spring was a poultice that had gone far to heal the wounds of the great flood. Now it was time for the Cimbri to begin their new life.

Hrolf, the Teuton boy I had met while fishing eels, greeted us as he tossed a bedroll and a small sack of belongings into the cart. He and his father had joined us this spring, and we became good friends. His mother had been killed in the flood and his father rode with the scouts, so Hrolf would travel with us.

We had learned from the chaos during the fearful and disorganized time when we left our homes. The Cimbri leaders, with the help of Vallus's experience in the Roman army, had spent time over the long winter carefully planning. We were now divided into ten trail groups of about five thousand people that were organized by clans and villages. Because we could spread out on the flatlands and roll- ing hills, the entire tribe could travel at the same time until we were forced to restrict the size of the march when we entered the higher lands to the south.

Each group included about one thousand carts pulled by oxen, and all the associated cattle, goats, chickens, and other living beings that made up the menagerie that accompanied the massive horde. The large herds of cattle had been broken down to several hun- dred head to travel in the center of each trail group.

The new calves and kids jumped and kicked their legs playfully beside their mothers as we shouted and waved leafy branches to encourage them all to begin the journey. Once they were moving along, we returned to our carts and every few days would swap out with others to manage the herds.

A line of five trail groups moved abreast, separated from each other by a mile or so. A second line followed a day behind to space them out on the march and avoid the bunching up that inevitably occurred when everyone tried to move at once.

Each trail group included about one hundred mounted warriors and one thousand warriors on foot. The groups were large enough to defend themselves but could move independently to take advantage of forage and terrain.

The new grass had grown enough to feed the large herds of cattle and horses as we moved. The trees had leafed, the wildflowers were blooming, and the rivers and streams had crested, while the spring rains had subsided. The land was finally dry enough to support the vast number of feet, hooves, and wheels that would traverse it, and we were ready to leave the homes that had sustained us through our first winter after the great flood.

Though we roughly followed the Amber Road, which followed the Albis River, we were spread to the east over many miles.

The road was no more than a path, not much larger than an ox-cart. Merchants, traders, and small war parties used it. Not a mass migration such as ours.

It was difficult to move this way through such untouched terrain, and it challenged the members of the caravan with passing through, around, and over the obstacles that appeared in our path. There was simply no way for the large travelling groups to keep pace with each other, and after a few days, some distance separated them. But the new organization worked well overall, and the entire nation continued to march.

The flank scouts kept communication between the groups and prevented them from bunching too close or creating too much of a gap, while the forward scouts watched for danger and marked the best paths. The warriors at the front of each trail group cleared the path and guided the following carts through the forbidding terrain. The forward scouts also watched for game to supplement the food stores and were often successful in bringing back a deer and even an occasional boar.

There were small streams and rivers to be crossed, lakes to go around, impenetrable swamps that had to be avoided, and dense thickets to pass through. But the knowledge that we were leaving nothing behind us, and our entire future lay ahead of us, kept us moving.

At night, the carts of each group closed up to form an encircling barrier that enclosed the herds and provided a perimeter for protection, if needed. I noted the many changes for the better in our method of travel and added them to my ever-increasing knowledge.

Freki and I walked with my mother and Hilgi to handle the oxen and carts, as my father had many duties to attend to. Skalla walked with Hedda who had moved her cart behind ours, and Hrolf followed with Vallus.

Everyone who was able to walk, did so, and no effort was wasted as we continually foraged for food. The smallest children could find wild garlic and onion just by following their nose. I occasionally saw Frida walking with her friends, carrying baskets and looking for roots, mushrooms, and herbs as we trudged along. They seemed to look my way more than looking at the ground and were always whispering to each other and giggling.

I thought it was odd that I kept seeing her, as her father's cart was much farther back in the caravan than ours, yet she often seemed to appear nearby. But I enjoyed catching a glimpse of her from time to time and did not think much of it.

After five days of travel over the scrubby plains we came to the edge of the foreboding Hercynian Forest. This was the border between the Teutones and the Langobards.

The dark tree line swallowed the caravan as it slowly disappeared between the immense trunks, but the darkness was deceptive. When we entered the canopy, the bright daylight took on an emerald glow. Our ears were bombarded by the twitter of thousands of birds, singing from their perches high in the tops of the giant trees.

There was rarely a break in the thick canopy, and everything had a rich green color, from the thigh high ferns to the thick moss that covered portions of the forest floor and spread up the massive trees. Silvery dust motes shimmered in shafts of sunlight whenever a breeze rippled the leaves far above and allowed some light to filter down to the ground.

I looked around with a nervous eye, half expecting to see fairies flitting about or gnomes hiding behind gnarled tree roots. After all, this magical place was their home.

Great stands of oak led to miles of beech forests and mixed hardwoods of ash, maple, hornbeam, and linden, which gave way to cedar swamps and mixed pineries of spruce, hemlock, and black pine.

I slept in the open most nights, and when it rained I slept under the cart that my parents and Hilgi slept in. I awoke before dawn one morning to the clank of a cooking pot banging against a rock.

My blanket was damp, the result of a heavy, wet fog that occurred in the early morning hours. I had an urgent need to pass water and threw back the wet covering. I performed an awkward dance as my bladder felt like it was about to burst before I reached the edge of the light cast by the flames of a cooking fire.

The light from our fires reached only a short distance before the complete blackness swallowed it. The thick foliage absorbed the sound, and people or animals would suddenly appear without being heard. The entire caravan was hushed, including the animals, almost as if they sensed they would disturb the forest gods if they were too loud. Combined with the damp, earthy smell of the primeval forest, these things created a claustrophobic fear in many of the travelers. It was a disquieting experience for people accustomed to the endless open vistas, bright sunlit days, near constant winds, and saltwater smell of an ever-present sea.

I had looked in the direction of the fire and it was taking my eyes a moment to readjust to the blackness as I stood with my back to the fire.

My entire body shuddered in the cool morning air as I sighed with relief, my eyes staring up at the lightening treetops. I had finished and redressed myself when I noticed a slight glow in front of me at about eye level. Curious, I walked toward it and when I stumbled on an unseen root, the light seemed to grow larger and then floated away, bobbing through the darkness. I watched and when it stopped again, I continued to walk toward it. My heart pounded in my chest and my brain told me to let it go.

"Could this be a fairy floating through the forest?" I thought.

The enveloping blackness was slowly lightening enough that I could make out the darker outlines of trees in front of me. As the veil of darkness lifted, I could make out the shape of a bird sitting on a low branch where the glowing light had been. Its feathers had an iridescent quality that reflected the light of the fire and made it appear as if it glowed on its own.

Relieved, but almost disappointed, I turned to go back to the caravan when I caught a glimpse of something else among the trees. Taking a few steps to the side, the gaps between the trees revealed several standing stones. Turning around slowly, I realized that in the dark I had wandered into the center of a large stone circle. Granite markers that rose out of the dense ground cover, deep in the forest near no settlement that we knew of.

We had passed several of these circles, as well as tombs and other great stone monoliths on our journey. These were the places of the ancients, men who had placed these stones to worship gods much older than Wodan. These were sacred and mysterious places, and we tried to give them a wide berth.

Despite my uneasiness, I felt compelled to walk up to one stone and place my open palm on it. I jerked it back in surprise; the stone was warm, even on this chilly morning.

Turning, I hurried back to the camp with an uneasy feeling of being watched.

---

During the winter camp, my father had again sent Lothar as ambassador, this time to the Langobards and the Semnones, two tribes whose land we would travel through on the way southward. Both tribes agreed to let us pass without trouble if we continued to move and did not delay. Our scouts regularly reported seeing their warriors watching the column from a distance, but there was no trouble.

When the caravan paused for a few days of rest, I woke up eager to get started on a hunt that I had planned for some time. Hrolf and the twins joined me and when we were out of sight of the caravan, we spread out and began walking slowly, looking for signs of game. We each carried a sling and small smooth stones with which we could kill a rabbit or squirrel at twenty paces. For larger game, we each carried a short wooden spear about the length of a man's arm that could be thrown with deadly accuracy. As we silently crept through the forest, Freki discovered a well-used animal trail. We followed the trail deeper into the forest until we came to a clearing with a mineral lick on the bank of a small stream. We each chose a spot where we could observe the lick and settled in. We waited silently for nearly an hour until we heard the soft steps of a deer moving along the trail. Materializing at the edge of the clearing, a young female red deer cautiously stepped out of the foliage, nervously twitching her ears and sniffing the air, watching for movement or other indications of danger.

Slowly, she approached the lick, bobbing her head with each step. Movement flickered between the leaves as two more hinds cautiously followed the first into the clearing.

We waited, blood racing at the sight of the deer so close. A passing shadow was all that announced the presence of a large stag that suddenly appeared at the opening of the trail. His nose held high, he tested the air but caught no scent of us downwind of the lick.

The stag was magnificent; tall, with a thick neck and a heavy body. An enormous set of velvet covered antlers reached back over its shoulders, nearly touching its rump with the tips when it sniffed the air.

With the hinds occupied at the salt lick and the stag drinking, I slowly rose from my crouch. My heart was pounding so loudly I was afraid it would spook the beast. I drew back my arm and my vision narrowed, focusing on the exact spot, willing the small spear to fly true, and I launched a perfect throw. The long hours of working the axe and the blacksmith's hammer paid off when the weapon sank deep into the stag's chest with a hollow thud, puncturing its heart. The large deer took one startled leap into the middle of the shallow stream and collapsed dead.

Almost at the same moment, the twins had each thrown a dart at the hinds, but only Freki's aim was true. Skalla cursed his luck that his dart had been deflected by interfering branches between him and the deer. We set to work immediately skinning and quartering the deer while Hrolf constructed a litter to carry it.

We washed the blood off in the stream, laughing and splashing each other, enjoying the warmth of the day and the success of the hunt. We were preparing to return to the caravan when Hrolf suddenly hushed us.

His eyes huge, he pointed past my shoulder to the far side of the stream where there stood a large, gray wolf. I turned slowly, then froze. It was only feet away from me, an easy leap if it attacked. The wolf stood impassively watching us, its gaze settling on me as I felt a sudden calm come over me. The world around me faded into the background, and I was only aware of the wolf and myself.

My friends were watching the link between us in wonder and when I finally blinked my eyes, the connection broke. I raised my hand in farewell and the wolf turned and loped off between the trees, disappearing without a sound as if it had never been there.

Movement in the grass where the wolf had stood caught my attention, and I crossed the stream to find a pup struggling to follow its mother. Its rear legs were bloody and missing patches of fur, and I realized it had been attacked by something and severely injured. Its mother, not able to care for it and knowing it would die in the forest, had left it in my care. She had asked me for help.

I reached down and picked up the pup. When I returned to the group, we all looked at each other, eyes wide in wonder.

"We must take it back," I said. "We need to bind its wounds, or it will die." Sensing that I meant no harm, the pup licked my hand and laid its chin on my arm.

All four of us were grinning with excitement when the twins lifted the litter filled with fresh meat and we started down the trail back toward the caravan.

My mother was not pleased when we finally came into sight. It was past midday and we had said nothing about where we were going. She called to my father, who came to stand beside her.

The sight of me carrying a bloody wolf pup caused quite a commotion in the camp. We attracted a small following as we made our way to where my parents stood. The twins set the litter filled with meat down as we all began chattering at once. My father raised his hands for silence, then looked at me.

"Tell me what happened," he said.

I told the entire story of our hunting trip, how we had downed the two deer and the wolf had appeared and left her pup. I did not speak of the connection I had felt with the she-wolf, preferring to speak with my father about it in private.

He looked at me gravely.

"You took a great risk. We are no longer in our homeland. There may be warriors about who will not take kindly to our presence.

You are not ready to defend yourselves against full-grown war-riors."

"Yes, Father," I said ashamedly, hanging my head.

"In the future, you are not to leave sight of the caravan without permission. However, you have done well in bringing us fresh meat. You should all be proud of your hunting skills," he said, looking at each of us.

We beamed from the praise.

"Now, what of this pup?"

"I hoped you would allow me to care for him, Father."

He frowned. "No. He is a wild thing and cannot stay with us. Wolves are not to be trifled with; they will kill a man in a second and cannot be tamed. You should have left it to die in the forest, it is their way."

My face dropped when I heard those words.

I looked up at him and said, "Father, before you make your final decision, may I speak to you in private?"

He paused. "Of course," he said, looking at me thoughtfully.

We walked to the edge of camp and sat on a cluster of rocks; the wolf pup still cradled in my arm.

"I haven't told you everything, Father. I wanted to wait until we were alone," I said. "When the she-wolf appeared, she stared into my eyes, and I felt her speaking to me. In my mind I mean, not to my ears."

He was looking at me strangely.

"For a few moments, we had a connection, and we understood each other. Somehow, I knew she was not there to claim our kill or to do us harm. She wanted me to help her pup.

"Our family is of the Wolf Clan; am I wrong to believe she picked me because we are her brothers? Is it not right that we help our brothers? I will care for the pup. I will bandage its wounds and ensure that it stays out of trouble until it heals. When it is well, I promise I will release it."

Hesitating, my father scratched his chin thoughtfully.

"You are wise beyond your years, my son," he said. "You remind me of the duty we hold as members of the Wolf Clan, and you are correct when you say that it is our responsibility to honor that connection."

My face brightened, and I opened my mouth to thank him when he interrupted me.

"However, you must always remember that this wolf is not a pet. Wolves are not dogs. It will show affection for a time, as you have shown it compassion. But you can never remove the wild from this animal. You have my permission to nurse it back to health, but as soon as it is healed and old enough to care for itself, you must return it to the forest."

"Yes, father. Thank you."

I was relieved that I would be allowed to keep the pup for now. I had worried that my father would kill it or make me leave it to die, and in my heart, there was still a small hope that I could tame it and keep it as my companion.

I named the pup Skoll, after the wolf of legend who chased the sun until the end of times.

---

Our westernmost traveling group did their best to maintain contact with the Amber Road, and occasionally they came across a small settlement. The villagers always disappeared into the forest in fear of the large groups of people emerging from the dense forest. My father maintained tight control to ensure these encounters remained peaceful. He issued orders that no one was to act aggressively, and there was to be no raiding. We were moving among people with whom we had made a peace agreement and he did not wish to start a conflict. But among thousands of people, there were always those that acted on their own. On several occasions he was forced to punish young men who disobeyed his orders and raided isolated farms.

We moved through the dark forest for more than a month when I noticed the trees were farther apart, the ground was firmer, and the daylight seemed brighter. Gradually we passed into a grassy plain dotted with small groups of trees and scrub brush. In the distance I could make out hills on the horizon that as we got closer, I realized were mountains.

When the entire tribe moved out on the open plain and there was enough room to establish an encampment near a small river, a halt was called for a week's rest to allow the herds to graze on the lush grass and recover their strength before we moved on.

Two days later, the Cimbri leaders held a council. Vallus, as always, was present to offer his knowledge of the lands we were entering.

"When we cross the mountain range in front of us, we will leave the lands of the Marcomanni and enter those of the Boii. You already know that your ambassadors were sent back with a refusal to allow you to enter their lands. They are a powerful tribe and will have scouts warning them of our approach. There is a large oppidum called Zavist here," he said, tapping a finger on his map. "Their king is hostile, but not suicidal. He will know that he cannot attack you outright, you will outnumber him several times over. However, he does not have total control over his subordinate chieftains, and they may raid the column. But I suspect we can bargain with him if he gets something he wants. He will see this as an opportunity for gain, and knowing that, we may be able to negotiate."

# Chapter Eight

## Entering Boiohaemum

## Mid July 119 BC

The caravan bunched up as we left the northern forest and marshes behind us to begin the slow climb into the hills that shouldered each side of the Albis River. Tall sandstone spires soared above the treetops as the terrain narrowed, forcing the trail groups to make camp on the near side of the pass. Time was required for the lead groups to pass through the hills and pause on the far side until the rest could join them. The caravan continued to grow as we gained more people from the various tribes we passed through, and it was taking longer for the entire procession to pass any given point.

The ever-present sights, sounds, and odors of thousands of people, cattle, and other livestock on the move competed with the more pleasant parts of early summer. Whips cracked, oxen lowed, goats bleated, and roosters crowed amidst the shouts of the drovers.

The going was fairly easy, and I walked with my friends, marveling at the steep hillsides so thickly forested with great oaks and beech. We had never seen hills so large, and we gaped as we passed a large basalt escarpment that jutted hundreds of feet up from the valley floor. In the distance, from time to time, I could see a range of snow-capped mountains that ringed the basin we were entering. After spending weeks in the confining forest, the sky seemed impossibly large as we came down from the passes and into the valley meadows. Towering white clouds floated across a bright blue sky as the vanguard passed through the hills and into the emerald valley.

Even the air seemed different at these heights. I filled my lungs, feeling the strength in my chest. I felt completely healed from my childhood sickness. Ever since I crawled from the river nearly dead, I had felt a difference in my breathing, and my newfound health excited me. For the first time I could remember, I was confident with what the future might bring. I looked up from my daydreaming to see my father riding toward us with Grimur and Lothar behind him.

"I want you boys to be especially alert today. I don't like the looks of these hills," he said. "Find your mother and the others and stay with them."

"Yes, father," I answered, scanning the forest with a renewed interest, imagining an enemy warrior behind every tree and rock.

---

The Boii were hidden on a hillside above us where the trail neared the dense tree line. A horn blast was the signal to begin the attack, and several hundred warriors launched a volley of spears, leaping from their hiding places and racing toward the caravan with a roar. The concentrated attack overwhelmed the nearby warriors and families, who had little time to react. When the Boii accomplished maximum carnage, two blasts called them back into the forest.

My father heard the commotion near the front of the line at the same time a horseman galloped up with the news.

"To me!" he commanded, leading fifty mounted warriors toward the sound of battle. When they arrived, they found twenty dead and twice that wounded. The mournful calls of wounded cattle mingled with the screams and sobbing of the survivors. The Boii had struck and disappeared back into the forest so quickly, they had not lost a man.

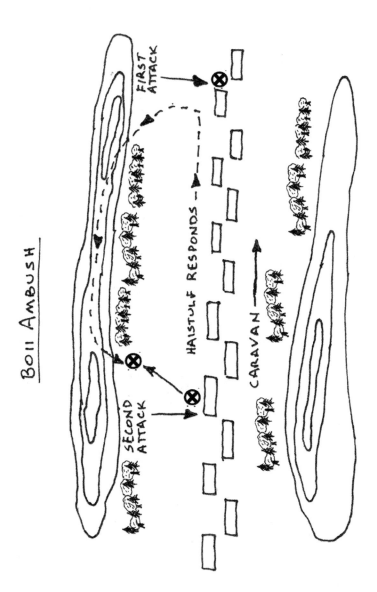

Figure 4.

We watched him depart with his warriors and remained alert to possible danger. Those around us reacted quickly when we heard a carnyx blow from the hillside above us. I shoved my sister and mother behind a nearby boulder as a cloud of missiles flew toward the column. A nearby ox took a spear to its belly and bolted, its cart careening behind until it tipped when the ox fell, legs kicking, and crying out painfully before it died. The din of the enemy rose from the forest, and in a moment, I could make out the brightly colored shields moving swiftly toward us in a headlong downhill charge.

Responding to the calls for warriors to assemble and meet the charge, my friends and I fell into the rear rank of defenders. A deafening crash arose when their charge came to an abrupt halt on our solid wall of shields. Our warriors pushed them backward, pressing them back up the hillside. I heaved my darts as hard as I could, throwing one after another over the heads of our warriors into the press of the enemy behind the shield wall. When the Boii realized they had lost the initiative and would not get another easy win, they withdrew into the forest above.

When my father heard the sound of battle rising from where he had just come, he realized the column was being attacked again. He called his men and turned back toward the rear. This time, however, they entered the tree line and climbed the hillside, swinging wide from the road. This brought them up behind the second war party.

Our defense held and turned the attack. As the Boii fell back, they were caught between the caravan's defenders and the counterattack, and they suffered heavy casualties. They were able to break away, but not before we wounded or killed at least half of them. The wounded were dispatched without mercy, except for one warrior who was brought to my father for questioning. The man was holding what remained of his right arm; a dirty rag soaked with blood covered the stump. He wore a bronze helmet and iron chest plate over a leather cuirass.

The man was dying and was too weak to answer our questions, but Vallus stood nearby and confirmed the man was a Boii tribesman. "We should expect more attacks. They are a powerful tribe and will not take kindly to an entire nation of people encroaching on their lands. It will look like an invasion to them. Their tribe is smaller than our combined strength and they are spread out over their territory, but with the caravan stretched out as it is, we will have difficulty defending against these types of raids. We will travel through their country for weeks."

My father turned and ordered the men behind him to account for the dead and wounded and sent word along the caravan of the attack and the tactics used, then he sent more scouts out to the flanks.

"The train will keep moving until we pass through these hills, and we will make camp in the valley ahead," he said. Then he sent two men forward to find a suitable place to stop the column.

---

Later, I joined the young men moving among the enemy dead. We collected the weapons and armor and anything else that was useful and left the bodies where they lay. Dumping a last armload into a wagon brought for that purpose, I turned with the others back toward the column. Mother set out smoked fish and cheese for the family, and I ate sparingly as I watched the senior warriors and leaders making their way to the ancient oak that had been designated as the council site.

My father walked past and growled, "You will come to the council with me, it's time you started learning about the business of leadership and war."

I was stunned. I had always assumed that I would not follow into his position as hunno of the clan, but this was a sign that it might be possible after all.

Each leader reported their losses. A third war party had attacked farther down the line and Lugius's people had suffered similarly but had not reacted quickly enough to punish the enemy, as we had done.

Several called for immediate retaliation.

"Vallus warned that the Boii would not welcome us," my father said. "I urge caution. We must try to negotiate safe passage through their lands. We do not want to have to fight them continually as we travel southward. It is too difficult to defend the caravan with it being so stretched out, especially while traveling through these narrow passes. This isn't about pride; we have to be smart."

I stood near the back of the tent, observing silently. I noted how he allowed the other leaders to have their say and how he listened to each of them, until at one point the group became agitated and began to talk over themselves, eventually shouting at each other.

"Enough!" he shouted after a few moments. "We are not here to quarrel amongst ourselves. We must defend the caravan, but we must also try to prevent these raids. We do not intend to stay in this country, and we need to convince the Boii of that. Remember our goal: to find new land where our people can live in peace."

"Yes, but how do we do that?" Lugius interjected.

"Vallus told us of an oppidum south of here that is the center of their power, Zavist, where their king resides. He has been there and has volunteered to go there to speak on our behalf."

After further discussion, the council agreed Vallus would lead an embassy to Zavist to negotiate safe passage while the rest of the tribe remained here until they returned.

Their response revealed to me the level of respect that my father commanded, and I recognized him as the leader that kept the tribe together through this troubling time. I silently vowed to do my best to earn that same respect.

The next morning, before the embassy could depart, a scout returned with news of a large party of warriors approaching on foot from the south. They walked in the open and were not attempting to conceal themselves. My father sent word to the other chieftains and hastily prepared his warriors for a battle.

After an hour, the Boii group came within sight of the caravan and stopped in the open, not threatening, but on guard. A man who appeared to be their leader came forward with several companions, one of which carried a spear with a dingy white bit of cloth tied to it.

My father looked questioningly at Vallus, who shrugged.

The Romans use a white flag to indicate they wish to talk. The Boii have fought with the Romans in the past and perhaps they learned it from them," Vallus said in reply.

He received a non-committal grunt in reply and with Grimur and Lothar beside him, my father walked forward, followed by Vallus and myself.

Father stood silently until the stranger spoke first. In a language that was surprisingly similar to ours he announced, "I am Theobald, sub-chieftain of the Boii. You are trespassing on Boii land, and I demand that you turn around and leave this area immediately."

My father replied, "We are travelling south and only ask to pass through your land. We do not intend to stay here; we only wish to continue southward until we find land suitable for farming and raising our cattle. Our home was destroyed, and we are seeking new lands to live in peace."

"We heard of your approach from the Marcomanni," Theobald said coldly. "I don't care why you are here, and I don't care what you wish to do. It is not our concern that you have lost the protection of your gods. This is not a request. I am telling you what you will do, or you will suffer the consequences of war with the Boii."

Angered, my father stepped forward. Theobald's guards bristled, but he motioned them back with a wave of his hand.

"You attack us without warning, like cowards! You slaughter women and children and cattle, and now you make more threats! We are not weaklings to be trifled with. We sent ambassadors to you to assure you of our intentions. We came here peacefully, and this is the reception we receive. We will not be intimidated by your boasts. We do not want war, but if war is unavoidable let it come, but fight us like men! Meet us on the field of battle. Do not call yourselves warriors and fight like women. What you see here is only the beginning. We are coming here in the tens of thousands. If we wish, we will take what we want and there will be little you will be able to do about it."

Theobald clenched his jaw and did not reply. I understood then that he did not want war, though he boasted as if he did. Maybe he did not have the authority to speak for his king, or maybe he knew the size of the vast horde coming his way, but whatever the reason, he backed down.

"You said that you were a subchief of the Boii," my father continued. "I am the chieftain of the Cimbri. I wish to speak to your tribe's chieftain. We will camp here until he agrees to speak with me. Go now, and tell him that Haistulf, chieftain of the Cimbri, wishes to parley with him. I warn you not to attack us again, or you will have the war you seek."

He turned on his heel and stalked back to the caravan. The two parties withdrew, and the Boii disappeared back the way they had come.

---

Several days later the Boii king Magalus arrived with a small party that halted a half mile away from the caravan and set up a leather tent on the grassy river plain. He sent word for us to meet him at dawn the next day.

Our camp had tripled in size as the caravan continued through the passes and they were still coming.

"You will be quiet and only observe," my father told me as we walked toward the king's tent. "You will be respectful and keep your distance from us. I do not want you to be a distraction to our talks, but you must listen and learn. Some day you will need to know how this is done."

"I will," I promised earnestly.

He glanced at me, and he saw how much I had changed. My breathing was stronger, my color was better, and I had grown and put on muscle. As a boy, because of my illness, I could not focus on developing my physical strength or combat skills as much as the other boys, and I became more thoughtful and observant. I absorbed information and had gained the thoughtful wisdom of a much older and more experienced man. Now sixteen, I was nearing my father in size, and I was learning much about being a leader.

When we entered the tent, the others stayed outside. Magalus offered my father a seat, and I sat in the shadows near the door. Roasted meat, cheese, and rye bread was served with a pitcher of ale, and after the two leaders ate their fill, Magalus spoke first without preamble.

"You must turn your people around and leave our lands. I don't care where else you go, but you cannot continue here. You were not invited, and I view your appearance as an invasion. My own people have barely enough to sustain them each winter, there are not enough resources here to feed your many thousands of people as well. There has already been bloodshed, and I do not wish for more, but if you try to continue, I will have no choice but to fight you. It will take you many days to cross our lands and we will fight you every step of the way."

My father paused so long before he spoke that I wondered if he was going to reply.

"Less than a year ago, my people suffered a great disaster. The gods sent a flood such as no man has seen before. Our fields were flooded, and our homes were destroyed. We had no choice but to leave. We only seek to pass through your lands on our southward journey. We do not intend to stay, and we do not wish to fight, but we will defend ourselves if we are attacked. Your people and mine were once part of a great confederation. We share the same ancestors that brought the Hellenes to their knees. Can we not find common ground that will satisfy both our peoples?"

"Brennus lived generations ago and the people of our tribes no longer know each other," Magalus said. "I am aware of why you are here, and that is not my concern. I only care about my people and your presence threatens their food and their security."

After a brief pause, he went on thoughtfully.

"But…my scouts have told me of your vast cattle herd. Perhaps there is something that we can come to an agreement on."

My father seized on the opening.

"You have said that your people are hungry. I would be willing to exchange some of our cattle for safe passage."

"Some cattle will not be sufficient. You will need to do much better than that," Magalus said.

My father thought for a few moments.

"I could bolster that with some amber. We have salt from the sea."

Magalus pretended to show his disinterest, and the haggling went on for hours. In the end, Magalus agreed to safe passage through the land of the Boii. It cost us a great deal and was a risk in itself, but the opportunity to continue on without an all-out war was too much to pass up. The final bargain included three hundred head of cattle to include ten prime bulls for breeding, one hundred each of goats, sheep and swine, twenty horses, eighty small bags of sea salt that we had carried with us from home, twenty clay pots of honey and ten small bags of amber for Magalus himself.

Magalus promised to stop the attacks by his men but could not guarantee against harassment from the smaller local villages. He offered an escort to ensure protection and communication with his people, but I realized its true purpose was to ensure we continued to move. My father promised to stop for only two days at a time to rest before we moved on, provided the weather cooperated.

When he told the clan leaders of the bargain, some were furious.

"You cannot possibly be serious! You would give away our food?" spat Lugius.

Father growled through clenched teeth. "The tribe has elected me as their leader, and I will make these decisions. If you are not happy with them, you are free to return to your lands. I will not put our people in jeopardy of more attacks when I can avoid it. We have their guarantee of safe passage, and we will make up the loss of food after we leave their lands. The bargain is struck. We will leave in two days at dawn. I expect your portion of the goods tomorrow."

---

When we began to move again, I kept an uneasy eye to the north where the steep hillsides came near the river, but there were no further attacks. The promised escort joined us two days later at the mouth of the Vltavus River. The warriors from both tribes warily eyed each other, but all went well enough. A week of passing rain showers dampened us but did not slow our progress, and after ten days of uneventful travel, the vanguard came to the foothills that announced the end of our journey along the Albis when the river turned north toward its source. The great river had become little more than a stream compared to the great tidal estuary where we had started.

The caravan rested for two days as agreed. On the morning of the third day, we crossed the Albis at the fording site and continued through the mountain passes that led us to the Marus River. The terrain narrowed again, only wide enough to allow one trail group to pass at a time. There were spots that narrowed down to just enough room for a few carts to pass side by side, stretching the caravan out for miles as we passed through the mountains. Like before, the last groups stayed in camp until it was their turn to cross, while the lead groups waited on the far side.

The caravan crossed the Marus River easily, and the caravan turned south for two more weeks. The weather cooperated and with no major problems from the local villages, we traveled with little trouble on solid ground until we came to where the Marus spilled into a large river that Vallus called the Danubius.

At the confluence of the Marus and Danubius, an old fort at the top of a sandstone bluff stood watch. The Boii escorts had already warned the fort of our approach and assured them of the caravan's intentions and of our bargain with Magalus. They watched us from their high walls, but no one came out. The caravan passed north of the fort and continued on its journey. A large party of warriors led the way, and none of the local tribes wished to take on such an adversary. The caravan had grown and was a formidable sight as thousands of warriors on foot and on horseback flanked the train of wagons, livestock, and people. It took ten days for us to pass the fortress.

Two days farther along the Danubius, we passed below another fortress of the Boii. Posonium was a large oppidum perched high on a hill overlooking the river. A busy trading site, it guarded the site where the eastern branch of the Amber Road crossed the Danubius River.

Trade ships from many lands traveled up and down the river and were docked at quays along the riverbank. The traders hired locals with strange pack animals that looked like a small horse, that Vallus called an ass, to transport their goods up to the fortress.

My father sent a delegation to the oppidum to trade for items we needed, and I and my friends accompanied the group under the supervision of Vallus. A long winding path climbed the escarpment to the hilltop fortress, and when we passed through the open gates, we experienced a sight that we had never seen before.

The village was larger on the inside than it appeared from below and was filled with buildings built close together. My senses were assaulted with the many sights, sounds, and smells that reminded us of home, yet so many that were unfamiliar and enticing.

Several blacksmith's hammers echoed across the grounds and seemed to answer each other with the constant ringing. The murmur of people talking was a constant hum, and a chorus of singers and musicians played to onlookers and dancers in the city's square.

Further along a man stood on a tree stump reciting stories to a fascinated audience next to a stall surrounded by children watching puppets argue and play with each other.

Walking on, we heard the shouts and groans of an excited crowd, and we worked our way forward to see two warriors in the center of a marked ring. I was astounded to see a large black man, taller than the largest warrior I had ever seen, his skin as dark as the night in the great forest. He was naked to the waist, and his broad shoulders and chest bulged with muscles rippling with great strength. His expression was so fierce it appeared as if he could kill his opponent with only his eyes. He was facing a diminutive brown man who looked as if he could be squashed under the larger warrior's foot like a bug.

The little man was leaping about the ring, tumbling on the ground, and waving his arms while his opponent simply turned in place, arms spread and knees bent, waiting for an opportunity.

"If he gets his hands on that little man, he will snap him in two,"

I said to the others.

Suddenly the little man darted in and just as his opponent tried to close his arms around him, the smaller fighter slid between the giant's legs and leaped onto his shoulders from behind, landing a strike to the side of the big man's throat. He appeared to barely touch him, but the giant's eyes went blank, and he crumpled to the ground in a heap, the smaller one riding his shoulders and leaping aside at the last moment. The victor raised his arms, and circled the ring playing to the crowd that let out a collective gasp, and then an uproar of cheers and shouts as bets were won and lost.

"I have never seen such a man as that, and to be taken down so easily by someone half his size," Hrolf said in awe.

"Did you see how fast the little one moved?" Freki asked. "I could barely see him when he attacked. And what did he do to so easily subdue the black man?"

The giant was coming around as the crowd dispersed and the little man crossed to help him to his feet. The big man's face cracked into a broad smile when his senses came back and he slapped the other on his back, knocking him halfway across the ring. His laugh was a booming rumble from deep within as the small man stumbled and fell to the dirt.

The two turned to leave the ring together, and we realized they were not the deadly opponents we thought but were in fact friends. Vallus walked up behind us and hailed the two as we looked on, surprised.

"Anik! Tala!" he called out.

They turned at the sound of their names and came trotting over to us, recognizing Vallus, who happily greeted them both. He introduced us four boys who stared in awe at the strange-looking men. None of us had seen people of such dark skin before.

Vallus explained he had met Tala years ago on one of his many journeys and they had become fast friends. The giant was Nubian. He had been my age during the siege of Carthage, and Vallus was on the opposing side as a young Roman soldier. Tala hated the Romans for the slaughter and destruction they had done when the city fell, but he loved Vallus as a brother.

Anik was from India. A strange and dark land far to the east. He was a warrior who had been cast out of his homeland for daring to marry a woman who was not of his caste. She was killed and Anik fled on a merchant ship that eventually docked at a trading port, where he met Tala. Tala introduced him to his friend Vallus, and the three traveled together, or independently, throughout the world. From time to time, they ran across each other as they had today.

Tala and Anik were wanderers with an unquenchable thirst for adventure and would sell their skills to anyone willing to pay, performing for their meals when necessary.

We found a tavern with an open table, and Vallus called for ale and a loaf of bread. We sat, and my friends and I marveled at tales that sounded too wild to be true, as the three friends all laughed and toasted to old times. Eventually we grew weary of the talk and slipped away to explore the city further.

We passed jewelry makers, potters, butchers, leatherworkers, cobblers, coopers, and farmers, all hawking for a sale. There were people here of every shape and size, dressed in both familiar and strange, colorful clothing. We wandered the streets, eyes wide and mouths agape at the many unfamiliar sights. I turned when I heard someone speaking Latin and I saw a Roman other than Vallus for the first time. He was dressed in a simple tunic and sandals and was haggling with a trader over horses.

Sme of the best horses came from Gaul, and Romans were willing to pay a great deal for quality horseflesh. There were even Romans with grand villas near the Danubius River who bred and sold horses, and this trader was one of those.

A second Roman, leaning against a nearby wall, observed us closely as we passed by. He spoke to his companion and nodded in our direction. I assumed it was because we appeared so different from most in the city, dressed in furs and animal skins, and we walked on.

There was wine and wheat from the south; ale, amber and salt from the north; silk and spices from the east; all changing hands for other goods or for silver and gold coins.

Eventually, we returned to find Vallus and his friends still at their table, eating a roasted goose which we happily helped them finish. Vallus had acquired space in the tavern's stable for us to sleep, and after a few tankards of ale, we turned in. In the morning we went to the docks and Vallus traded the amber my father had given him for several wagon loads of grain to be distributed when we returned to the caravan. We were pleased when he told us that Tala and Anik had decided to join us on our journey, at least for a while, as they were between employers and bored with their current situation.

When we left the oppidum, I noticed the watchful Roman walking in the crowd behind us, seemingly interested in everything along the way but us. I caught Vallus glancing back once and then he said to me, "Continue on, tell your father that I will return as soon as I can and make sure he gets the remaining amber. I will catch up to you in a few days."

He immediately turned without giving me a chance to ask anything else and after a few steps called over his shoulder for me to care for his ox and cart until he returned to the caravan. With that, he disappeared into the crowd behind us.

# Chapter Nine

## Posonium

Vallus found a quiet corner, and the man approached him. "Hello Vallus, it has been some time. How are you?"

Vallus smiled. "Hello Marcus, it's good to see you." Marcus was an acquaintance that Vallus had cultivated and valued for the news that he could provide. The man had excellent contacts back in Rome and throughout the far-flung provinces that helped fill in the blanks of Vallus's own information. They were not close friends; more like a business relationship that held the mutual respect of two men who had faced the hardships of war together. They both had served as soldiers, but these days they traded in information and they recognized the value of their relationship.

Marcus invested in a comfortable villa on a bluff that overlooked the Danubius a short distance from the oppidum. It was a beautiful place with whitewashed walls and cleared fields where he grew the feed he needed for the horses that he raised, as well as several other marketable crops.

Marcus asked if Vallus had the time to spend a night or two at his villa so that they could visit and share any news they might have. Vallus readily agreed, remembering that Marcus employed a superb cook. He looked forward to hearing news of Rome.

Marcus's companion, the man who had first noticed the boys, led the horses that Marcus had purchased onto the ferry. Marcus and Vallus followed them, discussing the weather and other mundane topics, leaving the more interesting conversation until they reached the villa.

Vallus took advantage of his host's hospitality and took a luxurious hot bath, washing off months' worth of living in the wilderness. A trio of female slaves entered to assist him, washed and trimmed his hair, cleaned his nails, and shaved his face as Vallus laid back and enjoyed the attention. Finally, he drifted off into a contented sleep as the girls massaged warm oil into his skin, working out the knots that had developed from sleeping on the ground for so long.

Later, the two men reclined on their respective lectus, the dining couches the Romans were fond of. Contented after a proper Roman dinner of roasted fish and vegetables, accompanied by soft white bread, boiled cabbage and several types of clams and shellfish, Vallus released a polite belch and patted his stomach. Marcus poured another cup of watered wine and got down to the reason he had invited Vallus to his estate.

"I am curious who you are traveling with these days," he said. "Yesterday I saw four strange boys walking through the market and today I saw you leaving in their company. I couldn't help but see the large group of travelers that have been passing by for days and, like you, I am always in the market for information."

Vallus told him of the Cimbri leaving Jutland and about their journey. The idea of an entire nation picking up and leaving everything they knew in search of a new homeland fascinated Marcus.

"Do you think they are a threat to Rome?" Marcus asked.

"No, I don't believe so," replied Vallus. "They were reeling from the assault on their lives and had little choice but to move or starve. Their consensus is to peacefully find a new homeland. They do not seek war; they are negotiating with whoever they encounter for peaceful travel and for whatever they need. They are led by a strong man whose focus is to provide for his people and he does not see war as a means to do that. At least for now. But make no mistake, if they are threatened or unable to avoid conflict, they are quite capable of defending themselves, or, if survival is in question, of taking what they need to survive."

Changing the subject, Marcus shared his news of Rome. He began with the trial and suicide of Gaius Papirius Carbo and that senior consul Lucius Caecilius Metellus had been dispatched to deal with the uprising in Dalmatia, along with his junior consul Lucious Aurelius Cotta who was currently fighting the Scordisci in Pannonia.

Marcus chuckled and leaned forward. "Do you know Gaius Marius? One of Scipio's young cavalry officers in Hispania?"

"I do," Vallus replied. "Well...not personally, but he has come to my attention several times since we left Hispania. What is he up to now?"

"He was elected as tribune of the plebs this year and immediately set about poking a stick in the eye of half the senate," Marcus laughed. "The man is extremely popular with the plebs, and he put forward a bill to regulate voting procedures, which would limit the power and influence of the senators. He is aware of what happened with the Gracchus brothers and Scipio, yet he seems determined to follow in their steps.

"It is well known that he is not a wealthy man and is a client of the Metelli. He borrowed heavily from them to finance his election and yet he risked their displeasure by proposing this bill, which they greatly opposed. He's trying to force the bill through, even at his own expense.

"Consul Cotta opposed him and persuaded the senate to declare the bill illegal and to hold Marius accountable for his actions. The senate summoned Marius to the Curia to defend himself and instead watched in shock as Marius, right there on the floor of the senate, confronted Cotta and demanded he recall that decree, and support the bill or he would have Cotta thrown into prison! Can you imagine? This man, an equestrian from Arpinum, who believes himself on the path to be Novus Homo, threatening a consul, a man whose family goes back generations as consuls and generals. Gods, it must have been something to see."

Vallus was intrigued and asked, "So how did it end? I suppose that Marius is the one who ended up imprisoned."

"No, my friend, nothing of the sort." Marcus chuckled. "Marius turned to the senior consul and asked his opinion on the matter. When Metellus sided with Cotta, Marius actually had the stones to call to a squad of legionnaires standing outside to arrest Metellus! My cousin was standing at the foot of the steps of the Curia and heard it himself. The crowd gathered outside the Curia roaring their approval was enough to cow Metellus and Cotta into submission, and the bill passed unanimously. The man is incredible. This was his first real test in politics, and he stood up to his more powerful opponents without fear.

"Those close to him know his military abilities, but this showed the masses and the senate that he is an astute politician as well, and one willing to stand up for the plebs. He may not be highborn, but he understands people, and that helps him win support. His soldiers love him, and now the plebs do. This will serve him well on his climb through the cursus honorem."

Vallus filed away that information in his mind and they continued their talk late into the night, until finally, he bid Marcus good night. He was looking forward to sleeping in a proper bed before rejoining the last of the caravan as it passed the oppidum.

# Chapter Ten

## Meeting the Scordisci

## August 119 BC

One evening our Boii escorts told my father that when we crossed the mountains ahead of us, we would leave their lands and enter those of the Scordisci.

About half of them chose to join us. Many had made friends among our people, and this helped with avoiding conflict with Magalus' followers and strengthened the caravan's defense. Along the way, families and, at times, entire villages of the Boii picked up and joined the caravan. It seemed there were many who sought change and moving with a large body of people was an opportunity that would not come again.

When the caravan neared the mountain passes that marked the end of our journey through the Boii lands, it was necessary for most of the column to pause again to allow those in front to move through the narrow pass. Before the first carts went through the pass, a large party of warriors secured the high ground on both sides of the trail to protect against attack. We had learned from the Boii ambush and did not intend to let that happen again. The scouts led the way through the pass and into the valley on the far side, followed by a large body of mounted warriors that would find a site for the caravan to make camp.

Coming down from the mountains, we saw a small city across the Danubius that Vallus said was Ak-Ink, a settlement on the edge of the great Pannonian plain. Known for its hot springs, it was founded by the Eravasci, a minor tribe and part of the powerful Taurisci confederation. The land across the river was called Noricum and was an ally of Rome.

After several days to traverse the pass, the caravan continued south to the mouth of the Dravus River and established another camp.

That night, another council was called. Vallus was asked to tell what he knew of the lands we had entered.

He unrolled his map and tapped it with a dirty finger. "As you can see, we have entered a vast plain, a region Rome calls Pannonia. Rome has been expanding their influence into Illyria, here, for decades and they want to conquer Pannonia for its rich land to grow wheat for the republic and its growing population. They currently control a narrow strip of land along the coast here, and are pushing north into Paeonia from the south, here," he said, tapping his finger.

"The Scordisci, whose land we are now entering, have been resisting this Roman expansion for decades along with the other tribes in the region."

My father picked up where Vallus left off.

"Our ambassadors have negotiated space for us here on the great northern plain, provided we assist the Scordisci with warriors to support them. The Romans are besieging them now at the oppidum Siscia on the Savus River. They have asked us to relieve them as soon as possible by attacking the Roman forces. I have sent Grimur ahead with fifty mounted warriors to scout the area and assure the Scordisci that we will be there as soon as our families are seen to. He will report to me when we arrive. In one week, we will take half of our warriors to Siscia. The rest will remain here to defend the camp."

After the council, my father and I walked side-by-side to our cart. He gave me a sideways glance and said, "You will accompany me to Siscia. I expect Hrolf and the twins to come as well."

I was excited, of course. Other than the Boii ambush, I had not seen battle, and this would be the first time that I would go to war. I had practiced with my uncle Grimur over the winter and learned the sword and spear and the use of the shield. I had put on muscle and gained endurance and my father now thought me ready to fight as a warrior in the ranks.

"Before we leave," he added, "I expect you to prepare your mother with firewood for several weeks. Vallus will stay here, and he has agreed to help her and your sister while we are gone."

---

Five thousand warriors crossed the Danubius and cut cross-country to the Savus. They followed that river westward to within a few miles of Siscia, the oppidum that defended the western entrance to Pannonia.

Consul Lucius Aurelius Cotta had marched two legions from the Roman held coast to push into Pannonia and destroy the seat of local power.

Grimur successfully contacted the besieged city, and when we arrived a war council was called. My father required my presence at all councils now. I was privy to the information that flowed and the decisions that were made, and I was learning the ways of leadership and strategy.

A large bend in the river had undercut a sandy bluff, leaving a wide beach in the floodplain that was left exposed during the dry months. I helped Grimur draw a map on the sand large enough for him to walk on, and he used a short spear to illustrate his briefing to the men gathered around.

"Siscia is here, on a hilltop between the Savus and Colapis rivers," Grimur began, pointing the spear at the mound of sand in the center of the map. An enclosure of upright twigs in a small circle represented the oppidum at the top of the hill.

"The Roman camp is situated here, between the two rivers and several miles north of the city," he continued, touching the rock that served as the Roman camp with the butt of the spear.

"The Romans have built a defensive wall with a ditch that separates their camp from the city." He pointed at the sticks and line in the sand that represented the fortification. "The barrier spans the entire peninsula between the two rivers, about a mile long, and effectively locks up the Scordisci."

"At this point, north of the camp, there is a shallow ford in the Savus," he continued as he touched the spear to a handful of pebbles that crossed the line I had drawn in the sand to represent the river.

"There is a full legion with auxiliaries in the camp, over five thousand fighting men. Half of them rotate at dawn and dusk to man the wall and keep the Scordisci contained. During the changing of the guard, the entire legion is out of the camp; half on the wall, and half moving toward the wall or back toward the camp. The people in the city are running low on food but are still strong and ready for a fight."

His description of the area completed, he looked at my father to continue. They exchanged the spear as he stepped onto the map.

"After midnight tomorrow, we will move north on the east side of the river to the ford and cross above the camp," he said, tracing the path with the point of the spear. "We will take up a position here, beside the path and halfway between the camp and the wall. The moon should be down before dawn, making the area very dark as the relief force moves toward the barrier.

"We will cut them off from the camp when we attack, then signal the Scordisci, who will attack the siege works from their side to fix the guards in place. They have been preparing ladders and plank bridges to cross the ditch and wall.

"When the Scordisci attack, we will have the Romans trapped and outnumbered between our two forces."

That night my father took me aside to speak to me about the coming battle.

"Tomorrow will be a fight like none you have seen. There is a reason these Romans have such a reputation. They do not lack courage, nor do they lack leadership. To win, we must be the smartest. We will beat them tomorrow; I am sure of it," he said confidently. "Tell me why."

The question was unexpected. I must have looked astonished, but he gazed at me steadily and waited for an answer.

"We...have the advantage of surprise," I stammered hesitantly. "And superior numbers," I added, although it came out like a question.

"We will win tomorrow," he said again. "And there will be many more battles; Rome does not give up easily. They have been at war with the world for a very long time and they have always survived. Do not underestimate them, you must always know your enemy. That is why whenever I can, I speak to the traders and travelers, the leaders of other tribes, to anyone who might have knowledge of Rome and their ways. You must do the same. With each new piece of information comes wisdom. Learn from this, Borr. One day you will be a leader, and this is a skill that will help ensure our people's survival."

"I will, Father," I promised.

"You have shown that you know how to fight, and that you can think under pressure," he said with pride in his eyes. "You know our battle tactics, and you are ready. When the day has ended, your reputation as a warrior will have begun. I am already proud of you, son. Tomorrow will only make me more so."
I felt the color rise in my face with the praise.

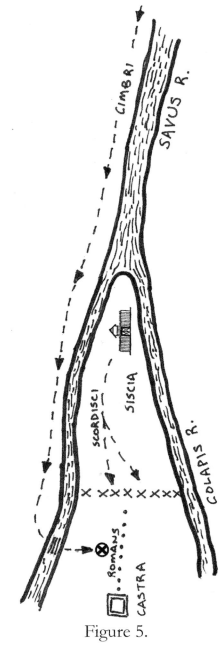

Figure 5.

Finish your final preparations for battle and try to rest," he went on. "We will move into place well before light. Eat and drink lightly tomorrow morning. We will feast after the battle."

The twins, two years younger than Hrolf and I, sulked in the rear lines again, holding the javelins they would hurl, waiting for the signal to attack. They wanted to join me in the front ranks but were told to remain in the rear. The stars were still bright as the moon slowly set in the pre-dawn hours. In the distance, we could hear the rhythmic pounding of iron shod sandals on the packed earth of the camp. A piercing squeal of iron hinges in the early morning stillness told us when the gates opened, and the soldiers emerged from their camp. When the torchbearers in the first rank reached the pre-arranged marker to our front, we launched our darts and throwing spears silently from the darkness.

The first the enemy knew of our attack was when the carnyx blew and we struck our shields once with swords and spears, creating a clap of thunder that sounded just before the missiles fell. Then began the barritus as our warriors held their shields up before their mouths, amplifying their voices into our fearsome battle song. Roman heads turned toward the sounds emanating from the darkness as their brothers fell around them. Their eyes grew wide with fear, finally comprehending that there was an enemy behind them.

"Aaarroooo!" At the call from an ox horn, our warriors raced forward to close with the enemy. When we collided with the flank of the relief force, there was no time for them to react.

My father looked like a god of war, the muscles in his shoulders and arms bulging as he swung his huge two-handed battle axe, cleaving through the Roman ranks. He called on Wodan and Donar to strike down his enemies, and he bellowed a barrage of curses at the soldiers who faced him, their eyes wide at the sight of this blood-covered bringer of death.

His long blonde hair, braided at the temples to keep it from his face, was stained red from the flying gore as he waded further into the breach he created. Grimur and Lothar were at his side, joined by Tala and Anik, and together they were terrible to behold.

Matching my father in size and strength, Grimur was a spear warrior of great skill. Thrusting his framea over his shield, the heavy ash shaft gave him a reach twice as long as the Romans had with their short swords. His nimble feet kept him out of range while he dealt quick death to one after another legionary that was foolish enough to face him.

Lothar, armed with a seax and shield, slashed his way through what was left of the Roman ranks. Anticipating each other's moves, Lothar knocked an opponent off balance with his shield, while Grimur thrust the fatal blow. Then Grimur would create an opening by thrusting high with his spear, and when his opponent raised his shield to protect his head, Lothar stabbed quickly under the shield and into the groin or slashed the unprotected thighs. Over and over again they piled up the enemy dead.

Tala and Anik brought their own unique skills to the battle. Tala wielded a spear, but with a different, yet highly effective technique than our warriors used. He towered over the terrified Romans who saw a giant demon from Hel before them. The sweat on his ebony skin shined in the torchlight, and the wicked smile showed his joy in the slaughter that he created.

Anik wielded two swords at once, spinning them while often fighting two or more Romans at once, keeping them at bay while seeking a weakness, then striking with the speed of a snake from his native jungles.

I killed several men that day, with Hrolf beside me, always guarding. When the close-up fighting commenced, Freki and Skalla made their way to me, each of them baptizing themselves in blood. Before it started, I had been more terrified of embarrassing myself than I was of dying. As I entered the fight, there were no thoughts of myself, only action and reaction; cut, slash, block, stab as we followed into the breach in the Roman formation, and I became lost in the blood-craze of my first battle.

A coppery taste lay on my tongue. The smell of butchered bodies, loosened bowels and bladders threatened to turn my stomach, but there was too much killing to be done before that could be indulged.

I saw a Roman, an officer judging from the crest on his helmet, who had killed several of our warriors and stood upon their bodies, calling for more to come to him and die.

I foolishly accepted his challenge and approached him at a run, thinking to bowl him over with my shield, when two legionaries stepped out of the rank to support him. Suddenly I was facing three warriors of much more experience than I. If not for Hrolf and the twins watching me, I would have been slain; outnumbered, and outmatched. But as I approached, my companions came at the three from their sides, forcing them to step back and defend their flanks. The press of our warriors behind us forced us into their reach and the Romans pushed and stabbed, but the longer reach of our spears proved the deciding factor. When the officer went down with a fatal wound to his neck, the other two folded back and succumbed to Hrolf and Freki's blades.

We had killed half the Romans before they began to rally. Just as they gained some sense of what was happening, the Scordisci emerged from the fortress. Panic set in. What remained of the Roman relief force turned to fight their way back to the camp and, seeing this, the men on the siege works ran to join them.

The Scordisci broke over the barricade like an ocean wave. The Romans, unable to organize their formations, were in a man-to-man fight, and the fury of the Scordisci, coupled with the numbers of the Cimbri, rained death upon them. We chased the last of the survivors into the Roman camp where the calones and lexae, the slaves and camp followers, defended the walls and barred the entrances. Our warriors checked their advance outside javelin range and jeered the Romans hiding behind their walls.

Consul Lucius Aurelius Cotta was among the survivors in the camp, and he immediately disappeared into his tent. Discarding his armor, he paced anxiously, grasping his head with his hands, despairing. Unable to comprehend the sudden loss of his legion.

Seeking orders, his legate entered the commander's tent to find him sprawled in a pool of blood where he had chosen to fall on his sword rather than face the reality of his abrupt defeat.

The tables had suddenly turned, and the Romans were now besieged in their camp. Cotta's legate negotiated with the Scordisci who agreed that the remaining Romans would be allowed to leave unmolested if they left empty-handed with just their tunics, sandals, and a few wagons of food and water, enough to get them to the coast. The allied tribes would divide the rest of the spoils amongst themselves.

---

The Scordisci, grateful for the assistance of the Cimbri, invited us to settle onto the southern plains of Pannonia where the winter was milder than on the large open northern flatlands. There was still a month of good traveling time to get there, and a feast would be held at the fortress of Singidunum to celebrate Samhain and our collective victory over the Romans. The Scordisci promised to help us through the winter, and we agreed to join them in the spring on another campaign against the Romans, this time to the south, in the mountains of Macedonia.

A few days after we returned to the encampment, the tribe was on the march again, moving southward, making good time as we were able to spread out across the grassy plains. The livestock were happy to have more than they could eat and were gaining back the weight they had lost. We encountered thick stands of oak, lime, elm, and ash mixed with hazel, beech, and hornbeam that at times pushed us away from the river.

Every so often we passed around a cart, or its oxen, or both, that had become mired in one of the sticky mudholes that formed after a day of rain. Groups of warriors roamed the length of the caravan to provide the manpower needed to assist so the rest could keep moving. Broken axles, or a yoke, or piece of harness were an everyday occurrence. The people as well as the animals were near exhaustion and the equipment sorely needed repair. The months of walking, fighting, and living in the open weather were catching up. Father had developed teams to mend broken carts along the trail, and they were kept busy. Men from Gorm's wagon assembly traveled with carts filled with spare parts and tools. They would conduct repairs as best they could along the trail. Injured animals had to be killed, butchered, and the meat eaten or preserved so it would not spoil and go to waste.

The summer heat gradually changed into cooler fall weather as we traversed Pannonia. Thankfully, the lack of biting insects was the first sign the seasons were changing. Colors were just showing on the trees and the rains were coming closer together and getting colder. The air in the mornings was cooler and the swans, geese, and ducks were moving about, preparing their young for the long flight southward by moving from lake to river to pond. Warblers, swifts, and wagtails passed over in clouds as they headed south, where the insects were livelier. The red deer stags rubbed the velvet from their antlers against the trees and pawed the ground to leave their scent on an enticing scrape. Their winter coats were changing to a light gray, and the males were developing a thick mane. On a cool, foggy morning we could often hear a dominant stag roaring, echoing through the forest, calling for potential mates.

As the clumps of forest merged into the open plains, it was easier going, and one day the lead scouts met with a small party of Scordisci warriors. Near the mouth of the Savus River, they led us into a sheltered area between two wooded ridgelines, a two-day ride from Singidunum, the Scordisci capital.

The caravan was well practiced in establishing camp by this time and in short order there were tents up, fires going, and all the activity of a village of thousands of people.

---

Glum was brewing a batch of mead when Skoll and I found him. The wolf pup was healing well and followed me everywhere now. Somehow, Glum had already discovered a few hives and had enough honey to get started. The brew master was in a cheery mood, and no wonder. He always seemed to have a mug of ale, or mead, or birch wine, within arm's reach. The big man greeted me with a hearty embrace and pounded my back so hard my teeth rattled. He offered a horn mug of ale he had brewed from wild wheat that he collected while on the march. Whenever the caravan paused, Glum was brewing something.

A wide grin parted his dark, bushy beard like the sun shining through a hole in the clouds. It was welcoming and genuine. Deep-set dark eyes were always filled with an infectious mirth, as they peered out from beneath a heavy brow forested with thick, bushy eyebrows that nearly connected above his nose. We sat on a log by his open fire, while Glum scratched Skoll's ears.

"So, what do you think of our journey thus far, my boy?" he asked with one eye squinted at me. "Do you think we have reached the end? It is a beautiful place, this Pannonia."

Looking south to the snow-capped mountains, I smiled. "It is beautiful, and I am tired of our journey."

"I could grow a never-ending supply of barley, rye, and wheat here." He grinned again, his unruly hair making him look a bit mad, and absently wiped a dribble of ale from his beard with a sleeve.

"It seems at long last we may have found friends that will grant us the land we need to settle down," I said. "In exchange for the strength of our warriors, of course. These battles against the Romans are not our affair. Yet, I'm grateful for the opportunity it presents us."

"Our people need somewhere to call home Borr, and the Scordisci have been generous. In the spring I will gather some swarms and get my hives going again. I've already found a grove of birch trees I can tap to make wine. I can harvest enough wild grain in a few weeks to keep me in bread and ale for the winter. It doesn't take much to make me happy," he said with a laugh.

I chuckled. "You've been busy."

Skoll took a step, then two, away from Glum so that his hand traveled from Skoll's ears toward his back end. The wolf pup looked back over his shoulder, his tongue lolling, ears back, and eyes watery with pleasure.

"Yes, I have. But then, you've not come here to talk to me about honeybees or ale, have you?" He patted Skoll on the rump and shooed him away, chuckling and shaking his head.

I looked down sheepishly. "No, I haven't."

"Well, she's gone to fetch water for me, but she will be back shortly. You have my permission to see her, Borr. You make her happy, and that makes me happy. There has been little enough to make anyone happy for the past year."

"You always seem to be happy," I said, smiling.

"Ha! That's just the ale boy!" Glum guffawed. "We all have hard times, but it doesn't pay to stay mad or upset at anything for long, one has to move on from the bad times. My wife died bringing Frida into this world. I lost the most precious thing in my life and was given something equally precious. It nearly drove me mad that I lost her, but Frida, she kept me sane. If it were not for her, I truly believe that I would not be here. No one would think that an ugly bear like me could father such a beautiful child, Borr, and that makes me happy too! Here she comes. You two run along, enjoy the rest of the day."

When Frida saw me sitting beside her father, she smiled warmly.

Skoll ran to her and licked her fingers when she bent to greet him. I felt as if the air had been squeezed out of my chest. She looked so different from when we left Jutland. We were little more than children then, but in only a year's time she had grown into a beautiful young woman. I had found new health and become a warrior. I had grown in body and mind and gained a confidence that was changing me.

Like me, Frida was shy and quiet. But at this moment there was no trace of shyness, and she stared at me with an intensity that drew me to her. Her long chestnut hair shone in the sunlight. It was parted in the middle and pulled back from her face in a braid that trailed down the center of her back. The deep brown of her dark eyes drew me into their depths. I wanted to speak, but I could not, and she saved me.

"I saw you watching me yesterday," she said softly. Her voice seemed as sweet as honey to me. "I was hoping you would come and talk to me."

Time seemed to slow as she stared up at me through delicate, long, black lashes that slowly closed, then opened again.

"I... wanted to talk to you, but...I... I didn't want to bother you."

She tilted her head and looked at me quizzically, not understanding what I meant, and neither did I. After a moment, she stifled a giggle with the back of her hand.

"You don't have to be shy with me, Borr, I like you," she said kindly.

I exhaled loudly, some of the tenseness leaving me, but I was still on edge, unsure what to say next.

I blurted out rapidly, "I like you too–you look very pretty–would you like to go for a walk?"

I felt like running away.

"Yes," she smiled. "Thank you, I would." When she turned toward me, her hand brushed mine and I flinched when I felt a fire course through my arm.

"Are those for me?" she asked.

Confused, I followed her eyes downward toward my hand. I had forgotten the handful of wildflowers I picked on my way to see her. Suddenly realizing what I was holding, my hand jerked up and brought them so close to her face she pulled back, smiling gently.

As we walked, I was unsure what to think or how to act, and she did most of the talking at first. Gradually I relaxed and could talk to her more easily as we became familiar. Skoll happily trotted ahead of us, occasionally finding something interesting to sniff at.

We walked along the riverbank, enjoying the early autumn sun, growing comfortable in each other's company, talking of nothing and everything. Our walk lasted a good portion of the day until I realized I would be missed if I was not home soon. We returned to her father's cart, where I bid them both goodbye with a heart that was lighter than I could ever remember.

---

Hrolf worked in a hypnotic rhythm, cutting a wide swath through the tall grass and leaving it to dry for the next day. Skalla raked and pushed yesterday's grass into a fresh pile for me. I pitched a large clump onto the tall stack of hay where Freki was arranging it around the center pole and stamping it down. As he worked, I used my fork to comb the outside of the stack so that when it rained, or the snow melted, it would act as a thatched roof and the water would run off and down the outside of the stack. A bed of crossed branches kept the haystack off the ground. Sweat rivulets ran down my skin, turning into a line of mud that dried and itched annoyingly. When the day ended, the four of us ran straight to the nearby stream to jump in and wash off the grass and dust that coated our skin and clogged our nostrils.

We were fortunate that it had been a dry fall and the rains held off this long. Many more crews of people were working quickly to cut the tall grass and pile it in haystacks to store for the winter. In a weeks' time there would be hundreds of stacks. The cattle would have to endure the winter outside again, but the weather here would be milder than in our homeland. The stacks of hay would see them through until spring.

When we arrived, the cattle had been released onto the vast prairie to fatten them up as much as possible, but the snows would come. After the slaughter, the remaining cattle would be rounded up and brought here to feed throughout the winter.

The nearby stream and small pond provided water. The cattle would do well on their own, as long as they had some protection from wolves, which the hounds would provide.

By now I had fully caught up to my friends in physical health and was surpassing some of them in height and muscle. We swam and wrestled in the stream for a while, and it was nearly dark when we arrived at the family's fire, where a stew pot simmered with vegetables and pork in a thick gravy. A loaf of warm bread sat on the hearth. We ate like starved beasts, finishing the pot. Then, realizing what had happened, I looked at my mother with concern.

"Don't worry, I already set aside enough for your father and the rest. I expected a pack of hungry wolves could not stop themselves when they came back today," she said lightly.

Smiling with relief, I sat back, patted my stomach, and released a loud belch.

"Mother, you are the best cook I know," I said with conviction.

"I'm the only cook you know, and all of you would starve if you had to cook for yourselves. Now get out of here so your father and his men can eat," she said as they walked up. We four boys scrambled to leave before my father saw fit to assign us another task. He gave my mother a knowing smirk as he watched us run off.

We built new cabins for the winter as the weather was already turning colder. Grimur and Hedda were now living on their own and Hedda was showing with child. The twins and I moved back in with my parents and Hilgi. Lothar, Vallus, Tala, and Anik had built a hut of their own to share but took most of their meals with us. They each took turns in teaching me and the other boys in sword craft, spear fighting, and other combat skills and Hilgi never lacked an uncle to play with. They each doted on her equally. Hedda and my mother had eventually broken through to Hilgi, who now seemed to have recovered from Nilda's death and had mostly returned to her old self.

---

The brilliant autumn sunrise broke over the eastern mountains and spilled onto the bright red, yellow, and fiery orange oaks, maples, beech, and poplar; splashes of dark evergreens amongst them. The colors seemed to glow in the morning light. I have always loved this time of year, as the heat of late summer gradually gives way to the cooler nights and comfortably warm days of the harvest season. I breathed deeply of the cool morning air, smokey from the smoldering fires used to cure the meat. The cattle, sheep, goats, and hogs had been culled, and the butchering was nearly finished. Culling the herds in the fall lessened the feed that had to be put up to get the remaining animals through winter, and the best were kept for breeding in the spring.

Women and girls bustled about, tending the meat that dried on smoking racks above the fires. Smoked and salted venison, boar, geese, ducks, and other wild game hung in the common food warehouses. Baskets of dried fish, apples, and various roots, and clay jars of milk curds covered the floors. Blocks of coarse cheese, smaller clay jars of honey, and bags of salt filled the shelves. Dried herbs used for seasoning food and healing hung in bundles from the rafters.

We had been busy in the fields; cutting, threshing, and winnowing the wild grains. After we separated the grain, we collected the straw for bedding and floor covering. The grains were stored in clay pots and placed in shallow cellars beneath the floors of the warehouses, to be ground later to make bread and porridge.

There was no end to the work to be done before the snows came, and it was not just the food that needed to be stored. Firewood had to be gathered into huge piles convenient for the people to use, clothing had to be replaced as well as tools and weapons that had been broken, worn out, or lost. The spoils from the battles with the Boii and the Romans had been distributed and some of our warriors now carried the higher quality Roman swords and daggers, as well as the occasional mail coat or helmet. Most of the armor did not fit our people who stood a head taller and weighed half again as much as a Roman. Most of our warriors still preferred our traditional weapons and used the heavy armor as valuable trade items.

Among all these preparations, I continued my training. On my way to meet Tala, I stopped by the fire where my mother and Hedda were salting and hanging fresh meat to smoke. Four-year-old Hilgi was playing with the other children not far away.

They smiled at my approach. Hedda had softened the wound of Nilda's loss and become another mother figure for Hilgi who would never be found more than a stone's throw from one of them.

"You had best be on your way or you will be late again, Borr," mother said with a smile as she handed me a strip of dried beef.

I grinned at her, tearing off a chunk and chewing.

"Father told me to come and tell you that a supply caravan is approaching the camp. The Scordisci took it all as spoils of war and are giving it to us in thanks for our help. He said there may be some wool or other items you might want in it."

Before she could answer, Hilgi came running up like a short blonde lightning bolt that nearly knocked me over. I had to reach out and grab the smoking rack to steady myself and keep from knocking it into the fire as she hugged my legs. Just as quickly, she disappeared into the passing swarm of running children.

"She needs to be put to work," I said with mock seriousness. Tearing off another chunk of beef, I tossed the rest carelessly to Skoll, who was sitting on his haunches expectantly. He deftly caught it and in two swift bites it was gone, and he was looking at me with the same questioning expression, waiting for more. The two women stopped abruptly in disbelief. They did not like to see their hard work gobbled up by a wolf. Eyes narrowed, lips were pressed tight, and faces reddened as they glared at me with malice. Feeling my life may be in immediate danger, I decided it was time to leave.

"She has done her share," my mother said testily. "There is a point that all children become more of a hindrance than a help," she said, tipping her head in my direction and raising her eyebrows.

I chuckled and nodded my head, turning toward the training grounds.

On my way, I passed the caravan entering the village. I knew how badly these things were needed and was glad to see the relief and joy in our people as they found replacements for items that had been damaged or lost since the flood.

---

Finally, the day of the Samhain feast arrived. My father and his retinue of fighting men, along with their families, were invited to join the Scordisci at Singidunum. I had not yet been to the city and was surprised to see that it was even larger than the oppidum at Posonium. It looked much the same, but the mood was different, as it was a festival to honor the harvest time and a last chance to celebrate and feast before the start of winter.

Vallus told us that the Romans referred to the Scordisci and the other eastern tribes as Celts and those people that lived north of the Danubius like us they called Germans, though we had common roots and told similar stories as the Scordisci. We shared many of the same gods and customs, but the Cimbri, because our ancestors had mixed with the Germanic peoples who lived in Jutland and to the north when we arrived, also worshipped many of the gods of the north such as Wodan and Donar. We had a harvest festival every year as well, but the Scordisci had prepared a celebration like none I had ever seen. There was an enormous feast with foods of all kinds everywhere I looked.

Many people wore strange costumes and as we walked through the busy streets, Vallus explained to us, "During the time of Samhain, the Celts believe that the veil is thinned between the world of the living and that of the dead. People disguise themselves to ward off the evil spirits that may have penetrated that veil."

We all looked at him in disbelief and after a moment Hrolf asked, "You are saying the dead can walk among the living?"

Vallus went on. "Many believe that these unseen malignant spirits travel about playing mean pranks on people, but I think it is just an excuse for mischievous children to have fun."

From then on, we were alert for anything amiss, but none of us reported seeing a dead spirit wandering about.

The feast lasted three days in which large quantities of food and alcohol were consumed, and worldly cares were cast aside for a time. Each day there were horse races, and a great deal of good-natured betting took place, though there was the occasional drunken brawl over a debt.

On the last day, there was a joint council. I accompanied my father and as I watched, Aodhan, the Scordisci king, opened the council.

"Welcome Haistulf and our northern brothers, the Cimbri. I thank you for your help in fighting the invaders. We have been resisting these incursions for many years and we look forward to building on the victory at Siscia with a new campaign into Macedonia in the spring."

He paused for a moment and was answered with a loud cheer.

I noted it was the same oratory trick my father used during his speeches.

Aodhan went on. "I pledge to you Haistulf of the Cimbri, that the Scordisci are your brothers, and we welcome you into our lands. Our tribal council has agreed to grant you the land you are now settled upon and wishes you to rebuild your villages. We hope to find common cause in our resistance to the Roman threat."

When Aodhan finished his speech, my father toasted the Scordisci, the agreement was sealed, and the final night of Samhain proceeded. The priests proclaimed the beginning of the new year and in the morning we all returned to our camps to settle in for the winter.

# Chapter Eleven

## Summer 118 BC

I was a scout now. A full warrior who had grown into a man's strength at seventeen years old. Experienced warriors had trained me in battle skills, and I had studied my enemy at great length under the tutelage of Vallus. I had learned woodland stealth from my friend Anik who was raised in jungle lands, and I was good. Very good.

I stood as tall as my father, who was taller than most men, and the maidens of my tribe whispered behind their hands that I was handsome. I stood apart from other men of my tribe with my long red hair and gray eyes and I had a respectable start on a beard, or at least I thought as much.

Skoll walked silently by my side. I nursed him back to health over the past summer, but by the time he had healed from his injuries, it was the dead of winter. I convinced my father that to release him then would either result in his starvation or possibly in having a predator that was unafraid of man living near our cattle and other livestock.

He was reluctant but agreed to allow me to keep him through the winter, provided I taught him to hunt wild game instead of cattle and that I released him in the spring. I readily agreed and hoped that by spring I could convince my father otherwise. But, in the spring, there was no exception, and he insisted I release him.

I walked Skoll away from the camp and hugged his neck, bidding him a tearful farewell while he licked my face. When I turned away, he simply followed me back toward our camp, not understanding

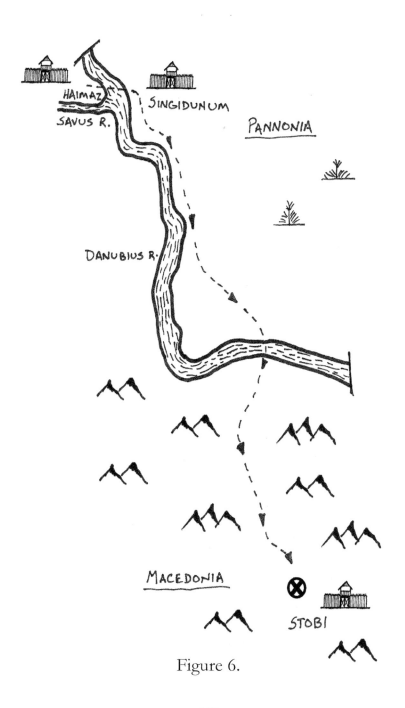

Figure 6.

what I expected him to do. I yelled at him, "Go! Go away!"

I stomped my feet and waved my arms, tears streaming down my face. "Go!" I yelled again. Finally, he understood. He turned away, took several halting steps, then stopped. He looked back over his shoulder with his ears back and tail tucked, unsure what was happening. Then he turned and disappeared into the forest. I was heartbroken, for I loved Skoll deeply.

Some weeks later I was cutting wood in the forest when I saw him watching me from a distance. I called him and he came to me. I scratched his ears, and we played for a while, then he moved off into the trees once again. It thrilled me to know that he was still nearby, and I felt reassured that he might come for a visit from time to time.

We marched south after the calving season; our herds replenished and growing fat on the lush grass of Pannonia. The spring flooding had receded along the Danubius and a combined force of warriors from the allied tribes, twenty thousand strong, marched south to meet the invaders.

When we left on our campaign, I often saw Skoll off in the distance watching, and whenever I left the main camp to scout, he joined me.

My adopted brothers Freki and Skalla also served as scouts and were on our flank, watching for enemy movement. Hrolf, as usual, was with me.

Hrolf and I were working our way along a ridgeline in the mountains north of the Roman encampment.

When I found a suitable spot to observe the Roman camp, Skoll lay beside me on the ground. Hrolf was behind us, watching for danger from our rear.

From my position looking down into the valley I could see two castra, the military camps the Romans used on campaign. Each contained one legion, over ten thousand fighting men in all including the auxiliaries, enclosed in large fortifications with significant defenses. After the battle at Siscia, Vallus taught us about the Roman camps and now I was observing one.

The ten-foot-high earthen berms were topped with wooden stakes and fronted by a ditch also filled with sharpened stakes. Though I was too far away to see them, the cleared ground surrounding the camp was likely seeded with caltrops, small yet vicious three-sided iron spikes that were spread on the ground to disable both infantrymen and cavalry horses that stepped on them.

Guards kept watch over the walls while the daily life of a field camp took place. Like in our camps, the steady sound of a hammer striking on a blacksmith's anvil rang out. There were infantry troops drilling outside the camp, the blaring of brass horns announcing a change in formation or battle tactic, and I memorized the purpose of each call. I watched for some time, marveling at their precision and the control their leaders exhibited over the formations as they marched, turned, launched pila, changed to the testudo and defended, then moved forward in the attack; stepping, shoving, stabbing, stepping, shoving, stabbing. Vallus's teachings became real before my eyes.

Our people fought as individual warriors massed together for strength. When drawn up for battle, our clans were organized into a wedge-shaped phalanx that was led by the highest-ranking and bravest warriors at the front. Each side swept back to protect the flanks, forming a wedge that resembled the shape of a boar's head. When the point of the wedge struck an enemy wall, the sides would come forward and meet the line.

The wedge was effective to charge the enemy and breach a line, but once combat was entered, control was lost, and the fighting fell to the individual warriors. We did not have the ability to control our warriors after the initial contact or to move and respond to orders the way these Romans did. In the defense we formed the shield wall and overlapped our shields to protect the front line while they were pushed from behind to provide weight to the line, but we always preferred individual combat over massive formations.

We used our horns to give the order to attack, or to fall back, or form the wall, but we did not maneuver tactically in the middle of a battle as an entire unit. We depended on surprise by using ambushes and by putting fear into the enemy with brute strength. Until the battle madness had passed, the fight tended to go its own way until the gods and the superior strength or numbers of one side or the other determined victory. We had no such control once a battle started, and I saw its effectiveness watching from my hidden position.

A formation of archers in strange clothing, all with the same dark skin as Tala, were practicing on a bow range set up to one side of the castra. A group of horsemen were practicing cavalry tactics farther away, screening their movement in a cloud of dust. These were the foreign auxiliaries Vallus told us about.

A sudden noise and a flash of motion to one side of the training ground surprised me as a pile of rocks and logs exploded. I looked back at the castra to see a line of strange devices that looked like a huge crossbow on a stand. A crew of two men were winding the powerful bowstring back using winches while another placed a bolt half the height of a man onto the bow. When they were ready, a command rang out, and the bolt sprang forward so fast it was difficult to see until it hit the target, hundreds of paces away, causing rocks and logs to fly into the air again.

I realized this weapon was the scorpion that Vallus had told us of. I and the others had scoffed at the idea of such a thing, yet here it was. The idea of this weapon firing into a mass of warriors and the destruction it would cause, gave me pause.

Vallus had schooled us on all these things, but to see them with my own eyes was both impressive and intimidating. The military strength and skill of these Romans must be respected.

I reflected how we had surprised the Romans at Siscia, coming from the darkness into their flanks and how their iron discipline broke in the face of the fear that we put in their hearts. Watching these soldiers, I determined that attacking them inside their castra could never succeed. They would slaughter our warriors before they ever breached the walls. Meeting them when they were prepared to offer battle on their terms, when their superior discipline and weapons would be to their advantage, could only lead to our defeat.

Developing tactics to counter the Romans' superior weapons and battlefield control would be key to our survival.

I backed out of my hiding spot and rejoined Hrolf. After telling him everything that I had observed, we turned to go. Returning the way we had come, Skoll stepped in front of me and blocked my way. I noticed his posture had changed and when I kneeled, he quietly split away from me into the trees. Suddenly, I heard a man's scream that ended abruptly, then another man screamed.

I realized too late that we had broken one of the strictest rules of scouting by retracing our steps along the same path we had used to enter the area. We crouched down in anticipation of an attack, when Skoll materialized by my side, his jaws and chest covered in blood.

We cautiously approached the area where the men had been waiting and found the two Roman scouts who had found our trail and were lying in wait. If Skoll had not sensed their presence, they would have killed us.

"Thank you, my friend," I told him as I knelt and scratched his ears, handing him a generous piece of dried beef as a reward. Hrolf and I shared a look of relief, and after rejoining the twins, we moved off on a more indirect path to return to our camp.

After reporting to the allied leaders, I joined my friends for some hot food for the first time in several days. I was looking forward to getting some undisturbed rest. I lay on the ground under a large tree, falling asleep immediately. Several short hours later, Hrolf shook me awake when the call went out to prepare to move. There were spies among the camp followers that had confirmed the legions would march in two days into the interior along the Axius River.

The mountainous terrain of Macedonia provided many locations that were ideal for ambushing any force that passed through the narrow valleys. The war council had chosen such a place near the village of Stobi.

The river valley the legions were following made its way through a narrow pass about two miles long, where a bend in the river brought the legions closer to the western cliffs. We prepared trees at both ends of the pass by chopping part way through their trunks and leaving them standing. When the lead Roman units reached the mouth of the pass, Aodhan gave the signal to begin the attack. The trees were felled, effectively trapping the legions on the narrow strip of land along the river.

The sound of the barritus spread fear among the Romans and brought courage to our warriors. The battle song stopped abruptly and was followed by a rhythmic clash of swords and spears against shields and a short war cry that echoed through the valley.

Crash . . . Crash . . . "Hoosh!" Crash . . . Crash . . . "Hoosh!"

An ominous rumble grew slowly, seeming to shake the very ground we walked on. The sound echoed between the hills, causing confusion among the legions as to where or how large the enemy was. The Scordisci brought war drums, something that we had not used before.

Aodhan allowed the sound to grow. The longer it went on with no attack beginning, the more nervous the Romans became. The unseen enemy that was creating the noise became more fearsome

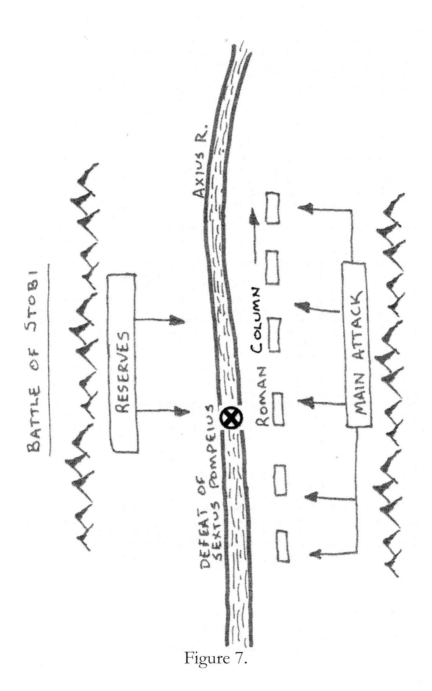

Figure 7.

with every moment.

The legions tried to mass from march formation into their familiar square phalanx, but the terrain restricted their movements. The centurions ordered them into the testudo with a clap of overlapping shields, limiting their ability to support each other while our warriors had the advantage of movement on the slopes, hidden by the trees.

The Nubian archers had no targets to engage, and their superstitions ran wild as they imagined the hidden enemies. The horses of the Numidian cavalry were snorting and shying, unnerved by the sounds, and feeling the apprehension of their riders.

Several large rocks tumbled down from the heights, crashing through the trees, and smashing into the testudo formations. The boulders were followed closely by thousands of screaming spearmen. The unprotected cavalry and archers milling about near the rear of the formation were the first to panic. We had the advantage of high ground, and the momentum of the charging horde crashed into the Roman lines, pouring into the gaps created by the boulders.

To their credit, the Romans reacted quickly and met the first charge with sword and shield, but the overwhelming numbers of warriors pushed them backward toward the river. Their fearsome scorpions had been disassembled for the march and could not be brought to bear.

Their leaders could not maintain control, and some legionaries threw down their weapons and fled. A panic spread rapidly through the rest of the legions and the men in front could feel the reassuring pressure at their backs lessen. In mass formations, when one man panics it spreads like wildfire and soon affects the entire group. When the centurions in the front rank called for relief, there was no one to step forward. The men in the front lines were tiring, and the ranks were breaking apart. Once a hole was created, our warriors poured through and widened the gap.

As if at once the Roman resistance broke. They fled to the river trying to escape the fury of our attack. The river was wide and shallow here, but deep enough to slow their rout as they waded through. As the survivors reached the perceived safety of the far shore, we applied the final blow. A large group of our warriors emerged from the forest on the other side of the river to massacre the mostly unarmed and totally disorganized survivors.

My companions and I faced a group of soldiers near the center of the ambush that had rallied and formed a defense around a small island that rose from the shallow river. The stone-faced soldiers knew there was no escape, but they were determined to sell their lives at a high cost. They had locked shields into a testudo formation. Their gladii, smeared with the blood of our warriors, poked through the gap at the top of the front rank's upright shields and the shields of the second rank which guarded their heads.

A senior officer stood in their midst, shouting encouragement. He had lost his helmet and blood from a head wound ran down his face, dripping from his chin onto his chest plate.

He called to Mars, the Roman god of war, as well as Jupiter, king of the Roman gods and promised his men that if they died valiantly, the gods would reward them. Vallus had taught me Latin and explained the Roman gods to me, and I called back to the Roman in his own language.

"Your gods have abandoned you to your fate!"

The soldiers froze at the sound of my voice. They had never encountered a barbarian who spoke their language.

"They have abandoned you! Rome has abandoned you! You will all die here today. Your blood will turn this river red, and your bodies will be torn apart and devoured by the animals of these mountains."

"Look above you." I pointed at the sky with my spear where a spiral of black birds circled high above. "Already the ravens await your deaths. They shall pluck your eyes and rip off your eyelids and your lips. Your bones will lie here and mark this place for generations. They will mark your failure to conquer this land."

The shield wall rippled as my words unnerved them. Many had taken their eyes from us to look skyward. Shields moved slightly as men shifted their weight, looking around them, seeking a way out, muttering among themselves.

"Do not think you will find yourself in Elysium! Your souls will be trapped in these mountains forever, cursed to wander this land. Wodan will see to that."

I slapped my spear to my shield and was answered by my men. Crash . . . crash . . . "Hoosh!" As they took a step forward into the river, the Romans took half a step back, startled by the sudden movement.

Recovering from his shock, the officer attempted to rally his men, but I had shaken their confidence. I nodded to Hrolf, who blew the attack on the bull's horn. Arroooo!

The group of soldiers stood like a rock in a storm off the coast of my native Jutland, and the wave of our warriors broke over them until they were no more.

It was slaughter, and in a matter of minutes, the last of two legions were destroyed, only a few surviving by playing dead and floating away down the river.

Despite my words, the Romans fought valiantly. I received a puncture wound to my thigh when a gladius stabbed between the shields. It was not crippling but was painful and bled profusely. When I fell, I was dragged to the rear of the line by Hrolf while Freki and Skalla closed the gap. Hrolf bandaged my leg with a strip from a Roman tunic and returned to the fight.

I later learned the officer's name was Sextus Pompeius. He was a praetor and the Roman governor of Macedonia. He was the leader of this expedition and he paid for it with his life.

The screams and moans of pain lasted throughout the day as our warriors roamed the battlefield, dispatching the wounded. We stripped the Romans of anything useful and left the bodies where they lay. We lost less than three hundred men to nearly ten thousand Romans. With the Scordisci we had broken the back of Roman expansion into Macedonia.

After the battle, Hrolf approached me, holding his hand out. In it was a beautiful torc made of twisted silver braids with a snarling wolf's head attached to each end.

"It belonged to the officer," he said. "You should have it."

I took the torc from his hand with admiration, running my thumb along its carefully formed lines. I had never seen an object of such craftsmanship.

I thanked him and placed it around my neck. Hrolf bent over and helped me to my feet. My leg was stiff, but I could walk without help.

"Have you seen my father?" I asked him.

"Over there," he pointed, and I limped over to him.

———————

When we neared the village, Freki rode ahead to tell my mother that I had been wounded. She and Frida were both waiting for me when we arrived.

Mother gasped when she saw my pale face. My wound was infected and inflamed. And painful. With Freki's help they got me out of the cart, and I limped weakly into our cabin. Frida placed a cool cloth on my brow and when mother unwrapped my leg, they both recoiled at the smell. It had festered on the march home, and I was in real danger. Mother immediately went to work cleaning the wound, probing the tender flesh as she did, and discovering a deep sack of puss in the wound. She worked the muscle and squeezed, then moved and squeezed again, as I bit hard into the thick piece of leather she had placed between my teeth, but nothing happened.

"I'm going to have to reopen it," she said matter-of-factly.

"Mmph," I groaned past the leather in complaint.

"Frida, boil water and bandages. Cut up some garlic, mash and mix it into a few spoonfulls of honey. Then warm that up too."

She opened Nilda's medicine box and rummaged around, coming out with a small clay jar. "This is Valerian root. Steep this in a small cup of boiling water as well."

"Haistulf," she called to my father, who had just walked through the door. "I need your small knife, the one you use for shaving and eating. Make sure it's clean and extra sharp."

As my father stropped the knife a few strokes, she fished a bandage out of the steaming pot Frida had brought over, wrang it out and folded it, then placed it on top of my wound. I winced in pain at the touch, but after a moment, the heat soothed the throbbing, and the pain faded a bit. She repeated this process several times until my leg was reddened from the heat and then reached for my father's knife.

As soon as the blade cut into the inflamed flesh, a pale greenish pus mixed with blood erupted from the wound and oozed down my leg. Frida turned green herself and looked as if she might faint. My father watched intently as mother started pressing the muscles in my leg again. She repeated the process, alternating more hot rags with pressure to draw out the poison and drain the wound until she was satisfied she had gotten the infection out.

"Bring me the honey," she told Frida. She smeared a generous dollop onto the wound, then bound it with several clean bandages.

"Drink this," she ordered, handing me the Valerian tea. "And eat this," she added, offering me a piece of bread with the honey and garlic mixture.

When I was finished, she stoked the fire as Frida propped my head and covered me with my cloak. I laid back, exhausted from the efforts of the last hour. My leg was feeling better already, and I fell asleep immediately.

We returned victorious to our villages, secure in the gratitude of our Scordisci hosts, and spent the rest of the summer rebuilding our life. We had finally found the home we searched for, and we built a new stronghold on our land by the Savus.

My leg healed well, and another winter passed.

---

In the spring, a group of riders approached the village from the north. We were all surprised and pleased to learn that it was Teutobod and a dozen of his retainers. My father sent me to gather the leaders for a council and the next day we held a feast.

Teutobod told us that the year after we left, they had an unusually cold and wet summer. Their crops rotted in the fields and a sickness decimated their herds. Their cattle, sheep and goats were all affected. Herdsmen noticed the animals staggering and trembling which developed into difficulty breathing, seizures, and bleeding from their mouth and nose. They died suddenly after one or two days of these symptoms, and the disease wiped out nearly half their livestock.

Some herdsmen who had close contact with the diseased animals had also developed similar symptoms and died.

After the outbreak passed, the Teutones followed our example, but they took a different route. They traveled south along the Suevus River, the eastern boundary of their lands, then like us they came to the Marus, but from the eastern side, then followed the Danubius.

Their trip had seen more conflict than ours, as they were forced to find food wherever they could. That often meant taking it from others. They had several clashes with the Boii who pushed them eastward into the Quadi, a smaller Celtic tribe that could not resist the concentrated might of the Teutones. The Teutones were starving, and the constant conflict with other tribes had taken its toll.

At Posonium, Teutobod heard of our passing and followed our path southward. They entered the Scordisci lands without permission and established a village near the mouth of the Dravus where we had camped two years ago.

Upon entering Pannonia Teutobod learned of our new settlement and came to ask us for help to get through the winter. My father was happy to return the favor they had granted when we were in such need and immediately assembled a large relief party. We drove hundreds of head of livestock along with a large caravan of food and supplies northward to the Teutones' new settlement on the Dravus, Teutobergium.

# Chapter Twelve

## Spring 117 BC

The sun's warmth finally returned to Pannonia. The spring rains subsided, and the last of the melt ran off into the streams and rivers.

The signs of new growth were everywhere, and the women were foraging for spring greens and roots. The first wildflowers were blooming, the hardwoods were budding, and the new grass was greening the vast plains.

We turned the livestock out from their winter stalls to wander about the homes and farmsteads as they enjoyed the tender shoots of new grass. After the spring festival, the animals would be released onto the plain to be pastured there until the fall slaughter.

The longhouse doors were braced open to allow the fresh spring air to come inside. Children helped their mothers bring belongings outside to lay in the sun and use the breeze to cleanse the stale smell of wood smoke and animals. A large bonfire burned dirty bedstraw, worn clothing, and other items that were no longer serviceable.

The celebration of spring was fast approaching, and the preparations for the feast were nearly complete. Hunting parties returned with as much meat and fowl as they could find. Fishermen doubled their efforts, and the children harvested freshwater clams, mollusks, and mussels from the Savus River.

The spring celebration began with a parade emerging from the sacred grove near our new village. The Spring Bride, chosen for her exceptional beauty, was dressed in white linen, her blonde tresses crowned with a wreath of flowers. She rode in a ceremonial cart covered in more flowers and evergreen boughs and topped with a canopy of woven branches and bright green spring buds. A pair of white oxen pulled the two-wheeled cart, each with a young maid walking at its head. Three bridesmaids walked on either side of the wagon, cradling evergreen boughs, and dressed in white linen and flowers. A pair of young acolytes, not yet priests, led the procession, blowing the bronze lurs used in religious ceremonies. The mellow tones of the horns carrying on the light winds announced the coming of the parade. The Spring Bride traveled about the countryside, bestowing the blessings of the goddess Nerthus and her gift of fertility on the people, the animals, and the fields.

Two priests followed behind with another cart to accept the offerings and prayers of the people as it wandered from home to farm to village. The people came out in numbers to witness the Spring Bride's beauty and to receive her blessings.

I was among the escort of mounted young men who followed behind, swains from around the countryside, dressed and adorned in our finest livery. No weapons or other metal objects were to be seen as they are forbidden to be near the Spring Bride, as all conflict and war was set aside during this time.

At dusk, the procession returned to the sacred grove as bonfires dotted hills on the horizon. The young people were gathered to spend the night out of doors, dancing, drinking, and welcoming the spring. From each hilltop, the twinkling lights could be seen in all directions, connecting the people as one tribe as their neighbors conducted the same rites at the same time.

This was a time for many a young man and maid to begin their courtship. Often there was rivalry for a particular girl, resulting in a fight, but ultimately the girl chose her own suitor.

My three friends and I drank and sang with the rest until late in the night and did not wake until mid-morning. With heads thick with drink from the night before, we stopped at my home to make a breakfast of whatever was available and wandered toward the district commons to watch the games.

This was the first time the tribe had celebrated the Spring Bride since the flood, and the unmarried young men from all around appeared to participate in feats of strength and skill in weapons, horsemanship, foot races, and grappling. The favorite competition, dancing with the bull, an ancient custom brought with us from Jutland, was left to the champions of each of the contests.

My friends Skalla and Freki were still young compared to most of the competitors and lost quickly to the older boys in the strength tests.

I was tall and lean with broad shoulders, while Hrolf was a head shorter than me, with a large chest and thick arms. I had not only caught up to my peers but had surpassed many of the young men in size and strength, and Hrolf was an equal in most events. The twins watched us and cheered loudly, betting with each other on who would win.

Again, and again, Hrolf and I stood out from the rest. He won the weapons contest outright. A clear victor over his closest opponents in sword and shield sparring, he far outmatched the others in strength and accuracy when he threw the spear, hitting his marks consistently. In horsemanship I bested most, only losing out to one of my good friends when I slipped while mounting a galloping horse, nearly getting trampled. I came in third place in the foot races, and in the grappling match I came close to besting a hulking young man we had not seen before, who in the end put me into a headlock that nearly choked me unconscious. After the match I learned he was called Ansgar, and that he was one of the Boii who had joined us.

After a quick break, the champions of each bout gathered for the final competition. A huge beast that had been chosen especially for this contest was driven into the paddock where the mounted champions waited. The bull, obviously not far removed from the wild auroch, was enraged by the prodding of its herdsmen and the shouting of the excited people around the edge of the paddock. With a snort and a fearsome bellow, the bull charged at Hrolf, clods of earth flying from its hooves.

Hrolf showed no fear of the certain death hurtling at him, and met its charge head on, veering his horse to the side just in time to avoid the razor tipped horns. But he could not reach the bull with a killing blow of his sword. The other men each took a turn at the bull, the crowd roaring each time they came near. When Ansgar saw an opening, he charged toward the side of the bull and leapt from his horse onto the back of the beast. Gripping its wide back with his knees as best he could, he reared up and plunged his sword down through its hump and into its heart. The bull's front legs collapsed, its chin plowing into the earth and throwing the young man over its head. He sprawled awkwardly on the ground and rolled several times before coming to a stop.

The crowd took a collective gasp, then, as Ansgar slowly got to his feet, a great cheer erupted. The other champions dismounted and hoisted him onto their shoulders, parading him around the arena for all to see.

That evening a light rain shower preceded a return to the heights by the unmarried young men and women for another night of drinking and dancing. I was hoping to find Frida, but she did not appear. Instead, I spent the evening sitting around the fire, talking, and drinking with my friends, recounting the events of the day. The older men retired to the great hall to do their drinking, singing of songs, and boasting, while their wives worked to prepare the feast for tomorrow; butchering and cooking the bull that was killed and gossiping excitedly about the events of the day and the coming wedding.

At midday on the third day of the celebration, Ansgar was escorted to the sacred grove, where the Spring Bride had remained after the procession. It was the champion that killed the bull who won the honor to wed the Spring Bride, creating the perfect union of strength and beauty. Hundreds of people gathered to watch as they laid their hands on the oath ring held by the priest, declaring their faith to each other as they were joined as man and wife. With the wedding complete, the couple climbed into the ceremonial wagon and were pulled to the edge of the open grassland where two large bonfires had been built. As the last official act of the spring celebration, the champion and the Spring Bride blessed the cattle, the living wealth of the tribe. The herdsmen drove the cattle between the fires and through the purifying smoke out onto the plains for the summer pasture while the Spring Bride stood in the wagon with her champion, dipping an evergreen sprig into a bowl of fresh blood from a slaughtered bull and sprinkling the cattle with the blood. When all the cattle had passed, the couple was pulled away in the wagon, farther out onto the plain to share their wedding night alone amongst the vast herd.

After everyone returned to the village, the feast could finally begin. Having been forced to endure the smell of baking bread and roasting meat for the past two days, and only being allowed to eat a porridge of fish and clams my mother had made the previous day, I was famished.

Frida suddenly appeared behind me. I jumped when her fingers brushed my shoulder as she sat beside me. I had two trenchers overflowing with food and a large mug of ale in front of me. She had just barely covered the bottom of hers with some meat and vegetables. She smiled sweetly, inviting me to speak, and as usual, I was tongue-tied. Or perhaps it was the large chunk of bread that I nearly choked on when she touched my bare shoulder. I could feel the warmth of her thigh so close to mine. She reached out and brushed a piece of roasted pork from my mustache that was still wispy, but finally long enough to droop past my upper lip. My heart leaped at her touch, and I could hear my pulse pounding in my ears.

She laughed softly at my discomfort and knew that if we were to speak, it was up to her to begin.

"I watched you during the games. I was worried Ansgar would hurt you during the wrestling match," she said.

My expression must have changed because she immediately went on apologetically.

"I...did not mean...I, I..." she stammered. For once she was the one who did not know what to say.

"It's alright," I said smiling.

"I thought he was going to kill me too," I laughed, and she laughed with me.

That exchange seemed to loosen my tongue, and we spent hours talking and laughing, long after the last people wandered off to their beds. She took my hand as we rose from the table and led me to the fire. When she turned toward me, her hair reflected the firelight behind her and shone with red and amber streaks.

As she looked up at me, standing so close, we locked eyes. Her hands were so small in my own. She seemed to have a question in her expression. I could tell she was waiting for something, but I had no idea what. I waited for her to speak, but instead she pressed her lips together in a line as if she were frustrated.

After a moment, she let out a sigh and said, "Come, let's sit by the fire." Her tone confused me as she almost sounded disappointed, and I did not know how I had upset her.

I spread my cloak on the ground and we sat with our backs to a large log used as a bench at the bonfire, stretching our feet toward the warmth. We reminisced about when we were children in Jutland and the hardships of our journey, of the loved ones we had lost and our hopes for the future. Deep in the night, she caught a chill and snuggled closer.

I decided to take a risk. I was not sure if it would be welcome, but

I summoned my courage and put my arm around her shoulders. She immediately laid her head on my chest, and I saw her smile, as if she were finally content. I was thrilled.

I had survived two drownings, been in battle three times, and I had killed several men in single combat, but I was terrified of this tiny girl who had captured my heart. I called Skoll to lie on her other side and he curled up next to her. Sometime during the night, we fell asleep beside each other with her head and arm on my chest, my hand covering hers. As the fire died and day broke to a clear sky, I woke, and I marveled at the peace I felt just sitting there with her in my arms. My buttocks and back ached badly from sitting on the ground all night, but I refused to move until she opened her eyes. When she did, her hand circled my neck; pulling my face to hers, she kissed me sweetly. When we parted, her face was flushed and mine felt warm as well. I saw a familiar look of invitation on her face, and this time, I had no hesitation, and kissed her again.

---

The ground squelched under Frida's feet as she approached my mother, who was outside struggling to coax a fire back to life in order to smoke some fish on a nearby drying rack. It had been raining off and on for a week and the ground was saturated. The hard-packed pathways had turned to mud, and everyone's feet suffered from the constant wet.

When she looked up, my mother smiled brightly. "Hello, Frida. How wonderful to see you this morning."

"Good morning," Frida replied brightly. "My father asked me to bring some honey for your family," she said, holding out a small container. "Is Borr here?"

"Please give your father our thanks, Frida. Yes, Borr is in the house drying out his feet. He and his father went fishing this morning, and as you can see, they were quite successful."

"Oh, would you like some help?" Frida asked helpfully, if unconvincingly.

"No," my mother said, smiling again. "I'll be fine. You go ahead."

Frida happily skipped a few steps and bent to enter the door to our longhouse as my mother smiled behind her, shaking her head, remembering the excitement of youthful love.

As Frida bowed her head to enter the low doorway, I was emerging at the same time. We knocked heads together, and both fell backwards, seeing stars and moaning.

"Ow!" we both said simultaneously. Recovering first, I reached out to help Frida to her feet, laughing at the site of her sitting in a rather large puddle. She glared back at me, clearly not amused. She had put on her best dress to come and see me and now she was dripping wet, and her entire backside was covered in mud.

When I reached down to help her, she grasped my hand with both of hers and pulled with all her strength. My feet kicked out in the slippery mud, and I fell face first in the muck right beside her. We both burst out laughing while my mother looked on at our foolishness, shaking her head all the while.

---

Frida laid beside me on my cloak sleeping, facing toward me, both hands under her cheek. When we arrived, I spread my cloak out on the stream bank and the clean smell of the crushed grass mingled pleasantly with the fragrance from the nearby wildflowers.

A large bumble bee delicately wandered about a golden dandelion flower, then droned to a small patch of white clover, collecting pollen for its hive. I ducked when a dragonfly buzzed past my head on the hunt for mosquitos and water bugs. An unseen sparrow sang from somewhere in the aspen tree above us.

She had brought us a small lunch and after we ate, we lay back content in each other's company. The babble from the nearby stream lulled us both into a nap in the springtime sun, completely at ease. Awakening first, I propped myself up on one elbow and watched her doze beside me.

A breeze stirred a single strand of her dark hair and caused the aspen's bright green leaves to shiver. If I had ever known a more perfect day, I would have been hard pressed to recall it.

I had been courting her in earnest for several months now. At times, it was still difficult for me to imagine that she loved me. We had already grown very close, and during our rare times alone, we found we could talk about anything. We anticipated each other's words and thought much the same about most things.

I was chewing the tender shoot of a long piece of grass, and grinned slightly, mischief on my mind, as I tickled her top lip with the feathery tip of the grass.

The petite nose snorted abruptly, and she opened one eye, immediately focusing on me smiling at her. She arched a questioning eyebrow, and I laughed. She smiled back as I leaned over and gently kissed her cheek, then her lips, as she rolled onto her back, pulling me over her. We kissed softly for a few moments, then passionately for a while longer, until we were forced to part in order to take a breath.

"I love you," I said softly.

She stared up at me and smiled, "I love you too."

Running my fingers along the line where her forehead met her hairline, I smoothed back the loose strands from her face. My fingertips continued along her temple to trace the outline of her ear, then behind her neck to pull her toward me, and I kissed her again.

Between our sessions of kissing and petting, we talked comfortably. Hours passed like minutes and before we noticed, the sun was setting. Curious heads turned in our direction as we made our way back her father's camp. Apparently, judging by all the knowing smiles, what we thought was our secret was obvious to anyone who looked our way. Glancing at Frida, I saw that her skin was flushed, and her hair still had bits of grass in it. I self-consciously ran a hand through my hair and found more than a few pieces, as well. I smiled at her with a feeling of contentment and completeness that I had never known. My heart was full. Frida had agreed to marry me by the end of summer, and my only thoughts were of spending every day and every night with her.

---

## Late summer, 117 BC

I beamed with joy and pride as I watched Frida approach through the gathering of friends and family. She walked to the tune of a flute playing in the background, mingling with the twittering of the birds in the meadow, and we joined hands below the spreading branches of an ancient oak. Her father, Glum, was nearly unrecognizable. He had cleaned his old tunic and even washed and combed his hair and beard for the occasion. Frida's hair was decorated with a wreath of spring wildflowers, and she was more beautiful than any woman I have ever known. Her fair skin seemed to glow beneath her brown hair, and her liquid eyes reflected her happiness. Bright yellow ribbons were woven into the braid around her crown and cascaded loosely with her hair down to her waist. Her white dress was adorned with bright green trim at the wrists and hem, and she wore a yellow sash around her small waist. A necklace of brightly polished amber hung from her neck, my gift to her for our wedding day, and she clutched a small bouquet of wildflowers in her hands.

The multi-colored cloak that my mother made for me hung from my shoulders. It was pinned with a special broach given to me by my friend Gorm, the blacksmith, for the occasion. I wore a leather vest and woven trousers, and I bore no weapons. My long red hair was tied at the nape of my neck with a rawhide thong. The wolf torc adorned my neck, and I wore bronze wrist cuffs that were a gift from my father.

A bearded priest droned on endlessly as I stared into Frida's eyes, oblivious to what went on around me. The priest directed us to grasp the oath ring while he wrapped our wrists with an embroidered strip of cloth, symbolically binding us for life as he said the final blessing. Finally, it was my turn to speak, and this time I had no hesitation.

"Under the watchful eye of Freya, goddess of marriage and family, I vow to watch over you, protect you, to love you and to be kind to you until the day of my death. I give to you this token of my love as a symbol of your independence."

I nodded at my father, who handed Glum a small bag of silver coins that he would pass to his daughter, and the leather lead attached to an ox. These symbolized her ownership of half my wealth.

After Frida recited her oath, Glum handed my father a beautiful new spear and shield, a gift from Frida to me, and an acceptance of my love and protection.

The priest raised his voice and declared, "By the strength of Wodan and the blessing of Freya, I declare these two joined forever as one."

We kissed and embraced, lost in each other, not hearing the celebration of our friends and family as music played and people moved to the banquet tables. Glum brought me back to the moment with a giant slap on my back and a bear hug that pressed the wind from me.

He was uncharacteristically speechless as he wept openly and engulfed his daughter in a tender embrace.

# Chapter Thirteen

## Haimaz

Before the wedding, my friends helped me construct a small hut in our favorite meadow by the stream. After the ceremony was complete, I was immediately focused on escaping the crowd of well-wishers as quickly as possible in order to be alone with my new bride. But Frida, who had taken on the role of the responsible side of my conscience, ensured that we stayed long enough to properly accept the gifts and blessings of the many friends and family that attended.

At long last we were able to slip away quietly as our guests focused more on the food and revelry than on us. By the time we reached our hut, the sun was setting behind the trees at the edge of the meadow. We sat near the stream for a few moments to enjoy the beauty of the evening, my arm spreading my cloak around her shoulders, holding her close within its warmth. As usual, we needed few words to communicate our feelings. We sat close, her head in the hollow of my neck.

A splash broke the silence as a trout captured its supper, leaving a spreading circle of ripples where it broke the surface. The crickets began chirping as day faded into evening and, overhead, several bats flitted about in the gray light of dusk.

I heard a sniffle and felt a wetness on my neck. I looked down at her, alarmed. "What's wrong?" I asked, fearing that she regretted her decision.

She sat up, wiped away a tear, and reassured me with a gentle smile. "I was just thinking of my mother," she said, looking into my eyes.

"She died the day I was born, and she could not be here to see me wed. I never knew her, but I spoke to her every day. She would have loved you, Borr." She snuggled back against me, and I held her close and rocked her in my arms, stroking her hair.

We sat there silently again for a bit, rocking gently back and forth in each other's arms before I found the words I wanted to say. "Your mother must have been very special, to have created someone as wonderful as you. She would be so proud of you for the strength you have shown and the way you have looked after your father. Today, you were the most beautiful bride anyone has ever seen, and she cannot help but have seen you from afar."

Tipping her chin up so I could look into her eyes, I made her a promise. "I pledge to you I will always care for you and protect you and our children. And I will always help you take care of your father as well, so that he is not left alone. He will always be welcome at our fire."

She wrapped both arms around my neck and pulled herself onto my lap. It felt as though our hearts melded as we kissed passionately. Unable to resist any longer, I rose with her in my arms and carried her inside the hut.

I placed her gently on her slippered feet, her arms still about my neck. As our kissing became more urgent, she stood on the tips of her toes and pulled my head down to her hungry mouth. She unpinned my cloak, and let it fall to the floor. Her hands slid along my chest to my shoulders, trying to shed the vest, but I was reluctant to take my hands from her to let it fall. I fumbled with the knot on her sash as she did the same with my belt. She pushed against my chest and stepped back. She reached behind her neck to pull the string that held the dress about her shoulders and allowed it to fall to the ground in one swift motion as the breath flew from my lungs. I kicked off my boots and trousers. We stood naked before each other in the cool evening air. The dim light of a crescent moon rising just above the treetops shone through the open door and provided the smallest bit of illumination, which was just enough to see how perfect she was.

I shook with excitement and we both took a step forward, this time with nothing separating our warm flesh. The fingertips of one hand slid across her shoulder and traced the line of her spine, creating gooseflesh as it moved downward. She stopped my hand with hers and led me to our marriage bed.

------

The moon was no longer shining through the door when I woke. It had moved across the sky and now cast a shadow on the ground before the entrance. When I heard a tiny rustling sound across the hut, I realized why I had awoken. I paid little attention to what I assumed was a field mouse looking for scraps and I had no intention of disturbing the head lying on my chest, or the warm arm and thigh that lay across my stomach and legs. I closed my eyes and returned to a peaceful sleep.

It seemed like a moment, but I really did not know how much time passed when I heard another rustle, this time louder and more urgent. Annoyed, I waited, now wide awake. Another rustle. Almost frantic this time. And now Frida awoke, startled and confused. I sat up, alert now for danger, pushing her behind me and against the wall. It was too dark to see anything, but my senses were on high alert.

From outside, I heard what sounded like a snicker. My brain did not register; I had gone from total contentment and being sound asleep to being on alert for danger. *Why would there be a snicker?* I wondered. Then I heard it again, this time there were two, followed by an outburst of laughter.

"You two had better get out of here before I catch you!" I bellowed. A loud thrashing noise followed as two bodies raced through the dark woods and underbrush back toward the camp, laughing hysterically all the way.

I lay back down, grinning, and pulled Frida close once more. "The twins?" she asked skeptically. "The twins," I replied.

"Are you tired?" she asked, an invitation in her voice.

"Not in the least," I answered, rolling toward her.

---

## Winter, 117 BC

Frida suddenly turned a sickly shade, put a hand to her mouth, and ran outside. I followed her, intending to help however I could. She waved me away with a hand behind her back, holding her braid to the side with the other hand while retching into the bushes. I was concerned for her as she had been fatigued and showing signs of illness for several days, and I decided it was time to do something about it.

When Frida returned, I sat with her, wordless. I was not sure how to approach the subject, when once again she put into words what I was thinking.

"I'm going to talk to your mother today," she began.

"Good, I'll come with you," I said, relieved she brought it up before I did.

"No, you won't," she snapped, unusually short with me. I was taken aback by her abrupt tone, and it took me a moment to compose myself. Before I could reply, she continued.

"I'm sorry," she said, looking down and fidgeting with the cloth she used to wipe her mouth. "This will be a conversation for women." The concern was clear on her face.

"I don't know what is happening, but I've not been feeling myself lately. I've been so tired, and the smell of food makes me ill. I never eat much anyway, but now I don't feel like eating at all. I'm going to see if your mother can give me something to settle my stomach. Why don't you spend the day with your father?"

I had not seen my father for a while and decided that was a good idea. We spent the pleasant fall day fishing and talking, but to my frustration, my father just smiled and nodded his head when I explained Frida's condition. He assured me that everything was going to be fine, and that mother could help but offered no further comment. We brought home enough trout for a fine dinner for the entire family, though I felt bad that Frida could not enjoy one of her favorite meals.

We found her smiling and laughing with my mother which left me more puzzled than ever.

"Come sit by me," Frida invited. "I've something to tell you." She was obviously feeling better and offered me the most charming smile. I sat by her, looking at my mother and father, who were both grinning broadly. I realized I was the last one to be let in on a very big secret.

Frida faced me, grasping both of my hands. Her deep brown eyes locked on mine, and she smiled happily. "You're going to be a father. We're going to have a child."

I blinked slowly. Despite the smiles, this was not the news I was expecting. I was genuinely worried about Frida. I glanced at my father, then mother, then back to Frida, not comprehending.

"Borr?" she asked. "Did you hear me? We're going to have a baby," she said, laughing. They were all laughing at my reaction.

With the sudden realization of what she had said, I jumped to my feet and whooped. I embraced her and swung her around in a circle. "I'm going to be a father!" I exclaimed.

My father and mother both stepped forward to embrace us. "I'm going to be a father!" I shouted at them.

---

X

On the day our son was born, the thunder god welcomed him with a storm that shook the heavens. Bolts of blinding light cleaved the sky, accompanied by deafening rolls of thunder.

He came earlier than expected. I was away on a raid against the hostile mountain tribes that still resented our presence, and the fury of the storm delayed my return.

The morning after the storm, I led a large band of mounted warriors from a billowing mist as we cantered homeward. We were heavily armed, bare chested, and wore a mixture of woven trousers and animal skin leggings. Most wore their blonde hair gathered into a horse's tail on the top of their heads and had thick beards. I wore my hair long and unbound and I was still working on a beard that was showing promise but was still an embarrassment, and the cause of good-natured ribbing from my friends. We rode easily, the severed heads of our enemies tied together by their long hair and slung over our horses' withers.

We travelled throughout the day, splashing across the Savus just west of the village as darkness fell. With our destination now in sight, we all sat straighter, shaking off our weariness. As we drew nearer, the night watch announced our arrival.

Our new fortress sat on a hill in an oxbow of the Savus River. A defensive ditch filled with water diverted from the river completed the natural moat that surrounded the earthen berm, which was topped by a wooden palisade. A bridge led across the moat and through the single gate.

Rows of rectangular houses lined the western wall of the settlement, each house made of timber-framed turf walls with a high-pitched thatch roof whose eaves nearly touched the ground on all sides. Inside the western end of each house was a living area with a raised hearth and clay floor. The eastern end was used to keep livestock during the winter months.

Dispersed among the larger family dwellings were several smaller buildings used to store food, tools, and weapons. The road leading from the gate passed the edge of the buildings and ended in the village square.

Haimaz was the largest of the new villages of the Cimbri, whose clans were spread out across the southern plains of Pannonia in smaller villages and farmsteads. It was a reasonable replica of Borremose, and it reminded all of us of home.

As the fortress came into sight, I urged my horse to a gallop for the short distance remaining. Crossing the bridge alone, I entered the village. It was time for the evening meal and smoke from the cooking fires lingered in the damp air. The sentries hailed me, and a man ran up to take my horse. I dismounted and handed him the reins. At nineteen years old, I stood half a head above our tallest warriors, and I was gaining reputation. I had grown into a heavily muscled frame, and my body bore the permanent scars of battles with man and animal alike. A fresh cut on the left side of my face missed my eye only slightly.

I wore a fur shoulder cape, and my seax and pouch made of fox skin hung from a thick leather belt with a bronze buckle.

Striding purposefully toward my house, my concern was evident. When I left for the raid several days ago, Frida had been near her time. Entering the doorway, I relaxed somewhat when I heard the excited babble of the women as they fussed over a newborn babe. They parted at the sound of my entrance. My beloved lay on a bed of straw, holding the newest member of the tribe. It had been a difficult birth, and she wore a weak smile on her face.

"Welcome home," she said simply to me.

I stepped forward and gently took him from her, so carefully, afraid that I might hurt him. I unwrapped his swaddling to better see him and was pleased at his healthy color and sturdy body as he stretched and squirmed in my hands.

"His name is Lingulf, and he will be a strong warrior, like his father and grandfathers," Frida said, smiling fondly at us both.

I was staring down at him proudly and was startled by a sudden stream of urine shooting past my ear. The women gasped as one and then tittered at my expression.

My mother touched my arm and reached for my son.

"Your wife and child will be fine, Freya has looked after them well," she said, "but she needs rest, and he needs to eat." Turning her back, she dismissed me and placed the babe at his mother's breast. When I started to reply, I saw that her head had slumped, and her eyes were closed. For a moment I thought the worst, and then saw her chest rise as she breathed. I stood for a moment longer. Then, with my chest swelling with pride, I turned and left the house.

As I returned outside, the other members of the raiding party were dismounting and upon seeing the relief on my face, began heartily congratulating me. Freki and Skalla excitedly pounded my back, and Hrolf hugged me tightly, grinning from ear to ear. The raid had gone well, and a new member of the clan was here to greet us on our return. We had finally pleased the gods. Or so we thought.

---

My father and I had just returned from our hunt when we heard my mother calling Hilgi for supper. We joined her, assuming that my sister was off playing with her friends, but now mother was getting worried.

"I haven't seen her since breakfast," she said, the concern apparent in her voice. "I asked her to bring me a bucket of water before she left to play. She didn't return, and I assumed she forgot, like she does when she has other things on her mind."

We looked everywhere in and near the longhouse with no luck. I called to Hrolf and sent him to rouse the rest of the village to look for her. My mother was becoming frantic.

"Don't worry," I said. "We'll find her."

I went to my house to tell Frida what was amiss; the house was empty, and the fire was cold. I frowned, assuming she was with Hedda or one of her other friends, but a sliver of fear formed at the back of my mind.

A search inside the village turned up nothing, but Rurik, one of our most experienced hunters, ran up panting for breath.

"I found a trail outside the gate," the small, wiry man reported. "A child's tracks wandered away from the stream. A woman's prints were on top of the child's as if she were running after, and as they entered the tree line, there were signs of a scuffle. It appears three men were watching the village from a short distance away and Hilgi may have wandered right into their arms. They took the woman as well."

My blood ran cold.

"Frida!" I exclaimed. "She has not been at our house for hours. Mother! Have you seen Frida today? Lingulf?" I said, my voice trailing off.

"No," my mother managed in a strangled voice. "Not since last evening."

"The child's tracks disappear, and the men headed off into the woods with the woman. One of them must have carried the girl. I found this," Rurik said as he handed my mother something. It was the gourd rattle I had made for Lingulf.

"Ohh!" she moaned, realizing that Hilgi, Frida and Lingulf had been taken. She was pale and her knees were weak. My heart sank. My mind was spinning.

Hedda came running up and embraced my mother as my father called for an armed search party. We followed Rurik closely as he traced the steps of the kidnappers. They had nearly a full day's head start, and we followed as quickly as we could. Skoll material-ized at my side soon after we left. Just as it was growing dark, we found where they had joined with a larger group. My father was not only worried about our family, but angry with himself. There had been an enemy scouting our village, and we did not know they were there.

---

My father sent Lothar back for more men and enough supplies for three days, and we made a cold camp for the night where the kidnappers linked up.

"We can't stop!" I protested. "We have to find them!"

"We can't follow the tracks in the dark Borr, we will lose the trail," he replied.

"But father...!" I cried in anguish. "If you won't follow them, I will. Skoll can follow their trail."

"And then what?" his face darkened with anger. "There are at least seven men. What will you do, fight seven men by yourself? No. If you follow in the dark, you will foul the trail for Rorik, and you will likely stumble upon their sentries and get killed. We will begin again at first light when we are certain to follow the trail. We've gained ground on them, and we will find them tomorrow."

I stood the first watch, unable to sleep, and stared up at the sky, fearful for what Frida and the children must be going through. A bright moon winked down as clouds skittered across its face, dark-ening the world from time to time.

With his anger faded, my father relieved me past midnight, and told me to lie down and get some rest. "You will need to be ready in the morning. It will be a long day and you'll need your strength. Try to get some sleep, or at least close your eyes and rest the best you can. We will find them, son," he assured me, gripping my shoulder.

I looked at him through tear-filled eyes and nodded. What was there to say?

At first light, we hurried on. The trail led into the mountains, back toward the tribe we had recently raided, and knowing this, we quickened our pace. Lothar caught up to us and in the afternoon of the third day we sighted the kidnappers.

---

As we came out of a low ravine, they ambushed us. Two of our men went down with mortal wounds. The rest of us charged right into the ambushers. I went mad, killing two within seconds, and my companions pursued the survivors into the trees.

We searched frantically, calling for Frida and Hilgi, fearing the worst. I was searching the ground for clues and looked up to see Frida appear from the undergrowth, walking beside Skoll. Hilgi was grasping the thick fur at the back of Skoll's neck, tears flowing freely.

Overcome with relief, I ran to Frida. Lingulf was sleeping in his sling and protested loudly when I embraced his mother. She seemed to stiffen at my touch, but in the excitement of the moment, I thought nothing of it.

"Are you...did they hurt you?" I asked her.

She looked down, shaking her head. "No, we were moving quickly," she said. "There was no time. Only scratches and bruises."

Hilgi was sobbing and hugged my legs. I sensed something was wrong, but the relief at finding them overcame my thoughts and I assumed it was the fear and trauma. "I got scared when the fighting started," she said in her little girl voice. "I saw them kill two of our people and I thought they were going to win. Auntie Frida hit the man that was watching us with a rock, and we ran away. We hid in a thicket and Skoll came and found us."

My father ran up and swung Hilgi into his arms, hugging her tightly, relieved to find her safe. After our initial embrace, Frida said nothing to me on the way home and seemed to avoid my gaze. We returned home to my mother, who sobbed so heavily she could not speak. Other than being scared and hungry, the children were fine. But Frida could not meet their eyes as she hugged herself tightly. My mother and Hedda shared a knowing glance as they turned to follow her into the longhouse.

That night, my family gave thanks to Wodan and to Freya for watching over our family and returning them home safely.

Skoll stayed by Hilgi's side for several days before he wandered off into the forest again, giving her comfort that he was watching and protecting her.

# Chapter Fourteen

## Late Summer 116 BC

My father lay in his bed, wavering between shivering and sweating as a fever ravaged his body. Everyone knew what was approaching, though his tortured mind was elsewhere. His body was covered with painful pustules and his lips and fingertips were a sickly shade of grayish blue.

He struggled for breath, the rattling in his lungs becoming worse with each passing day. He coughed again, a horrible hack that spasmed his entire body and made me cringe in sympathetic pain for him. The coughing fit went on until it seemed to loosen what was choking him and he turned his head to spit out gobs of the infection, too weak to rise from the bed. Then he took a deep breath, only to repeat the process again.

The whole thing reminded me of my childhood illness, and it scared me witless. I now knew the fear that my mother and father must have felt when I was a child, as they watched helplessly, thinking each breath would be the last.

He muttered in his sleep, his mind trying to provide comfort where his body offered only pain and suffering. He called out lovingly to my mother, then spoke to my grandfather as if he stood nearby.

He had been a large man, tall, covered in powerful muscles. Now, he had been reduced to a sickly weakling struggling for breath in just a few weeks' time. His eyes were sunken and dark, and his skin was pale. He soiled himself and vomited until he had nothing left in his body. It was a horrible death for a warrior and leader, and I pitied him, though that would have been the last thing he wanted.

I was watching him from across the room when he spoke.

"Borr," he said, his voice raspy and dry.

I crossed to him and sat on the bed, offering him a cup of water.

"Here Father, I'm here," I whispered.

I held his head up as he sipped from the cup, and during the coughing fit that followed.

"Borr." Almost a whisper this time. "My time is near. You must prepare yourself to lead our people. They will need a steady hand in the future, or they will be lost."

I fought back tears and struggled to keep my voice from trembling when I replied.

"I'm not ready."

"You've grown into a man, wise beyond your years," he managed to say before his body spasmed with another coughing fit. He leaned over the bed and spit into the bucket.

He took a few wheezing gasps, and when he regained his breath, continued.

"Borr, the people respect you. You have proven yourself as a warrior, and you are a thinker. Remember what I have taught you, and don't be afraid. Surround yourself with reliable men and continue to prepare yourself. Your time will come. Grimur has been my rock. He will help you as well."

He succumbed to another coughing fit, then, totally exhausted, fell into a restless sleep.

Across the room Hilgi lay on her own bed, sweating through the first days of her fever. I cared for them both, as there was no one else to do it. My mother had succumbed to the illness just days before.

Father never regained consciousness, and that night the coughing stopped abruptly. I feared to look at him, for I knew what had happened, but forced myself to walk to his bed. In the feeble light from a dying fire, I covered his face. I did not wish to remember him as he was now, but as he was when he led the Cimbri from our destroyed homeland and provided the leadership we all needed to endure the journey.

---

My father's companions helped me construct his funeral pyre. There was little talking as we gathered the logs and stacked them waist high. I stuffed the interior of the stack with smaller kindling, bark, and chunks of wood soaked in oil.

When the pyre was ready, we placed his body atop the logs. We dressed him in his finest clothing, as befitted the chieftain of our people. His hand gripped the hilt of his sword, and his shield and spear lay on either side. He lay upon his cloak. A mail coat, taken from a Roman soldier at the battle of Siscia, draped loosely over his thin frame.

I sent out word to the surrounding villages and a few people had come, but the sickness kept most away. Still, there was a respectable amount of people present for his funeral.

Gudrun also died, and the new high priest, Eldrik, conducted the rites that would assure my father's ascension to Valhol. After the religious rites, Eldrik spoke of his leadership and wisdom, and how he led us during the aftermath of the great flood, along our journey to Pannonia, and through the challenges ever since. When he was finished, I touched the torch to the kindling. The flames grew quickly, the seasoned wood catching fire and burning hot. Long after the mourners departed, I remained. I stood until the raging flames had subsided, staring into the glowing embers.

My father was such a powerful presence in my life. How could I go on without him to guide me?

My mother and father, Nilda; all were gone. I felt lost.

---

The disease had touched me as well, but it was a light touch. I only felt ill for a few days and never suffered from a fever. A few of the painful blisters developed on my face and arms, but nowhere else. And now they were gone, leaving only scars in their wake. Those who recovered from it did not get it again.

Frida was still nursing our son and somehow both were spared the sickness.

Hrolf recovered, as did Freki; his twin, Skalla, had died.

Hilgi recovered but lost her vision and completely retreated into her own mind, and I took her into our home. She allowed herself to be led about and she responded enough to allow Frida to help her eat and care for herself, but little more.

She spent her days sitting alone, humming to herself, and rocking back and forth. After some time, she began having dreams. At first, they were normal dreams about everyday things, causing her an unrestful night at worst. Usually, she would not remember what they were. Eventually, she began remembering them. Soon, nearly every night, she was reliving the memories of our lives since the flood. She kicked or lashed out suddenly or whimpered in her sleep. She even woke up screaming about the destruction wrought by the flood, Nilda's death, my near drowning, being attacked by the Boii, mother and father's deaths from the plague, and the many things that had caused fear and uncertainty ever since.

She was afraid to go to sleep and would sit by the fire for hours, staring into the darkness that was now her world, rocking and humming, while everyone around her slept. Frida and I tried to help her, but we fell short. Remembering how Gudrun had helped me understand my dream, I sought Eldrik. When he could not help her, he suggested the priestesses might.

Skyld, the high priestess, convinced me that Hilgi would be better served by staying with her. She said that Hilgi was special, that she deserved a place of honor among the priestesses. She would learn their ways, and they would care for her better than we could.

I hesitated. I just wanted them to help her, not take her from us. The priestesses were revered and respected, but they were also feared. They tended to be old crones, workers of magic that no one else understood. Not someone who would be chosen to raise a child. But Hilgi took to Skyld immediately, and though Frida had provided her a home and helped her cope with her blindness, she did not feel like she belonged with us any longer. We were at a loss as to how to help her get better.

Skyld assured me that Hilgi would be cared for and that they would train her in their secrets. Through their guidance, she would become an honored member of the tribe.

---

Grimur was weak, but recovering, and while Hedda was attending him, she fell ill. She suffered from a terrible fever, which suddenly disappeared and stayed gone for a few days. We thought she was getting better, but then the fever returned, and she died in great misery. Their two-year-old son died a few weeks later.

It was as if something broke inside my uncle with the loss of his wife and child. Grimur was no longer the steady and reliable uncle that I had known. The easy smile and quick wit had disappeared, and he was always angry.

He hardly ate and he drank himself into a stupor every day. Consuming great quantities of ale, mead, or wine; whatever was at hand. He tried in vain to escape his misery, never forgetting his pain until he passed out, only to repeat the process the next day.

One morning, Frida and I were walking about the village, visiting those who were still sick, when Grimur approached us, his upper lip curled into a sneer. I thought he would pass me yet again without saying a word, as he had not talked to me in weeks. But he deliberately stepped close when we passed and shoved his shoulder into me, knocking me off balance and into Frida, causing her to stumble.

"Get out of my way, boy," he growled.

His shirt was stained with old vomit and his hair had bits of grass in it, left from wherever he slept last night.

I had finally had enough of the way he was acting and confronted him.

"What is it, Grimur? What have I done to make you so angry?"

"What have you done?" he asked. "What have you done?!" he almost screamed this time.

"You live! Your wife lives! Your child lives! Isn't that enough?"

I was astonished. I knew he was grieving over their deaths, but I had no idea he felt so about me. I stood rooted to the ground, speechless, as he stalked angrily away.

After that I kept my distance, hoping that time would heal his heart. But days later, without a word, he rode out the gate and did not return.

---

The sickness finally passed. A full half of our people fell ill and half of those died. We slowly regained our strength and mourned our losses. Leadership of the Wolf Clan passed to me upon my father's death.

The crops had suffered without the people to tend them, and the storehouses were low on food. We were facing another hungry winter. Without my father to lead them, the people were returning to the dejected state that they were in after the great flood.

Eldrik spoke up. "It is another sign that we have angered the gods. They sent this affliction upon us, and if we stay here, they will try again until they kill us all. It is a sign that we must abandon this land and continue our quest."

Our relations with the Scordisci had soured as well. They were not happy that the Teutones had entered their lands and settled in without so much as a request. They felt we were complicit in this, knowing that we helped them on their arrival. The Scordisci now thought of us as an advance party for an invasion of their territory and saw us as an enemy and a threat to their security.

The plague was a last sign to the Scordisci that their gods did not want us here and their priests agitated for our removal. Like our own priests, they blamed the sickness on our disfavor with our gods and theirs. They warned their people that further contact with us could bring the anger of their gods upon them, and they advised Aodhan that we could not be allowed to stay.

He sent several messengers, telling us we were no longer welcome, but our people were still too weak and unable to just pick up and move. Then came the raids on local homesteads. They began as cattle raids and farmstead burnings but gradually became worse. Soon, our people were being assaulted and killed.

After my father's death, the people looked to Claudicus for leadership, for he was our most senior leader. But he was not up to leading the entire tribe. He remained focused on his own clan, and we could never organize an effective defense against the Scordisci raids.

Lugius, Caesorix, and the other hunnos, who were older and more experienced than me, followed Claudicus's lead and only concerned themselves with their own clans. Their warriors chafed with the lack of an organized response and called for action.

I became disgusted with our inaction to the Scordisci aggression, and I led several mounted patrols that ambushed the raiders

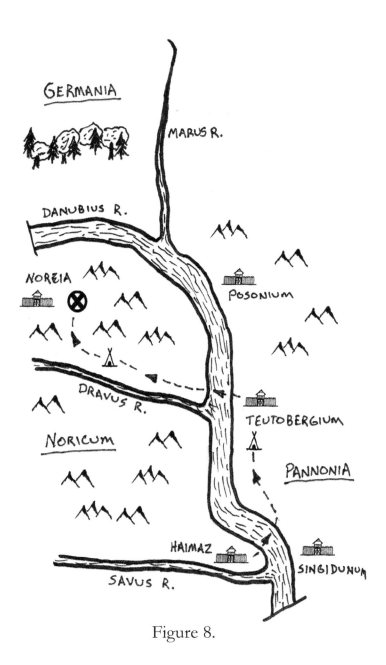

Figure 8.

and avenged the unprovoked attacks. Warriors from all the clans flocked to me when they saw we were finally responding to the Scordisci. I had just turned twenty years old, and I was now a clan leader and a war chief of the Cimbri. In the absence of an elected chieftain, many warriors of the other clans looked to me for leadership, and I was comfortable in the role.

I established a network of scouts to warn us of impending attacks as well as mounted patrols to respond quickly. We became very good at thwarting their attacks and could defend against most of them, avenging the ones we were unable to stop. I did not wish to provoke an all-out war; we were not strong enough for that yet. So, we stayed away from their strongholds, and we did not attack their people, but claimed the areas where we lived as our own and protected them as best we could.

These defensive actions allowed us time to regain our strength and to develop a plan for the future. Our relationship with the Scordisci was fractured beyond repair. We could not go on like this forever, so we prepared to leave our homes once again.

Late in the fall, we packed our belongings and hitched the oxen to the carts. We retraced our steps northward along the Danubius to Teutobergium and renewed our close friendship with the Teutones. We stayed through the winter, still in Scordisci territory. In the spring, our former allies continued to harass us. We resumed our resistance, but we were growing tired of the endless raids. One day we learned of a stronger effort to remove us permanently from Pannonia and we held a council. As usual, the clan leaders were indecisive and could not agree on what was to be done. I walked away in disgust and called my warriors to me. I was determined to organize a defense, and I sent scouts out to gather more information.

The Scordisci were moving northward in large numbers. They wanted both tribes out of their lands and were willing to go to war to achieve it. Teutobod and I planned a defense along their approach, and our warriors moved quickly to take up their positions.

The other clan leaders followed along without acknowledging any single leader.

As the enemy army approached, they saw a wall of brightly painted shields silently awaiting them. They could see that they outnumbered the defending phalanx of warriors, and they immediately attacked, throwing themselves against our shields. They soon enveloped our warriors and were pressing in on the flanks; they knew it was only a matter of time before they were victorious.

When I was sure the Scordisci had fully committed to their attack, I gave the pre-arranged signal and the carnyx blew. When the sound of our battle horns replied from all around them, the Scordisci looked about, confused, as they could not see any reason for the sound.

The land we had chosen to meet them on was deceptively flat but was in fact cleft with deep ravines and dry waterways. This allowed the rest of our warriors to remain hidden until I gave the signal to join the battle.

Thousands of Cimbri and Teutones warriors appeared to rise out of the ground and attacked the exposed flanks and rear of the Scordisci army.

The sight of thousands more warriors appearing out of thin air panicked the Scordisci, and the battle turned into a slaughter. When it was clear we were victorious, I called for a halt to the fighting and spoke to the remaining Scordisci.

"We do not wish to fight our brothers. We have shared battlefields with you against the Romans and we have feasted together in your halls. We only wish to be left in peace. Cast down your weapons and go home. Tell your king that we will leave your lands, but it will not be yet this year. Tell him that we will leave next summer, when we are as prepared as we can be. But if he continues to attack us, we will bring the battle to his people and we will not stop until the Scordisci exist no more."

There were no more raids, and we were able to adequately prepare for winter.

---

In the spring, Vallus returned. He had left to continue his wandering shortly after we returned from Macedonia four years ago. Not ones to settle down permanently, Tala and Anik left with him to seek out new adventures. Vallus had returned one time since then and stayed the winter two years ago but left again before my son was born and the plague killed so many.

He was saddened to hear of my parent's death from the sickness and overjoyed to learn of the birth of my son, now two years old and full of energy. Vallus flirted unabashedly with Frida as he had my mother, and he doted over Lingulf.

Vallus brought me the news of the world like my father before me. As he spoke, I remembered my father's words, that it was important to gather as much information as possible, whenever, and however one could.

"Ah, my dear, you are a magnificent cook," he complimented Frida as he sopped up the last of the grease from the roasted beef with a large slab of warm bread slathered in butter. She blushed and smiled at the compliment.

After dinner he pulled out the ancient vellum map that he always carried. There were smudges and corrections where the map had changed over the years. He wiped his hands carefully on a rough cloth to ensure he got the grease off, so he did not transfer it to the precious map. He took a large drink of ale from his cup and began.

"We are here," he said, pointing to the map, and belching. "This is Rome. Between us, in the north of Italy, is a land claimed by the Carni, a Celtic mountain tribe that descended from their mountain strongholds more than a century ago. Between the Carni and the Danubius is the land claimed by the Taurisci. These tribes, along with several others, make up the kingdom of Noricum. Its capital city is Noreia, here.

"Last year, the Roman consul Marcus Aemilius Scaurus defeated the Carni and their Taurisci allies in one great battle, near Aquileia, here, on the Veneti plains. After this defeat, the Carni and Taurisci were tamed and became allies of Rome. The kingdom of Noricum, specifically the Taurisci, control several large salt and iron mines, as well as gold and silver mines. The high-quality iron ore is smelted into Noric steel for the weapons and armor of the Roman army, in trade for wine, grain and other goods. The Roman settlement of Aquileia receives the gold and silver and mints it into coins."

We were almost ready to follow Eldrik's advice to leave, but before we departed Pannonia, Vallus and I had several more weeks to discuss our situation.

To prepare for our departure, we sent a delegation up the Dravus River into Noricum. They were intercepted by a large group of Taurisci warriors who escorted them back to the Danubius. There would be no welcome, and if we entered the kingdom of Noricum uninvited, there would be war between us.

Claudicus called for an immediate council of the clans and allied tribes, and it was unanimous that we move into Noricum, regardless of their threat. We were being pushed out by the Scordisci and our people were in no mood to be refused by the Taurisci.

Teutobod informed us that his people would remain at Teutobergium. The Scordisci's attention had turned toward the south where Rome was encroaching on their territory, and they had ignored us since our last conflict. The Teutones were tired and wished only to be left alone to build a new life in this land. They had no desire to move again into hostile territory.

We decided that when the Danubius receded sufficiently we would cross it to follow the Dravus north-westward into Noricum. We had been through a great deal since the flood and now we felt betrayed by the Scordisci. Many felt that the time for asking for things was over. The combined strength of the Cimbri, and those who had joined us on our journey, was greater than any of the local tribes. There were many voices calling for us to simply take what we wanted and move on.

---

## Summer 114 BC

In the summer of the sixth year since the great flood, we bid farewell to our friends, the Teutones, and the Cimbri once again picked up our entire population and continued our journey. Since the council meeting, we had spent considerable energy in building hundreds of boats and ferries to get the many thousands of carts, people, and animals across the large river.

We sent fifteen thousand warriors across the Danubius to establish a secure crossing for the rest of the allied tribes. The remaining ten thousand stayed behind to guard the rear against further attacks from the Scordisci.

There were over seventy thousand women, children, and others along with more than a million head of various livestock.

The Cimbri accounted for three quarters of those numbers, along with the numerous smaller tribes, clans, families, and individuals that had joined us over the past five years. Thousands more Cimbri had followed and rejoined us in the years since we left home, as well as Ambrones and Boii, Quadi and Marcomanni. There were Langobards and Cherusci, Semnones and Saxon, and many others. Some remained independent, while others placed themselves under our tribal leaders and melded into the greater tribes.

I sat alone on my horse on a bluff above the river and watched the massive gathering waiting to cross. The far side was crawling with those who had already reached the shore, and the ferries were steadily traveling back and forth across the river.

I remembered the day I stood beside my father when we left Borremose. It seemed like a lifetime ago, and here I was again, this time without his guidance or my mother's strength. Now I had a family of my own to provide for and protect, as well as several thousand members of my clan. I descended the hill and rejoined the mass of humanity, finding my wife and son with some difficulty amongst the many thousands of carts. I was not surprised to find Vallus nearby to lend a helping hand if needed.

The crossing took days but was not challenged. Just as a drenching rain began, the last of our people made it across.

We moved up the Dravus and onto high ground. The rain continued for several days until the water crested, then returned to its normal level for the middle of summer.

We gave the ground a few days to dry out, and then we continued our journey.

---

On a hill high above and west of the Danubius River, the Taurisci chief, Epatus, silently watched as the massive horde spilled across the river into his lands. He had known for some time this would happen, and he knew there was little he could do to stop it. The Taurisci were dwarfed by the numbers that were crossing below.

Across the river, he could see a lone rider on a hill watching the crossing. He wondered if this was the leader of this invasion.

Turning to his retainers, he ordered them to spread out and instruct any of his people in the path of this foreign invader to retreat to the mountains for safety. As rain clouds ominously gathered on the horizon, he turned his horse and silently descended to the Dravus and followed it back to the city of Noreia. His guards followed at a respectful distance, careful not to disturb their chieftain's mood.

---

The allied tribes continued westward for a few weeks along the

Dravus River as we entered the eastern end of the Alpes Mountains. Almost immediately after we crossed the Danubius, the land began to climb toward vibrant green foothills with fertile mountain meadows and rocky limestone outcroppings. We often found signs of livestock herds and abandoned villages, but seldom ran across the inhabitants of this beautiful country. As we moved further on, jagged, snow-covered peaks rose above the crest of the foothills. Sparkling streams came down from the heights of every side valley and spilled into the Dravus. We came upon a lush alpine valley with rich green meadows that were large enough to accommodate the huge caravan. Without any kind of direction or decision, the people spread out and claimed their homesteads or gathered to create a makeshift village.

I claimed the area around a small stream for the central village of the Wolf Clan. The other clans of the Cimbri were spread in clusters about the valley and the allies took up their own areas as they pleased. We turned the livestock loose into the valley and the people immediately went to work felling trees from the foothills to build their winter homes as they had done so many times before.

The mood had changed again among our people and as we settled into the area we had claimed as our home, I and the other clan leaders led bands of warriors to patrol the area and forage for anything we could use. We found planted fields of grain that were nearly ready for harvest and brought our people to occupy the buildings near them, to guard the fields and harvest them when they were ready. The occasional abandoned village or farmstead offered storage pits or buildings that still held food or tools. We took what we found back to our settlement, and we rounded up strays from the vanished herds. As the patrols roamed farther and farther, they came across more villages, some of which were still occupied.

We raided the Taurisci as the Scordisci had raided us and took whatever we wanted as we ranged the countryside, burning and looting. With our unchallenged raids, we became bolder and more aggressive. Our people were turning from victims and survivors into pillagers and raiders, and though I was troubled at how fast we had turned, it was difficult to resist the pull of the success we were having. We were finally the ones who were to be feared. For the first time in years, we would have enough food to comfortably last the winter.

However, this change came with uncertainty. The Taurisci had done nothing to us, and in moments of quiet, I suffered from self-doubt, wondering if I were leading my clan down a path that my father would not be proud of. In any case, I justified to myself, as the leader of one clan of people among these many thousands, I did not have the power to guide the behavior of all. I dismissed these doubts and was satisfied that my people were prospering, regardless of the source of that prosperity.

# Chapter Fifteen

## Aquileia

## August 114 BC

Marcus Aemilius Scaurus, princeps senatus, and victor over the Carni and Taurisci alliance less than a year ago, was in Aquileia. He was inspecting the mint that produced the gold coins from the ore that was mined in Noricum.

He was enjoying a sumptuous meal at the home of a wealthy Roman investor in the Noric iron mines, when he received an unexpected request for an audience with a messenger from the Taurisci chief, Epatus.

The messenger was brought before the princeps senatus and presented him with a letter with Scaurus' name scrawled on the outside.

With a look of curiosity, Marcus Aemilius Scaurus broke the seal and read. The letter was written in Latin in a legible but unpracticed hand.

*Most honored Marcus Aemilius Scaurus. It is with great hope that I address this letter to you to ask for the assistance of Rome. I have chosen to communicate with you directly as you showed yourself to be a generous and honorable victor over the Taurisci and have treated us with respect since the battle that decided our fate.*

*A month ago, a great horde of barbarians crossed the Danubius River at our eastern border and followed the Dravus River into our central highlands where they have established a colony. They call themselves the Cimbri. Their numbers are bolstered by several smaller tribes and lesser groups from lands far removed from ours. These invaders have murdered many of my people and stolen their homes and livelihoods, leaving many in a perilous situation as winter approaches.*

*I have pulled as many of my people back to our strongholds as possible, but we are not able to give them all safety. Many have found refuge in the high mountains and will be trapped there to die when the snows arrive. The warriors that I have sent out to defend our lands have been badly outnumbered by this vast alliance of tribes, and I am unable to protect my people.*

*They have already found one of the gold mines and intercepted a large wagon caravan of gold ore headed to the smelters at Noreia. There are several iron mines and another gold mine in the area, and it is only a matter of time before their scouts find them.*

*They have taken many of our eastern villages and established a large colony along the Dravus. It appears they intend to stay there. They have refused all attempts at communication and continue to pillage our countryside.*

*My people do not have the strength to repel these invaders who number in the hundreds of thousands!*

*I implore you to please send us help. I anxiously await your reply.*

It was signed Epatus, chief of the Taurisci, friend and ally of the Roman people.

---

Scaurus looked up from the message and scowled at the messenger. The man blanched under his gaze.

"How did you know to find me here?" he demanded.

"M...my chieftain gave me orders to fly with all haste to Rome to find you and deliver this message, sir," the messenger stammered. "I had to pass through Aquileia to get to Rome and as I was travelling, I saw the troops of your escort. The talk of the town is that you are here, sir, in Aquileia, and when I found you were here, I approached the commander of your guards who brought me here. I did not know you were in the city when I left from Noreia."

Scaurus grunted his acknowledgement. There was no end to the gossip, he knew.

"Return to your chieftain," he said. "I will take your letter before the senate. This will take some time. Do not expect an answer for several months." He dismissed the messenger with a wave of his hand.

After the man left, his host spoke. "Marcus, you must do something. This is very bad."

"I know, Paulus," Scaurus replied. His mind was already considering the consequences of this invasion.

"I must return to Rome immediately. I will leave in the morning. I'll send a messenger ahead with a letter to notify the senate and to call an emergency meeting. Thank you for your hospitality, but I must take my leave and prepare," he said, rising from his lectus.

---

Two weeks later, Marcus Aemilius Scaurus stood before the senate.

"Conscript fathers, honored senators and magistrates of Rome. I stand before you today to speak of a significant threat to a friend and ally of the Roman people. However, this is not just a threat to one of our allies. This threat includes the possibility of cutting off our supply of Noric steel, which, as I am sure you all know, is used to produce our superior weapons and armor. They have already seized one gold mine and a large shipment of gold destined for our mint in Aquileia.

"I am doubtful that the numbers of the barbarian horde are as astronomical as the letter relates, nevertheless, it is a genuine threat. As you know, consuls Gaius Porcius Cato and Manius Acilius Balbus are otherwise occupied in Thrace and Macedonia. There are no current armies in Italy able to respond with military force.

"As these barbarians have not threatened Rome directly, I propose that a delegation be sent to the German tribes that have entered Noricum to make them aware of the consequences of their attack on an ally of Rome.

"As the victorious general over the Carni and Taurisci, I treated them with honor and allowed them to retain their pride. They became a friend and ally of the Roman people and made further trade concessions in return for our protection. They trust me and have asked for my help. As princeps senatus, I volunteer to lead that delegation."

It did not take long for the senate to grant Scaurus the authority as princeps senatus to represent Rome as the head of a delegation of senior senators to intervene on behalf of the Taurisci. Many of the senators had financial interests in Noricum and were concerned over any threat to those interests. Several of those volunteered to join the delegation. Others had no concern over events in a far-flung, backwards kingdom of Celts who most considered no better than the barbarian Germans who invaded them. Many saw the delegation as a way to dismiss the problem and get back to more important dealings, and if Scaurus was willing to waste his time negotiating with barbarians, they were fine with that.

# Chapter Sixteen

## Noricum

### Late September 114 BC

Skyld, the high priestess, came to me one evening and bade me to follow her. She took me to the grove that the priests and priestesses claimed when we arrived in Noricum. A small hut stood off to the side of a cleared area and I ducked my head as we went in through the low door. Hilgi sat on a mat on the ground before a small fire, rocking back and forth and humming. She wore a dirty white shift, and I saw that her hair was disheveled. There was dirt, or soot, smeared on her cheeks, and streaks where tears had fallen earlier. Her sightless eyes stared off into the smoky darkness of the hut.

I sat on a mat across the fire from her, and Skyld sat between us. Hilgi abruptly stopped rocking and was now jabbering incoherently. I was afraid and thought she had slipped into madness when she suddenly whispered my name.

"Borr, my brother, how are you?"

"I am... well, sister," I replied hesitantly. "Are you? Are you happy here?"

"I am content," she said. "Skyld treats me well, and I have learned much. The others look after me and I have learned to control my dreams. My mind is settled, and I am at peace."

"I'm very happy for you." I looked questioningly at Skyld who turned to Hilgi and instructed her to tell me about her dream.

"Last night," she began, "Freya appeared to me. She revealed the source of our troubles, and knowledge that will shape our people's future.

"You see brother, in the beginning of time, the sea god Njoror married Nerthus, the goddess of fertility, who bore him a daughter, Freya.

"Over the centuries, Njoror and Nerthus drew apart, and Njoror fell in love with the goddess Skadi, the beautiful giantess and goddess of winter. But Skadi could not return his love for Njoror was ugly. His hair of seaweed hung limply to his shoulders, and his face and skin were gray and disfigured from the sea and wind that he ruled. Skadi left Njoror in the sea, and married Wodan the sky god instead, and bore him many sons.

"Later, Njoror's daughter Freya also became a wife of Wodan, which infuriated the sea god further.

"Njoror swore revenge against Wodan but he knew he could not defeat his powerful enemy, so he plotted against Wodan's children, the Cimbri. When Njoror saw Wodan was not watching, he spoiled our crops and scared away the fish and sea animals, and little by little he pushed the sea ever nearer to our homes. All this was done slowly to avoid Wodan's attention, and the Cimbri suffered.

"His anger pent up for centuries, Njoror sent the great wave in a final attempt to destroy us. Wodan, learning of Njoror's plan, tried to warn us through your dream, Borr, but the warning came too late.

"Wodan was angry with Njoror for the attack and punished him severely. Undeterred, Njoror next enlisted the aid of Lokke the trickster, who also disliked Wodan and is ever agreeable to making trouble. Together the two designed a curse that would doom the Cimbri forever.

"Freya learned of this curse and revealed it to me:

*Out of the northern mists, the Cimbri appear;*

*wagons and oxen, shields and spears.*

*Cursed by Njoror, to forever roam;*

*they search for a land, to call their home.*

*If one summer they rest, in any land;*

*they shall be punished, by Njoror's hand.*

*The Red Wolf shall rise, as king he becomes;*

*and defeat the red soldiers, while the tribes fight as one.*

*The curse will be lifted, from this great host;*

*when Lupa welcomes, the people of the coast.*

Hilgi had related her dream and abruptly started rocking and humming again. I looked at Skyld who gestured toward the door with her head.

Outside, Skyld drew me aside.

"Njoror has cursed our people, Borr. Condemned us to wander forever. Promised that if we tarry more than a winter in one place, we shall be punished. He demonstrated his power to do that when he brought the plague upon us.

"In a cruel twist, he promises us a champion, the Red Wolf, and assured us victory over the red soldiers. This can only be the Romans, whose soldiers wear red. But this assurance stands only if we continue to wander, ever seeking, but never finding our new homeland. And only while the tribes are united.

"You are the Red Wolf, Borr," she said, reaching up to touch my hair. "Your red hair – you are Hunno of the Wolf Clan. Njoror has prophesied that you will lead our warriors to victory in battle against the Romans. He has said you will be king."

I stood back and stared hard at her. What she was saying hit me like a sling-stone.

"It is our fate to wander the world, Borr, and it is your fate to lead us. You will bring us great victories, and you will lead us through great trials. But only as we suffer through our journeys.

"Yet there is hope. Njoror's curse can be lifted if we determine who this Lupa is. She is the key to finding our new homeland. We must receive her welcome to lift the curse, or we are left with forever wandering the world."

I thanked Skyld for caring for Hilgi and for sharing the dream with me. I asked her to tell no one of it for now.

---

That night I walked the riverbank alone, lost in thought. The curse and its prophecies foremost in my mind. The threat of our destruction, the promise of lifting the curse, and the revelation that I was the Red Wolf who was destined to lead our people, was troubling me.

The plague scourged us because we had stayed too long in Pannonia, and the Scordisci had turned against us. It was obvious the curse was at work. We had moved into Noricum, but if we stayed through next year, our people would once again be punished.

She said that I would lead our people to victory if I followed the prophecy. But how? I was already hunno of the Wolf Clan, and a respected war leader, but I was not the chieftain, no one had been since my father died. And I certainly was no king. How was I to lead our people away from here, I thought, when I was not the chieftain? The Cimbri had not elected another chieftain, and the clans had reverted to their individual hunnos for leadership. I was deeply troubled, and I had no answers.

---

We prepared a leather tent with one side rolled up to allow the spectacular view of the valley, and to impress the Roman delegation with our numbers. The tent wall broke the autumn winds that were becoming a nuisance, especially this high up in elevation.

We shared a laugh when the Roman's togas blew about uncontrollably in a sudden gust, exposing their pale legs. They made a futile attempt at preserving their dignity, holding the edges down as they approached the tent.

Lugius, and the other hunnos attended the meeting. I was there as well, but as the youngest hunno, I was relegated to a silent role, which suited me fine.

The meeting began with a round of introductions, assisted by an interpreter brought by the Romans. No one knew I understood the language of the Romans, and I did not make any effort to inform them.

When Epatus was introduced, I looked at him with interest. He was not a man who commanded respect through his physical appearance or his demeanor. He was short and balding, flabby, and pale. His days as a warrior were obviously long past, if in fact they ever existed. If his red-rimmed eyes, bulbous nose, and ample midsection were any indication, he spent far too much time in his fortress drinking and feasting.

He appeared nervous and deferential to the Romans. He seemed to feel the contempt with which we regarded him for never meeting us in battle and allowing his people to suffer with no actual attempt to stop us. The fact that he called for the protection of Rome without any kind of response to our presence told us all that he was a coward.

I looked upon the Romans with interest. Other than in battle, I had never seen their like up close before; clean shaven and close-cropped hair, and their snowy white togas. Their leader wore an officer's leather cuirass and greaves as did their guards, but the men who accompanied him, these senators, looked ridiculous in their flowing robes blowing about when the wind whipped. I wondered that these were the men so feared by the rest of the world.

Scaurus began by directly addressing Claudicus.

"You and your people have invaded the lands of our allies, the Taurisci. We, as delegates of Rome, demand that you return to your own lands and return what you have stolen from them."

Most in our delegation chuckled when this was interpreted. I remained plain faced, waiting to hear more.

Scaurus looked surprised. He was unaccustomed to the lack of respect he was receiving. Many were grinning at him. They even appeared to be amused.

Attempting to regain control of the meeting, Scaurus continued, "You have seized a gold mine that is the property of the Taurisci, and a gold shipment destined for Aquileia. I demand that this be returned. You will immediately abandon the area that you have seized and return across the Danubius out of Taurisci lands."

Claudicus lifted his chin toward Epatus, "Why doesn't he make demands? Why is the chief of the Taurisci silent? Did Rome cut out his tongue?"

The chief's face reddened, and he opened his mouth to speak, but was cut off by Scaurus.

"Epatus is our ally. That is enough for you to know. Now, I have presented our demands. What is your reply?"

"Why?" Claudicus said.

Scaurus blinked at the one-word answer. He was accustomed to speaking from a position of recognized authority and being listened to, and these people did not seem to understand him.

"What do you mean, why?" he asked.

"Why should we leave? Claudicus asked amiably. "We like it here. The land is beautiful. We have already built homes for the winter and obviously there is no one living here with the strength to defend it. There is much gold and iron for the taking. Why should we leave?" he asked again.

The others looked at Scaurus wolfishly, content to allow Claudicus to speak for them. I continued to watch Scaurus without expression, thinking of my sister's words.

The typically unflappable Scaurus was becoming angry. Never had he come across anyone so flippant, so arrogant.

"If you do not do as I have demanded, you will feel the power of Rome and you will know why. You will understand why having Rome as a friend is desired by all and why having Rome as an enemy is feared by all. If you do not immediately leave this land, our armies will be here by summer."

"Bah, send your armies," Claudicus replied. "We have bested them twice already, at Siscia and again at Stobi. We are not afraid of your soldiers. I think we will stay, and we will keep this land for ourselves." He nodded at Epatus, "He is weak. By summer we will have conquered all his lands and taken possession of all his mines. We will rule this land in his place and then the Romans can bargain with us for their gold and iron."

The meeting certainly did not go how Marcus Aemilius Scaurus had expected, and he was angry at the way he was treated. The senatorial delegation was irate by the way they were slighted, and Epatus was dismayed. The threat of Rome seemed to have no effect.

About a week or so after the Romans left, the first snowfall of winter blanketed our encampment much earlier than we were accustomed to. Soon, the passes were blocked, and travel was nearly impossible. The raiding slowed to a stop, and our people settled in for the winter.

In the absence of a chieftain, Claudicus reluctantly prepared to lead the usual council of the clans during the yuletide celebration. While he had boasted weeks earlier at the meeting with the Romans, he was wise enough to understand the threat they posed and was unsure what to do about it.

I sat back during most of the council, allowing the older and more experienced leaders to discuss their concerns. Eventually, the idea of electing a new chieftain was introduced.

Caesorix, hunno of the raven clan, asked to be heard.

"I believe it is time to elect a new chieftain. Haistulf served us well through the challenges we faced when we left Cimberland. His courage and strength gave the people hope after the great disaster. His skill at negotiating kept us from constant conflict on our journey and his cunning and ferocity in battle brought our people respect from our allies and victory over our enemies.

"His death was a great loss to our people, and he is sorely missed. Since his death, the clans have not elected a new leader, and that has left us fractured, indecisive and vulnerable. Though we have thus far been successful in our journey into Noricum, it is not because we were organized, or that we had an overall plan. We have allowed our warriors to run rampant, and we reaped the rewards of our sudden attack on the local populations, but I am concerned with the coming of spring. The Taurisci themselves are not to be feared, but their allies the Romans need to be recognized as a dangerous enemy to have.

"We have fought the Romans twice and won, but we all know the history of Rome and how it continues to raise armies again and again, until it eventually defeats its enemies and annexes whatever land it decides that it wants.

"The Romans warned us that if we stay in Noricum, we will become the focus of their attention. I do not shy away from conflict with the Romans, but I believe that in order to best address this challenge, we need to elect a new leader of the Cimbri, and as hunno of the raven clan, I nominate Claudicus as chieftain. As the most senior of our clan leaders, Claudicus is the most experienced and most logical choice."

There was some discussion amongst the assembly and little enthusiasm came forth, as Claudicus was not one that many looked upon as someone they wished to answer to. True enough, he was the leader of his clan, and he was a respectable warrior. Unremarkable, but effective, and better suited to carrying out orders than making them. He lacked the ingenuity for planning and strategy, and he had little support from men who had been through the challenges we had faced since leaving home. Most did not view him as someone they would want to lead the nation. It was obvious by his face that Claudicus was as surprised as any at Caesorix's words, but he was insulted by the debate. Although I suspect he had his own doubts and was aware of his own limitations.

I was deep in my own thoughts when I realized the assembly had quieted and I turned my head to see what the others were looking at. Skyld was standing at the edge of the gathering, my sister behind her, holding the arm of another priestess who was guiding her.

In our culture, women have the same right to speak at an assembly as any man. There were a few women who attended all the assemblies, and they were welcome. Some were warriors, some war leaders, and some wizened elders. Skyld was the high priestess, equaled only by the high priest in prestige. She was very thin in her dirty shift, and a thick sheepskin cloak covered her shoulders and back. She normally walked barefoot, but it was the dead of winter and she had sheepskin lined boots on her feet.

There was no sound from the assembly as she shambled out into the center of the group, using a walking stick to steady herself and began to speak to the outdoor gathering. As she did, it began snowing lightly. The fire reflected from each flake, and they sparkled in the darkness as they fell to earth.

"You are debating the election of a chieftain without my presence? Since when are the priests and priestesses left out of such a decision?" she chided.

Her voice was strong but tempered, with no hint of anger, yet many in the gathering looked down and could not meet her gaze. Since leaving Cimberland our religious leaders had taken less of a role in our existence. They were always there on the edge of our daily life, but in our minds, they were less present than before. We had been more preoccupied with finding food and fighting off enemies than attending ceremonies.

"It is my duty to tell you of a prophecy that has come forth. One that will guide our lives for many years into the future. Weeks ago, this girl had a vision brought to her by the gods," she said pointing to Hilgi, who was now seated behind her, near the central fire, rocking back and forth, and humming quietly to herself. Her blind eyes stared into the distance.

"She has revealed that Borr is the one chosen by the gods to be our next chieftain, as his father was before him. It has been prophesied that Borr shall lead the Cimbri to great victories and through challenges not yet imagined. Though he is young, he has shown wisdom and is respected as hunno of the Wolf Clan. His courage in battle is unmatched and his ability for strategy has been proven. Who among you would argue with me that Borr is the proper choice?"

Someone from the crowd called, "She is his sister. How do we know she is not simply supporting her brother? How do we know she is telling the truth?"

Skyld turned on the speaker, and though she could not see him clearly, fixed him with a stare that he shrank away from. "I have interpreted her dream. I say to you, she has received this message from the gods. Do you doubt my word?" There was no reply.

While we had been listening to Skyld, the snowflakes had gotten larger and were falling steadily now. The temperature dropped significantly, and many were shaking the snow from their heads and shoulders and rubbing their hands together for warmth.

"Hilgi, tell them what you have dreamed," Skyld commanded.

My sister stopped her rocking and recited what she had told me, only she left out the words that foretold my kingship.

The assembly listened with rapt attention. As she came to the end of her tale, a distant rumble echoed across the mountains. The people looked around fearfully, as did I. Never had we heard thunder in the dead of winter, but there was no mistaking the sound as it carried to us from afar. Skyld showed no such surprise at the sign. In fact, her mouth curled into a satisfied, toothless smile. The sound came closer and grew louder. A bright flash of lightning split the night sky and struck a tall pine standing on the slope above us, lighting it afire. We all jumped, and an outburst of nervous chatter arose when, by the light of the burning pine, a large wolf appeared at the tree line. In the flickering light from the fire, his light-colored coat reflected the flames, making him appear reddish in color. Skoll stood there silently for a moment, then raised his head and released a long, mournful howl, as if acknowledging the prophecy. Then he turned and disappeared back into the trees.

Skyld reappeared and cried out, "You have seen and heard the signs sent by Donar! Is there anyone that doubts the gods have made their choice? If there is anyone who thinks that Borr should not be named chieftain of the Cimbri, say so now!" Silence was her only answer.

"Then if you support Borr as chieftain, let me hear your voices!"

There was a roar of approval that reverberated off the hillsides and followed the sound of the thunder off into the distance; suddenly, I was chieftain of the Cimbri.

The next morning was the last day of Yule and I received the oaths of each clan leader beginning with Claudicus. I met him standing face to face, as equals, and accepted his pledge. He held his seax by the blade, offering me the hilt, which I accepted as he pledged his loyalty.

"On my life and honor, I give you my oath and swear loyalty to you, chieftain of the Cimbri people. May Donar's hammer strike me down should I violate this oath."

I nodded solemnly and reversed the seax, handing him the hilt, "I accept your oath, and am grateful for your loyalty."

This exchange was repeated dozens of times throughout the morning as each of the hunnos pledged their oath. The individuals and small groups that had joined us were accepted into the clans of their choosing and swore allegiance to their hunno. The tribe was regaining its identity, and for the first time since the plague, there seemed to be a sense of common purpose.

---

There was much time after Yule, to think during the long and dark days of winter, and I held many private meetings with my trusted advisors. I met separately with each of the clan leaders to learn their thoughts, as well as the high priest and priestess. It was a time that I greatly missed my father and my uncle. I wondered what had become of Grimur. I longed for his counsel and regretted how we parted.

Vallus heard Hilgi recite the prophecy and later informed me that Lupa was the she-wolf that suckled Romulus and Remus, the founders of Rome. Lupa represented Rome. This meant that to lift the curse, the Romans must welcome us into their land, to make a home for ourselves.

From Vallus, I had learned that Rome employed many mercenaries and foreign auxiliaries in their military, and I had seen them in battle. A plan began to take shape in my mind, and hope began to rise. Maybe there was a path forward after all.

Yet, the prophecy also said that wave after wave of Rome's soldiers would come, and that I would defeat them. Skyld assured me that time would reveal the answers and that all I needed to do was be patient. She said that fate would shape my decisions, but I felt my decisions would shape our fate, and I feared making the wrong ones.

One evening, I sat staring at the embers of our fire, brooding over the future. Hilgi's words, as ever, weighed heavily on my mind.

Frida had finished cleaning up after our supper and after she put Lingulf to bed, took out her materials and began quietly spinning wool. A slight noise when she shifted her weight intruded on my thoughts. I blinked as if waking from a deep sleep, sucked in a breath, and looked at her as my mind shifted to the present.

Her brow was furrowed in concentration as she went about the repetitious task. From the booty we had captured, I had provided her with a sack of sheep's wool that she had washed to clean it, and to remove the natural grease in the wool, then dyed it red with the roots of the madder plant. The wool was then combed to orient the fibers in the same direction and wrapped around a distaff to manage it more easily.

I watched as she teased out a length of fibers from the roving and tied it to the spindle. Then, holding the distaff in her other hand with the spindle hanging between her knees, she gave the spindle a twist and began drawing the fibers out of the roving, as the spindle dropped, forming a strand of yarn.

When the spindle nearly touched the floor, she paused, wrapped the yarn that had been spun around the spindle, and repeated the process, again and again, until the spindle was full.

She was beginning a second spindle when she caught me watching her. She smiled at me warmly, her dark eyes gazing at me questioningly.

Finally, she spoke. "You are troubled, husband. Are you still unsure of what to do in the spring?"

"The prophecy is clear," I said quietly. "We have to move on, or we tempt fate. After our last meeting I do not believe the Romans will welcome us into their lands. They made it clear they want us to leave. But...I must try. They may welcome our strength against the Scordisci."

I had made my decision, and she was the first to hear. "When winter passes into spring, the Romans will come, and I will ask them to grant us land. If they do not, when the land is ready for us to travel, we will depart.

"We shall travel over the mountains, to the north and back to the Danubius. We have learned of a path that leads up and over the high mountains. Then we will turn westward, toward the setting sun, and place our fate into the hands of the gods."

"You have been given a great responsibility; Donar selected you. The people elected you chieftain. That's because they trust you. They knew your father always led them with honor, and they believe you will do the same. They will respect your decision."

Her conviction settled my troubled mind, and her belief in me warmed my heart. My somber mood was broken.

I stood and embraced her tightly, and she sighed as she nuzzled against my chest, the top of her head just reaching under my chin. Her hair smelled like flowers, and I marveled at how it could in the dead of winter.

I was thankful for the comfort I always felt in her presence, through the troubling times of the sickness which took my parents, and the time since. With a finger under her chin, I tipped her face toward me and bent to kiss her, but she pecked me on the corner of my mouth and pulled away.

My relationship with Frida had changed since she was kidnapped. I had always suspected that she was abused at the hands of her captors, and on certain nights when she would whimper and cry in her sleep, I knew. At times she seemed her old self, and then, like now, she turned distant and cold. We were seldom intimate any longer. It was as if she deliberately avoided being too close to me, and she turned her attentions away from me and toward our son. I tried to understand, but I did not, and if I was caught off guard, at times I became angry.

I tried to talk with her about it on several occasions, but she refused, the only result being an uncomfortable companionship and her continued silence. I knew that she blamed me for what happened, and I knew she was hurting inside. But despite my efforts, I could not break through.

I still loved her deeply and hoped beyond hope that we could return to the happiness that we had before.

We went to bed, her back to me and a space between us, and I lay awake long into the night, still pondering the future.

---

We spent the rest of the winter preparing ourselves. We refitted wagons and carts, leather harnesses were repaired and replaced, and weapons were cleaned, sharpened, and oiled. Hrolf became my second in command and oversaw the training of our young warriors. In council, we developed tactics designed to counter what we had learned about the Roman ways of war, and we trained in their use. We created and constantly improved communications on the battlefield through horns, drums, and flags. We established a messenger system that would allow me to communicate my wishes to subordinate commanders. We trained our warriors in these new ideas and at first, they resisted. But over time many realized the value of being able to respond to actions made by an enemy. We would never equal the Romans in discipline, but it was an improvement.

Gradually, we added these new skills, but still valued our ancient ways of combat and we would rely greatly on our superior strength and numbers, coupled with stealth and surprise.

# PART III
# ROME

# Chapter Seventeen

## Rome

## Nones of January 113 BC

The Noric ambassador had crossed the Flavus River into the center of the city many times yet still was not accustomed to Rome's grandeur. Viranus was careful to keep his face a mask of indifference, but no one could ignore the fabulous wealth and power of this shining city, where the buildings were faced with white marble and glittered with gold inlays.

Lifelike statues and busts of some god or great man seemed to be everywhere, and beautiful fountains overflowed with cold and clear mountain water. The streets were paved with smooth stone and constantly cleaned by an army of slaves owned by the state; their sole job to pick up the litter and horse dung that accumulated. The side streets and alleys on the other hand were ankle deep in trash and refuse. Most Romans walked everywhere, but the occasional riding horse or carriage, owned by some rich or important man, made its way through the city. And of course, the many merchant's carts had to get to the shops to bring in the latest fashions from Greece, exotic fruits from Africa, amber from the northern seas, and so many other trade goods from all over the Roman world and beyond.

Flanked by four legionaries, he was the object of many shocked stares and whispered comments. The soldiers served more as escorts than bodyguards, as Viranus was a head taller than them, and his physical size alone would have given any petty thief second thoughts before accosting him. He wore leather soled shoes and multicolored leggings with a belted tunic. He kept his hair cut short but maintained the thick, drooping mustache common to his people. A plaid, woven cloak over his shoulder, pinned with a silver brooch, kept the January chill at bay, and a thick torc of twisted gold around his neck made it obvious he was a man of wealth and influence.

His weapons were left in his residence outside the city proper, as it was illegal for anyone but a Roman soldier to come into the city under arms.

They climbed the Capitoline Hill to the Temple of Jupiter Optimus Maximus, where the first Senate meeting of every new year took place.

A terra cotta sculpture of Jupiter being pulled in his chariot by four horses crowned the apex of the temple's soaring roof, and delicate acroteria traced the roof lines. An open colonnade stood in front of three red doors that led to separate rooms holding the enormous sculptures of the Capitoline Triad of gods: Jupiter, the king of the gods, Juno, his wife, and Minerva, his daughter.

The temple was a place of worship and sacrifice to the greater Roman gods and served as a repository for treasured artifacts. The Sibylline Books and the shield of Hasdrubal Barca, Hannibal's brother and general of Carthage, were stored in its lower levels, among many other treasures.

Viranus climbed the stairs to the colonnade and paused for a moment to gaze upon the Forum Romanum below, and the city beyond. A chill wind blew across the hilltop and ruffled his cloak as he gazed toward the Palatine Hill. Its expensive homes and numerous temples allowed the city's greatest citizens to live above, and look down upon its poorest, from their hilltop, high above the common people, as if they were gods on Olympus.

The sun had just risen above the Apennines to the east and warmed his face as a golden light spilled over the city. In the distance he could see the Circus Maximus, and past that the Aqua Appia, a two-century old marvel of engineering that brought water from dozens of miles east of the city to hundreds of thousands of citizens. As much as he disliked these people, one had to admire the civilization they had built, and their armies who had conquered so much of the world. He knew how good those armies were; his family still told stories of the battles that occurred before he was born and the many friends and family that had been killed before the two nations had become allies.

Though he was treated to several distasteful looks and many curious stares, he was largely ignored until a chime sounded and the senators began to take their seats. They waited while the newly elected senior consul, Gaius Caecilius Metellus Caprarius, conducted the required sacrifice and read the auguries to ensure the gods favored the day's meeting. With the preliminaries concluded, the newly elected magistrates and senators were introduced. Immediately after, a lengthy discussion took place over the assignment of the new senior consul who was being sent to Thrace to renew the campaign against the Scordisci.

Last year's consul Gaius Porcius Cato's army had been wiped out in a one-sided battle in the mountainous terrain of Thrace. After the army was defeated, the Celts turned to the Roman fortress Heraclea Sintica on the upper Struma River; the camp being used as a base for the expansion into Thrace. The garrison was lured out and away from their fortress and two cohorts were destroyed, including their commander, Lucullus.

The senior consul was another disciple of Scipio Aemilianus, a career military man with experience against the Numantians and the Gauls and was well respected by the army. He and his officers would travel to Macedonia to assume command of the legions there and renew the effort to subdue Thrace.

By the time they finished discussing Thrace, it was mid-day, and the assembly was dismissed to return in two hours.

Viranus was frustrated by the delay, but maintained his demeanor, and had to admit, he felt better with something to eat and drink and a moment to stretch his legs. Finally, when the Senate reconvened, they called Viranus to speak.

With the typical disdain that Romans held for the rest of the world, many of the white-robed senators paid no attention to him as he stood and faced them. They continued their private conversations, the babble in the room a constant thrum.

Viranus, not in the least bit surprised, stood patiently, waiting for acknowledgement. He had been involved in trade and defense negotiations with Rome before. He was well aware of how these people thought themselves the betters of everyone else.

Eventually, the senior consul called for silence, leaving only the steady crackle of the braziers in the background. Beneath the colossal, red painted statue of bearded Jupiter on his throne, Viranus began his speech.

"Consuls, Senators, citizens, I bring you greetings from the Kingdom of Noricum, friend and ally of the Roman people.

"My name is Viranus of the Taurisci. I will do you the honor of getting directly to the reason for my presence here today.

"I come before you to officially invoke the treaty of protection and to request your military assistance."

He paused as a low murmur went around the room.

"As you know," Viranus continued, "this past summer, a large tribe of barbarians arrived at our border from the east by way of the Dravus River. They claimed to be a northern tribe that migrated from their homeland years ago and have been traveling ever since. You would call them Germans, but they call themselves the Cimbri, and they most recently have come from the plains of Pannonia. These Germans were at first allied with and living among the Scordisci and were involved in the battle of Siscia when Lucius

Aurelius Cotta was defeated. And again, in Macedonia, near Stobi when they together defeated a large Roman expeditionary force.

"Two years ago, they suffered from a plague, and had a falling out with the Scordisci who ordered them away. There was fighting, and the Germans moved on. When they first arrived at our borders, they requested land to settle on. As you know, we have precious little land for farming and settlement as it is, and it is not possible for us to accommodate such a large group of people. We refused their request, and at first, they remained beyond the Danubius River, but that did not last. They crossed into our lands, establishing a camp in the foothills of our mountains, southeast of our capital, Noreia.

"Raiding parties roamed our lands and killed many of our people, robbing and burning our settlements. They have stolen our cattle and grain. Our people are afraid to leave the fortresses and the mountain fasts. Many were trapped above the passes and surely have died from the weather. The Germans have found only one mine, but in the spring, it is likely they will find and capture more and cut off the flow of Noric steel and gold to Rome."

Another outburst of voices interrupted him, this one louder and longer than before.

Raising his voice to be heard over the babble, Viranus continued.

"Last year, Princeps Senatus Marcus Aemilius Scaurus came to you with a letter from my king, asking for your help. This senate sent a delegation to speak with the invaders led by the same Marcus Aemilius Scaurus. The delegation returned to Rome with their answer that the Germans intended to stay. They continued killing our people and stealing our property and kept the gold for themselves.

"The raids have stopped for now because of the heavy snows in the mountains, but the Germans did not leave. They have built homes where they camped and appear to have no intention of leaving. In the spring, they will begin raiding our communities again to supplement their own food supply, and we are fearful of what the coming summer will bring.

"My friends, you must understand. This is not a small tribe of people, but a massive horde of hundreds of thousands. Men, women, children, young and old, cattle and other livestock. They carry all their belongings in carts and wagons pulled by oxen. It is an entire nation on the move. Even now they sit a short distance from the Amber Road. As of yet, they have not restricted the trade route, they are content to raid for subsistence, but my people count only in the thousands.

"We are no match for the numbers of warriors they can field, and it is only a matter of time until they decide to take what they want. When that happens, we will be unable to stop them. If they take our lands, the city of Aquileia and the northern regions of Italy will be next!"

His voice rose in volume, becoming forceful.

"If they are not stopped now, you may very well see a return to the days of Brennus nearly three hundred years ago, when Rome was sacked, thousands were killed, and the citizens retreated to this very place on Capitoline Hill, to starve and suffer pestilence while the Senones burned this city to the ground!"

This time there was an uproar as the senators finally realized the seriousness of the situation. Everyone talked over each other, asking questions, making points, questioning the truth of the matter, and throwing accusations about not doing enough before. Viranus returned to his seat, confident that he had reached these men with something they were subject to as much as any other man – fear.

The delegation they sent last year was the least they could do to say they were helping their ally and resolving the situation. And that was the point – it was the absolute least they could do. In their arrogance, they believed the north men would listen and obey them.

Viranus knew these Romans' weaknesses, and he had struck a nerve. To ask for Rome's help simply because his people, people for whom Rome cared little, were being attacked was not enough. But if he framed the request with the actual possibility that the Romans would also be at risk if they did not act, he knew they would not simply look away.

The suggestion that they might experience an interruption of trade, and especially the flow of money into their own coffers, got their attention. Even worse, the idea that they themselves might be in danger of physical harm spurred them to action.

This was not the first time the Senate had heard of the German migration, and not the first time they had heard Viranus speak of it. He had been speaking with anyone he could get an appointment with for months, preparing for this very meeting, especially anyone that was on track to become a magistrate. He already had the support of Marcus Aemilius Scaurus, and his voice was valuable, but he needed more.

Despite their prejudices, there were many in the Senate who listened, and the junior consul Gnaeus Papirius Carbo was one of them. Viranus knew Carbo's personal motivation was an asset he could exploit to gain support for his request, and Carbo did not disappoint.

Carbo had been lobbying for support, especially since the election. Not just because he was invested heavily in the mines of Noricum, but because he recognized the opportunity that was laid before him, and he was not about to let it pass. He saw his election as consul as the fulfillment of his destiny. He was of noble birth, did his time in the army, had served in all the required positions, moved up the cursus honorum, and now had reached the pinnacle of his career. If he was granted an imperium to remove the Germans, to be a protector and savior of Rome, it would be his opportunity to finally cleanse the stain on his family name after his brother's ignoble death. He was already envisioning himself leading a triumph through the streets of Rome, his face painted red, riding in the victor's chariot with his vanquished foes in chains behind him, followed by his grand army and the spoils of his victorious campaign.

The uncontrolled debate went on for several minutes until the senior consul called for order.

"Honored senators," began the senior consul. "You have heard the Taurisci ambassador's request, and now I place it before you to debate. Who will be first to speak?"

Immediately hands went up; a dozen senators stood to be heard.

"I recognize Princeps Senatus Marcus Aemilius Scaurus to speak first."

Scaurus rose. "I stood before this body just four months ago and suggested the delegation that subsequently traveled to Noreia. At the time, I doubted the vast numbers that were suggested by the Taurisci king. I can assure you I have seen them with my own eyes, as have the senators who accompanied me. We met with these Germans and demanded they return beyond the Danubius River and leave Noricum in peace. They refused our demand and scoffed at the threat of our legions. They even dared us to respond. The Senate ignored that slight.

"It is my belief that we cannot allow this to continue, because of the harm they have already caused to our ally the Taurisci, and because of the threat posed by so many barbarians so close to our borders."

Another senator, a man made very rich by trade that moved back and forth on the Amber Road, was recognized next.

"I am very concerned with the situation in Noricum, and I feel we must immediately address this threat. The Noric mines are a constant supply of gold that feeds our city's economy, and the largest source of quality steel for our legion's weapons and armor. The trade that travels through that region is lifeblood to our city. I said a year ago that a delegation sent to merely speak to them would not be enough. I say now that we must force these barbarians to leave Noricum on threat of their destruction. We have little choice. I nominate the junior consul Gnaeus Papirius Carbo to the rank of general, and I move to grant him an imperium to remove the Germans from Noricum with all due haste."

Marcus Junius Silanus, newly elected praetor and appointed as Governor to Hispania, but not yet departed, agreed. "I second the motion of Piso, and I would add that the imperium give Gnaeus Papirius Carbo the authority to petition the Italian allies to raise the men and arms for one legion, the other to be raised from Rome itself. I also stipulate that this effort includes at least two thousand fighting men from the Taurisci."

Quintus Caecilius Metellus spoke next.

"I agree with all that my distinguished colleagues have said thus far but would add that we do not need to seek more conflict if it is possible to remove the Germans peacefully. We have been deeply entwined in Thrace for years and we have lost thousands of men and many talents of gold in an effort that is yet to be concluded. These Germans have not directly threatened Rome. While I recognize the threat and share all of your concerns, I do not wish to commit our forces to war unless it is unavoidable."

The speeches continued as Viranus watched impassively from his seat. Some were concerned with the additional cost in manpower and gold to raise more legions. Some thought it was the responsibility of Noricum to defend themselves. Others were afraid of a repeat of Brennus's invasion.

Some questioned his information and felt he was exaggerating the situation. The senators that Carbo had garnered support from agreed with Piso and Scaurus and spoke in favor of Carbo.

Through it all, Gnaeus Papirius Carbo only observed. He was confident he had gained enough support to assure a vote in his favor, and he saw no reason to appear over-anxious. Gradually, the opinion to send an army to Noricum under Gnaeus Papirius Carbo held a majority, and when all spoke, he finally asked to be recognized.

"We have heard from the Taurisci ambassador and the princeps senatus who both describe the threat," he began. "I too, felt that only sending a delegation last year to talk to these barbarians was not enough, and I believe it was foolish to allow the Germans to strengthen their position. I sympathize with our friends the Taurisci for their suffering."

Nodding toward Piso he continued, "I accept your nomination and the responsibility to force the Germans to leave, at sword point if necessary, and to return to their homelands, or anywhere that is not within the borders of Rome or her allies."

When Carbo took his seat, the senior consul called for a vote. It was a safe majority that granted Carbo imperium to remove the Germans, peacefully, if possible, by force if necessary, no later than the Kalends of Iunius.

# Chapter Eighteen

## Hispania Ulterior

## February 113 BC

Gaius Marius, pro-praetor and outgoing governor of Further Spain, and Marcus Junius Silanus, newly elected praetor and Marius' replacement, sat in the governor's palace sipping a delicious Italian wine brought by Silanus to his new appointment. They reviewed the Spanish legions earlier in the day and changed over the command. Marius provided a delicious meal prepared by his Spanish chef, made up of the spicy dishes favored by the Iberians, after which they retired to his study to continue their conversation.

Marius had spent the past several days bringing Silanus up to date on his campaigns in Lusitana and Baetica against the Celt-Iberian rebels and bandits. He had been heavy-handed and beat them into submission, taking many slaves. He assured Silanus that they would not be causing trouble for some years.

What he did not apprise Silanus of, was that during his year as governor, Marius secured interests in several new mines and enriched himself on the superior gold and silver that came from those mines, as well as the slaves and other chattel that was his right to claim as praetor and as a victorious general. But the real money was in the investments of the businesses that provided the ongoing support of those activities. The food, tools, and materials required to build and run the mines. They would provide even more gold to his already stuffed coffers. Marius was going home a very rich man. He was leaving in the morning, but tonight's conversation was about recent events in Rome.

Silanus told Marius how Marcus Aemilius Scaurus led the failed attempt to get the Cimbri to leave Noricum last fall, and of the Taurisci request for assistance – and now the senate had voted imperium for the newly elected consul Gnaeus Papirius Carbo.

Marius had already received word of the elections of this year's magistrates and was aware of the ascension of Carbo. Remembering the new consul's brother, Gaius Papirius Carbo, he scoffed at the idea of the younger brother being tasked with removing the Germans.

Despite his reservations about the competence of the consul, Gaius Marius recognized another opportunity for furthering his own political career and returned to Rome immediately, where he sought out Carbo to request an appointment as his legate. Carbo, who had already chosen his legates and the rest of his staff, did not even bother to see Marius, who he considered to be a simple country farmer. A turnip eater. A novus homo. A "new man" with no famous ancestors, who rose to his position through luck and association with more competent men.

This of course infuriated Marius, who knew that every time he dealt with these pompous asses, these patricians, they looked down their aquiline noses and thought themselves so much better than him. He did not care about anyone's status at birth. What Gaius Marius cared about was competency. Bravery. Initiative. Intelligence. These were the things that mattered, not that you were the descendent of some great man who did great things a century ago, or how much old money you had, or how many marble busts of famous ancestors stood in your atrium.

That is why he loved his soldiers so much. Why he preferred a good campaign, months or even years of sleeping on the ground, eating coarse food; talking with, and working beside soldiers, real men, who appreciated good leadership. They wanted nothing more than an officer who cared for their well-being. A general who knew how to win battles and who lived and fought beside them and gave them the respect and reward they earned with their loyal service. That is the kind of officer Marius had always been, and this brief return to Rome had reminded him how tired he was of the cesspit that was Roman politics. Maybe, he thought, what he needed was to return home for a while, just to get his head clear, far away from the political intrigues and manipulation. Yes, home.

# Chapter Nineteen

## Rome

## February 113 BC

Gnaeus Papirius Carbo knew little of these Germans except the names of several of their tribes, which meant nothing to him. They were, after all, barbarian tribesmen who wore animal skins and ate raw meat. How could they possibly resist Rome's shining legions?

Many Romans feared the people north of the Danubius River and likened them to the Carthaginian threat of decades ago. Though they were fearsome warriors, Carbo knew they were no Hannibal. They were no threat to what he knew was his own superior military abilities.

He was tired of constantly hearing of his co-consul's experience in the army under Scipio in Numantia. Everyone was always comparing generals to Scipio, the destroyer of Carthage and conqueror of the Numantians. With Carbo's family history, he was eager to show everyone that he was every bit as capable as that annoying group of so-called professional soldiers who served under Scipio.

Carbo knew that this was his chance to restore the family name after his brother's ill-fated consulship and defense of Lucius Opimius, and his subsequent suicide. Gnaeus would not let a chance for his own triumph slip through his fingers.

The red flag had been raised above the Capitoline to notify all that the new levies were to report for duty on the Kalends of March. Word was filtering out of the city with travelers and official messengers were sent out to the Italian countryside to raise the conscripts needed to fill the ranks. The new recruits would have to be trained and equipped, and that took money.

Fortunately, the bill that Gracchus passed, the one that led to his murder by Opimius, required the state to pay for their arms and armor. Carbo chuckled to himself that this move, which he opposed, ended up saving him talents of gold from his personal fortune.

---

### Kalends of March 113 BC

Young Lucius arrived at the Campus Martius before dawn. There were thousands of young men already milling about, nervously watching the large tent on one end of the field. A centurion in full regalia stood outside the tent, the light of the torches glistening off his highly polished armor. The primus pilus.

His face was screwed up into a dark scowl as he watched the activity, tapping his vitis menacingly against his greaves. Behind him stood ranks of junior centurions and behind them their optios. A group of aeneators, horn players assigned to the legion, stood on one side. On the other stood a rank of signifers, the standard bearers of the legions, holding their various standards.

As the first gray light of dawn announced the day, the strident sound of horns filled the air, sounding assembly. Thousands of heads snapped toward the sound and eyes widened as the primus pilus and the other centurions strode purposefully toward them. The confused levies did not know the meaning of the call to assemble or what they were expected to do. Resplendent in his scarlet cloak – his helmet, cuirass, and greaves reflecting the rising sun – the primus pilus bellowed his commands echoed by the other centurions.

"*Ad signa! Ad signa!* Fall in! *Silentium!* Silence!" They waded into the boys, swinging their vitis like madmen. Pushing and booting them out onto the field where they had chalked lines on the grass.

"Line up! Line up, you sons of whores! Get your feet on the line! Arm's length apart! Eyes front! Stand tall! What is wrong with you?! Are you stupid?! Wipe your chin, you've got milk from your mother's teat on it!" The centurions shouted in their faces, nose to nose, spittle flying.

"Are you crying?! By Jupiter, he's crying!!" With that announcement, several centurions surrounded the hapless boy, screaming obscenities into his face. The levy stood frozen in fear, shaking, the tears continuing to flow.

The shocked young men finally assumed some semblance of a formation and the primus pilus strode to their front, glaring at them from under the visor of his helmet. The other centurions stalked the ranks, the occasional smack of a vitis sounding as the levies were introduced to the discipline of the legions.

"*Dirige frontem*! Dress the ranks! Straighten that line!"

When the primus pilus was satisfied with the formation, he issued his instructions. "Welcome to the Legions, goat humpers. As of now, you are no longer free men. For the next six years, your life belongs to the legions. You will do what you are told to do when you are told to do it. There will be no hesitation, no questions. You will be silent until you are asked a question or told to speak. When I am done with you, if you survive, you will be soldiers of Rome, feared by the entire world. But for now, you are goat humpers. Now, your first task will be to take the sacramentum."

"Signifer!" he bellowed.

The senior standard bearer ran forward to the primus pilus's right and stood at attention, his SPQR standard facing the assembled men.

A tribune emerged from the command tent and walked to the front of the formation. The primus pilus turned about and saluted smartly, then moved to the rear of the formation.

In a more cultured voice, but one equally accustomed to authority, the tribune said loudly, "All of you place your right fist over your heart and repeat after me."

As he recited the oath of the legionary, the men repeated the sacred promise:

*"I swear on my life that I shall carry out all that my consul and his officers' command. I swear that I will never desert my comrades nor seek to avoid death, for fear or for flight, and will not quit the ranks save to fetch or pick up a weapon, to strike an enemy, or to save a comrade. I swear loyalty to my fellow soldiers, my legion, and the republic. On punishment of death."*

When they finished the oath, the primus pilus reappeared and assumed command. The tribune returned to the tent.

"When I give the order, you will fall out and reassemble according to age. Those of you between the age of seventeen and twenty will be assigned as Velites, twenty-one to twenty-five Hastati, twenty-six to thirty Principes, and thirty-one to forty will be assigned as Triarii. If any of you are over forty years old, you will be assigned to the reserve.

"If you have had prior military service, that will be taken into consideration."

There were forty ranks of one hundred and twenty-five levies; five thousand men, many wondering what the Hades they had just stepped into. A legion consisted of four thousand eight hundred men, but the extras provided for those who would be released for various reasons, or died, before they completed their training.

Of course, there were the veterans of other campaigns mixed in each rank, especially the Principes and Triarii, who knew exactly what to expect, but most had never served. Lucius fell in with the Velites as he had just passed his seventeenth birthday.

Lucius had already realized that his world was no longer what it had been a few short minutes ago. That, of course, was the goal of the primus pilus. To shock them into the reality that they were men, no longer boys. Their world now consisted of the legion and only the legion. Nothing else existed.

The junior centurions moved to the right end of each rank.

"You will be under the command of the centurion in your rank until further notice. Follow his orders." He paused for effect. "*Ad gladio, clina!* Face to your right!" he shouted. "Move!"

The day began with a run around the Campus Martius, returning to the awnings where a score of actuarii sat at tables to take their personal information. Name, age, next of kin. Their height and weight were recorded. Identifying marks such as tattoos, birthmarks, and scars were noted. A physician assessed their overall physical, dental, and mental health and fitness. Some were deemed unsuitable on the spot and told to return home, the reasons noted by their names on the roster.

They were issued white woolen trainee tunics and caligae, the legionary's hobnailed footwear that would see them through thousands of miles of marching by the time they completed their service. They were assigned a tent where they dropped the extra clothing, sleeping gear, cooking equipment, and the pack they would use to carry their personal equipment.

At midday they were marched past a series of tables set up with bread, cheese, and watered wine. They ate ravenously, having been kept too busy to think about their hunger until the food appeared. Whenever there was a pause between stations, their centurion would lead them around the field on another jog, do some stretching and physical exercise, or instruct them in basic military drill such as standing at attention, at rest, saluting, marching, how to recognize rank, and more. Never were they given a moment to think about anything except what they were told to do.

When they had completed all the stations, the remaining men were again assembled on the field. As daylight faded, the primus pilus strode out onto the field to address the men.

"*Mandata captate!* Attention!" he shouted. The men moved to the rigid position of attention, shouting a weak and disjointed "For Rome!" Those not fast enough received a whack on the backs of their thighs from their centurion's vitis.

"You sound like sheep, not Roman soldiers! Once again! And this time snap to! I want them to hear you in the Forum! *Mandata captate!* Attention!"

This time knowing what was expected of them, they thundered as one, "FOR ROME!!" as they snapped to attention.

"Better, now you sound like cattle," he said. "Your centurion will count off eight-man groups in your rank. This will constitute a contubernium. This will be your unit, the men who will be closest to you in training and in war. Tomorrow morning, a legionary who serves in the training legion of Castra Piacenza will join every contubernium. This legionary will be responsible to begin your training. You will listen to them, and you will learn about the life of the legionary. Tomorrow, you will begin marching to the Castra Piacenza on the Padus River where you will receive your initial training. You have been instructed on what to bring with you — bring nothing else." Pausing for effect, his head pivoting, eyes surveying from one end of the formation to the other and back to the center, he shouted, "*Mandata captate!* Attention!"

"FOR ROME!!" echoed off the Servian Wall.

"*Dimitto!* I dismiss you!" All the centurions and other soldiers disappeared, leaving the recruits to themselves for the night.

The young men mingled for a while, learning more about each other that they had not had the chance to do during the day. Lucius was exhausted and exhilarated at the same time. It was not what he expected, but the sight of the centurions in their shining glory, the order, the discipline, and the camaraderie of the surrounding men had all caused him to feel the pull of what he now belonged to. He realized that this was what he wanted to do with his life. His father had fought against the Arverni and his grandfather had seen Carthage fall. Like Lucius, they had been levied into the army, but once their campaigns were over, they were dismissed. Now enlistments lasted six years.

When he was a boy, he used to take down his father's sword and don the bronze helmet and chest plate and pretend to be a soldier conquering distant lands for the glory of Rome. Once his father whipped him good when he was caught with the valuable weapon. His father and grandfather had to purchase their own arms and armor from their own pay. The laws passed recently now provided these from the state treasury. He still had to pay for his own food and clothing and other incidental needs, but at least the most expensive items were not taken out of his pay.

His grandfather had bought the family farm with the booty gained from his service, and his father had expanded it with his, paying off all the family's debts. But Lucius was not content to be a farmer. Having been raised on their stories of combat against the wild Gauls and crossing the sea to destroy the Carthaginian Empire, tales of war elephants and great generals, he had more in mind for himself than growing wheat.

---

Their training began before dawn the next morning with a sound that would become a part of their daily lives for the next six years. A chorus of buccina horns woke the new recruits as the centurions stalked the camp shouting orders. A legionary was standing outside the entrance of Lucius' tent when the occupants emerged, and he immediately took charge. He lined up the men and introduced himself as Titus Romanus. He demonstrated how each recruit was to pack his bedding and other belongings for the march, then instructed them on how to strike the tent and properly roll it up for storage. Mule teams pulling wagons were staged along the edge of camp, and the recruits were instructed to load the baggage wagons.

Another call from the buccina announced breakfast. The recruits were assembled and marched to the last meal that would be prepared for them until they reached Piacenza. They were instructed to eat as they moved through the line and given what seemed like moments to finish, then picked up their packs and reformed into march formation. By the time the sun had lightened the sky, they were moving north along the Via Flaminia, away from Rome and toward their new life. At Ariminum they would continue along the Via Aemilia to Piacenza.

At noon, the march halted, and they filed past a wagon that passed out bread, boiled eggs, and water to refill their canteens. Their new caligae were stiff, and though Lucius was accustomed to walking everywhere barefoot, he sported raw, red hotspots on his feet from the new leather. During their halt, Titus inspected the feet of each of his recruits and showed the group how to soften the leather by rubbing bee's wax into the straps, and to cover the hot spots to avoid blistering. Several recruits had caligae that were too large, and Titus had them step into a nearby stream to wet the leather so they would shrink to fit as they dried.

When the column moved off the road in the late afternoon Lucius could just make out an area staked out up ahead, and Titus told them they were stopping to make camp.

They had marched twenty miles, and while they were tired and footsore, they were in a good mood when they came to a halt, thinking that their first day wasn't so bad and they would soon eat and rest. The mood did not last long when they were formed into work and guard details and told they would construct their first castrum, the uniquely Roman march camp that provided the legions defensive protection every night while on campaign.

The work details were divided up and assigned to dig and construct fortifications, cut trees, and gather wood, level the inside of the camp, build watchtowers and gates, and construct the principia. Lucius and his tentmates were issued spades and picks and designated a section of ground to dig the trench and build the wall behind it that would surround the camp. After four hours of digging the ditch, throwing the dirt, and packing it into a solid wall behind the ditch, the men were amazed to see that a large fortification had been built including the deep ditch and wall that created a barrier more than the height of two men and twice as wide, with defensive wooden stakes, and solid log watch towers and gates.

Titus came up behind them and addressed the group.

"This is the first of many marching camps you will build. When you are on the march, the castrum provides you with security from enemy attack and a defensible location from which to rest and recover during war. Now that the wall is completed, you will pitch your tent, prepare your evening meal and care for your equipment. One century has been tasked with guard duty for the night."

"We have built a city in just a few hours. Do we just leave it in the morning when we depart?" Lucius asked.

Titus' eyebrows raised nearly to his hairline, amused.

"Oh no," he replied. "Before we leave in the morning, the castrum will no longer be here. The ditch will be filled back in, the palisade stakes will be loaded back on the wagons, and the towers and gates burned. In just a few weeks there will be no trace there ever was a castrum here."

Darkness had fallen on their second full day and as soon as they ate their supper, the young men fell into their bedding, exhausted.

---

Lucius and his tent mates were getting to know each other. There was Vulca, an Etruscan, whose countenance was always serious and almost never smiled. Decius, an Oscan who loved to gamble, and Foligio, who was an Umbrian with a sweet voice that brought a tear to many an eye around the evening fire. Large Porcius was of Celtic lineage from the Padus River valley, whose belly and laugh that sounded like a snort probably earned him his name.

From Rome came Aulus the quiet one, who listened, laughed occasionally, and seldom spoke. Then there was Marcellus, an annoying, musclebound, loudmouth who rubbed the others raw with his overbearing attitude and physical size. And of course, there was Titus; older and more experienced, he was quiet, and left the younger men to their antics. The men became closer over the next several weeks, and after a while Lucius realized that despite some slight differences in speech and manner, they all were very much alike, and got along well enough, excited about their adventures to come.

Even Marcellus seemed to be a little easier to stomach as time went on and they learned more about each other. During the march, the new recruits shared many evening conversations and worked with each other to learn the lessons that were already being taught. For most, cooking meals over an open fire was new, as was mending sandals, or caring for their tent and other equipment. Across the fire in the evening, they boasted of how many barbarians they would kill in their future campaigns. Foligio and Decius had been levied for the six-year enlistment and only intended to complete their term, as did Porcius and Aulus. But Vulca and Marcellus, like Lucius, planned to make a life of the Army. The prospect of a standard wage, promotions for exemplary service, regular food and medical care, and even a pension after twenty years was intoxicating. Not to mention a life of adventure, camaraderie, and the opportunity to amass wealth from one's share of booty and the sale of slaves and other captured goods.

By the time they reached their destination, the blisters on their feet and hands had turned to calluses. The ache in their legs and backs had faded, and they had become stronger.

After they marched through the massive gate at Castra Piacenza, they formed up on the parade ground. After a quick welcome briefing by the camp commander, Titus marched them around the camp to show them the legion headquarters, the canteen, the latrines, the quartermaster, and other buildings. Lucius noted that this permanent camp was a larger reflection of the march camps they had constructed, and everything was already familiar, though now the buildings were permanent structures made of wood and stone.

They were assigned to a century barrack in the same group they had traveled with. The long building had a dozen doors, each entering a large room, ten of which were sleeping rooms. One room at the end of the building was for weapons and equipment, the other end for a common area and gathering place. Each room had four double bunk beds, a crude table with four chairs, pegs on the wall to hang clothing, and a small window. Each bunk had a trunk at each end for personal belongings. A message was posted on the door, indicating there would be a formation at dawn the next morning.

After eating dinner at the common mess and a trip to the latrine, Lucius joined Marcellus, Aulus, and Decius in a game of dice. It quickly became obvious that Decius was a man to be careful with when gambling as he produced his own dice and won most of the throws until Titus came by and instructed the candles be snuffed.

Just as on the march, the talk continued quietly, wondering what was in store for them tomorrow until Vulca snapped at them.

"Knock it off! How is anyone supposed to get any sleep?"

There was a moment of silence, broken by a mocking "ooooooohh-hhh" and a snort, and a giggle, before the room was finally quiet.

It seemed to Lucius like he had just closed his eyes when the door crashed open against the wall behind it and the loud clatter of a gladius striking an ancient bronze shield woke him with a start. He jumped out of bed, not sure what to do first. A centurion was silhouetted in the doorway by a torch held behind him and began shouting at the top of his voice.

"Out of bed, you festering boils! Half the day is gone, and you are still sleeping. Get outside, century formation, now!"

The men scrambled to lace up their caligae and throw on their tunics, bumping into each other as they rushed the door all at once. Outside the building they formed up in ranks, coming to attention as they lined up. As the last men were running toward the formation, they faced to the right and moved out at double time. Lucius looked at the sky and realized he was getting used to beginning his day well before dawn and was thankful for the fact there were no ditches to fill in this morning. They only had to endure a brisk five-mile run.

When Lucius and his century returned from their run, they were released to clean up and eat. The centurion would be back in one hour.

The first day began with an accountability check and several briefings with information they needed to know. An actuarius told them when and how much they would be paid, and what was expected for them to purchase, such as shaving and hygiene equipment.

An armicustos told them what to do about broken, worn out, or lost items.

A medicus gave them a briefing on sex with the local prostitutes and how to protect themselves with condoms made from sheep intestines if they partook. There were punishments if they could not work due to contracting a disease, and there were some diseases that the cure was worse than the punishment. Then there were those diseases that were incurable and even deadly. Diseases were rampant in the local town and many of the new men would likely contact the local ladies, so it was a serious matter, and there could be serious consequences.

After the noonday meal, another run was in order. Some men who had eaten too quickly or too much wound up ducking out of the formation and vomiting, earning a quick strike from a vitis as well.

Lucius felt he was in his element. He was fit enough to stay in the front rank and not be shamed by falling behind, although his muscles ached from the new demands he made on them. He exhibited a knack for learning the various skills of the legionary, and for helping his tent mates who might have a problem with something. Titus appointed him as second in command of the contubernium.

During the first several weeks, every day was filled with fitness exercises. From dawn to dusk they ran, marched, carried logs, swam rivers, climbed trees, and ran obstacle courses. They cut logs, dug trenches, carried stones, and did calisthenics and stretching. Lucius led his contubernium through these basic tasks.

It was not long before they were developing the thighs, chest, and arms of a legionary. As they became more and more fit, they learned the meaning of the battlefield commands of the horns and banners. They conducted battlefield maneuvers on the march and on the run. They learned military customs and regulations, and how to stay healthy and clean, and to prevent and treat sickness and injury.

One morning after breakfast, they were ordered to retrieve their training weapons and equipment. As Velites, they would be in the front lines of the legion. They were skirmishers, used to harass the enemy by throwing their short spears, hastae velitares, about as long as a man's arm. After throwing their spears, they would then withdraw behind the first line of Hastati. They were not supposed to see close quarters battle with the enemy, but they carried a gladius and a small round shield in case they did.

The practice equipment was heavier than their actual gear in order to strengthen the men. This was what most had been waiting for, and there was great excitement among the men as boredom had begun to set in with their routine. Their enthusiasm waned quickly, however, when they found out they would not be training with any of it yet, just carrying it on their marches and runs from now on.

Finally, the day came when they were marched to the practice field with all their training arms and armor. The men were thrilled to observe several pairs of Principes demonstrating individual combat, and two maniples in full combat dress conducting battlefield drills. One maniple took up a defensive posture, locking shields as the opposing maniple threw pila to demonstrate the strength of the shield wall. Then the wall began to move forward, shields pushing forward with each step, gladii thrusting from between their shields, the centurion calling out the battle rhythm, keeping time with the march. When the demonstration ended, the new recruits began their training with sword, shield, and spear.

For the next few weeks, their fitness training continued but the focus was now on weapons training and hand to hand fighting, both in formation and as individuals. Shortly, they were issued their combat equipment and were trained on how to use and maintain it. They were proud to finally be carrying iron tipped darts, a gladius of steel instead of wood, and a real parma, the small round shield the Velites used.

---

After the second month in training, the recruits were allowed one evening pass a week if they stayed out of trouble and completed their training satisfactorily. Each century drew lots for two lucky soldiers to get an overnight pass. One such evening, Lucius and his friends wandered among the market stalls, laughing at the enthusiastic merchants hawking their wares, competing for the soldier's attention. The men had just been paid, and the merchants knew it.

There were jewelers and smiths, seers and holy men, food vendors of every kind, and, of course, prostitutes. The girls smiled and batted their eyes at the passing soldiers, baring their breasts, and inviting them into their hovel for a quick romp. But it was early, and Lucius and his friends were hungry and above all, thirsty, after a long week of training.

They made their way to their favorite taberna. The owner served a drink that passed for wine but was closer to vinegar. But the reason they liked the pub was not the wine, it was the ale. The young men had developed a taste for the ale that the Celtic host brewed, and it was a favorite among the hard-working legionaries. The roasted meat was expensive but was a pleasant change to the boring rations of the legion, and there was a wide variety. Some of it rather questionable as to the species, but when it was washed down with a large draught of beer and a loaf of freshly baked brown bread slathered with butter, who cared?

The Italians, the Romans especially, were accustomed to watered wine and the lighter, white bread of the south. They did not eat butter like the Celts did, but instead mixed it with honey and used it on their wounds. As soldiers on the edge of a foreign land, the legionaries enjoyed the many tastes available.

After a couple hours of boasting, laughing, and telling raucous stories, Lucius and his friends prepared to return to the camp. As usual, Marcellus was drunk early and making quite the fool of himself. He never could seem to handle his alcohol, yet he would partake in any type as often as he could. Vulca and Foligio wound up walking him back to the camp, one of Marcellus's large arms over each of their shoulders. But Decius was the lucky one this evening. He had won an overnight pass, and he intended to use it for its full worth.

It would cost half his month's pay, but he intended to spend the night with the beautiful prostitute that he fancied loved him. His friends tried to convince him she only loved the money he threw at her, but he could not be reasoned with and became jealous any time his friends brought it up, so they had learned not to discuss it.

---

During their third month of training, they learned about basic tactics and battlefield movement in large formations and continued to hone their individual skills.

One day they were woken up in the usual manner but told to gather all their arms and armor and assemble outside rather than go for the customary run. Once they were assembled, they marched out the gate and followed the river plain twenty miles away from the camp. Here they were ordered to set up a campaign camp and to prepare for battle. This was to be their final training exercise, observed by the senior tribune himself.

The following morning, they were simulating a pitched battle when the tribune called a halt to the exercise. After the men were formed up, the tribune addressed them directly.

"It appears that your training will be cut short. I have received a message from Rome that we are to join the consul Gnaeus Papirius Carbo in Aquileia without delay, to prepare for a possible battle with the barbarians threatening our borders. Your primus pilus has assured me that you have completed your training satisfactorily and will serve Rome honorably. Therefore, I am concluding this exercise and ordering you to prepare to depart for Aquileia the day after tomorrow."

A great cheer erupted from the assembled legions as they realized the endless training was over and they were about to embark on the expedition they had dreamed of for so long.

# Chapter Twenty

## Arpinum

## June 113 BC

Gaius Marius, senator, praetor, commander of legions, governor of Hispania Ulterior, victor over the Celt-Iberians, New Man of Rome, and one of the richest men in all of Italy, shared a drink of cool water with the slave that he stood beside, sweating in the summer sun.

The two had been digging post holes for a new fence line along the road that approached his family's farm. The rich dark brown of the freshly planted wheat fields around them contrasted with the cloudless blue sky. Marius took a deep breath in through his nose, expanding his chest, taking in the smell of the tilled earth, and exhaled loudly through his mouth. Gods, he had missed this more than he realized. It was good to be away from the stink of the crowded cities, and he vowed to return to the fields and forests of his youth more often to rejuvenate himself.

His companion was astounded by how hard the general worked side-by-side with the slaves and tenants. He had never seen such a thing. Marius was no longer a young man and had not been back to the estate since he was elected plebian tribune almost ten years ago, but he was fit and strong from a soldier's life, and he enjoyed physical work. His father had always been fair and kind, at least to the point that a slave owner could be, but never had he lowered himself to work beside the slaves.

Marius' father had passed several years before while Gaius was on campaign in Gaul, and his mother kept the estate going with the help of a trusted freedman who oversaw its activities.

His brother Marcus was home for a short time between military postings, and the brothers had been carrying on as if they had never parted. Like Gaius, he had also signed up to join the legions at seventeen and had served in Thrace and Gaul. Twelve years Marius' junior, thirty-two-year-old Marcus had put in his time in the military and was rising swiftly through the cursus honorum, serving last year as military tribune. He had benefited from his brother's wealth and sponsorship and was thankful for it.

Their sister Maria and her husband, Marcus Gratidius, an official in Arpinum, were also visiting the estate. Their mother was ecstatic to have all three of her children home at the same time. With them was their twelve-year-old son Marcus Gratidius, the younger. Marcus the younger was very close with his uncle, Marcus Marius, and they had gone riding together today.

Dinner that evening brought the whole family together, and the wine and laughter flowed deep into the night.

After retiring to his rooms, Gaius sat reflecting. He opened a large trunk that sat at the foot of the bed he had slept in as a youth and removed a small wooden box. Reaching into the box, he withdrew an eagle feather that lay on top of the other contents. Slowly, his mind drifted back to the day when he realized how special he really was.

That fine summer day in Arpinum he had been playing alone in the woods behind his father's farm fields when a strong wind suddenly whipped up, swirling grass and leaves and dropping limbs down from the tallest trees. After the wind had passed, he heard the piercing scream of an eagle and excitedly raced through the trees to find its source. As he made his way toward the sound, he could see a pair of eagles circling high above, screeching their frustration, over and over again.

As Gaius neared, he could see a large nest lying upside down at the base of a tall tree. Keeping one eye on the soaring eagles, Gaius carefully approached the nest, noticing slight movement under it, and a muffled squawking coming from amongst the grass and twigs that formed it. Taking a stick, Gaius reached out and flipped the nest over. Underneath were four featherless eaglets that appeared to have hatched only recently. The sudden gust of wind had knocked the nest to the ground.

As he stood motionless, contemplating what to do, he heard more sounds like the ones coming from the nest. Carefully walking around the area, he found three more eaglets that had fallen away from the nest. Miraculously, all seven birds were uninjured from their fall, and the three strays allowed him to pick them up and return them to their nest. His heart nearly pounding out of his chest, Gaius raced home to tell his father and mother.

Both of his parents were in awe and were adamant that the nest be returned to its place immediately. It disappointed young Gaius that he could not keep them, but he reluctantly agreed after a talk from his father that eagles were meant to be free and not to be pets for young boys. Gaius and his father returned to the tree that the nest had fallen from. Gaius climbed high into the tree with a rope slung over his shoulder and found the spot the nest had fallen from. Meanwhile, his father laid a cloak out on the ground and placed the nest and the eaglets onto it. Drawing the corners of the cloak together, he tied it at the top with a piece of rawhide. Gaius dropped the end of the rope back down through the branches, and his father tied it to the cloak. Gaius pulled it carefully back up into the tree, placing the nest and its inhabitants where they had fallen from earlier.

Gaius and his father kept close watch on the adult eagles as they soared above, no longer crying out, but watching intently. As the boy reached the ground, the eagles alighted at the top of the tree and rejoined their babies. In a few moments, the male flew away to find a meal for the hungry brood, while its mate watched the humans who saved her young depart.

His encounter with the eagles was no insignificant event, and Gaius was so excited he slept little during the night. His father and mother sat up for hours discussing the possible meaning of the incident and concluded that they needed to consult with someone that knew of such things.

The next morning the family traveled to the home of a local priest who listened intently as they recounted the story. Looking at Gaius, the old man explained the meaning of the omen.

"The eagle is a noble creature; strong, beautiful, graceful. When we see the eagle soaring in the skies above, our hearts are filled with joy at its freedom and beauty.

"With its powerful vision, the eagle sees what a man cannot. He floats on the winds of the heavens, and he has been granted the wisdom of the gods.

"By helping the eagles, your destinies have been joined. This omen portends a great future for you, Gaius.

"Like the eagle, there is great strength in you. You are not destined to be just a farmer.

"As the eagle is fierce and brave, so shall you be in the face of danger. Like the eagle who knows no earthly boundary, you too shall travel the world without limitation.

"As the eagle soars amongst the clouds high above, so shall the new man rise to the greatest heights: soldier, senator, general, consul.

"And as you found the seven eaglets, so shall you claim the highest of honors seven times.

"But beware. Just as the nest fell from the treetops, it is from the greatest heights that the mighty shall fall."

Gaius was so overwhelmed he could not speak. His father and mother could not stop asking questions, but the priest had no more information to give, sending them away, still babbling with excitement. From that day forward, Gaius had been different. He was no longer interested in the things that boys his age thought of. His father hired a weapons master and a tutor to ensure the boy had as much advantage as the father could afford. He learned horse riding, tactics, military discipline, leadership, history and much more.

Gaius Marius, the man, knew without a doubt that he was destined to become the most powerful man in Rome, and to repeat that feat over and over again.

If he were to repeat these words aloud, he knew that most would dismiss him outright or even think him insane. All would doubt that a man of his humble beginnings could ever aspire to such greatness. Some might become jealous enough to openly stand in his way or attempt to prevent him from achieving his destiny, so he had never shared this knowledge with anyone save the old priest who had died shortly after, and his parents, who were both sworn to secrecy on his behalf.

He thought of how far he had come from his humble beginnings as a boy joining the army the day he turned seventeen. His father had presented him with the gold finger ring of the Equite, and he was aware that his family's equestrian status and clientage to the powerful Roman Metelli family assured him a beginning in a cavalry unit and a chance for a military and political career.

In his early years in the legions, he had taken part in several small military actions, gradually building a reputation as an excellent horseman and capable fighter. Even at a young age, Marius displayed an understanding of leadership and was soon elected by his men to the position of optio, second in command, and then decurion, commander of his cavalry turma. Eventually, recognition of his intelligence brought him to the attention of his commander.

Marius set the feather aside and reached back into the box. He picked up a silver medallion and held it in his hands, absently running his fingers over the relief and admiring the work of the craftsman that made it.

Marius was awarded command of an auxiliary cavalry ala in Hispania under Scipio. After the fall of Numantia came his election to military tribune, followed by the Battle of the Rhodanus River against the Arverni where he covered himself in glory with his audacious cavalry attack.

He remembered as he had stood at attention in the general's tent as Fabius Maximus himself slipped a chain suspending the medallion over Marius' head. The award represented his promotion to praefectus alae, commander of a unit of five hundred auxiliary cavalry troops. Maximus said a few words of praise and gripped Marius' forearm proudly, smiling and congratulating him with a clap on the shoulder.

Marius wrapped the medallion in its linen cloth, and gently replaced it in the small wooden box that held his military awards and other memorabilia.

After another year in Gaul, Marius had returned to Rome and, after a short time, was assigned as a general staff officer in the consular army of Lucius Calpurnius Piso during the slave revolt in Sicily. On Piso's staff, Marius honed the skills of supply and logistics as well as his planning and organizational skills. It was no small feat to move legions of men across the Mare Nostrum and keep them supplied with food, equipment, and reinforcements.

His rise through the military ranks had been swift, but his elected offices had taken their time in coming. There were moments he doubted he would ever fulfill the prophecy.

Finally, feeling the effects of the long night of wine and memories, he closed the lid, then rose to prepare himself for bed.

When Marius returned home from the fields the next day, he found a letter had arrived from Rome. Breaking the seal, Marius saw it was from his friend Gaius Lucilius. He called for a servant to get him a cup of wine and walked into the library, reading the news.

*Greetings my friend, I hope this letter finds you in good health. I am writing to tell you some news that will be of great interest to you, as it is regarding our mutual acquaintance, Jugurtha of Numidia. You will remember him as Scipio's brash young auxiliary cavalry commander in Numantia.*

*You will likely recall that Jugurtha killed his younger brother Hiempsal several years ago, and attacked Adherbal, the third brother, in an attempt to consolidate Numidia for himself. Adherbal was no match for Jugurtha in battle and fled to Rome to request help from the senate. They tasked Lucius Opimius to lead a commission of senators who negotiated a peace and divided the kingdom between the two remaining brothers. Rumors still abound of the bribery of Opimius and the other senators by Jugurtha to ensure that he got the better half of the kingdom, but nothing was proven, and nothing was done.*

*As you know, as praetor, Opimius destroyed the Latium city of Fregellae in response to their uprising, and he was the consul responsible for the deaths of Gaius Gracchus and thousands of his supporters. He was later successfully defended in those murders by Gaius Papirius Carbo. He was rather obviously not the best choice the senate could have made.*

*That peace lasted three years, and this spring Jugurtha attacked Adherbal once again. Jugurtha's military performance sorely outmatched Adherbal, who retreated to his capital city of Cirta where he was besieged.*

*Once again, Adherbal appealed to Rome to intervene. However, this time, the senate was preoccupied with the threat in the north by the German barbarian tribes that have entered Noricum, and with the ongoing wars in Thrace, Macedonia, and Pannonia. So, the senate sent a small delegation of junior senators to demand that Jugurtha withdraw his forces and honor the peace agreement that was formerly arranged.*

*Of course, seeing that Rome was no longer interested in the goings on in Numidia, Jugurtha has continued his siege of his brother in Cirta, and the delegation returned empty-handed this past spring.*

*Another commission led by Princeps Senatus Marcus Scaurus himself is currently in route to frighten Jugurtha into complying, but I am sure you would agree old Jugurtha does not frighten easily.*

*Incidentally, I am not sure if you know that Marcus Scaurus also led the delegation that negotiated with the Germans in Noricum last year while you were still in Hispania. They also ignored his demands and even now, Consul Gnaeus Papirius Carbo is marching to stop them.*

*It appears, my friend, that you may have missed your chance to fight the Germans, but you may yet get an opportunity to apply your military genius in the near future.*

*For the life of me I cannot imagine why you have exiled yourself to be a farmer, but if you have had your fill, now may be the time for you to return to Rome.*

*Whatever you decide, I wish all the best to you and to your family Gaius, and I look forward to hearing from you soon. Your friend,*

*Gaius Lucilius*

Marius read the letter again, then leaned back with a frown. Tenting his fingers and tapping his chin, he thought about what he had read. If he returned to Rome now, he thought, he would have enough time to run for consul for next year. If he won, and the senate declared war, he would likely be granted the imperium to deal with Jugurtha.

On the other hand, he had spent little time in Rome in the past few years, and that would hurt him in an election. His time as praetor did not make him any friends in the senate and a year in Hispania as governor meant he needed to build up his supporters before he could win an election.

He had thoroughly enjoyed the summer as the simple master of a country estate, without the headaches and concerns over politics and the self-serving politicians. The clear air and clean water had done wonders for his mood. But, if he was honest with himself, he was also getting bored.

Marius neatly refolded the letter and placed it with his archived papers. His mother had taken ill recently, and he decided he would stay until she felt better, and then pay a visit to Gaius Lucilius. It would be good to talk things over with his old friend.

Having reached a decision, he realized he had not eaten, and was famished. He followed his nose to the source of the smell of freshly baked bread.

# Chapter Twenty-One

## Noricum

## June 113 BC

Having deciphered the prophecy, I planned to ask the Romans for a place for our people to settle, but I also felt it was unlikely, given the way our last meeting ended. I issued instructions to prepare to leave Noricum, in case they denied my request. If I was wrong and they accepted us, we would need to move anyway, so no effort would be lost.

We would move as soon as the passes were clear, and the swollen rivers had crested and fallen. Because of the heavy snows this past winter, that took nearly until the end of the midsummer moon. I made the unpopular decision to refrain from raiding and terrorizing the countryside, at least until I spoke with the Romans. But I had no intention of returning what we had taken.

Gorm had built smelters where his men converted the ore we captured into ingots.

As when we left Borremose, his smiths and carpenters built more carts and improved the designs to travel better with heavier loads. Soon all our families had several carts, one to live in and others to carry gold and iron ingots, salt and weapons, and iron tools and pots. Dozens of carts were built to store the wealth that I claimed as chieftain, and they were guarded by my most loyal warriors.

No longer were we the poor and needy people that left Jutland with nearly nothing. Many were clothed in the better garments of the Celts, though most still wore leather and animal skins and rough woven clothing. Some sported helmets and swords and even mail coats taken from our defeated enemies.

Spring passed quickly. The date of our departure neared, and I gave the order to prepare to move with the new moon. The people had all been made aware of the prophecy, and my plans were passed down to the last person. When I walked among our camps as I often did, they were eager to be moving on and the camps buzzed with renewed energy.

I sent some of the Boii tribesmen, who fit in better with the locals than any of the northern tribes did, to Aquileia and to Posonium to inform me of any movement of the Romans or other news. I expected them to arrive with a military force soon, and I intended to reach out to them first.

Before we could set off, one of my spies from Aquileia arrived with the message that a delegation of Romans had arrived in the city ahead of several legions who were marching from the west. The delegation was asking around the city for the best route to our camp and would arrive soon. We needed more time to prepare to leave anyway, so I waited for them to see what word they brought.

Several days later, they rode down from the passes, escorted by a few of my outlying sentries. We received them at the same place that we talked with Marcus Aemilius Scaurus the year before.

The tribune leading them reported the legions marched two days behind them, and that consul Gnaeus Papirius Carbo wished to parley with us at a site he had already chosen.

# Chapter Twenty-Two

## Noricum

## Late September 114 BC

Consul Gnaeus Papirius Carbo, pale, paunchy, and balding, sat straight-backed in the curule chair placed on the dais built for the occasion. A frown of displeasure that he had often practiced in his polished silver mirror sat comfortably on his countenance. His lips taught, brow wrinkled, and his eyes slightly narrowed, he watched the approaching Cimbri delegation. It was an expression that he thought would sufficiently impress upon the half-naked barbarians his displeasure at their actions.

A maniple of hand-picked soldiers, selected for their superior size and bearing, stood at attention a hundred paces behind him. On their right, a selection of artillery pieces and to their left an ala of auxiliary cavalry sat on their mounts.

Another hundred paces behind those, the rest of his two legions were drawn up in battle order, a sufficient example of Roman military might to impress even the most backwards tribesmen of the north, Carbo thought.

The white canopy that shaded the dais was not so large to include his guests, ensuring they would stand in the sun for the length of the meeting, further adding to their discomfort and the impression of his superiority over them.

He watched the German warriors approach, a large wolf stalking beside them. They slowly walked their horses to within a few feet of the waiting legionaries of his personal guard, who stood in a line in front of the consul. Carbo was disappointed to see that the expected expression of awe was not apparent on their faces. Instead, they wore a mask of stoic lack of emotion, even bored, as they surveyed the legions behind him. The legionaries of his guard had to tip their helmets back to look up at the giants that sat on these enormous horses so close to them.

A tall, red-haired young man dismounted after a moment, followed by the rest. His hair was unbound and fell behind his broad shoulders. A thin braid descended from each temple. Unlike the rest of his companions, he was clean shaven, no thick beard like the rest, and his chest was completely barren of the thick carpet of hair that seemed to be common to all Germans. He spoke softly to the wolf, who laid down in front of the wary legionaries, his tongue lolling, ears up and watchful.

He wore simple buckskin trousers and leather-soled shoes. Linen strips wrapped his legs from his ankles up to his knees, holding the leggings tight to his muscular calves. A leather belt held up the trousers, a badger skin pouch hung from it, and a seax was tucked behind it. He was bare chested save for a wide leather baldric that crossed it and held his scabbard and long sword, and he wore nothing that identified him as any different from the rest of the men behind him, though from their deference it was obvious who was the leader.

The men strode confidently up to the centurion of the guard, who barred their path. "You may not approach the general with your weapons," the officer announced.

He was about to reach for the chieftain's weapon when he noticed the murderous glare in his eyes.

"Leave them be, centurion. They may keep their weapons," Carbo ordered. Relief washed over the soldier as Carbo went on. "After all, they are not defeated enemies, or subjects of Rome." Thinking to himself that if they were to try anything, they would never leave this place alive.

The flame-haired leader walked up to the dais. There were several stools on the ground, intended as seating for the Germans. The difference in height would have given Carbo an impression of superiority over anyone sitting on the stools. Instead, the barbarian stood before Carbo, his steel-gray eyes at the same level as the seated consul on the raised dais.

Marcus Sosius, Carbo's legate, stood to the right of the dais. An interpreter stood opposite, and a scribe sat at a table with quill and parchment at the ready. Sosius opened the meeting with formal introductions.

"Gnaeus Papirius Carbo, consul of Rome, welcomes you to this meeting and asks that you introduce yourself so that we may begin our discussion as friends."

The interpreter translated the question.

# Chapter Twenty-Three

To his credit, Carbo reacted only with a raised eyebrow and slight tilt of his head when I replied in his own tongue. His legate, however, was obviously shocked.

"I am called Borr. I am the chieftain of the Cimbri."

"Ah," Carbo said, leaning back, looking at me with hooded eyes. "Well then, let's get on with it, shall we? Since last summer, you have been trespassing on lands that belong to the Taurisci and the Kingdom of Noricum, who are allies of Rome. I am here as the representative of Rome to tell you that you must immediately return everything you have stolen from the Taurisci people and withdraw from Noricum and beyond the river Danubius."

I said nothing and stood with arms crossed, my expression noncommittal. Irritated at my silence, Carbo went on.

"You were asked to do this last summer by the delegation sent to you from Rome, but instead you stayed in Noricum and have continued to raid the Taurisci and other local tribes and have disrupted trade along the Amber Road.

"I am here to ensure that this time, you do what you failed to do last year, either voluntarily, or by force if necessary."

Carbo's demands came as no surprise, I had already determined what was likely to be Rome's position.

"Seven years ago," I began, "we were deluged with a great storm brought upon us by Njoror, god of the sea. Our homes and our lands were destroyed, and we could not stay, for to stay was to

265

starve.

"Our entire nation began a journey of great hardship, through the northern forests and swamps, across wild rivers, over wide grasslands and tall mountains. All we wanted was a place to call home. We were rejected by the Boii, and after settling among the Scordisci, suffered a terrible plague that killed many of our people and scarred the rest of us," I said, pointing to the pox marks on my arms.

"We were betrayed by the Scordisci and forced to leave. Before we entered Noricum, we asked for land from the Taurisci and we were refused. With no other choice, we came anyway. Your ambassadors refused to listen and only insisted that we leave. We did not agree to leave, those are your words.

"Since your delegation came last year, I have been elected as chieftain of the Cimbri. We seek a land on which we can settle our families and create a new life, where we can grow crops and raise our cattle. We have heard there is fine land in Italy, and I am told that you Romans employ many thousands of warriors from other nations around the world. I can see some now, standing with your legions," I said, jutting my chin toward the mounted auxiliary troops.

"We know that you are fighting the Scordisci. We have no love for them, and we would be willing to join you in that fight. I ask you; will you grant us land in Italy in return for our service in your armies?"

# Chapter Twenty-Four

Carbo was shocked. He had anticipated belligerence, not an offer of alliance. He rubbed his chin for a few moments and thought. What if he were to bring this horde of barbarians under the influence of Rome? What if he were responsible for ending the threat of the invaders without conflict, while providing the means of defeating the celts that had been defying Rome for decades?

"I will consider your request," he said. "Return here in two days and we will speak again."

Carbo called an immediate meeting of his advisors.

Marcus Sosius reminded him, "The Senate's wishes were to remove the Germans peacefully, if possible. I believe their request demands serious consideration; this may be a way to solve the problem without war."

A senior tribune cautioned against inviting such a threat into Italy.

"I feel it is a risk to Rome itself to have such a large contingent of unknown warriors within our borders."

The Taurisci king, Epatus, forcefully demanded the barbarians leave Noricum and pay for the damage they had done.

Carbo's mind was reeling. The implications were many. He was intrigued with the idea of ending the conflict without a fight, but he did not have the authority to make such a promise without the senate's approval. He knew that if he returned this request to Rome that he would have to share in the outcome, and he did not wish to share any resulting credit for resolving this problem.

More importantly, he thought, he would lose his chance at a military victory while he was consul, and there would be no triumph if he granted their request. No opportunity to cover the family name in glory and prestige. Just a request from these barbarians, passed through him to the senate for their decision. He would be pushed to the side, and he could not stand for that.

After he dismissed his advisors, he considered his options. Late in the night he decided on a course of action and as the sun dawned on a new day, he managed a few hours of sleep before he called another meeting.

"How can we trust the word of these northern barbarians who have led an unprovoked attack on our friends and allies of Noricum and laid waste to so much of their land and people? No, we must ensure that they are held accountable for their actions, not forgive them and invite them into our lands where they will likely do the same to our Italian allies, and very possibly threaten Rome herself.

"Our legions in Thrace and Macedonia are capable of defeating the Celts without the help of these savages. Our responsibility is here. Now. And I intend to put an end to it once and for all. I will not allow them to leave and become a threat in years to come.

"As Epatus has said, they need to be punished and they need to pay for what they have done. Tomorrow they will return, and I will refuse their request for land. I will demand that they return to Germania to find their own way, far from the borders of Rome and outside the borders of our allies.

"But I have planned a surprise for these barbarians. If they refuse to leave, we will march on them and crush them in their camps. If they agree to leave, we will allow them to move, and then set upon them unexpectedly. Either way, we will punish them, and we will recover all that was stolen. Their defeat will ensure that there is no future concern from these tribes, and it will send the message to others that there is no place in Rome for bandits and thieves."

# Chapter Twenty-Five

When I returned to Carbo, I was disappointed, but not surprised at his refusal of land, and I agreed to his demand to leave Noricum. I had little choice, as the prophecy assured our destruction if we stayed in Noricum, and I had no wish to start a war with the Romans. I would have to wait for another opportunity to lift the curse.

I refused to give up any of the wealth that we had captured, and I was surprised at how little he and Epatus argued that point, as it had been such an important part of the discussion yesterday. Their willingness to drop it raised my suspicion. Yet, I agreed to move immediately, and Carbo promised to withdraw his legions from our path. We accepted his offer of guides, as I knew it was his attempt to keep informed of our movement, and ensure we followed the most direct route back to Germania.

# Chapter Twenty-Six

After returning to his camp, Gnaeus Papirius Carbo called his senior officers and the Taurisci leaders to plan the coming battle. He outlined his plan to attack the barbarians and ordered the legions to prepare to march at first light. They poured over the maps and consulted with Epatus to determine a suitable site for the ambush, and a route to it that would keep them out of sight of the Germans. Carbo instructed Epatus to have two of his men report to him. When the two arrived, they were told that they would act as local guides for the Cimbri, and he showed them the route by which he wanted them to guide the barbarian horde straight into his trap.

# Chapter Twenty-Seven

## Noricum

## July 113 BC

Gnaeus Papirius Carbo was pleased with himself; his deception had worked. He had convinced the barbarian chieftain that he would allow them to pass unmolested back to the frontier. Seated atop his stallion, he rode at the front of his troops, lost in a daydream. He could already hear the cheers of the citizens as he rode through Rome, dressed in the purple and gold toga picta, the red boots, and laurel crown of the victorious general, his face painted a bright red. He imagined leading his armies through the city in the red chariot drawn by four white horses as he tossed silver coins with his likeness stamped upon them to the grateful crowds.

Carbo pushed his army hard for the next two days to reach the area he had chosen for battle. When they arrived, the legions immediately went to work setting up their camp. His scouts kept visual contact with the Germans and reported their location often. Carbo knew that he still had several days before the slow-moving caravan arrived. While his men erected their castrum and readied themselves for battle, he rode the surrounding terrain with his officers, preparing for the coming battle.

Several of his officers offered suggestions, and he had to set them straight on who was in charge, but in all, there was little opposition.

Sitting in his tent on the second night, Carbo smiled to himself as he poured another cup of wine and reflected on the situation. He was confident that he had done everything he could to ensure victory in battle and a triumph when he returned to Rome.

―――――――――

Not far from the consul's tent, Lucius was trying not to show his apprehension of the coming battle, as he sat with his tent mates around their cooking fire. The other young soldiers were equally anxious and were trying just as hard not to let it show in front of their friends. Their commanders had spoken to them when they were assembled earlier in the day and reminded them of Rome's proud record of victory, but these young men had yet to meet an enemy in battle and lacked the confidence of those veterans.

It did not help that word had passed through the camp about the frightening size of the enemy force and the ferocious appearance of the warriors themselves. Since they were children, they had heard the stories of the huge barbarians that lived in the north. The Germans were reported to be even more ferocious than their southern cousins, the Celts, who generations ago had sacked Rome and allied with Hannibal. Even though Rome had emerged victorious, it was a costly time in lives and treasure for the Republic.

The steady rasping sound of the sharpening stone helped calm him as he slid it along the length of his gladius. His friends were keeping their minds busy by cleaning their equipment, sharpening their weapons, and otherwise preparing for battle.

Foligio was singing softly to himself off to one side and Marcellus was quiet for once, not boasting as was his custom. After they had eaten, their centurion gathered them together for a final briefing and ordered them to write letters home in case they fell in battle. They would leave the letters in the camp when they departed in the morning.

It was not long before the last horn sounded, signifying the end of the day. They put up their battle kit and turned in, anticipating a short night.

# Chapter Twenty-Eight

My lead scouts returned at a gallop. Breathlessly, they reported the presence of the Roman camp and I finally understood why I still had a lingering worry over the way Carbo and Epatus had acted.

I ordered the Taurisci guides brought to my tent immediately and sent for the hunnos. The guides were questioned and fearful for their lives, admitted the betrayal.

"This is an outrage!" Lugius roared as he pounded his fist on the table. "If this is how the Romans keep their word, we will show them what it means to betray us!"

We strategized well into the night and stayed encamped for another day to allow preparation for the coming battle and time for a proper sacrifice.

Skyld presided over a ceremony in an oak grove east of the village of Noreia. Our warriors gathered before a great bonfire and as they looked on, the two guides who had been tasked with leading us into an ambush were off to the side, hands bound behind their back and ankles tied together, kneeling on the ground beneath a large oak tree. Each wore a wreath of beech leaves and woven grass. On the ground beside each of the prisoners was a bronze cauldron. Ropes were tied around their necks and thrown over a thick branch.

Skyld, her shift hanging loosely on her scrawny frame, stiffly mounted the hastily built platform behind the prisoners. At her signal, a warrior heaved on the first prisoner's rope until his feet left the ground, kicking and spinning around, suspended in the air.

Turning the struggling man away from her, she reached from behind and slashed his throat; the blood spurting outward in a crimson circle as his body resumed spinning, the rope around his neck stretching the cut wide. The blood gradually slowed and ran down his body into the cauldron below. His spasms became weaker until his body finally hung limp at the end of the rope.

The other prisoner watched in horror, wide eyed and slack jawed, sobbing uncontrollably, his face and chest spattered with his companion's lifeblood. He would have collapsed flat on the ground but for the warrior at the opposite end of the rope, keeping his head up. When Skyld signaled, the warrior heaved on the rope and the second prisoner was hoisted. Suspended by the neck with his hands and feet bound, his struggles reminded me of how the eels wriggled when I picked them up the night I met Hrolf.

Skyld turned him toward her, looked deep into his terrified eyes, and slid the razor-sharp blade into his gut just above his belt, pulling it upward until it stopped at his breastbone. His entrails slithered wetly into the cauldron beneath him, another reminder of the eels. He tried to scream, but the rope only allowed a few choking gasps to pass his lips. After the second prisoner's shuddering death throes ended, the ropes were tied off to the tree, and they were left hanging, blood slowly dripping from their corpses.

Skyld looked down and observed the contents of each cauldron and when she lifted her gaze to the assembled warriors, she shouted in her toothless, loose lipped voice, "Wodan smiles on us this day! The signs portend a great victory over the treacherous Romans and their allies! Wodan points his spear, Gungnir, at our army. A sure sign he favors us in battle. Rejoice! Have confidence that tomorrow we will be invincible!" A great cheer rose from the grove with a thundering of spears beating on shields. The ceremony ended with the prisoners left spinning from their ropes as an offering to the gods.

# Chapter Twenty-Nine

The next morning, the legions marched out of their camp and took positions within the tree line on the hillside above the valley that the Germans were following. Carbo's plan was to allow the caravan to stretch itself out in the valley below and the legions would attack from the trees in their maniples against the enemy center. The Velites would launch their darts and retreat, followed by the Hastati throwing their javelins and then engaging in close quarters, supported by the Principes and Triarii.

Carbo's artillery hid in a small draw and would cut off reinforcement from the front of the caravan while his cavalry served the same purpose at the rear. His infantry legions would hit the center and each turn outward against the remaining enemy. The Taurisci warriors would descend from the opposite side of the valley to trap the caravan between the two forces.

He was convinced that his surprise attack would guarantee victory over the superior numbers of the barbarians.

Lucius could make out the tops of the trees across the valley as the sky slowly lightened. He knew the Taurisci concealed themselves in those trees, poised to attack the exposed caravan from the rear when they turned to face the legions. The usual sounds of the forest awakening were eerily silent, all the birds and animals aware of the men in their midst; except for an irritated red squirrel who kept busy scolding them and dropping pine nuts on the men below his tree. Soon the sun would be up, and the battle would be upon them. He shifted his weight from one foot to the other and nervously readjusted his grip on the darts as he waited for the rest of his legion to move into place. His palms were clammy, and a shiver

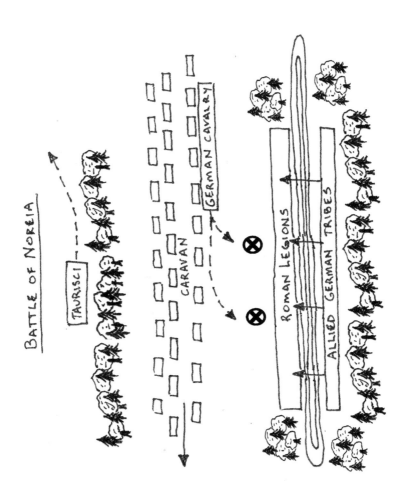

Figure 9.

ran through him as a trickle of sweat ran down the middle of his back. He looked to his left and right down the line of Velites, the youngest and least experienced soldiers in the legions, and acknowledged his tent mates with a nervous smile and a nod. Vulca returned the look with something as close to a smile as Lucius had ever seen the man give. The slight creaking of leather or a metallic clink were the only sounds that could be heard while they waited anxiously for the barbarians to appear.

Commanders passed word down the lines for the soldiers to make themselves ready as the rising sun slowly dissolved the white mist blanketing the valley. Shortly after sunrise, the lead riders of the Cimbri host could be seen making their way into the far end of the valley.

---

Across the valley, Epatus, the Taurisci chieftain, was also preparing his men for the attack. He knew better than the Romans the enemy they faced and had no illusions as to the difficulty of the coming battle. However, the Taurisci were descended from generations of warriors and had fought many battles in their own right. They also knew the reputation of the Romans, who were constantly at war. After defeating the Italian tribes, they moved on to the Gauls. Most recently they defeated the Arverni and Allobroges. Though they had suffered a defeat at the hands of the Scordisci and Cimbri in Macedonia, these Romans had a way of losing battles but winning wars. It had been less than fifty years since the Taurisci themselves had ceased fighting with Rome and become allies.

Epatus realized that their world was changing and if they planned to survive, alliances had to be made. He hoped their alliance with Rome would be enough to assure their survival.

---

Lucius wet his lips nervously and stared in growing fear at the huge caravan that filled the valley floor. There seemed to be no end as he looked down the length of it; mounted warriors, carts and wagons pulled by oxen, children and animals running in and about all of it.

"Something's not right," he whispered to himself. There seemed to be fewer warriors than expected. They were told the German's strength was their foot soldiers, but he only saw mounted warriors.

---

Judging what he thought to be the center of the line, Carbo raised his arm to give the signal to attack. His trumpeters took a breath in preparation, and the legions steeled themselves in anticipation of the fight to come.

Just as Carbo was about to initiate the ambush, a low, mournful sound drifted from the forest behind them that grew into a chaotic trumpeting that echoed between the trees. Carbo's head snapped toward his own horns, thinking they had anticipated his command before he realized it sounded nothing like the Roman horns. His officers and soldiers looked about with uncertainty as the sound of the horns faded. The realization of what was happening suddenly came when the sound of spears and swords clashing in unison on shields was heard. Then came a rhythmic crash . . . crash . . . crash, as the Germans moved up the back of the ridge.

In the valley below, the caravan had quickly formed into defensive formations, and an ominous rumble grew. The Cimbri had stretched leather tightly between the staves of their carts and created large drums which they now beat upon.

The terrifying sound of the barritus erupted from thousands of throats hidden behind the ridge top. It grew louder and louder until suddenly the forest exploded with the wild screams and howls of men, mingled with the sounds of a mass of warriors racing downhill toward the rear of the Roman formation.

Lucius turned toward the noise coming from behind, cold fear gripping his heart as he saw the first surge of warriors crest the ridgeline behind the Romans. There was a crash as shields and bodies met with a great impact.

The veteran Triarii, stationed in the rear of the legions, were quick to react to the unexpected attack from behind. They turned and faced uphill to meet their attackers even as the first wild-eyed warriors reached their lines. Veterans of many battles, they gave a good accounting of themselves but were doomed by an overwhelming number of barbarian warriors crashing into their lines and swarming in and around their maniples.

Lucius watched, unable to move, as he saw the barbarians overwhelm the Triarii. The Principes were now joining the battle, backed by the Hastati having overcome their initial shock at the turn of events. They were holding in sporadic clusters, but the downhill momentum of the Germans had allowed them to break through the lines and they were turning the flanks of the maniples. It was becoming a chaotic hand to hand battle that favored the Germans.

The Romans had broken up their normally close formations in order to hide in the forest. Now this worked against them, as they could not lock shields.

Several of the Principes commanders ordered volleys of pila, but these were ineffective due to the uphill angle and thick forest. Before they knew it, the Germans had decimated the Triarii and were among their ranks. Lucius and his companions now stood in what had been the front of the formation and watched wide-eyed as their older and more experienced comrades were falling to the furious onslaught. By attacking the rear of the legions, the Germans had reversed the order in which the Romans were accustomed to fighting and the veterans, who were the backbone of the legion, were destroyed before the eyes of the younger soldiers. The bile rose in Lucius' throat as panic's cold fingers gripped his heart.

Huge, half-naked warriors, deep in their battle fury, were laying death and destruction about them as they cut through the ranks.

The Roman cavalry turned and tried to attack uphill, but the thick forest prevented the massing and speed of horses and riders that made cavalry forces so deadly. Their counterattack broke up and was ineffective, allowing the Germans to deal with them individually.

The battle cries of the barbarians mingled with the screams of wounded and dying men and horses.

Lucius' head swam as time appeared to slow. When he looked to his left, he could see the cohort commander's mouth moving and his arm waving as he was shouting orders to advance uphill. Lucius could not hear him through the noise, and while he watched, a German spear took the centurion under his raised arm, piercing his chest above the armor.

The veteran Triarii and Principes were decimated and the men in the ranks of the Hastati, the last between Lucius and the barbarians, had given in to panic and thrown down their weapons and shields, racing downhill as fast as they could to get away from the snarling, howling barbarians that were hacking their way through the Roman ranks. In moments, the hysteria spread, and men everywhere were doing the same.

Lucius watched, frozen by fear, until Titus Romanus ran past him, nearly bowling him over trying to escape the carnage. Titus was wide eyed, running headlong down the slope, while looking over his shoulder in terror, his responsibility to the men of Lucius' contubernium forgotten. The collision woke Lucius from his trance and as he looked up, a huge warrior who had been pursuing Titus changed his focus to Lucius.

The warrior's face was twisted into an animal-like snarl, his long hair streaming behind him as he leapt over dead and wounded Romans, bearing down swiftly on his new victim.

Lucius took a terrified step back, away from the figure of death that was descending upon him. He tripped on a fallen branch at the base of a tree and fell backwards, landing hard on his backside. When he fell, his darts braced against the ground, and the warrior racing toward him could not stop or change direction, running himself upon the darts, two of them piercing his chest with such force they were driven all the way through his torso.

Lucius swatted his small shield desperately at the German's seax as it sought to skewer him, even as the warrior slowly died. The German hung in the air above Lucius for a moment, his arms hanging limply down, the seax falling from his nerveless fingers. Bloody spittle dripped from the barbarian's mouth in long strings, until he finally fell all the way on top of Lucius, knocking him momentarily senseless.

Lucius suddenly woke in terror, realizing his arm was being pulled and jerked, thinking there was another warrior trying to kill him. When his eyes focused, he saw it was a blood covered Vulca pulling him out from under the huge warrior.

"Come on! We've got to get out of here!" his friend spoke in almost a whisper. "They've gone through us and are pursuing the survivors into the valley."

Glancing around, Lucius suddenly became aware of where he was. He kicked the German off of him and jumped to his feet.

They were surrounded by the dead and dying of their legion, and Vulca shook him again, pulling him away. As they made their way across the battlefield, Lucius saw the bloodless faces of his friends, Porcius and Decius, both with horrendous wounds. There was no sign of the others.

# Chapter Thirty

I was the first to reach the Roman lines, followed closely by Hrolf and my companions, penetrating deep into their formation. The men behind me turned to the left and right, working the flanks of one century after another as we pressed the attack.

A spear was driven straight through one legionary and into another behind him by sheer momentum of the charge. Unable to recover his spear, the warrior drew his seax only to be gutted by a Roman before he could use it.

Skoll, followed by dozens of our war hounds, leaped among the Romans, wreaking havoc within their lines.

With the quick success in the center, more Cimbri broke through the Roman line and continued their advance.

I was lost in the glory of battle. No longer did I doubt myself; no longer did I fear the enemy; no longer did I doubt that we would win. My sister's prophecy gave me confidence, I knew we would be victorious, and I was a reaper of souls.

With my friends beside me, we laid waste to the Roman formations. Blood covered every part of our bodies, most of it from our enemies, some of it our own.

Lothar suffered a grievous wound, but the rest fought on, and the Romans fled from our fury.

# Chapter Thirty-One

When the German attack came from their rear, the Romans had turned and forgotten the caravan coming through the valley. Hundreds of panicked soldiers stumbled downhill and emerged from the tree line into the long grass of the valley. The German cavalry riding with the caravan met them at full gallop and were amongst them in seconds, impaling them on their spears and hacking at the unarmed men with their long swords and axes, slaughtering them by the hundreds.

On the opposite slope, Epatus watched as men began to emerge from the forested hillside in a panicked rout only to be run down by the enemy on horseback.

"That arrogant Roman has somehow lost the battle before it started," he muttered to himself.

Realizing the Romans were already defeated, he made an immediate decision to leave the battlefield with his army intact. Turning to his subordinates, he gave the order, and they slowly faded into the trees behind them.

---

Carbo lost control immediately and could only watch helplessly as the realization of what was happening overwhelmed his senses. He had miscalculated badly, and he knew there would be no recovering the victory he had so anticipated. The commander of his personal guard was pleading with him to leave the battlefield before the advancing Germans cut him off. Snapped back into reality when the commander grasped his shoulder, Carbo viciously whipped his horse around and made his way across the path of his retreating men, his personal guard forming up around him and clearing the way.

They came upon a wash that dropped out of sight of the main battle and they turned uphill, traveling with great haste until they could cross the ridge without being seen. They dropped down the opposite side of the ridge and rode away at breakneck speed.

---

As the battle raged on, the morning sky that had broken so bright and clear quickly darkened with heavy, wet clouds. A wind stirred the trees as the first large patters of rain fell through the treetops. From behind the ridge came the low rumbling of thunder and flashes of lightning. Within moments, a violent storm added its fury to the battle in a heavy wind and torrential downpour that drenched the combatants. The tops of the trees swayed in the high wind as branches fell amid the fighting and trees broke off midway up their trunks, killing and crippling men of both sides.

The warriors that had come over the ridgeline emerged from the forest into the valley, leaving scores of dead and dying Romans behind them, and the rest running before them. The mounted warriors that were with the caravan picked up the chase as the Romans broke into the open, running down hundreds more. Without warning, a lightning bolt struck the ground between the fleeing Romans and the German cavalry with a great flash and a deafening concussion, knocking several horsemen to the ground. With the wind and downpour limiting their vision and the threat of the lightning, the horsemen ended their pursuit of the fleeing Roman soldiers and returned to the caravan. The storm raged for another hour, by which time the surviving Romans had reached the safety of their castrum.

Those who had been left to defend the Roman camp, and those who made it back to the safety of its defenses, could only watch helplessly as the Germans picked over the battlefield. The mule handlers, quartermasters, bakers, and slaves armed themselves and manned the walls as they all waited fearfully for an attack that never came. Having won the battle, the Germans were content to treat their wounds and collect their dead.

---

When they had traveled far enough west to ensure their safety, Carbo's small band of fleeing horsemen turned southward and slowed their pace until they came upon a stream swollen by the sudden storm and too large for them to cross. Carbo called a halt and wearily dismounted. Having outdistanced the barbarians, his mind had been working furiously to understand what had happened. How could he explain the loss of two legions? His guards and the few of his staff who had escaped the slaughter quietly busied themselves with establishing a camp, leaving their consul to his thoughts.

Not far from the site of his defeated army, Carbo did not sleep, and morning brought a renewed urgency to get to safer ground. With the dawn, they mounted their horses and continued their flight back toward Aquileia.

They topped a saddle ridge between two large hills and came upon a small group of survivors making their way southwest on foot.

---

Lucius was overcome with relief when he saw that the horses they had heard coming in their direction were Roman and not barbarians who came to finish the job. He and Vulca, along with a few others, had spent a long, wet, and fearful night expecting at any moment to be discovered by the Germans, afraid to light a fire and not sure what to do next. All their leaders and veterans, save the party of senior officers that had just joined them, had been killed in the one-sided battle. All that were left of the over ten thousand troops were several hundred scattered, bedraggled young men.

Lucius had been cut badly along the side of his rib cage by the warrior he had killed, and Vulca helped him bind the wound and slow the bleeding, but he was weak, and the wound now pained him with every breath. He was so filled with fear, and covered in the German's blood, he had not even noticed it until they stopped to rest.

After pausing a few hours to allow more stragglers to be gathered up, Carbo struck up the march again. As they continued on, they came across groups of five or ten men, adding to their numbers throughout the day. They had lost everything on the battlefield, most of the men now unarmed. They had no food or water, and most were on foot. By the time the remains of the broken army limped through the gates at Aquileia three days after the battle of Noreia, they were starved and broken men.

# Chapter Thirty-Two

After the battle, I ordered the caravan to set up camp on the river plain to care for our dead and wounded and consolidate our victory. We had destroyed two legions, allowing only a few hundred to escape when the storm separated us. I left the castrum alone, as I had no desire to face the defensive weapons of the Romans, and there was no need for more killing. The Romans were soundly defeated, and the Taurisci were fleeing for home as if their hair were on fire.

Less than four hundred of our men were either seriously wounded or dead. The Roman dead numbered around eight thousand men, with many more wounded and dying. The two legions were destroyed along with their cavalry, artillery, and auxiliaries. A very successful triumph over the more heavily armored and trained Roman infantry. I grieved at the loss of Lothar, who had died from his wounds. He was the last of my father's companions and with him passed the generation of warriors that had been my mentors and my strength.

Though our new battle tactics were forgotten at the height of the battle, some had served us well. It was a base to build upon, and the clan leaders were aware of it as they each came to congratulate me on the victory.

Our young men wandered the battlefield, dispatching the enemy wounded as the ravens and vultures began their grisly dance with the dead.

Looking over the vast killing field, I was reminded of my flight with Wodan and of the raven goddess. My dream had become a reality.

The women and children were already scavenging the field for battlefield trophies: the armor, chain mail, helmets, and weapons of the defeated enemy; coins, silver rings and necklaces, and other valuables. The standards of both legions had fallen on the hillside, and we affixed them to the wagons that carried our gold. Their flags and other captured markers flew high from the staffs and spears of many of our warriors.

That night we held a celebration to mark our victory, and to indulge the priests and priestesses with a sacrifice to give thanks for our victory.

The heavy storm clouds had settled into a flat, iron-gray with a break just above the western treetops, enough for the setting sun to show through with brilliant orange, red, and purples lighting the edge of the evening sky.

In a ceremony borrowed from the Scordisci, several oak logs were sunk into the ground as a framework, and a wicker structure was affixed to them to create the shape of several gigantic men. A dozen or so Roman prisoners were encased inside each and tied to the oak logs. Piles of tinder and dried branches were placed around its base and stuffed inside the structure as the prisoners screamed and moaned, anticipating their fate.

As day became night, the people gathered near the wicker men to witness the prayers and incantations of the priests, giving thanks to the gods for this victory.

Eldrik was dressed in animal skins with a ram's skull covering his head. He carried a flat round drum, beating on it with a human shin bone as he scampered about, leaping and crouching, stamping the ground and screeching like a madman. He invoked Wodan and Donar and half a dozen other gods, thanking them for this victory and offering the lives of these prisoners in return. With a final flourish, he touched a torch to each of the pyres. The flames

swiftly climbed the wicker men as the cries of the prisoners became louder, screaming shrilly. Their vocal cords shredded as their
hair caught fire and their skin blistered and turned black. Slowly,
the screams fell silent, and all that could be heard was the roar and
crackle of the inferno that reached skyward. The smell of burning
flesh carried to the Roman camp, where the survivors watched in
horror as the extreme heat distorted the air. The towering flames
shone brilliant in the twilight, replacing the setting sun, the thick
black smoke rising toward the heavens in a windless evening sky.

# Chapter Thirty-Three

## Arpinum

## July 113 BC

A messenger galloped through the gate of the estate while Marius was going through his morning exercises. His horse slid to a halt on its hind legs as the rider pulled savagely back on the reins. He had ridden with all haste from Rome where Marius had hired and posted several such to keep him informed of current events. A slave appeared and took the lathered horse to the stables to be cared for, and another took the messenger away to rest when Marius took the dispatch into the house.

His face paled, then turned red with anger, and he cursed aloud as he read the dreaded words. His mother came into the room just as he struck out in anger and knocked a pitcher of water crashing to the floor, her hands going to her throat when it startled her.

In the familiar handwriting of his friend Gaius Lucilius was a brief message that he had feared all along:

*I am afraid, dear friend, that you were correct in your concerns about the ability of Consul Gnaeus Papirius Carbo to deal with the Germans in Noricum.*

*It has been reported this very day that Carbo was defeated by the Cimbri and their allies at a battle near Noreia. Most of two legions were lost and Carbo is as yet unaccounted for. He was last seen fleeing the battlefield, pursued by the Germans.*

*According to the Taurisci, Carbo met the leaders of the Cimbri alliance upon arriving in Noricum and secured their agreement to leave Noricum without*

297

*a fight. But then, apparently not satisfied with that, Carbo set an ambush for them along their route. He was set to attack the Cimbri by surprise, but, instead, they attacked first from his rear and wiped out most of the legions.*

*The only thing that saved the rest were the walls of their castrum and a freak storm that separated the two forces during the battle. The Germans broke off their pursuit and left the area.*

"I'm sorry for startling you, mother," he said. "A catastrophe has happened, and I must return to Rome immediately. I'm afraid our visit is over."

Fulcinia looked at him, concerned, a tear welling in each eye as she realized he could never have been happy to live the life of a country farmer, and would always return to the dangers of a soldier's life and the intrigues of the senate. Since he was a boy, she knew he was destined for greatness, and though he had excelled at everything he attempted, she knew he was far from finished.

"When will you leave?" she asked.

"As soon as I can gather some things and saddle a horse," Marius replied, calling for his guards to prepare to leave. "Please, have the rest of my things sent to my house in Rome as soon as you can."

# Chapter Thirty-Four

## Rome

## November 113 BC

The noise of the gathering crowd in the Comitium faded as the heavy doors of the Curia Hostilia swung shut. After the preliminary ceremonies were completed, Quaestor Marcus Antonius Orator opened the proceedings.

"We are here today to determine the guilt or innocence of Consul Gnaeus Papirius Carbo, and if he is found guilty, to determine his punishment. He stands charged with violating the imperium granted him by the Senate; provoking an avoidable conflict with the German barbarians known as the Cimbri that resulted in the complete destruction of two legions; of incompetent leadership; and of cowardice before the enemy.

"Less than a year ago, he was elected consul and charged with defending the borders of the Republic against the barbarians who invaded Noricum. This imperium was in response to the request for assistance from our ally, the Kingdom of Noricum, and specifically the Celtic tribe of the Taurisci, who had resisted the advance of these barbarians but could not stop them.

"The charges have been read and I now call Gnaeus Papirius Carbo to plead his guilt or innocence."

Carbo stood in the area reserved for the accused, his knees weak, his hands gripping the railing in front of him so hard his knuckles were white. He tried to lift his head but could not, his shame an insurmountable weight. His defense counsel spoke for him.

"Consul Gnaeus Papirius Carbo pleads innocent to the charges as read," Varus stated.

The quaestor sniffed with contempt and continued speaking.

"Enter the accused's plea into the record. We will begin by hearing the testimony of a witness to the charges read. The court recognizes Publius Cornelius Cethegus, quaestor to the defeated legions."

Cethegus swore to tell the assembly the truth and began his story.

"From the very beginning," said Cethegus, "the senior staff knew that the consul's imperium gave him the responsibility to reach a peaceful solution, if possible, with the invading tribes. At first it seemed as if he had succeeded in that effort. During the meeting with the tribal leaders, the consul received their concession to cease hostilities with the Taurisci and to immediately begin moving back across the Danubius. We were all aware of the enormous size of this gathering of tribes and the time that would be needed to get it moving in another direction.

"The consul, however, deliberately deceived the Germans and instead used that time to move to intercept them and set up an ambush. He even provided them with guides to be sure they were led directly into his trap. His stated intent was to permanently defeat the Germans and eliminate the threat they posed to Rome and her allies. A notable goal, to be sure, but unnecessary given their assurances.

"His ruse might have been successful, despite his defiance of the imperium, if he had heeded the advice of more experienced military commanders. However, he chose to believe in his own ill-conceived ideas to the exclusion of all others. He established an ambush in a mountain valley that did not take advantage of our strengths.

"The legions were concealed on a steep hillside among the trees. Just before the order for attack was given, we were ambushed from behind. Our disbursement among the trees meant we could not properly assume defensive formations, and the men were forced to fight as individuals, which as you know plays to the strengths of the barbarians.

"I do not need to explain to this house that the legion's strength is its ability to fight in its formations, infantry supported by artillery and cavalry. The melee that ensued prevented a coordinated defense. The cavalry could not see the battlefield clearly or form a counterattack due to the density of the forest. Our artillery was unable to fire for fear of killing our own men in close contact with the enemy. A deliberate attack by the Germans subsequently destroyed it. The consul's choice of terrain and tactic went completely against every principle of warfare that Rome has employed for over two hundred years.

"From the very start of the ambush, the consul never had control of the battle. The legions were on their own and there was no effort to coordinate a defense or counterattack. The consul was overwhelmed and out of his element. When it became apparent that the Germans had the numbers and the advantage, he took to flight, followed by most of his staff. The soldiers who saw their general fleeing the field dropped their weapons and ran, only to be slaughtered by the German horsemen attacking from the valley toward the trees.

"The Taurisci allies, who were the reserve force across the valley and were to attack on the consul's signal, saw what was happening, and never even entered the battle. They just rode away across the far ridgeline as the legions died.

"The surprise was so complete and the slaughter so great, you may ask how it is there were any survivors. It is only by divine intervention that anyone lived to tell the tale. At the beginning I was on the far left and out of sight of the consular staff. When the consul quit the field, I was the last senior officer left. I tried to form a defense and regain control, but it was a lost cause. The panic had set in, and our men were in flight for their lives. During the height of the battle an unexplained, sudden storm came upon us with terrible winds and hail and rain. Lightning struck the trees and the ground between the fleeing legions racing for the safety of the camp and the pursuing Germans.

"The storm separated the two forces and was likely perceived by the Germans as a message from their gods to cease the battle. I saw it as a bolt from Jupiter that saved what was left of our army. Whatever the reason, the Germans broke off and left us on our flight to the castrum. At first, I assumed the consul had fallen until a messenger made his way to me and I heard of his panicked flight. Later I learned of his hasty return to Rome in an effort to hide his own disgrace.

"I assumed command and consolidated the few clusters of soldiers left on the field that had survived intact. We gathered as many wounded as possible and made our way to the camp where we treated the wounded, sent out details to bury the dead, and prepared to march back to Aquileia. I immediately dispatched riders to Rome to inform this house of the disaster."

There was no shortage of witnesses presented to the impeachment court and for several hours the senate heard of Carbo's incompetence and cowardice. Carbo's case was sealed tighter and tighter with each one who spoke. His defense was nearly non-existent, and he was barely able to speak on his own behalf. It was obvious he had already accepted his fate. Finally, it was time for the prosecutor to present his closing argument.

"It is clear," he began in a quiet voice, "what transpired at the battle of Noreia and the disaster of that inglorious day."

His voice rose in volume as he went on.

"The mindset of Gnaeus Papirius Carbo has been proven, and the results of his selfish actions has placed Rome and her allies in a position of vulnerability. He defied his imperium and squandered an opportunity to prevent this disastrous conflict."

His voice rose in force and volume as he concluded.

"He has proven to be an incompetent coward, and I put it to this court of impeachment for a decision. You must find Consul Gnaeus Papirius Carbo guilty of all charges and punish him with the harshest sentence available in our law."

---

The heavy doors of the Curia Hostilia opened to the crowd that filled the Forum. A centurion appeared, followed by a contubernium of legionaries escorting the former consul. The crowd parted at the commands of the centurion leading the way as Carbo stared at the ground, his shoulders stooped, defeated.

Marcus Antonius Orator meticulously arranged his toga before climbing the steps of the Rostra. At his appearance, the din faded, and faces lifted expectantly toward him. In the strong, baritone voice that earned him his cognomen, he began.

"Citizens of Rome! Today the Senate has found Consul Gnaeus Papirius Carbo guilty of the charges of defying his imperium as decreed by the Senate; of provoking a conflict with the Cimbri that resulted in the complete destruction of two legions; of incompetent leadership during a time of war; and of cowardice before the enemy.

"It is decreed that as a result of the shame Gnaeus Papirius Carbo has brought to Rome and upon his family, and in accordance with deportatio, he is stripped of his citizenship.

"His estates and property shall be confiscated by the state, and he shall forever be exiled from Rome."

---

Gnaeus Papirius Carbo, impeached consul of Rome, sat with his elbows on the table, his forehead resting in his clasped hands, staring at a white vapor rising from the cup of pure vitriol.

The soldiers waiting for him certainly did not pity him, if anything they hated him. Hated him for being born rich; being born a patrician. Hated him for his incompetence. They hated him for leaving Rome vulnerable, and for leading his legions to an untimely death. Most of all, they hated him for his cowardice in running from the battlefield and deserting his men, their brothers.

If it were up to them, they would have been happy to strip him naked and send him away with absolutely nothing. Or better, stick a knife in his gut and slit his throat and throw his worthless body into the Flavus river. But it was not up to them. They were soldiers. Soldiers followed orders. They were simply executing the orders of the court by taking him back to his home and allowing him to pack a few bags of belongings and supplies and then escort him and his family to the outskirts of Rome, to be exiled forever. They cared nothing for him; he meant less than nothing to them. Just a few months ago, he was one of the most powerful men in Rome. Now he was their prisoner, with no value whatsoever.

His wife and children were weeping in the next room, having been told the terrible news. He had risked everything to restore his family name and instead had doomed them all. He knew that they too would be exiled no matter what he did, possibly even killed, but he could not bear to live with his shame. Had he acted before his conviction, as his brother did, he might have saved his family, but he did not have even that much courage. There would be no redemption. His family would forever have the stain of his brother's disgrace, and now, his own.

In his final act of cowardice, he swept the cup to his lips, threw his head back and swallowed the entire contents. His lips, gums, and tongue burned as the caustic liquid flowed down his throat and into his stomach. An unbearable heat seared his guts as the acid reacted with the moisture in his body, slowly burning through his esophagus and stomach walls. A spasm threw him sideways off the chair, jarring the small table and spilling the larger container of remaining acid over himself. He twisted in agony on the floor, gasping for air, the pain slowly fading as a final darkness closed in.

# Epilogue

Once again, Njoror's curse was forced upon us. We had been refused by Carbo and then betrayed by him. According to my sister's prophecy, our only hope for survival was to continue searching.

Standing on a rock outcropping above the river valley, I was reminded of the day we left Borremose, when my father and I stood on a hill much like this one, watching our people leave their homeland.

The great caravan was now more than twice the size of that original band of miserable refugees who had lost everything. Now among us walked bands of Teutones, Boii, Marcomanni, Quadi, and even some Scordisci, as well as many small groups and individuals of lesser tribes.

Many of our warriors were now armed with iron-tipped spears and carried swords of Noric steel. Though most still wore the animal skins and rough woven clothing of our past, many wore helmets and chain mail taken from the Romans and Celts we had fought, and we proudly displayed the symbols of our defeated enemies.

The caravan was on the move once again, stretching for miles, truly a sight to behold. We had wagon loads of gold and silver, and other booty taken from the Taurisci and the Romans. Our carts were full of food plundered from Noricum, and our herds were healthy and fat. We were far from the people who left Cimberland with little hope for the future. We had learned to survive in the wilderness, and we had regained our strength and our pride. Though the curse of Njoror meant we must never stop for long, our people now marched with their heads high.

In time, we would return, and we would try again. For now, we would leave Rome in peace. And they had our gods to thank for that.

# Historical Notes

The Roman Warm Period was a time of global warming that was active during the 2nd century BC and may have contributed to the rising sea levels and increased precipitation of rain and snow during this time period. These changing climatic conditions would have had an adverse effect on agriculture and other food sources and may have contributed to the mass migrations and other cultural conflict recorded during this era.

Geological evidence of layers of sand and gravel between layers of peat in Denmark, Scotland, and areas surrounding the North Sea, indicates a sudden unexplained rise in sea levels near the end of the 2nd century BC. While the great flood in Borr's story is fabricated, a tsunami caused by an underwater earthquake, volcanic eruption, or landslide could be an explanation for this evidence. A cataclysmic event such as this could have precipitated an evacuation of lowland communities such as where the Cimbri and their allies lived. Coupled with over-population, the changing weather conditions of the time, and dwindling food supplies, I believe it is a plausible explanation for their migration. In fact, in 2015 the University of Caen Lower Normandy, the Geological Survey of Denmark and Greenland, and the University of Copenhagen published a study in the scientific journal Geology that provided physical evidence of tsunamis reaching as far south as the west coast of Denmark over eight thousand years ago, when a large piece of seabed slipped off the continental shelf west of Norway. This event is known as the Storegga Slide. There are many recorded events of sudden catastrophic flooding on the Denmark peninsula and surrounding areas including the St Marcellus's flood of January 16, 1362 which took the lives of more than 25,000 people.

Rediscovered in 1929, the village of Borremose was one of several Iron-Age fortresses in Denmark abandoned in the 2nd century BC. Its description in this story is accurate based on archaeological evidence.

The Gundestrup Cauldron was found in a peat bog near Borremose in Denmark in 1891. Archeologists believe it was manufactured by Thracian silversmiths. It was likely deposited in the bog as part of a sacrifice. There are many bog bodies found in Denmark showing examples of ritual sacrifice like those described in the story.

Modern and ancient scholars are divided on whether the Cimbri and Teutones were Celts or Germans. Some say that they may have been immigrants from the Celtic regions of eastern Europe and part of the armies of Brennus. Many believe that they practiced religious and cultural habits of both Germans and Celts.

Ancient scholars recorded that the Teutones and Ambrones joined the Cimbri on this great migration as well as smaller whole tribes and many individual members or small groups from other Germanic and Celtic tribes.

Rome had contact with many places around the world at this time, including India and Africa, from where they imported spices, silk, fruit, grain, and exotic animals via well-traveled sea routes. It would not have been uncommon to see people of many different races and cultures at any given location.

The Amber Road was an ancient trade route that existed centuries before the Cimbri began their journey. It was a well-known route through the continent at the time. The large oppidum at Posonium was built upon the plateau now occupied by the Bratislava Castle, near where a branch of the Amber Road crossed the Danube River. Goods from all over the known world traveled to and from Rome through this important trade center.

Greek historian Plutarch wrote this about Gaius Marius: "For when he was only a boy and was still living in the country, he had caught in his cloak an eagle's nest, with seven eaglets in it, as it was falling; his parents had been amazed at the sight and had consulted the prophets; and the prophets had declared that he would be the greatest man in the world and was fated seven times to hold the supreme power and authority."

Greek historian Appian wrote that the Cimbri, among other tribes, suffered a series of devastating plagues sometime after their failed invasion of Greece and their later journey to the Pyrenees mountains. I chose smallpox as the disease but there is no way of knowing its true nature. I also chose anthrax, a common disease of the time, to motivate the Teutones to join their allies.

Regarding the Wicker Man: Greek geographer Strabo wrote "... having devised a colossus of straw and wood, throw into the colossus cattle and wild animals of all sorts and human beings, and then make a burnt-offering of the whole thing." Julius Caesar wrote "Some of them build immense effigies with limbs woven from wickerwork, and they fill these with living persons. A fire is then lit underneath, and the people inside are overwhelmed by the flames and die."

A memorial stone discovered near Thessalonica stated that Sextus Pompeius was slain fighting against the Scordisci near Stobi in 118 BC. He was possibly the grandfather of the Triumvirate Pompey the Great.

The battle of Noreia took place in Noricum, southern Austria, near modern Klagenfurt. We know that Carbo refused the Cimbri and ambushed them as they turned back toward Germania. Ancient historians tell us of a great thunderstorm that separated the combatants and ended the battle. It was the only thing that saved the Romans from complete annihilation. It remains a mystery why the Cimbri and their allies repeatedly turned away from the rich and fertile Roman valleys that were laid open time and again by their victories over the Romans.

The Romans knew Boiorix as the king of the Cimbri. Other than his name, and his later battles with Rome, little is found in the historical record. His name is spelled in several different ways: Boiorix, Boriorix, Boirix. The suffix "rix" means king or chieftain. Since the story begins when Boiorix is a boy, he obviously was not a king or chieftain yet. So, I invented the name Borr, which was the name of Wodan's father, the creator god Bor, or Borr, depending on the source.

Gnaeus Papirius Carbo was impeached and exiled for his failure to stop the Cimbri and for the loss of two legions. Rather than suffer the shame of his sentence, he took his own life by suicide with poison.

# Glossary

## MAJOR TRIBES/NATIONS

ALLOBROGES – A Gallic tribe dwelling in the area today known as France defeated by Domitius Ahenobarbus and Fabius Maximus in 121 BC.

AMBRONES – A Germanic tribe whose homeland is unknown but suspected to have been south and west of Jutland. They joined the Cimbri and Teutones years after their journey began.

ARVERNI – A Gallic tribe dwelling in the area today known as France defeated by Domitius Ahenobarbus and Fabius Maximus in 121 BC.

BOII – A Gallic tribe in Cisalpine Gaul centered around modern-day Czech Republic, Bavaria, and Bohemia. Shortly after the time of this story they moved northward as far as Poland.

CELTS – The Celts migrated into the areas of central and western Europe in pre-Roman times and the term is generally interchangeable with Gauls.

CIMBRI – An ancient Germanic tribe originating in Jutland, today's Denmark. They were possibly of Celtic descent and combined traits of both cultures. For unknown reasons, the Cimbri nation migrated throughout Europe coming into contact with Rome in the second century BC.

ERAVASCI – A Celtic people who lived near modern-day Budapest in the late second century BC.

GAULS – In the second century BC, the area today known as

France was known as Gaul and the tribes from that area generally referred to as Gauls, though they referred to themselves as Celts.

GERMANS – The area north of the Danube River and east of the Rhein River was referred to by the Romans as Germania and the tribes from that area as Germans.

LANGOBARDS – A Germanic tribe living on the eastern bank of the lower Elbe River during the second century BC.

MARCOMANNI – A Germanic tribe dwelling along the Elbe River in the second century BC.

SCORDISCI – A Celtic tribe living in what is now Serbia, Croatia, Bulgaria, and Romania. They successfully resisted Roman incursions for decades.

SEMNONES – A Germanic tribe dwelling along the Elbe River in the second century BC.

TAURISCI – A Celtic tribe that came down from the Alps mountains. They warred with Rome for several years which ended in their status of "Friend and ally of the Roman people".

TEUTONES – A Germanic tribe living south and east of Jutland among the sea islands and rocky shores of the Baltic Sea. They joined the Cimbri on their epic journey throughout the known world.


# IMPORTANT PLACE NAMES

AK-INK – Established by the Celtic Eravisci, it is located at today's Budapest, Hungary on the west side of the Danube River and is famous for its natural hot springs.

AQUILEIA – An ancient Roman frontier city founded in the early second century BC. North of today's Venice.

ARPINUM – Gaius Marius' birthplace in the Roman state of Latium.

BAETICA – Roman province in today's southern Spain.

BOIOHAEMUM – Latin name for the homeland of the Boii people.

BORREMOSE – Iron age fortress located in present day Denmark near the village of Aars.

CARTHAGE – Ancient capital of the Carthaginians. One of the most important trading hubs in the ancient world and hereditary enemy of Rome.

CASTRA PIACENZA – Roman fort and city in northern Italy on the Po River.

GALLIA TRANSALPINA/GALLIA/GAUL – The area of Gaul north of the Alps mountains. Today's Switzerland and southern France.

HERACLEA SINTICA – Fortress in Thrace used as a base of operations for Rome's invasion of the region.

HERCYNIAN FOREST – An ancient forest that stretched from the Rhine River across southern Germany into the Carpathian Mountains and formed the northern boundary of the area known to Rome at the time.

HISPANIA – Today's Spain and Portugal.

JUTLAND/CIMBERLAND/CIMBRIAN CHERSONESE – Present day Denmark and the German state of Schleswig-Holstein

LEUPHANA – Mentioned by Ptolemy and believed to be located along the Elbe, between Hamburg and Berlin.

LUSITANA – Roman province in second century BC corresponding to present day Portugal.

LYNGSMOSE- Iron age fortress located in present day Denmark.

NOREIA – The capitol city of Noricum and the Taurisci people near Klagenfurt in today's Austrian Alps.

NORICUM – Celtic kingdom located in modern-day Austria and Slovenia.

NUMANTIA – An ancient Celtiberian town in Spain near the modern city of Soria.

NUMIDIA – An ancient kingdom located across much of North Africa.

PANNONIA – An area encompassing parts of modern-day Hungary, Austria, Slovenia, Croatia, and Serbia.

POSONIUM – Modern day Bratislava, Hungary. A Celtic oppidum on a hill high above the Danube River.

SINGIDUNUM – Fortress of the Scordisci that is now the city of Belgrade, Serbia, near the confluence of the Sava and Danube rivers.

SISCIA – Celtic oppidum southeast of modern-day Zagreb, Croatia. Located on the Sava River

STOBI – A city in the contested area of Macedonia that was fought over by the Scordisci and the Romans in the second century BC.

TEUTOBERGIUM – An ancient settlement at modern-day Dalj, Croatia where the Drava River meets the Danube, believed to be founded by the Teutones.

THRACE – An undefined region north and east of Macedonia in the southern Balkans.

TREVA – Mentioned by Ptolemy and believed to be located near present day Hamburg, Germany along the Elbe River.

ZAVIST – A large oppidum of the Boii south of Prague, Czech Republic, on the Vltava River.

# ROADS, RIVERS, and SEAS

AMBER ROAD – An ancient trade route that led from the northern seas to the Mediterranean. Precious amber as well as many other trade goods traversed the continent from north to south for centuries.

VIA AEMILIA – A Roman road from Ariminum on the Adriatic coast to Piacenza on the river Po. Completed in 187 BC.

VIA FLAMINIA – Constructed by Gaius Flaminius in 220 BC. It ran northward from Rome across the Apennine Mountains to the east coast of Italy ending at Ariminum.

VIA POSTUMIA – A Roman road running from Genoa to Aquileia through Piacenza, along the river Po. Completed in 148 BC.


ALBIS RIVER – From the Czech Republic through Germany to the North Sea, the Elbe is one of the largest rivers in Europe.

ALSTER RIVER – A tributary of the Elbe that joins the larger river at Hamburg, Germany.

AXIUS RIVER – The Vardar River is the longest river in Macedonia.

CALAPIUS/COLAPIS RIVER – The Kupa River is a tributary of the Sava River and is a partial border between Croatia and Slovenia.

DANUBIUS RIVER – The Danube River is the second longest river in all of Europe rising in the Black Forest of Germany and traveling to the Black Sea. It stood as the frontier of Rome for centuries.

DRAVUS RIVER – Tributary of the Danube that leads from Dalj, Croatia, into Austria.

FLAVUS RIVER – The Tiber River is where Rome sits today.

ISARA RIVER – Located in north central France.

MARUS RIVER – Latin name of the Morava River, a tributary of the Danube that runs between Slovakia and Austria.

PADUS RIVER – The river Po in northern Italy.

RHODANUS RIVER – The Rhone River of Switzerland and France.

SAVUS RIVER – The Sava River joins the Danube at Belgrade, Serbia.

STRUMA RIVER – A river in modern day Bulgaria, part of the border between Thrace and Macedonia in the second century BC.

SUEVUS RIVER – The Oder River forms the border between Poland and Germany and was the eastern border of the Teutones.

VLTAVUS RIVER – A tributary of the Danube River that runs southward throughout the Czech Republic.


MARE SUEBICUM – Roman name for the Baltic Sea.

MARE NOSTRUM – Today's Mediterranean Sea.

OCEANUS GERMANICUS – The North Sea.

# GODS/RELIGION/MYTHS

AUGURIES – The art of divining events of the future by interpreting omens.

Believed to control the fates of men, or at least to foresee their fate.

BOG BODIES – Many bog bodies have been found in today's Denmark amazingly preserved by the acidic water. Most were victims of violent death and sacrifice.

CAPITOLINE TRIAD – The trio of supreme gods in Roman mythology; Jupiter, his wife Juno and their daughter Minerva.

CERUNNOS – Gaelic god of beasts and wild places.

DONAR – The Germanic thunder god, later known as Thor

DRAUGAR – An undead creature, usually the soul of a long dead king or great warrior.

ELYSIUM – In Greek and Roman mythology, the fields of paradise where the dead went to live forever among the gods.

ERCINEE – A mythological bird found in the Hercynian forest. Its feathers were said to glow at night.

FREYA – Wife of Wodan and mother of Donar. Goddess of family, love, life, and fertility. Frija, Freyja, and numerous other spellings.

GUNGNIR – Wodan's magical spear created by the dwarves.

HEL – Goddess who rules the land of the dead.

JUNO – Wife and sister of Jupiter, goddess of marriage and childbirth.

JUPITER – King of the Roman gods, god of the sky and thunder. Equivalent to Zeus in Greek mythology.

LOKKE – Early Germanic version of the Norse god Loki.

MINERVA – Daughter of Jupiter, goddess of wisdom and knowledge.

MODRANICHT – "Night of the Mothers" celebrated on what is now Christmas eve.

NEHALANNIA – Goddess of seafarers.

NERTHUS – Germanic goddess associated with peace and prosperity.

NJOROR – God of the sea and father of Freya

SAMHAIN – Pagan festival to mark the end of the harvest season and to usher in the dark half of the year.

SHIP SACRIFICE – Iron age sacrifice to the gods. Weapons and armor were thrown into a ship which was then buried in a bog or sunk into a lake.

SKADI – Germanic goddess/giantess associated with hunting, winter, and mountains. Married the sea god Njoror who she later left to marry the sky god Wodan.

SKOLL – Borr named his wolf Skoll after the warg Skoll that chases the sun through the sky each day.

SLEIPNIR – Wodan's eight-legged steed.

SOL – In both Germanic and Roman mythology, the god/goddess of the sun.

SPRING BRIDE – The spring bride represented the goddess Nerthus and welcomed spring each year by accepting the prayers and gifts of the people and blessing the tribe's cattle.

STANDING STONES – Neolithic monuments used for social and religious practices in the ancient world.

SYBILLINE BOOKS – A collection of prophecies consulted during times of crisis. The last Roman king, Tarquinius, purchased them and placed them in the Temple of Jupiter Optimus Maximus for safekeeping.

TANNGRISNIR and TANNGNJOSTR – The magical goats that pull the chariot of Donar/Thor. Later Norse legend tells that Thor would slaughter the goats for his own sustenance, then resurrect them using his magical hammer, Mjolnir.

TEMPLE OF JUPITER OPTIMUS MAXIMUS – Ancient Roman temple on the Capitoline Hill dedicated to the Roman king of the gods.

THREE MATRONS – Also referred to as the fates, common in many continental religions.

VALHOLL – Wodan's mead hall where he receives the souls of his warriors. Later known as Valhalla.

WARG – A mythological family of wolves including Fenrir and his children Skoll and Hati.

WICKER MAN – Ancient Roman historian and author Florus documented human sacrifice of prisoners of war by the Scordisci by burning. Strabo and Julius Caesar document the wicker man as a Druidic sacrifice.

WILD HUNT – A north European myth of the god Wodan and other gods conducting a hunt across the winter sky.

WODAN – An ancient Germanic god of war and king of the gods. Later known as Woden, Wotan and Odin.

YULE – Pagan Germanic holiday of the winter solstice, marking the beginning of the new year.

# GENERAL

ACTUARII – An official charged with the distribution of wages and provisions to the Roman military.

ADHERABAL – Son of Micipsa and grandson of Masinissa. He was a king of Numidia between 118 and 112 BC.

AENEATORS – A Roman soldier who was attached to a military unit as a horn player.

ALE – A type of beer brewed in ancient Europe.

ALPES MOUNTAINS – The Alps Mountains in central Europe.

APPENINUS MOUNTAINS – The Apennines Mountains in Italy.

AQUA APPIA – The first Roman aqueduct constructed in 312 BC.

ARIMINUM – Roman city on the Adriatic coast.

ARMICUSTOS – A Roman soldier tasked with the administration and supply of weapons and equipment.

AUXILLIARY – Non-Roman citizens attached to the army as cavalry and other special troops.


BARRITUS – Battle cry of the ancient Germans and Celts.

BATTLE OF NOREIA – Battle between the Cimbri and Roman Consul Gnaeus Papirius Carbo in 113 BC, near modern day Klagenfurt, Austria.

BRENNUS – Celtic chieftain who led his people on a plundering expedition throughout Greece and Macedonia in the third century BC.

BOAR'S HEAD – A wedge shaped military formation used by the Germanic and Celtic people.

BUCCINA HORNS – A bronze horn used by the Roman army.

BURIAL MOUNDS – Ancient European cultures buried their heroes, kings and other important people in large tombs of rock covered with earth called tumulus mounds.

CALONES – Slaves that were owned by the Roman state and served in support of the military.

CALTROPS – Iron spikes used to deter infantry and cavalry troops by injuring their feet.

CAMPUS MARTIUS – A military exercise ground outside the walls of Rome in second century BC. Later drained and covered with large public buildings.

CAPITOLINE HILL – One of the seven hills of Rome, site of the temple of Jupiter Capitoline.

CARNI – A Gaulish tribe living in the Carnic Alps in the second century BC when they moved into the Venetti Plain and founded the city of Akileja (Aquileia).

CARNYX – A bronze trumpet used by the Iron Age Celts and Germans. The bell was usually styled as an open-mouthed boar or other animal.

CASTRUM – Roman military camp/fort.

CAVALRY ALA – Roman cavalry unit of 500 – 1000 riders

CAVALRY TURMA – Roman cavalry unit of 30 riders

CENTURION – Roman officer. Commander of a century, about 100 men.

CHERUSCI – A Germanic tribe living in northwestern Germany in the second century BC.

CIRCUS MAXIMUS – A chariot-racing stadium in ancient Rome.

CIRTA – Capitol city of Numidia, known today as Constantine, Algeria.

COGNOMEN – A sort of nickname given to ancient Roman citizens that could have been passed from father to son or earned through military or other notable service.

COMITIUM – An area in the Roman Forum where the government communicated with the people.

CONSUL – The highest elected official of the Roman Republic.

CONTUBERNIUM – The smallest organized unit of soldiers in the Roman Army. Composed of eight soldiers.

CURIA HOSTILIA – The Senate house of ancient Rome.

CURSUS HONORUM – The succession of political offices required for a Roman of senatorial rank seeking advancement.

CURULE CHAIR – The official chair used by Rome's highest magistrates.

CURULE MAGISTRATE – Executive officer of the Roman state.


DALMATAE – A group of Illyrian tribes living in today's Croatia and Bosnia/Herzegovina.

DALMATIA – The region lived in by the Damatae during the second century BC.

DECANUS – The leader of a squad of eight men, or contubernium, in the Roman army.

DECURION – A Roman cavalry officer in command of a turma, or squadron, of 10 mounted men.

DELPHI – The ancient site of the oracle of Delphi. Located near modern day Greece.

DEPORTATIO – Banishment from Rome that also included confiscation of property and loss of citizenship.

EQUESTRIAN – The equestrian order of ancient Rome was a middle class of citizens who ranked just below the senatorial class. Often served as the Roman cavalry during the late Roman republic.

FALCATA – A style of sword used by the Celt-Iberians of Hispania, modern Spain.

FORTNIGHT – A period of time of fourteen days.

FORUM/FORUM ROMANUM – A plaza at the center of ancient Rome that functioned as a marketplace and gathering site for various civic activities.

FRIEND AND ALLY OF THE ROMAN PEOPLE – A status that Rome used to incorporate former enemies or belligerent tribes into the republic, and later the empire, by recognizing their sovereignty and providing defense, while requiring them to pay taxes and be subservient to the Roman senate.

GLADIUS – Sword of the Roman legions.

GRAECIA – The ancient area of, as opposed to the modern nation of, Greece.

HADES – Referred to by both Roman and Greeks as "the place of the dead", or Hell.

HASTAE VELITARES – A thirty-inch wooden throwing dart employed by Velites, the front-line skirmishers used in the republican Roman legions.

HASTATI – Roman legionaries who made up the front rank of the republican manipular legions once the Velites had launched their darts. Usually fought as spearmen.

HELLENES – Name for the Greek people of ancient history.

HIEMPSAL – Son of Micipsa the king of Numidia. He was assassinated by his adoptive brother Jugurtha in his efforts to consolidate power.

HISPANIA ULTERIOR – An ancient region that encompassed modern day Portugal and part of southern Spain.

HUNNO – The leader of a Germanic clan or tribe that lived in a village or series of villages that made up a district. Also, the military leader of his district, responsible for raising his "hundred" in times of war. The "hundred" was a term used to denote the military unit formed from the Hunno's clan and stems from the fact that it was generally around one hundred warriors that made up the "hundred".

IBERIA – The peninsula that encompasses today's Spain and Portugal.

IBERIANS – The Celtic people who lived on the Iberian Peninsula.

ILLYRIA – A region of the Balkans directly across the Adriatic Sea from Italy.

IMPERIUM – A form of authority granted by the Roman Senate

that provided the scope of a general's power as well as his military mission, such as removing the German tribes from Noricum.

INDIA – Ancient Rome not only knew of India but had a lucrative trade arrangement with them. Cane sugar and popular spices such as pepper, cinnamon, ginger, turmeric, and many other items were exchanged for Roman gold and goods.

JUGURTHA – Adopted son of Micsipa, the king of Numidia. Jugurtha killed both of his adopted brothers to seize the throne, and in the process became an enemy of Rome. Jugurtha was defeated by Gaius Marius and eventually killed. He was familiar with Marius from having served together under Scipio Africanus in Numantia.

LOOM – A device used to weave fibers into fabric to create clothing and linens of all kinds. Looms could be large and heavy, or made so that they could be disassembled and transported.

LAAGER – A circular formation of wagons used by caravans on the march. A laager was more defendable than a column and provided security while at rest.

LATIUM – The land on which the Italian tribe of Latins lived, before the city of Rome was founded. It later became known as Latium and was extended further to the south along the left bank of the Tiber River.

LECTUS – In ancient Rome the lectus was used for eating in a reclined posture, sitting, or sleeping. It was a couch of sorts, built with a wooden frame and leather straps that supported a mattress stuffed with straw.

LEGION – In the Roman republic the legion consisted of 4,200 infantrymen broken down into ten cohorts and 300 cavalrymen broken down into ten turma. Each infantry cohort consisted of four maniples which were further broken down into two centuries, each divided into ten contubernia. At this time the four maniples were organized one as Velites, one as Hastatii, one as Principes, and one as Triarii.

LEVY – A form of the "draft" used in ancient Rome to raise troops for the legion. When a new legion needed to be formed, the Senate would authorize a levy to raise the troops required to fill it. Also used to identify a new soldier in the legion, and as a verb as in: The senate levied the troops needed.

LICTORS – An officer or bodyguard that accompanied Roman magistrates. They bore a bundle of rods bound around an axe. They had the authority to beat or even execute offenders that interfered with or offended the magistrate they served.

LIMFJORD – A shallow fjord in the north of Denmark that nearly cuts off the northern tip of the Jutland peninsula. In 18 the western end of the fjord broke through to the North Sea.

LUR – A long, curved, bronze trumpet used during the bronze and iron age by Celtic peoples throughout Europe and Central Asia.

MACEDONIA – Became a Roman province in 146 BC. Rome fought with the Celtic Scordisci and other tribes in the area for control of the mountainous interior for centuries. Corresponds roughly to modern day Macedonia.

MANIPLE – A Roman military unit of 120 men during the late republic. There were four maniples in a legion.

MEAD – An alcoholic drink made by fermenting honey with water, and sometimes adding various flavors by using spices, fruits, or other.

MEDICUS – A physician or combat medic in the Roman army.

MILITARY TRIBUNE – An officer in the Roman army who ranked between the centurion and the legate. Usually the first step on the cursus honorem.

MISSIO CAUSARIA – Medical discharge out of the Roman army.

NOVUS HOMO – Latin for "new man". The term used for the first in a family to serve as a senator or elected consul. Sometimes used by the patricians and old families as a derogatory term for someone up and coming.

NUBIA – A region along the Nile River in Africa, the former kingdom of Kush.

OATHRING – A ring of metal; it could be bronze, iron, or even gold and it could be a finger, wrist or arm ring. Because it is sacred to the users, when an oath is sworn upon it, it becomes an unbreakable promise. Used in ancient Egypt, Greece, and Rome, as well as Germanic and Celtic cultures and carried forward through the centuries into Christianity, symbolized by the wedding ring.

OPPIDUM – A fortified settlement in central Europe during the Iron Age. They were built as far apart as Spain and the Hungarian plain. Hundreds were built during the second and first centuries BC.

OPTIOS – The second in command of a Roman army unit, compares to today's executive officer.

PAEONIA – An undefined region roughly corresponding to Northern Macedonia today.

PALATINE HILL – In legend, the earliest center of Rome. It became a place for the privileged and important to have their luxurious homes and religious temples.

PANNONIA – An undefined area north and east of the Danube. Roughly corresponds to parts of present-day Hungary, Austria, Croatia, Serbia, Slovenia, and Bosnia/Herzegovina.

PATRICIAN – A member of the aristocracy of ancient Rome.

PILUM/PILA – A javelin used by Roman soldiers.

PLEBIANS – Free Roman citizens that were not part of the aristocracy. The commoner.

PLEBIAN TRIBUNE – The tribune of the people was an election of a common citizen, who provided a check on the power of the Roman Senate and magistrates.

POPULARES – A political faction led by the Gracchi brothers during the late Roman Republic. They supported the agendas of reforming Rome's policies in favor of the plebeians, or common citizens.

PRAETOR – The commander of an army, or an elected magistrate.

PRIMUS PILUS – The senior centurion of the first cohort in a Roman legion.

PRINCIPES – Spearmen in the late republican army. Men in their late twenties and thirties. They were in their prime both physically and financially, and could afford better equipment. The fought in the second battle line between the Hastati and the Triarri.

PRINCIPIA – The legion headquarters in a Roman military camp.

PRINCIPS SENATUS – A prestigious office that was awarded to the most respected and capable of Roman senators.

PYRE – A funeral pyre is a structure made of wood filled with combustible materials that were often soaked in oil. Used for cremation and religious observations.

QUADI – A smaller Germanic tribe living in the area of Moravia and western Slovakia.

RED FLAG – A red flag was raised over the Capitoline Hill in time of war. It signified the calling of new recruits to raise a legion.

ROMAN CALENDAR – The Kalends was the first day of the month. The Nones was the seventh day of March, May, July, and October, and the fifth of the other months. The Ides fell on the fifteenth day of March, May, July, and October, and on the thirteenth of the other months.

ROSTRA – A large platform near the Forum Romanum where speakers would stand and face the senate house to deliver orations to the assembled citizens of Rome.

SACRAMENTUM – The oath of loyalty to Rome that legionaries took when mustered into the military.

SALONA – Capital of the Roman province of Dalmatia. Today's Croatian town of Solin.

SCANDIA – Ancient name for the Scandinavian peninsula that includes present day Sweden and Norway.

SCORPION – A Roman field artillery piece that functioned like a large bow and arrow. It fired bolts as long as a man at high velocity.

SEAX – Usually associated with later centuries, the seax was a small sword, or large knife, also used by the Germanic peoples of the Migration Period.

SIGNIFERS – A standard bearer in a Roman legion.

SPQR STANDARD – An abbreviation for the "Senate and People of Rome". A symbol of not only the legion, or cohort that carried it, but also the citizens of Rome and its polices.

SWAIN – A young, eligible bachelor ready to begin the search for a wife.

TABERNA – A type of stall or shop, sometimes a street vendor, who usually sold alcoholic beverages and food.

TALENT – An ancient measurement of weight equivalent to either 75 or 100 pounds.

TESTUDO – A Roman military formation where soldiers used their shields to form a tortoise-shell-like protection against the enemy. Especially effective against thrown weapons.

THRALL – A slave, captive, or servant.

THUNDERSNOW – A rare weather phenomena in which thunder occurs during a snowstorm. It most recently occurred in Germany and Austria in 2021.

TOGA PRAETEXTA – A white toga with a broad purple stripe on the border worn by curule magistrates.

TOGA VIRILIS – A plain white toga, worn on formal occasions by adult make commoners, and by senators.

TORQUE – A large neck ring made of rigid metal. Symbolizes the strength and virility of the wearer. Usually awarded for bravery or special action.

TRIARII – The third line of troops in the manipular legions of the Roman republic. They were the veterans, the oldest and wealthiest men in the army and could afford the best equipment.

TRIUMPH – A huge public celebration to acknowledge the success of a military commander.

VELITES – The skirmishers in the Roman legions of the republic. They were light infantry and spearmen who carried thirty-inch wooden darts, a gladius, and a small shield. They rarely wore armor as they were the youngest and the poorest soldiers in the legion.

VELLUM – A prepared animal skin that was used for writing in the ancient world. It is scraped thin and manipulated until it is very pliable, then rolled and stored carefully to prevent rot.

VITRIOL – Basically sulfuric acid.

VITIS – A centurion's staff made from a grape vine about three feet long. Used for discipline in the Roman army.

JEFF HEIN

# A Word from the Author

DEAR READERS:

I am inviting you to join the tribe, and I am asking you for your help.

Thank you for reading my debut novel, "The Cimbri Appear", the first book in the historical fiction saga "The Cimbrian War".

"The Cimbrian War" has been a story that has existed only in my mind for more than twenty years. Over those years I collected source material; historical magazine articles, academic papers by modern scholars, writings by the ancient historians, books on Rome and the barbarian invasions, books on ancient Germans and Celts, and so much more. All of these things went into a large cardboard box labeled "Book Research" and was stored in my attic, with the intent of someday writing this story.

In the spring of 2020, during the height of the COVID-19 pandemic, I decided it was finally time to put these ideas on paper, and well, here we are.

I hope that I have done this story justice, and that I have created a world and a story that the reader finds as fascinating as I do.

Now, a word about creating a self-published book. Unlike being published in the traditional manner by a publishing company, the entire process is on the shoulders of the self-published author. All the costs of publishing are paid up front. Editing, formatting, cover and other art, website, advertising, social media and many other costs are the responsibility of the author. In traditional publishing, the author typically is paid an advance, and these costs are picked up by the publisher. A self-published author receives no payment until the book begins to sell and must cover all costs long before they see any profit.

Many authors today choose to publish on their own in order to keep more control of their creations. The opportunities presented today give self-publisher's the tools to produce books on a professional level and to reach readers all over the world. However, one of the biggest challenges authors face, continues to be the marketing of their books.

So again, thank you for buying this book. If you enjoyed it, please help me by taking a few moments to leave a review on Amazon and Goodreads (see below) whether you bought the book on-line or in a store. Reviews on both will help if you have the time. Reviews are the way all books, self-published or traditional, gain momentum for more sales. Many readers buy books based on reader reviews, and the algorithms used by book sellers compound the sales and reviews to sell more books. Comments are always welcome, but you don't have to write anything if you don't want, you can just rate it using the five-star system. A few moments of your time will help me immensely. Thank you for your help!

## HOW TO LEAVE A REVIEW

Amazon

- Go to your order detail page

- In the US – Amazon.com/orders

- In the UK – Amazon.co.uk/orders

- Click the "Write a product review" button next to your book order

- Rate the item and write your review and click "Submit"

Goodreads

- Go to Goodreads.com

- Search for the author or book title

- Click on the star rating under the book cover and leave a review

Follow me at:

Facebook:      https://www.facebook.com/jeffheinauthor

Instagram      https://www.instagram.com/jeffheinauthor

Twitter:        https://www.twitter.com/jeffheinauthor

LinkedIn:       https://www.linkedin.com/in/jeffheinauthor

Webpage:       https://www.jeffhein.net

Jeff Hein grew up in northern Wisconsin. After serving twenty years in the US Army, he returned to Wisconsin where he now lives with his wife Dawn and their two lab/shepherds Daisy and Annie.

During his service in Germany Jeff first became aware of the story of the Cimbri and was fortunate to visit many of the places described in "The Cimbri Appear".

More than twenty years passed before Jeff was able to complete his debut novel "The Cimbri Appear" and he is pleased to finally bring it to publication.

In his spare time Jeff enjoys reading, camping, fishing, and gardening, and is currently working on his second book.

# Coming Soon!

# Rise of the Red Wolf

## Book 2

### The Cimbrian War

JEFF HEIN

RED WOLF BOOKS

# Chapter One

## Noricum

## July 113 BC

Pillars of smoke rose from the smoldering embers of the sacrificial fires as the head of the caravan climbed into the soaring limestone peaks of the Alpes Mountains.

Farther to the south, a spiraling column of squawking, black birds reached down from the sky to mark the battlefield at Noreia where we had defeated the Romans. The ground undulated as thousands of carrion birds feasted on the Roman dead, flapping, and hopping around from one delicious morsel to another.

After the battle we returned to the valley of the Dravus River, renewing our journey. The alpine valley rose gradually as we followed the river toward its source and on the morning of the third day we turned northward into the mountains.

A few of the local Taurisci tribesmen decided it was better to join us than fight us and now served as guides. The narrow trail forced the caravan to stretch out for miles as it trudged slowly upward, ever upward. The caravan was so large that it was several days before the last of the carts still at the battlefield could begin the journey and by then the vanguard was well into the mountain passes.

Freki, my childhood friend and adopted brother, now led my scouts and almost immediately after passing through the foothills, I received reports of the caravan being watched from a distance. There was no contact, just an occasional glimpse of movement among the rocks, or a brief reflection of sunlight from a spearhead. The Taurisci warned us of the wild mountain tribes who were fiercely independent, warlike, and trusted no one.

As darkness fell the caravan was caught on the trail and unable to set up our usual defensive formations. Carts stopped and oxen were unhitched so they could lie down in the trail. People slept on the ground or in their carts and the cattle herds bedded down wherever they found themselves. The rocky ground provided little forage for the animals and most laid down hungry, protesting their empty bellies with a constant bellowing.

My horse carefully picked its way along the path in the twilight as my retainers Hrolf and Arnulf followed behind me, speaking softly to the people they passed along the way. Arnulf found his wife and I returned to my cart where my wife Frida and our three-year-old son Lingulf traveled alongside her father, Glum, the brewmaster.

Glum had managed a small fire for light and as Hrolf and I dismounted, he offered us a horn of ale. Frida handed me a piece of dried beef and a chunk of stale bread as I sat beside her, offering the same to Hrolf.

"How does the trail look ahead?" Glum asked.

I chewed silently for a moment, considering the question.

"Steep," I replied with a half grin.

Frida chuckled softly beside me, rocking a sleeping Lingulf on her lap.

"Huh," Glum huffed impatiently. "I meant are there any dangers to be wary of."

"No more than usual," I said. "Steep hillsides on one side with rocks balanced precariously above us, precipitous drops on the other that one misplaced step can send you off into an abyss. Nervous, unpredictable animals all around. Nothing to be worried about."

"What about people? Word is passing that we are being watched,"

Glum persisted.

"I've heard the reports. So far as I know they are only watching us. I've issued orders for everyone to be alert tonight." I stood up and held out my hand to help Frida up. I glanced over my shoulder at Glum as we walked to the cart. "We'll be moving again at first light," I said. "The guides tell me we have at least five more days to the top."

---

I woke in the night to shouts coming from up the trail. When I arrived at the scene, I found that a family had closely escaped disaster when their cart went careening down the trail and off the side of a steep cliff. When they stopped for the night, the oxen were unhitched, and the cart was parked on a slight incline. No one had chocked the wheels and during the night, it rolled away, narrowly missing the family's young children sleeping on the ground.

In the morning several men climbed down to what was left of the cart and recovered whatever was still useable, but the cart was destroyed. Family and friends offered to carry their belongings in their own carts, and we moved on.

The following night, I was awakened again by Hrolf shouting for me. "There's a disturbance back down the trail at the cattle herd," he said.

I threw back the covers and jumped up, belting on my sword. It was too dark for the horses, so we left on foot, gathering men as we went. The herd was agitated and milling about dangerously, threatening to stampede. If they bolted, it could be disastrous. Several men circled them with torches trying to calm them down.

"What happened here?" I asked the nearest man.

"We were raided," he said, pointing at a nearby spot. "Several men came out of that cleft over there and cut out a dozen or so cattle. We tried to follow but they had men on the cliffs above who dropped boulders on us. One man has a broken arm. We were lucky no one was killed."

"Wodan's eye!" I swore. "I was afraid of something like this. We have a long way to go through these mountains. We can't have this happen every night. Hrolf!" I called. "Double the guards on the cattle. In the morning I need to figure out how to talk with these people."

Printed in Great Britain
by Amazon

42345938R00209